A STIRRING IN THE KREMLIN

He returned to his desk, seated himself once again, and on the lighted map studied with growing satisfaction the pulsating lights that marked the new advances he had ordered in the final conflict that he was supremely confident would eliminate the United States, decide the fate of all mankind, and assure for the Soviet Union the final conquest of the world.

The CIA had anticipated nothing.

The National Security Agency had received no inkling.

The various military intelligence units had drawn a blank.

And the whirling satellites had found nothing unusual, being unfortunately unable to photograph the one area that confounds all predictions and upsets all prognostications, namely the mind of man.

THE ROADS OF EARTH

ALLEN DRURY

PINNACLE BOOKS NEW YORK

THE ROADS OF EARTH

A Pinnacle Books edition, published by arrangement with Doubleday & Company, Inc.

Doubleday edition/September 1984
Pinnacle edition/September 1985

ISBN: 0-523-42611-9
Can. ISBN: 0-523-43558-4

Printed in the United States of America

PINNACLE BOOKS, INC.
1430 Broadway
New York, New York 10018

9 8 7 6 5 4 3 2 1

To
Clare Boothe Luce
with much
affection, admiration and respect

MAJOR CHARACTERS IN THE NOVEL

In Washington

Hamilton Delbacher, President of the United States

Elinor, his wife

Chauncey Baron, Secretary of State

Roger Hackett, Secretary of Defense

Arthur Hampton, Vice President of the United States

Anson McUmber, National Security Adviser

James Rand Elrod, senior Senator from North Carolina

James Monroe Madison, senior Senator from California

Mark Coffin, junior Senator from California

Linda, his wife

General Rutherford "Smidge" Hallowell, U.S. Army, Chairman of the Joint Chiefs of Staff

General Martin "Bump" Smith, Chief of Staff, U.S. Army

Admiral Harman Rydecker, Chief of Naval Operations

General Bartram C. Jamison, Chief of Staff, U.S. Air Force

General Robert "Gutsy" Twitchell, Commandant, U.S. Marine Corps

Major Ivan Ivanovich Valerian, a defector

In Moscow

Yuro Pavlovich Serapin, President of the Soviet Union

Ekaterina Vasarionova, his mistress

The Foreign Minister

The Defense Minister

Other members of the Politburo and Council of Ministers

Various marshals and admirals of the Army, Navy, Air Force and Strategic Rocket Forces

General Mikhail Cyrilovich Yarkov, head of the KGB

At NATO Headquarters
The member nations

In Taiwan
President Li Yuan

In Havana
The Maximum Leader, President of Cuba

At the United Nations
Ju Xing-dao, Vice-Premier of the People's Republic of China
The Prime Minister of Britain
The Prime Minister of India
Other heads of delegations
Fabrizio Gulak, a friend to mankind
The media

In South Africa
James Lytton
Henrik van der Merwe
Nkeze Sukuza

NOTE TO THE READER

The coming to power of Hamilton Delbacher in the United States and Yuri Serapin in the Soviet Union, and their first confrontation across the lands and seas of the globe, will be found in the predecessor volume to this, *The Hill of Summer.*

A number of frantic reviews were written of that novel, conditioned by a visceral fear of facing up honestly to the constantly proclaimed and absolutely undeviating intention of the Soviet Union to destroy the United States and conquer the world if it possibly can.

This aim has been candidly announced and steadily maintained for almost seven decades; and still there are many in America who refuse to believe it, just as many refused to believe Adolf Hitler when he proclaimed, and attempted, the same two ambitions. Yet the record of the Soviets, like his, is there for all who have the courage to look, and to accept what they see.

Deliberately self-blinded critics are not worth arguing with; but one earthshaking point should probably be responded to, since it illumines a whole school of approach to criticisms of the Soviet Union. Some individual who was described as being the "assistant foreign editor" of a major metropolitan publication made much of my "annoying habit" of having my fictitious Soviet officials refer to one another and to foreign leaders as R. Nixon . . . J. Carter . . R. Reagan and the like.

Everyone who has ever read any official Soviet publications knows that this is exactly how the Soviets do refer, in both written and spoken work, to their colleagues and to foreign leaders. Apparently reading what the Soviets themselves write and proclaim is not a prerequisite for being an "assistant foreign editor." It should, however, be at least a minimal requirement for being a critic of novels involving the Soviet Union.

A.D.

The Roads Of Earth

BOOK ONE

1

SINO-SOVIET PACT:
RUSS, CHINESE SIGN FIVE-YEAR ACCORD "TO RESTORE SOCIALIST HARMONY AND REPEL IMPERIALIST AGGRESSORS."
U.S. ISOLATED.
WORLD STUNNED BY AGREEMENT BETWEEN COMMUNIST GIANTS, ONCE BITTER ENEMIES. MANY LEADERS BELIEVE "IT MEANS WAR."

So began the Labor Day weekend.
So began the end of summer.
And perhaps—the next few weeks, possibly days, would tell—all else.

It did not take long to find out.

On Sunday morning, five days later, the fragile structure of world peace—such as it was—began to fall apart.

At three A.M. Washington time the President of the United States, Hamilton Delbacher, was asleep.

At ten A.M. Moscow time the President of the Soviet Union, Yuri Serapin, was wide awake, happily anticipating successes in the opening stages of what official Soviet doctrine describes as "the

3

climactic battle between communism and capitalism that will decide the fate of all mankind.''

Yuri Serapin was doubly happy because, exactly as planned, his country was nowhere directly involved.

Hamilton Delbacher, awakened five minutes after the first satellite pictures began to come in to the National Security Agency, was unable to be so sanguine.

He knew with a rueful certainty that his country was everywhere involved.

An hour after Yuri uttered his first grunt of satisfied triumph and Hamilton Delbacher his first angry expletive of dismay, the world heard the news.

A wave of foreboding raced across seas and continents.

Scarcely a week after their first great clash of wills, the Presidents of the two superpowers faced each other again.

This time there seemed to be no way out for the United States save complete disaster.

Or the final destruction of the earth.

Hamilton Delbacher was determined that neither would occur.

Yuri Serapin was determined that the first should occur but that the second must be avoided so that the Soviet Union might achieve its lifelong goal of establishing hegemony over the entire world.

Given his own character and the still considerable resources of the United States, President Delbacher was not about to yield or surrender.

And President Serapin, who felt that the new crises he had just created were only logical and inevitable steps toward rearranging the world in a form satisfactory to communist ideology, was not going to be easily discouraged either.

In fact, Yuri thought, all this was only the inevitable development of history growing out of the correlation of forces patiently created by his country with planning, foresight, treachery, deceit— and the willful blindness and weakness of the West—for more than four decades.

Most of it, Ham Delbacher told himself unhappily, was the inevitable result of the shortsightedness, lack of planning, lack of firmness, failure of will—and inability to give the West the calm, steady, consistent leadership it needed to counteract the Soviet advance—of his own eternally optimistic, eternally hopeful, determinedly self-deluding and self-defeating countrymen . . . and of those of his predecessors who, for what they believed to be their own political safety, could never quite bring themselves to acknowledge the fact, proclaimed incessantly by the Soviet Union itself, that it did indeed, genuinely and in truth, intend to achieve decisive conquest of the world if it possibly could.

It was also, he reflected as he hastily dressed and prepared to go down to the Situation Room in the basement of the White House, the direct outcome of his own first titanic struggle with Yuri that had brought the world so close to cataclysm in the two months just past.

2

Their confrontation, played out on the seas, the continents, in the United Nations, in Moscow, in Washington, NATO, Cuba—in fact, the entire world—had begun when his own complaisant and ever-hopeful predecessor in office had dropped dead of a heart attack on the Fourth of July.

The event occurred in the same week in which, in Moscow, Yuri Pavlovich Serapin finally succeeded in his long, murderous climb to power in the Kremlin and emerged, at age fifty, General Secretary of the Communist Party, Chairman of the Council of Ministers and President and Commander-in-Chief of the Soviet Union.

His accession to power had been hailed by the late naively hopeful Chief Executive as a good omen for the world. It had been regarded by Hamilton Debacher as an incipient and probably inevitable headache.

Within two days of his own accession to power his forebodings had been completely justified.

Yuri, product of the pitiless system of Soviet advancement, was the first of the "new generation" that had followed the late Leonid Brezhnev and his ailing successors. He was a born gambler. He had at his command a worldwide network of diplomats, officials, spies, terrorists and goggle-eyed sympathizers—Lenin's "useful idiots of the West." He also had an overwhelming military establishment that encouraged him to think he could browbeat into sub-

6

mission the portly, gray-haired grandfather who, ten years his senior, now faced him in the White House.

Probably no two men could have been better chosen by history to represent their widely differing, inherently antagonistic systems: Hamilton Delbacher (pronounced "Delbahcker"), the sixty-year-old former Pennsylvania farm boy, highly intelligent, tenaciously ambitious, temperamentally unflappable, who had grown up to become first Congressman, then Senator, then Vice-President and now, suddenly on the death of his predecessor from a heart attack, President; reared in the old American virtues of tolerance, decency, goodwill . . . And Yuri Pavlovich Serapin, the short, stocky, half-Asiatic offspring of a Mongol mother and a Great Russian father, highly intelligent, fiercely ambitious, utterly cold-blooded product of communist training who had been selected because of his brains to receive special attention from the Party; had been assigned first to the armed services political section, then to the KGB, then to six years as the KGB's top man in the Soviet embassy in Washington; had been called home to join the American and Canadian section of the Politburo, had intrigued and murdered his way to the post of Minister of Defense; and now finally, on the deaths of Leonid Brezhnev's elderly successors, last of the Bolshevik "old generation," had achieved at last his lifelong ambition and become the feared and all-powerful General Secretary of the Communist Party, Chairman of the Council of Ministers and President and Commander-in-Chief of the Soviet Union.

Ham Delbacher was easygoing but tough, shrewd, humorous, a veteran of thirty years in the give-and-take of American democracy, which works best only when operated by goodwill, willingness to compromise, respect for basic human rights and some essential concern for one's fellow beings. Yuri Serapin was cold-blooded, sardonic, completely ruthless, a survivor in the jungle world of the communist hierarchy who had lied, cheated, killed, used every trick and every deceit necessary to achieve his ambitions and his present supreme power; a believer, conditioned from earliest youth and all his subsequent training, in the two supreme articles of Soviet faith: that his country's hegemony of the world was an inexorable and inevitable certainty of history; and that the

United States, as the only obstacle left standing in the way at the end of World War II, must be destroyed as completely as Carthage.

Hamilton Delbacher was a father, a grandfather, a family man who, with his brothers and sisters, still had an active interest in the Pennsylvania farm and still found his basic strengths in the American earth and the traditional American Purpose—however often poorly achieved—of "one nation indivisible, with liberty and justice for all." Yuri Serapin had a wife he despised, two children he rarely saw, and a mistress, Ekaterina Vasarionova, who was the only person in the Soviet empire who dared treat him with contempt and upon whom, as a result, he relied heavily. His basic strengths came from a deep, visceral love, as profound as Hamilton Delbacher's, for his native earth; a contempt for its people whose undisputed master he now was; and the teachings of the ideology whose mastery had given him great material comforts denied all but an infinitesimal number of his countrymen. He also believed absolutely in the inevitability of the Soviet conquest of the earth.

To the Soviet purposes of destroying America and achieving complete hegemony of the world, Yuri at fifty brought all the resources of a brilliant mind, an unswerving purpose and a gambler's instinct. To the American purposes of thwarting Soviet ambitions and trying to preserve some basic freedom for the peoples of the earth, Ham Delbacher at sixty brought a shrewd intelligence, a dogged and tenacious character and a basic goodwill toward humankind which was part of his American heritage as surely as Yuri's contempt for humankind was part of his. Each had great strengths, each had some weaknesses—Yuri's principally the weakness of arrogance, Ham's basically the weakness of almost too much goodwill . . . and the lingering feeling, in common with most of his countrymen, that against all the historical evidence, it might yet be possible to work out a really genuine and good-faith means of existing peaceably on a small planet with those who were determined to ride roughshod over it, finally and absolutely.

That this had not been the case, Hamilton Delbacher reflected grimly as he gave Elinor a hasty reassuring wave, opened the door and stepped out into the great hall on the second floor to be greeted by the national security adviser and a phalanx of guards to escort him swiftly downstairs, had been due partly to luck, partly to world pressure and partly to his own dogged character and stubborn refusal to knuckle under. It had not been due in any great measure to the military strength he could field in response to Yuri's, nor could he truthfully say that it had been due to any overwhelming support from America's allies or even from America's own leading opinion-makers.

The American people, on the whole, while frightened, had backed him up, and some allies, such as Britain, had worked long and hard to stave off confrontation. But in the final analysis it had come down to his will against Yuri's.

Five short days ago he had felt that he had won, though it had been Yuri with his sudden, dramatic "withdrawal of forces" who had received the most plaudits from an hysterically grateful world. The intervening days swiftly informed the President that he had not "won," only postponed further clashes. Now, as it turned out, he had postponed them not even a week.

Thus fast were events moving in the ever-accelerated pace of civilization's headlong rush toward some unknowable, but very possibly unpleasant, destination.

"Mr. President," the national security adviser said breathlessly at his side as they strode along, "it would appear that the Chinese are moving only in their own interests. They are not cooperating in any of these other Soviet-backed adventures. That is some consolation."

"It is?" he inquired gloomily, turning to glance down at the sleek little figure that bustled along so importantly at his side. Why did I ever let *you* stay on, he wondered, and was stopped by the practical fact of it, which was that there simply hadn't been time since he took office to find a replacement for his predecessor's notoriously nit-picking and not really very good appointee. "How come we didn't know China was up to this in the first place?"

"You will remember, sir," the national security adviser said stiffly, "that *you* conducted all the negotiations with Ju Xing-dao at the United Nations yourself. I wasn't invited to be present."

"It wasn't possible," he said shortly, thinking back to his talks with the wispy, elusive little Chinese leader who had drifted gently in and out of United Nations debate, only to terminate an apparently sincere encouragement of the United States by suddenly presenting the world with the new Sino-Soviet treaty that had obviously opened the way to what was happening at this moment around the globe. "He was so hard to get to, in any event."

"Deliberately, as it turns out," the security adviser remarked with the slightest edge of triumph and the implication: *which should have been a tip-off.*

"So what do we do now?" Ham Delbacher inquired, ignoring it as they entered the waiting elevator. "Declare war on them both? You're supposed to think up solutions, aren't you? I assume you have several to offer me."

"Mr. President," the security adviser said solemnly, obviously not quite sure whether this was plea or jest, "my staff and I expect to have several courses of action outlined for you by six A.M. My top aides have been alerted and are already on their way in. By the time you request position papers—"

"By the time I request them," the President said tartly, "we may have eight or ten more little episodes on our hands."

"No, I think not," the national security adviser said. "I think the Soviet Union intends to concentrate on those they have just started. They are quite sufficient to . . ."

His voice trailed away and the President finished for him.

"Quite sufficient to tie us down all over the globe, if we respond as Yuri obviously expects us to."

"We have to make *some* response," the security adviser said. "The appeals for help are already coming in."

"Things," the President said grimly, "have been happening too damned fast ever since that tricky bastard came to power."

And so they had. Forty-eight hours after Ham's accession, Yuri had requested a summit meeting between himself and the new President. It had been held at the United Nations and had resulted in the first of their bitter personal clashes. The Soviet leader had in effect told the American President that the Soviet Union possessed such superior military power that the United States might as well surrender at once and get it over with—or at least surrender any pretense of opposing the Soviet policies and thereby bring itself swiftly into line with Soviet desires and ambitions.

Hamilton Delbacher's response had been to return to Washington and, addressing a joint session of Congress, lay out exactly what the situation was for his own people and the world to understand. He had put into immediate effect the ten-billion-dollar emergency increase in defense spending authorized in the bill introduced by Senator Jim Elrod of South Carolina but allowed to lie unused by Ham's predecessor.

Yuri's response had been to declare this "an act almost of war," and to order an immediate worldwide military exercise by all the land, sea and air forces of the Soviet Union. As part of his overall strategy, he ordered a flotilla of eighteen atomic submarines to join the six "normally" stationed at the Cienfuegos naval base of his Cuban satellite.

Ham Delbacher had issued an immediate ultimatum that unless they were removed the gravest consequences would follow. In a dramatic public meeting in Havana, Yuri and his errand-boy President of Cuba had asserted that the submarines were there to defend Cuba against American attack. Ham had remained unflinching in his ultimatum and had put United States military forces on worldwide war alert.

Yuri's response had been to withdraw six of the submarines—to a Soviet base in Nicaragua, as it turned out—and ask for an immediate United Nations Security Council meeting. With a great rush of relief the world had hailed his statesmanlike move, and the meeting had been held.

Heading his own delegation, President Delbacher had introduced a harshly worded United States resolution demanding immediate termination of the Soviet maneuvers and withdrawal of all Soviet Forces. President Serapin had countered with a harshly opposing resolution denouncing United States "imperialism." Both powers used the veto. Matters were at a crisis standstill when Britain, India and the People's Republic of China combined to seek a compromise. At the last moment, in a plague-on-both-your-houses speech, the P.R.C.'s Ju Xing-dao moved to discharge the Security Council from consideration and turn the matter over to the General Assembly, where the veto does not apply.

In the General Assembly things finally began to turn against the Soviet Union and in a dramatic last-minute gesture Yuri announced that he was ending the maneuvers and withdrawing his forces.

The world relaxed and again showered him with great applause and approval for his statesmanship—even though, as the President of the United States remarked disgustedly to his associates, the tricky bastard had created the crisis in the first place.

Within hours Ham was receiving satellite and other information that many Soviet units had been left in place under screen of the much-fanfared "withdrawal." And just as he was wondering with a tired exasperation how to meet with this new threat, Ju Xing-dao arrived at the Kremlin with papers from Peking and the world was once again struck numb with: SINO-SOVIET PACT!

The elapsed time between then and this day's new crises, Hamilton Delbacher thought grimly as he entered the Situation Room to face the grave faces of the Secretaries of State and Defense and the Joint Chiefs of Staff, had only been from Monday to Sunday. So swiftly was the challenge renewed and the battle resumed. And what did he intend to do about it?

There was not very much H. Delbacher could do, the President of the Soviet Union told himself with grim satisfaction as he occupied his favorite position, seated behind his enormous desk in the Kremlin, staring at the lighted map of the world that occupied most of the wall directly opposite.

Across its face ten days ago long red lines had spanned the seas and continents: the Soviet Air Force. Over the plains of Eastern Europe and into the conquered satellites of Southeast and Southwest Asia, other red lines stretched: the tank and artillery forces. Little lighted red dots had clustered off Washington, New York, London, the coast of Europe, Cuba, Nicaragua, the Panama Canal, Hawaii, San Francisco, Los Angeles, Seattle, the Bering Strait, the Mediterranean, the Strait of Hormuz, both ends of Suez: the atomic submarines. Blue dots hovered in strategic locations in the Atlantic, Pacific, Indian and Mediterranean oceans and the Persian Gulf: the Navy. Clusters of small diamond needles pointed toward the United States and South America from Cuba and Siberia, commanded Asia and Africa from the Kuril Islands north of Japan and the bases in satellite Afghanistan and South Yemen: the missiles. Above in the skies, unmarked on the map but known secretly to him and his military leaders, the satellite-and-communications killers and the atomic-armed space stations swung in their deadly, patient orbits.

Never had there been such an array of military force in all the history of the world, he had told himself then with a fearfully exciting sense of triumph: never had one man commanded so much sheer power. Only he, Yuri Pavlovich Serapin, the man chosen by destiny to preside over the final downfall of hated America and the last vestiges of freedom which her presence in the world made viable and protected, had been given overwhelming command of the world's destinies by the inevitable forces of historical development.

In that giddy moment, with the globe literally helpless at his feet had he desired to give the word, he had accepted the plaudits of the Politburo and his chiefs of staff, gracefully turned down the suggestion that he be named "President for Life," and instead had harbored in his secret heart the title he had chosen for himself when the United States was gone and he was finally in place above the entire world: Supreme Ruler and Arbiter of All Mankind.

He had no doubt that the United States soon *would* be gone; and now as he contemplated the map and the additional brightly pulsating lights that flashed from the four places he had chosen for the start of the final contest, he told himself scornfully that there was absolutely nothing his despised antagonist in the White House could do about it.

He had chosen four allies the United States could not possibly afford to abandon. He had made sure that they were separated by such vast distances and encumbered by such logistic complications that the United States could not possibly save them all at the same time. He had with great calculation and shrewdness invited the United States to spread its forces across the world on an utterly impossible task until they ran too thin to be effective—or do nothing and go down in ignominy before superior Soviet strength and the loss of faith in America that would inevitably result from failure to make adequate response.

And he had done it all against the background of the forces which he had, with practiced, skillful duplicity, left secretly in place around the world after his dramatic announcement of withdrawal delivered to the General Assembly. He had been decisively fortified in his strategy by the new Supreme Socialist Understanding Pact—as, he noted with wry amusement, it was being called in

Peking—which he and Ju Xing-dao had signed at this very desk scarcely a week ago.

The Soviet-Chinese Treaty of Cooperation, as he preferred to have it referred to in the Soviet and satellite press—having carefully considered and for good reason rejected the additional words "and Friendship"—still seemed to him something of a miracle. But had not his entire life, from its humble beginning through its murderous middle stages as he had risen by superior intelligence, guile and murder to the supreme pinnacle of Soviet power, been blessed with such miracles? Had not Yuri Serapin been favored from the first? Had not his destiny been inevitable? He had always believed so, and events had never failed him. The logic of history had been on his side; and so it was now, though he knew, with all the instincts of suspicion and self-preservation that had saved him in so many perilous situations before, that he must not rely too heavily on his newfound Chinese "friends."

This was strictly a temporary truce between two blood enemies so that they might eliminate a third. He knew it, they knew it, the world knew it. But while it lasted, it permitted him to achieve what he wanted. First would come the elimination of the United States, which he had been taught from childhood to believe was inevitable and to which he was completely and implacably dedicated, as was the entire Soviet system. And then would come the elimination of the People's Republic of China, which, having served its purpose, could be dealt with as its many insolent and and insufferable challenges to Soviet power and influence so richly deserved.

For the moment the treaty stood sufficient for the purposes to which its co-signers wished to put it: he to destroy America, China to draw the Soviet Union and the United States into a conflict in which they would destroy each other so that China could then emerge chief scorpion in the bottle—the Middle Kingdom, alone and unthreatened by foreign barbarians at last.

He thought of the gently whispering, frail little figure of Ju Xing-dao, and a contemptuous smile crossed his face. Such cordial encouragements as they had given one another, such suave congratulations and bland pledges of cooperation, such fervent promises of mutual love and brotherhood! And such deep, viscerally ineradicable mistrust and hatred underneath it all!

Their countries had been uneasy neighbors for centuries, active enemies for the past one or two. In a world increasingly technological, he and Ju Xing-dao, sworn to each other's eradication, were well within sight of the goal—at least he was. Not yet the P.R.C., for all its craft and bombast—but soon—soon.

He was working, he knew, within a narrow time frame. The Chinese already had the bomb. They were rapidly increasing their supply of missiles to deliver it. Their other technologies were keeping pace under the prod of an iron dictatorship that drove China's amiable people, as they had always been driven for the purposes of one set of rulers or another through all their long history, toward ever-increasing goals of production and preparedness.

For years now, ever since the American President Nixon had made his dramatic visit to Peking, Moscow had been taunting the United States with the potential perils of playing "the China card." In constant broadcasts, editorials, official speeches, the warning had been repeated ad nauseam: watch out—you are embracing the dragon—you cannot trust its friendship—you will not be so happy when it grows its teeth.

And, he reflected now, he and the Politburo had been right. Now China had swung again, and what was happening today was proof that the shift was not, for the moment at least, just a gesture. That it was devoted exclusively to the furtherance of Peking's own interests was characteristic and exactly what he had expected; but that was all right. It helped to throw the Americans off balance. Without it the worldwide net into which he was inviting them would not be complete. He did not care about the motivation as long as the result suited his purposes.

By the same token, however, it served to strengthen his conviction, ingrained in all top Soviet leaders, that China would have to be dealt with, when the time came, as ruthlessly and pragmatically as China was now dealing with a nation she had pretended to befriend as long as it suited her.

Meanwhile he had no intention whatsoever of furnishing the P.R.C. with the heavy machinery, the billions in credit, the military aircraft and the naval vessels it had been promised during the intensive secret negotiations that had preceded the treaty. Delivery on these promises could be stalled for a month or two on the pretext that the Soviet Union was too busy directing its puppets in the great task of bringing down the United States.

Two months should be long enough to do it, unless Hamilton Delbacher came up with a miracle—or several. Yuri did not see how he was going to accomplish this.

His impressions of the American President were extremely strong as a result of their recent worldwide contest of wills; and while he recognized that H. Delbacher was a stubborn and resourceful man who had finally managed, despite America's sagging military strength, to stand up to Yuri as vigorously as Yuri had stood up to him, Yuri still felt that he himself was far the superior in intelligence, shrewdness and skill.

As a result of their face-to-face discussions during the crisis, he had a further, more personal reason for destroying obdurate H. Delbacher and his declining country: he had come to feel a real hatred for the tall, portly, unimpressed man who had looked him in the eye at Fabrizio Gulak's apartment in River House, New York, and told Yuri flatly that he was *"Evil, evil, evil!"*

Yuri had not heard that kind of talk from anyone for many, many years; and although the life of murder and deceit he had led while clawing his way to the top of the Soviet hierarchy over the careers and bodies of so many upstarts who had thought they could block his destiny had made him almost impervious to such insults, in the case of Hamilton Delbacher he found it impossible to dismiss them with the contempt they deserved.

The President's words rankled, and they would continue to rankle, Yuri suspected, until the Soviet Union dictated a peace of annihilation to the United States. And he suspected the reason, though he thrust it angrily aside every time it came to mind and its recurrence only made him hate the President more. It rankled because Hamilton Delbacher was beyond question a good man, and so his strictures upon one who knew that by Western standards he *was* evil came with a righteousness that stung because it could not successfully be challenged.

In his youthful years a "second secretary"—actually, like most of the staff, a top-level KGB representative—in the Soviet embassy in Washington, Yuri had taken occasion to give much thought to the Senator from Pennsylvania who had risen to become Vice-Presi-

dent and now, so unexpectedly, President. The tall, powerfully
built, powerfully effective former farm boy from York County had
been one of the most influential members of the Senate Foreign Relations Committee. As such, he was a prime object of Yuri's study.
Yuri had not known him well—they had only met on the most fleeting occasions, since Hamilton Delbacher was impervious to the social invitations, luncheons and other flatteries with which the
embassy wooed so many of his colleagues in Congress—but well
enough to realize that he was a formidable antagonist of the basic
Soviet intention to dominate—and in time completely control—the
world. The Soviets had never made the slightest bones about this
intention, any more than Hitler had; and in similar fashion their
words and obvious deeds had been indignantly denied by the intel-
lectual community of the one nation above all others that they must
destroy if their plans were to succeed.

American apologists for the Soviet Union were everywhere—in
academe, the media, the arts. Their frantic denials of Soviet purpose and their frantic scorn for the Soviets' critics were never more
hysterical than when the Soviets gained some obvious new advantage in their patient, steady, implacable drive toward world dominion. Denial and scorn had a field day in America on such
occasions; it was so necessary, in those frightened minds, to deny
the reality of what they might have to do if they ever faced up to the
situation that really confronted the United States. And there was
still the lingering feeling, implanted so skillfully by the Soviet
Union in so many influential Western minds over so many years,
that the communist experiment was somehow "nobler" and "better" and "more human" than the democratic; and that therefore its
cold, plodding, merciless destruction of all freedom and all human
happiness over an increasing portion of the earth's surface should
somehow be excused and covered over.

Hamilton Delbacher was not such a one. Accordingly he had always been subject to the attacks that inevitably followed refusal to
accept the true gospel on these matters as laid down by Soviet apologists in America. He had always been considered in Moscow to
be a formidable force in opposition. When he had so abruptly succeeded to the Presidency—just when he was within hours of being
removed from the ticket in his late predecessor's campaign for

reelection—it had caused substantial dismay. The final humbling of America was not going to be quite so easy as everyone had thought. H. Delbacher stood in the way.

Yuri had done a great deal, in his own estimation, to minimize Delbacher in the last two months since they had both come to power. But America still existed as a major entity in the world, and so did her President. Therefore these new moves today, designed to place them both at a final disadvantage from which neither would recover.

He could not help but feel, as he contemplated the four bright areas of crisis pulsating on the map, a great satisfaction at how cleverly and with what consummate skill their unhappy surprises had been prepared for the despised United States of America and its stubborn leader, whom he hated so much.

3

$\mathbf{Y}$et for five days Hamilton Delbacher, while as taken aback as most of the world by the unexpected Sino-Soviet pact—as much of a shock to the West as the Hitler-Stalin pact just prior to World War II, and representative of exactly the same ruthless Soviet duplicity—had proceeded as calmly and effectively as he knew how to shore up his country and his country's allies against whatever the future might bring. His only mistake had been in overestimating the time in which he would be allowed to do it.

His initial precautions had been practical, matter-of-fact and conducted with an imperturbable calm which in itself had been a great strengthening to the West.

He only hoped now that he could continue in the same fashion.

In fact, he had to.

His first reaction upon learning of the new alliance had been to draw around him the principal advisers who had strengthened his hand in his first contest with Yuri. He consulted with Senator James Elrod, new majority leader in the Senate; Jim's son-in-law, Senator Mark Coffin of California; the ex-Senate Majority Leader, now his new Vice-President, Art Hampton; the Senate Minority Leader, Herb Esplin of Ohio; Chauncey Baron, Secretary of State; Roger Hackett, Secretary of Defense; the Joint Chiefs of Staff; the Speaker of the House; the charming, elusive and possibly equivocal Major Ivan Valerian, the Soviet defector who had consistently given him accurate information in advance concerning Yuri's

plans; and above all Elinor, his wife of almost forty years, whose
sharp New England common sense and level view of things had always helped him meet the many challenges of his long political career.

They were all agreed on one thing: he must make some public
comment. Most of his friends from Capitol Hill felt that this should
be in the form of an address to a joint session of Congress; others
were not so sure. Ivan Valerian, consulted more out of curiosity
than because the President thought he could contribute any in-
sights, had flashed his charming smile and inquired cautiously,
"But have you not already addressed Congress sufficiently in recent days, Mr. President? There is a possibility of too much sameness, is there not?"

And Mark Coffin, who had assisted in Ivan's defection and had
become a reasonably close if still suspicious friend of the lively
young defector, had agreed:

"You *can* overdo it, Mr. President. I think people are pretty
well exhausted by the events of the past two months. Do you want
to keep them at that pitch or should you let them relax a little?
Maybe they should be allowed to come down off the high. There
may be a lot ahead for them to cope with."

"I'm sure," he had said grimly, not realizing then how soon this
might be true; and after further consultation and a talk with Elinor,
who commented, "I think I'd go with the young," he had made up
his mind to side with Mark and Ivan and keep it relatively low-key.
He asked the press secretary to line up the networks. On the evening of the Sino-Soviet pact at nine P.M. Eastern Standard Time, six
P.M. Pacific, he spoke briefly to his countrymen and, through
them, to the world.

"My fellow Americans," he said gravely, "we were all startled
today to learn of the new Chinese-Soviet pact, which I notice is already being interpreted by many in the media as a great setback for
the United States.

"Your government is not prepared to accept this interpretation
until we know more about the intentions of the two parties. Certainly we do not intend to let it panic us into either an excessive
caution or an exaggerated response. Neither would serve American

purposes or the purposes of those nations with which we are associated that do not believe in the communist form of government.

"You may rest assured that your government and your President, having just come through such a protracted and dangerous confrontation with the Soviet Union, do not intend to foster or encourage any hasty reaction to this event. A new element has been introduced into international affairs, true enough; but it is one that has long been considered a possibility by the United States.

"We do not intend to let it throw us off course in our constant search for ways to strengthen the stability of world society. If this means the beginning of a more peaceful cooperation between the Soviet Union and the People's Republic of China, we would welcome it as we welcome anything that serves to decrease tension in the world. If it is the beginning of a new military adventurism on the part of the Soviet Union, or of the P.R.C., or both, then we are prepared to meet it when, and as, we have to.

"We have not been notified of any change in our diplomatic, cultural or commercial relations with the P.R.C. Therefore we will proceed as we have done in recent years on a course that we hope will continue to strengthen the ties between ourselves and the great Chinese people. Our relations with the U.S.S.R. must inevitably undergo a period of revision and readjustment following the recent international escapades of President Serapin; but even here, we must hope that in time some reasonable normalcy may be restored.

"For ourselves, we will be, as ever, vigilant and alert and prepared to deal with all comers on the some basis on which they wish to deal with us. We hope that this will be a basis of continued friendship with the People's Republic of China and, eventually, of renewed respect for, and cooperation with, the Soviet Union. Meanwhile we will continue to put our own house in order, strengthen necessary defenses and be prepared to treat with friendship those who want our friendship.

"The others we will attempt to live with, reminding them that coexistence can be either friendly or unfriendly, and that we are prepared for whichever suits them. The choice is theirs."

His short speech ended, his calm, determined visage faded from the screen, the video lights went out and the camera stopped.

"And now," he said, beckoning Chauncey Baron over, "see if

you can get me through to Peking. I want to speak to Ju Xing-dao personally, so don't let them fob you off.''

"I rather doubt—'' the Secretary of State said.

"So do I,'' Ham agreed, ''but try.''

Back in the Oval Office fifteen minutes later, he was surprised and pleased when the phone rang and Chauncey said calmly, ''Mr. President, the Vice-Premier.''

"Excellency!'' he said. ''I appreciate your courtesy in returning my call.''

"How could I not, Mr. President?'' the wispy little voice replied, clear and distinct via satellite across twelve thousand miles. ''It is always an honor to speak with you. I must congratulate you, he added with the faintest, but detectable, of ironies, ''on your magnificent address just now. It expressed the aspirations of all the world.''

"It did?'' the President inquired dryly. ''I thought it expressed the determination of the United States and its President not to be dismayed or thrown off course by any alliance between Moscow and Peking.''

"Not just 'any alliance,' Mr. President,'' Ju Xing-dao said gently. ''An alliance of understanding—''

" 'To restore socialist harmony and repel imperialist aggressors,' '' the President finished for him in the same dry tone. ''Exactly what does that mean?''

"It seems self-evident,'' Ju said softly. ''When the wind blows, the trees shall stand together.''

"Yes,'' Hamilton Delbacher said, mimicking more dryly if possible, than before, ''And when the woodsmen join hands, the pine must drop its needles.''

"Not on us, I hope,'' Ju said with a faint little chuckle. ''Surely not on us!''

"That depends,'' the President said. ''What do you think you stand to gain from this alliance, Vice-Premier?''

"Must there always be 'gain' from such things, Mr. President?'' Ju inquired with some disapproval. ''Cannot they simply be arrangements between friends for a more amicable relationship?''

"Not in today's context,'' the President said. ''In any event, I did not know you and the Soviet Union were 'friends.' ''

"China is friends to everyone," Ju observed. "It is our desire to have friendship with the whole world."

"I am afraid," the President said, permitting his voice to become cold, "that we cannot take so innocent a view of this matter. Or that we can quite believe in China's friendly intentions."

"Mr. President," Ju said with some severity, "China has done everything possible to assist you in these recent hectic weeks. What more could we do?"

"You could have refrained from tying yourselves by treaty to the world's greatest troublemaker," Hamilton Delbacher said sharply. "You see how it has been received around the world. 'It means war,' a lot of people say. Well: does it? I'd like to know. It might have some bearing on my plans."

"How could it mean war?" Ju inquired, voice a little stronger now, expressing some righteous indignation. "China is not going to attack you. We do not have the military strength. How could we reach you? It is absurd."

"I am not saying China will attack us," the President said. "I am simply pointing out the obvious, which is that you have now freed Serapin to move with considerable flexibility wherever he pleases without having to worry about China on his flank."

"Need he not?" Ju inquired with the faintest of chuckles. "I wonder if he is really that complacent now."

"I doubt it," the President conceded with a rather grim chuckle himself. "But for the moment the practical fact is that he *is* freer to move than he was. Look what he did when he was worried about you. Imagine what he will do now that he is somewhat relieved of that worry."

"It relieves China of some worry, too," Ju reminded gently. "Perhaps now his multiplicities of energy will be directed elsewhere. At least for a time."

"And after that?"

"Five years, as the treaty says?" Ju dismissed it comfortably. "Much can happen in five years."

"Too damned much can happen in five minutes," Hamilton Delbacher said. "Don't be too sure he won't turn on you again when it suits his purpose."

"Or we on him," Ju murmured. "It is a game we all play, is it not?"

"Not so much the United States," its President responded. "Not so much the U.S. We are not quite that—adaptable. It takes us much longer to formulate a position, and normally we stay with it for some time."

"Too long, perhaps," Ju remarked.

"Have we tried to be friends with *you*—'too long?' " the President inquired sharply.

"You have not been friends in some important aspects," Ju said smoothly. But the President refused to take the bait.

"We have done everything we could consistent with our principles and other obligations," he said calmly. "And so it will remain if you wish to continue to be friends with us. You just heard my speech. I said we had not been notified of any change in our diplomatic, cultural or commercial relations with the P.R.C. Are we being so notified now?"

"Mr. President," Ju said softly, "It was you who initiated this conversation, do you not remember; it was not I. There has been no need seen here to communicate with you at this time. Therefore the assumption must be that all remains as it was between us, must it not?"

"Put it down to my typical American lack of tact," Hamilton Delbacher said dryly. "I found it hard to contain my curiosity. We can rely upon it then, that you are planning no overt moves of any kind at this time?"

" 'At this time,' " Ju echoed with a wispy little chortle. "That favorite escape clause of so many of you Westerners. Yes, at this time, you may rely on this. And," he added, "for some time to come, I think. Unless, of course," he went on gently, "I find that I am being overruled by my colleagues here, or that some action is being taken that I may not know about."

"Which leaves you in a position to stand clear and continue to deal with me as needed, of course," the President said. "Good thinking. It is well to retain a bridge to America."

"There are many bridges to America," Ju Xing-dao objected.

"Drawbridges," the President said. "Subject to being raised at any time."

"But better than none," the Vice-Premier noted. "He who would span the raging river needs many bridges."

Hamilton Delbacher snorted. "Particularly when the flood is rising."

"Talk to President Serapin," Ju Xing-dao suggested with again the wispiest of chuckles, a sound of amusement so faint the President barely heard it. "Ask him whether he is sure which way the flood is going."

"I do not intend to talk to President Serapin," Hamilton Delbacher said shortly, "until he precipitates something that makes it necessary. As I assume," he added with a trace more gloom in his voice then he really intended to reveal to the Vice-Premier, "he presently will."

"Oh, I think not for a time," Ju Xing-dao said with what appeared to be confident certainty. "He has too much to take care of now. There is a limit to even his duplicity, I think."

The President was tempted to utter an obvious and ironic guffaw but restrained himself.

"I hope so," he said gravely. "Otherwise I shall be impelled to take the most drastic measures."

"Oh?" Ju inquired, not quite hiding a sudden quickening of interest. "In what way, Mr. President?"

"The direction of the wind determines the wave of the wheat," Ham Delbacher said promptly. "And he who has the compass finds the north. Or something . . . You will discover in due time, Vice-Premier, should it become necessary. Just tell your friend in Moscow that he underestimated me last time on several occasions. He must not do so again."

"He is not 'my friend,'" Ju Xing-dao said, voice coming as close to asperity as its fragile strength permitted.

"Ally, then," the President said. "Socialist partner. Fellow hegemonist. Whatever."

"Mr. President," Ju said sharply, "I do not think you should use the word hegemonist, which you know is repugnant to us. Its use will not help to preserve *our* friendship."

"Such as it is now," the President observed. "Good-bye, Vice Premier. Pass the word to Yuri. Tell him to be very careful. I am a patient man, but my stock of patience has been just about exhausted in these recent weeks. I should not like to have to draw on it again.''

"I think he knows that, Mr. President," the Vice-Premier said stiffly. "In any event, it is not my place to advise him. I am sure he understands your position well enough."

"I hope so," Ham Delbacher said, "because I do not intend to spell it out further."

"Good-bye, Mr. President," Ju said, voice becoming remote both in volume and emphasis. "Perhaps we may talk again another day."

"Perhaps," Ham said. "Sometime."

The days between then and now had, on the whole, gone with much the same inconclusiveness. He had considered several times, and finally rejected completely, any idea of trying to communicate with his opposite number in the Kremlin. Yuri was busy playing host to half the world, it seemed, as delegation after delegation came to Moscow to express official thanks for his statesmanlike actions in saving humanity from the crisis he himself had created. The irony of this was not lost on some members of the Western press, who commented acridly and at length, but there were many journals and commentators who joined the hallelujah chorus. And there was no doubt that, as Variety put it, **YURI BOFFO IN BUSH. THIRD WORLD FLOCKS TO VIDEO OF WAR GAMES END.**

And so, indeed, did almost everyone else. There seemed to be an endless fascination with the crisis and its conclusions. The highlights were run and rerun on television not only in the bush where Yuri was boffo but on all the networks and cable outlets. Endless media analyses accompanied this. From them Yuri Serapin definitely emerged the hero, Hamilton Delbacher not exactly the villain but certainly, in the opinion of many commentators, the one who by his blundering had very nearly blown up the globe.

His reaction to this at first had been harsh and explosive. He had been tempted to issue a statement, hold a press conference, make some sarcastic comment to the media. His own common sense and that of his advisors stopped that.

"Let him put on the show," Jim Elrod advised from the Senate.

"Even the dumbest of 'em will stop and wonder one of these days. He can't hide all he did just because there's a big foofaraw now."

"I hear there's a movement afoot by some jerks on the Hill to put in some kind of resolution praising him for his statesmanship," the President said in a disgusted tone. "How stupid can you get?"

"Well, seein' as how it's James Monroe Madison," Jim Elrod said, rolling the names in the same orotund tone as that used by the pompous and mightily egotistical senior senator from California himself, "I don't think there's much limit. However, we've got him squelched, I think. Leastways we told him he'd never be able to claim another damned cent for California throught the Appropriations Committee if he didn't knock it off. He couldn't stand the thought of Mark gettin' all the credit, so I think he's calmed down . . . I *think*."

"I don't want any postmortem debates up there," the President said. "I've got enough headaches as it is. The Speaker told me he'd put the cork in the House."

"If he says so," Senator Elrod said with a chuckle, "he will. I think we've got things pretty well under control here, too. It's a time to go forward, now, and not keep lookin' back."

"Say that to the public, will you?" Ham requested. "Very brief and to the point—a time to look forward. Because God knows we have to."

"I'll do it," Senator Elrod said. "Right away. But tell me, Ham—Mr. President. What do we have to look forward to?"

"That," the President said somberly, "is the rub. Constant provocations from the Soviets, more aggressive and open now than they have ever been. A further falling away of the weak and cowardly around the world. A greater snuggling up to Moscow by all the fainthearted. Higher defense spending. The draft. Perhaps a civilian draft. Sacrifice, which is something the American people in the last three decades have become psychologically almost unable to accept. Maybe gas rationing. Maybe food and clothing. Maybe even housing. Constant vigilance. Constant tension. Constant strain. A fortress mentality, perhaps, for a while. The Israeli syndrome, on a much bigger scale: always on edge—always on guard—always watching—never at rest. Do you think we can do it here? I wonder."

"If you say we have to—"

"Jim," he said patiently, "it's going to take a lot more than just the President saying it. It's going to take a national agreement, a national determination, a unified will, a whole new mind-set. Everybody who believes in the danger will have to help. But how many do?"

"The way my mail's running," Senator Elrod said, "a whole hell of a lot."

"Oh, sure," Ham Delbacher said. "But give the termites a chance to work on them for a while, let the clever weakening voices begin the doubts, the undercutting, the usual attempts to force the country's thinking into the pattern some of our frightened know-it-alls think is best for us, and we won't have a unified position very long."

"We've got to," Jim Elrod said somberly. "Don't they realize what we're up against?"

"You know how well they realize it," the President said. "You read them and listen to them. I wouldn't give you two cents for what *they're* trying to do to the country."

"It baffles me," Jim Elrod said. "But, then, it always has. How they can want to see their own country so weakened in the face of what we're up against—"

"Oh, I don't think they exactly *want* to see it weakened," the President said. "They just can't bear to admit that somebody else's judgment of the danger is better than theirs. It goes against the grain of a lifetime. Plus the fact they're scared to death that we'll have to do just exactly what I've outlined if we really face up to it . . ."

"So what will you do about the Sino-Soviet pact?" Senator Elrod inquired. "It still leaves it up to you, doesn't it?"

"Pray like hell," the President said, "and carry on."

The advice on how to do so came from many voices. So, too, did the intelligence reports which made it obvious that he must not be too long about it.

He received emphatic admonitions from expected quarters, falling neatly into two predictable categories, as always.

"In the wake of the crisis just past," the *Times* said, "in which humanity seems to have been saved at the last moment by an exercise in restraint on the part of the President of the Soviet Union, it would seem to behoove President Delbacher to reassess his own approach to world affairs in the hope that another such exhausting confrontation can be avoided in the future.

"Certainly no American can fault the way in which he refused to knuckle under to Soviet pressure skillfully manipulated and applied by President Serapin. It is quite possible that his refusal to be bluffed by the worldwide show of Soviet force was the key factor in bringing about a Soviet backdown at the last possible moment. But basic questions as to the wisdom of his own sometimes provocative conduct remain. He should seek answers and learn from them.

"His ultimatum concerning Soviet submarines at the Cuban naval base of Cienfuegos, for instance, seems in retrospect a reckless and unnecessary provocation which might well have prompted the most devastating Soviet reaction. So, too, do his harsh responses to every overture by President Serapin to find some compromise way out of the situation. It is true that President Serapin to a large degree created the situation himself. Nonetheless, once created, it was incumbent upon President Delbacher to cooperate in finding a way out that would permit both sides to gradually defuse the crisis with dignity and international esteem intact.

"Unfortunately he did not do so, and the initiative was left to Mr. Serapin to find the solution that is now bringing him such universal plaudits from a relieved world.

"President Delbacher, it seems likely, still needs much seasoning in the office which he has occupied, after all, for only two months. He needs to moderate his toughness—which he has now amply proved—with the skill, delicacy and willingness to compromise of a true statesman. It is one thing to be macho. It is another to exercise power safely, and with grace.

"We hope, for the sake of his own country and all humanity, that from here on he can find it in himself to do so."

To which Ham Delbacher, reading the editorial aloud to Elinor at breakfast in the family room on the second floor of the White House, remarked, "Hmph!"

"I agree with *that*," she said with a smile. "And what say the *Post*, and dear Anna Hastings in the Washington *Inquirer*?"

"The same," he said. "I won't bore you with further dissertations on what a dangerous dolt I am and what a statesman Yuri is. You can read them later."

"Doesn't *anybody* like you?" she inquired with mock wryness. He nodded.

"Oh, yes, quite a few. I'm not without friends. For contrast, let me give you the *Wall Street Journal*."

" 'President Serapin of the Soviet Union may be collecting plaudits of a nervous world at this moment, but we suspect in history's perspective it will be seen that President Delbacher is the man to be credited with saving mankind—if not from nuclear holocaust, then from permanent and irreversible Soviet domination.

" 'President Serapin obviously had the intention of precipitating the surrender of the West by an overwhelming show of that force which the Soviet Union, by design and deceit, has carefully built up during these recent decades of 'detente.' President Delbacher refused to be bluffed. The world eventually came around to his support. The threat was withdrawn. Iron nerves and a steady purpose—in which, it might be pointed out, the courage of a majority of the American people played an indispensable part—carried the day.

" 'President Serapin picked up his dangerous marbles and went home to collect, in our opinion, much more credit than is due. President Delbacher now faces the fundamental and overridingly vital question: where do we go from here?

" 'A program of specifics is called for now. This should include a further strengthening of American arms; the development of a steady, consistent, *non*belligerent but *firm* policy toward the Soviet Union; the calling of a new international disarmament conference to take advantage of the urge—which may not last long—to reduce the threat of ever-growing armaments; a sensible civil defense program that will recognize the futility of mass evacuations but still provide on-site shelters to which citizens may repair if worse comes to worst and time permits; a new round of strong, affirmative diplomacy designed to strengthen ties with our NATO allies and with all other nations who may now be more disposed than before to seek a reasonably lasting peace.

" 'These, taken together with a strengthening of national purpose, a reaffirmation of human rights and human values in America and the noncommunist world—values which must be preserved if the word "civilization" is to have any meaning at all—plus an agreed national desire to live and go forward as a free people—and we will emerge in fairly good shape.

" 'Central to all of these plans and purposes, of course, is the President of the United States. So far, in our estimation, he has done a remarkable job under terrifyingly difficult circumstances. He does not have the flash and glamor of his predecessor, or of some others who have occupied the White House in recent years. Neither does he have the fey innocence and appalling incompetence of one or two others. He does have solid and unflinching character, and that is what America needs most right now.

" 'We are not worried about the future under Hamilton Delbacher, providing he moves and moves fast to shore up America's defenses not only militarily but in all those areas of national purpose and conviction that form a nation's greatest inner strength. We are confident he will.' "

"Which is a tall order and a flattering confidence," Elinor observed as they finished their customary light meal and he prepared to return to the Oval Office while she prepared to depart for a much-publicized national Red Cross board meeting on emergency medical measures to be taken in the event of attack. "But you can do it."

"I am fortified," he said with mock solemnity, kissing her lightly on the nose, "by such implicit faith in my poor old battered talents." His expression turned grim for a moment. "I'm glad you're going to the Red Cross. We've got to keep up the sense of urgency. Too many people everywhere are letting down."

And so they were, he reflected as he returned to his desk and the many calls that were waiting.

The great crisis had inevitably produced the great letdown. All over the world people, including his own, were making the relieved assumption that now they could relax. Governments as well as citizens were reverting swiftly to life as usual. It was human nature, but it did not make his task easier.

Some of his waiting calls he shunted aside, passing them on to Chauncey Baron in Foggy Bottom or to Secretary of Defense Roger Hackett across the Potomac in the Pentagon. Some from the Hill he accepted. Most were from former, older Senate colleagues pledging their support for whatever he now deemed necessary. A few were from nervous younger members of the Senate and House, conditioned by their education to be antiwar, antistrength, anti anything that might indicate the slightest show of continuing firmness or run even the remotest risk of renewed confrontation. He answered all as best he could, thanking his former older colleagues, attempting without much success to put what he regarded as some minimal backbone into his nervous younger callers.

Two calls he delayed returning for a while, debating what he might say to the determined people at the other end. Finally he notified his secretary. In a moment the soft, emphatic voice came over the wire from London.

"Mr. President!" she said. "How nice of you to return my call."

"I would not dream of doing otherwise, Prime Minister," he said cordially. "I need all the help I can get—and certainly you have furnished me with magnificent support in these recent weeks."

"I have done my best. The reward is that we now have a breathing space."

"But for how long?"

"Exactly what I was going to ask you," she responded. "My own guess is: not very."

"Mine, too," he agreed rather more gloomily than he had intended, not knowing then how brief it would be. His mood must have transmitted itself, because she uttered a cheery little chuckle.

"Now, Mr. President! This is no time for despondency and despair. You have just put the genie back in his bottle. It is only a matter of keeping him there." Her amusement increased, a wry note entered. "Very simple, really. Very simple!"

"Exactly, he said. "Particularly when he is not all back in the bottle. As you know, he has left his web all over the earth."

"And probably assumes we don't know it," she said scornfully.
"What kind of fools does he take us for?"

"I doubt if there is a limit," he said. "His ego is so great that it
cannot concede much intelligence to anyone else. Plus the conviction that history has singled him out to put an end to all of us—at
least to all our silly pretensions to liberty and justice and individual
freedom and the rule of decency and law."

"We have taken the measure of his kind before," she said tartly.
Ham Delbacher grunted.

"True. But we only did it this time through sheer luck and God's
good grace."

"*And* your character, and that of your people. *And* our character
in this island. *And* the character of a few others who stood beside us
when it was most necessary. It was not all happenstance, you
know."

"True enough," he said. "I didn't intend to demean all that or
sound ungrateful for it, God knows. We all did it together. But we
didn't really get rid of the Soviet military presence, which still
crawls about the seas and continents in its usual slimy fashion. He
didn't 'withdraw' everything. He has plenty still in place for the
next time around. Where do your intelligence services tell you it
may come?"

"We expect something in Western Europe," she said promptly.

"That is conventional wisdom," he agreed, "but I suspect it's
too obvious."

"Continuing maneuvers are going on in Bulgaria and Rumania.
They seem to have stepped them up a little since the big 'withdrawal.' "

"Too simple," he said. "Too predictable, too easy, entirely too
pat. I'm convinced it will be somewhere else."

"Where, then?"

"I don't know," he confessed. "But I just don't think it will
be somewhere that we're prepared for, as—to some degree, at
least—we are for Western Europe. Yuri prides himself on the unexpected. Why would they strike where we have the heaviest armor
and a fairly good organized force to stand against them? They
might make a feint there, but I certainly wouldn't expect the real
attack to come anywhere so obvious."

"That leaves many possibilities," she observed dryly. "Can Western intelligence keep an eye on them all?"

"I rather doubt it. Which poses some problems for us, doesn't it?"

"Would you like me to convey a warning to him?—not that he has been notorious for paying attention to me, but just to place a small cautionary note on the record?"

"By all means," the President said. "It can't do any harm. I've already sent him one myself through Ju Xing-dao."

"Ju called you?" she inquired with considerable surprise. "Now, what did he do that for?"

"He didn't," the President corrected. "I called him just to see what he would say about the pact."

"And?"

"Equivocal as ever," Ham Delbacher said. "Full of assurances that it means nothing except innocent friendship. Plus veiled implications that we should not worry because of course China is quite capable of turning on her newfound friend if in her opinion it becomes necessary."

"And vice versa," the Prime Minister observed. "So what else is new? What did he indicate might happen militarily as a result of it?"

"Staunch promises that nothing would," the President said. "I conveyed the impression that it would not be advisable and suggested my sentiments be passed along to Yuri. Your added advisory would not be a waste of time, I should think."

"You don't care to talk to him yourself?" she inquired. "I could assist in setting it up if you don't want to approach him directly."

"I'll approach him directly if it becomes necessary," he promised grimly. "For the moment, I think the best medicine is to leave him strictly alone, pending some overt action. Maybe there won't be any for a while."

"Maybe not for a while," she said, "but before long, I'm afraid."

"Within a year," he agreed, a prediction he looked back on now with rueful irony. "But for the moment I think he needs a breather as much as we do. I'm wondering about the advisability of holding NATO exercises in the next month or so, possibly in the North Atlantic. Just to show them we're still around. How would that appeal?''

"We could to it," she agreed. "If the others will cooperate."

"If they don't cooperate after the lesson we've just had, they don't deserve to survive. They'll cooperate."

"I expect so—with grumbling, but they will. Should we do something in the East also?''

"If you would care to," he suggested, "we might hold joint maneuvers out of Diego Garcia."

"That would upset our friend in Delhi," she said wryly, "but, then, she's always upset. I daresay we can stand it."

"She does upset very easily," he observed.

"Perhaps you should check with her and get back to me," she suggested. "Just for protocol's sake."

"Then the word *will* get right back to Yuri."

"Don't we want it to?" she inquired. "I thought that was the purpose of it all."

And so it was, he reflected as he waited for the call to go through to India's imperious lady. Once again he was facing Yuri without a great deal more to go on than his own will and a large amount of bluff. The United States was not helpless in a military sense, but neither was it equipped to fight all over the world wherever the Soviet Union might choose to exercise its many options for trouble. Despite diligent efforts in recent years, the forces he led were still not large enough to fight worldwide, still not flexible enough to meet any and all challenges that might be posed. And his military, like the British Prime Minister's, were still basically locked into the idea that the greatest challenge of all was most likely to come in Western Europe. He himself was not so sure; a premonition in which, he now knew, he had been unhappily all too correct.

As of the moment of his return call to New Delhi, however, this had not unfolded. The Indian Prime Minister was as tart and scornful as he had expected her to be.

"Prime Minister," he said after formal greetings had been exchanged and the conversation had progressed to the point where he felt he could broach the idea, "it is quite likely that we will hold NATO exercises in the North Atlantic sometime next month—"

"Why?" she demanded sharply. "What are these 'exercises'?

Why would you feel it necessary to renew aggravations and provocations that have already come close to destroying the world?''

"*We* 'renew' them?'' he demanded with equal sharpness. "We didn't start them in the first place; how could we 'renew' them? You deny NATO's right to hold whatever exercises it pleases, Prime Minister? On what grounds, may I ask, do you try to interfere with NATO?''

"Well,'' she said, taken aback by his tone. "Well! I am not saying that I interfere with NATO—''

"I am saying you do,'' he said coldly. "And by what right?''

"Well,'' she said again, retreating into indignation. *"Well!"*— and he could hear the jangle clearly as she shook her head and tossed her giant earrings and the gold bangles on her arms—"I was not aware that my friendly call of encouragement was to be turned into an occasion to berate me—''

"You have begun berating me,'' he pointed out, unyielding, "and so far in this conversation the words of encouragement have been very few. I have been congratulated on bowing to the peace-loving desires of the President of the Soviet Union, when all along, as you admitted yourself in the United Nations, it was the President of the Soviet Union who precipitated the crisis in the first place. We and the United Kingdom,'' he added without missing a beat, "also intend to hold exercises out of Diego Garcia.''

"What?" she cried, her voice sailing upward in righteous indignation at the mention of the British-owned, U.S.-developed island. *"What?* Exercises out of Diego Garcia? *In the Indian Ocean?* What—what—''

"Don't screech, Prime Minister,'' he said, deliberately unimpressed. "The satellite transmission is perfect; I can hear you very well. I believe it was President Serapin who told you in the Security Council that just because the ocean bears India's name for the convenience of cartographers, it does not mean the entire ocean belongs to India. The United Kingdom and ourselves have a perfect right to conduct exercises out of the base at Diego Garcia and we intend to do so.''

"India will regard this as an unfriendly act!'' she cried, and in his mind's eye he could see her sweeping one of her gorgeous saris around her shoulders with a dramatic gesture.

"I would hope not," he said calmly. "I would hope second thought and sound reflection will persuade you not to react in quite such a hostile fashion. The thought is, after all, to protect India, among other things."

" 'Among other things,' " she echoed scornfully. "And what are these 'other things'? Renewed imperialist aggression against Southeast Asia, perhaps? A move on East Africa? An attempt to shore up Pakistan and encourage rebellion in Afghanistan?"

"Prime Minister," he said patiently, "you are an extremely intelligent woman and you *know* those statements are nonsense. You are not addressing the Lokh Saba now, you are addressing me, so please let's refrain from exaggerated political rhetoric. It has no bearing here."

"But it will have in the Lokh Saba," she said with some relish, picking up his reference to India's unruly lower house of parliament. "It will be very pertinent there, even if I do not raise it myself. Many others will."

"I'm sure," he agreed. "That is inevitable. It will make some difference, however, if you oppose these ridiculous interpretations rather than join in them."

"Why should I not join in them?" she inquired, "particularly when I am not convinced that they are such 'exaggerated political rhetoric,' as you would have me believe?"

"Well, Prime Minister," he said, "if that is really your belief, then I see no further point in this conversation. When you are in a more reasonable mood and have something constructive to suggest to me—"

"No, wait!" she said, sounding more mollified. "It was not my intention to argue with you, Mr. President, only to give you my best wishes in the new era following the crisis. It seems to me there is a great opportunity to achieve much in the way of genuine moves toward peace, in the wake of the confrontation between you and President Serapin. The world is expecting this. I only wished to proffer India's services in whatever way we can be of help. That is all."

"If that is all, Prime Minister," he said dryly, "we seem to have strayed rather far off the mark. However, if you really do wish to be helpful, you can do one thing for me."

"Yes?" she asked, instantly wary.

"Yes. You can join in warning Mr. Serapin in the strongest possible terms that any new attempts to disrupt the peace and threaten the world with further Soviet domination will be met with even stronger action than last time. Tell him he would undertake such a course at a very great peril to himself and his country."

"I could do that, yes," she said slowly, "though I am not sure he would listen. In any event, I do not think he will wish to move in my area of the world—"

"Out from Afghanistan?" he interrupted. "Over from Ethiopia? Up from South Yemen? Subs off Bombay and Calcutta, as they were just a week ago and probably still are? Come, Prime Minister! It is all very well for India to be idealistic and optimistic and hopeful of all good things in the world, but it is not very practical, now, is it?"

"I should not worry about India, if I were you," she said stiffly. "India can take care of itself. I should worry about Western Europe and your threatened allies, if I were you. They are much more at risk than we are. Who could ever conquer India? Worry about Western Europe, Mr. President, and do not lecture *me!*"

"I'll grant you no one could *rule* India for long," he said, "but I'm not so sure about conquering. As for Western Europe—"

"As for Western Europe, it would crumble in a day!"

"Not quite."

"Let us say a week, then. Surely you would not claim longer."

"It would depend."

"On the will to resist," she said scornfully, "and we all know what that is. Particularly with the pipeline now in place. They could be cut off in ten minutes, and then where would the will to resist be?"

"It would not be gone altogether," he said sharply, "and certainly it would not be gone here. Surely you have no doubt of that."

"No," she conceded, "no doubt of that. But meanwhile Western Europe will be gone and the Soviet Union will be at Calais, and what then of fine words and high intentions?"

"I don't think a new crisis will come there," he said stubbornly. "It is too obvious."

"Well," she said tartly, "it will not come in India, I can assure you that. So you wish me to warn President Serapin, I take it. I can do that."

"With conviction," he suggested.

"Mr. President," she said with a rather wintry chuckle, "I do everything with conviction."

"Yes," he agreed.

"And if not Western Europe, where?" she inquired.

"I couldn't say," he replied. "But I just have a hunch."

"It will be Western Europe," she said flatly, "if it comes any-where. Everyone expects it. It is the only logical place."

"That's why I have the hunch," he said grimly, though he could not have put his finger on why or have accurately predicted what had now occurred.

After they had parted with mutual assurances of continuing to consult, in which she placed little intention and he little faith, he sat for a while considering the problem he faced because of exactly this skepticism on the world's part.

It existed, he knew, in the British command, in the United Nations, in NATO, in his own chiefs of staff; it seemed to be prevalent all over the world. The conventional wisdom said the Soviet Union would confront the West militarily, if it ever did, through Western Europe. Endless books had been written about it, endless fantasies contrived. For that very reason—and because other options would be so much more attractive to him, were he sitting at Yuri's desk in the Kremlin—he found it very difficult to believe.

Why strike at the most obvious spot when so many other attractive opportunities begged to be exploited in places where the West was much less prepared and where risk of its armed response was so much less?

He did not of course know, at the moment of these conversations coming immediately after the announcement of the Sino-Soviet pact, how correct he was; and so found himself confronted with a difficult problem with both the country and his own military advisers.

Mark Coffin summed it up as well as anyone when the President decided to call him at home later that evening. Linda answered, sounding pleased to hear from him.

"Uncle Ham!" she said, reverting for a moment to the name she had called him ever since she and her father, Senator Jim Elrod, had first come to Washington two decades ago; then, with a chuckle, "Mr. President! How are you feeling? More relaxed?"

"Not very," he said, a little more grimly than he had intended. She reacted at once.

"Why not?" she inquired quickly. "Is something else happening already that we don't know about?"

"Now you're sounding like a mother," he said more lightly, "which is what you should do, of course."

"It's my job," she said with a still uneasy cheerfulness, "and I'll bet you'll find almost every parent in the country still just as jumpy as I am. You haven't answered my question. *Is* there something new?"

"Not yet," he said, "and with a little luck, not for quite a while if I can possibly prevent it. But I am *not* relaxed about it. How can I be, knowing my opponent's capacity for mischief? He's not a very nice fellow, you know."

"I despise him," she said shortly. "And the Chinese too."

"They're playing their game," he said, "and it's not one that should really have shocked anybody very much. It's to their practical interests, and they've always been a most pragmatic people. Maybe they'll switch back again one of these days. It wouldn't be surprising."

"But in the meantime it poses a real problem for us."

"Oh, yes. It frees Yuri to move around a bit. For a while, anyway."

"Damn them anyway!" she said fiercely. *"Why won't they leave us alone!"*

"Because they intend to destroy us," he said simply. "A difficult concept for many of our countrymen to accept, but there it is."

"I suppose you want to speak to Mark," she said. "Hang on. He's busy writing a speech, but I know he'll be more than happy to get away from it for a while. Is it anything I can know about?"

"Nothing in particular," Ham Delbacher said. "Just a tired old President, touching base with the young."

"Sorry I can't be more cheerful," she said, "but I'm still getting over the last couple of months."

"Aren't we all."

"Hold on. I'll get him."

In a moment the calmly efficient voice of California's junior Senator came over the line.

"A nice break in the evening. What's up?"

"Nothing much. I understand you're writing a speech, so I thought you might like an excuse to interrupt it."

"Love it," Mark said. "Love it. I have to speak to the Commonwealth Club in San Francisco on Friday. I'm going to try to simultaneously calm people down and keep them on their toes."

"My problem exactly," the President said with a chuckle. "How are you going to do it?"

"By assuring them that you have everything under control but we still have a lot of difficulties to face," Mark said promptly. He laughed a little ruefully. "Doesn't sound very original, does it?"

"No," the President agreed, "it doesn't. But like you, I can't think of a clever way to say it."

"Is it true?" Mark inquired. "That you have everything under control, I mean?"

Ham Delbacher sighed, an unhappy sound he made no attempt to conceal from this young confident on whose reactions he had come to rely a good deal in recent weeks.

"Just between you and me, I'd hardly say so. I've just conveyed the message, through our ladies of Britain and India and Ju Xingdao—"

"Oh?"

"Yes, equivocal as ever and full of ancient wisdom—to friend Yuri, that any attempt at new adventures will be met with a most vigorous response from here. Whether this will do any good, I don't know. But the try had to be made."

"Yes. Are there any signs that he's going to break out again soon?"

"Not aside from the forces he's left in place around the world," the President said, "which are substantial."

"Really?" Mark inquired, sounding shocked. "You haven't told us about them."

"No, not yet. We're making some moves of our own to neutralize them as much as possible. I thought I'd wait a bit and see what happens. No need to get the world upset again needlessly. The time may come," he added grimly, "soon enough."

"They *are* tricky bastards, aren't they?" Mark observed. "Do you suppose Ivan Valerian would know anything?"

"I don't know," the President said thoughtfully. "I had the impression he's about run out of information, but it's possible he may have heard some predictions about future plans. I don't suppose you can be a military aide to the Soviet dictator without hearing quite a bit. And he was very helpful during the crisis, certainly. I'm still not entirely sure he's a genuine defector."

"I'd like to think so," Mark said, "but the doubt always remains about such people. The way the Soviets work, they could plant him and let him lie dormant for a decade before it came time for harvest."

"I sometimes wonder if we have a decade left," the President said somberly.

"Not an entirely original feeling," Mark agreed. "Half that or less, it sometimes seems to me. But one has to keep hoping. For the kids' sake, if nothing else."

"Yes," the President agreed in the same sober tone. "For the kids' sake. And my grand-kids, too. . . . And all kids, everywhere."

"What's NATO going to do about this?" Mark inquired. "Anything? Or just sit on their duffs and be difficult, as usual?"

"The British Prime Minister and I think it would be a good idea to hold exercises in the North Atlantic, just to show we're still around—if we can get the others to cooperate."

"They'd better," Mark remarked, "since they're the ones who are under the gun."

"You think that?"

"Don't you?"

"Everybody does except me," Hamilton Delbacher said. "It's the agreed faith. Which is why I'm looking elsewhere. Wouldn't you, if you were the Soviets?"

"I might if I were Serapin," Mark said slowly, "but when you talk about 'the Soviets' you get into all that ponderous machinery of theirs—Politburo and so on. *They* like to be predictable, too, it seems to me. Particularly the older ones."

"I'm old," the President said with a chuckle. "Moderately. And I'm not all that predictable. But I know what you mean. However, there *is* Yuri, and as we have learned extensively, Yuri is a born gambler. He is also, I believe, in command there in a way nobody has really been since Stalin. They're scared to death of him, from what we hear through our sources. He can carry the Politburo with him if he really wants to, as witness what has just happened in the worldwide maneuvers. There was a lot of uneasiness underneath, but they went along. And now he has succeeded brilliantly—in their eyes—in what he set out to do, which was to scare the hell out of the world and come out of it with a lot of his forces still in place. He's riding high, really high. I don't think there are any restraints on him now. I think what Yuri wants, Yuri gets, from the Politburo. Which is why I think he can jump anywhere. He has that kind of mind."

"Even with their economy in the shape it's in? We got the CIA's report on them in the Senate Foreign Relations Committee this morning. The harvest is terrible again this year, industry is sagging, consumer goods are scarcer than ever, drunkenness is almost a universal curse, morale in the armed forces is low, racial minorities are getting restless, particularly the Moslems—"

"And still he was able to order worldwide military maneuvers and his forces were able to do it," the President reminded. "When you sacrifice everything to the simple aim of conquest, as the Soviets have for at least the last four decades, you can go a long, long way."

"On a tightrope," Mark said.

"Yes, but he got there, didn't he? And a lot of their stuff is still out there. And if the tightrope is shaky enough, sometimes if you run really fast because you have to, and never stop to look down, you can get across to the other side. He may be a very desperate man at heart—and so may they all in the top leadership. Which could make them extra dangerous right now, and propel them into new adventures anywhere. Or everywhere."

"But Western Europe is still the industrial heart of the continent," Mark objected. "It's the nearest industrial complex; it's the most logical one for them to try to absorb into their system, which badly needs a shot in the arm economically. It's contiguous, which

I'm sure appeals to their military, as it eliminates a lot of headaches present in the global picture. No, I think you're mistaken. If anything comes, it'll be there.''

"I won't argue," the President said, "but I'm not at all sure but he's convinced himself that that gloomy picture is an entirely false reading, and that everything is in good shape. There's an enormous ego there, as well as desperation—a fearful combination. Anyway, I'm certainly going to instruct every intelligence operation we've got to be on the alert everywhere . . . Why don't you talk to Ivan again, sound him out a bit? He'll see you coming, so be frank about it; no point in playing coy. I'd like to know what he has to say, for whatever it's worth.''

"We have a tennis date tomorrow. I'll talk to him."

"He *is* getting Americanized. Next come jogging and health foods, I suppose. Let me know what he says. And if your distinguished colleague in the Senate gets any more crazy ideas about praising the statesmanship of Y. P. Serapin, sit on him, will you?''

"That old ass," Mark said flatly. "If the voters of California don't kick James Monroe Madison out of office next year, they're crazy.''

"Well, they are," the President said with a chuckle. "We all know that, don't we?" At least we Easterners do. Meanwhile, I'd appreciate anything you can do to keep him under control.''

"Oh, I'll oppose him if he tries to put in a resolution or anything. We barely speak as it is, except on things directly affecting the state. Let me know if there's anything I can do to help. Of course I'm always available.''

"Your speech to the Commonwealth Club Friday sounds like exactly what's needed," Hamilton Delbacher said. "Keep sounding positive notes every chance you get. And also help me keep up the sense of urgency. We've got to maintain a certain level if I'm to have room to maneuver.''

"That NATO exercise should help."

"Yes. We and the British are also going to conduct some exercises out of Diego Garcia next month, which sent our lady from Delhi into near-hysterics when I told her. But I think it's necessary—again, just to show we're still around.''

"That will probably mean another fuss in the United Nations.''

"Let 'em fuss," the President said. "I don't think I'm going up there again for a while. They can scream their heads off if they want to. I have more important fish to fry, right now."

"Good luck," Mark said.

"Thanks," Hamilton Delbacher responded. "I'll probably need it."

Next morning, facing the Secretaries of State and Defense and the Joint Chiefs of Staff in the Oval office—a discussion eerily prophetic of the one he was about to have with them now in the Situation Room—he had found himself up against the same conviction that if anything happened it would happen in Europe. The reasons for this conviction, he suspected, were not entirely based on a dispassionate assessment of probabilities. Like the British and NATO, his military leaders were also conditioned by the fact that Western Europe was where they were best prepared to fight. Contemplating other possibilities made them uncomfortable to the point of stubbornness.

General Rutherford ("Smidge") Hallowell, U.S. Army, Chairman of the Joint Chiefs, finally spelled it out quite candidly.

"It isn't that we wouldn't like to be able to fight all over the world wherever that bastard wants to light a fuse," Smidge Hallowell said, "but we just aren't able to. So we have to concentrate on where we're likeliest to be most successful."

"You didn't hesitate a couple of weeks ago when the Soviets were everywhere around the world," the President pointed out. "What's the problem now, Smidge?"

"You know how thinly we were spread, Mr. President," General Hallowell said. He shivered suddenly. "I hope we never get in a spot like that again."

"We will if he pulls another stunt like that one," the President said bluntly. "At least, I hope you'll respond if I request you to."

General Hallowell gave an unhappy shrug.

"You're the Commander-in-Chief. But it won't be easy."

And he looked somberly around at his colleagues, all of them still tagged in typical American fashion with the nicknames they had acquired in student days—General Martin ("Bump") Smith, chief of staff, U.S. Army; Admiral Harman ("Snooze") Rydecker, Chief of Naval Operations; General Bartram C. ("Bart") Jamison, chief of staff, U.S. Air Force; and General Robert ("Gutsy") Twitchell, commandant, U.S. Marine Corps.

Bart Jamison was the first to respond in his deceptively lazy, actually shrewd-as-a-razor fashion.

"Everything we get, Mr. President," he said in his offhand way, "every piece of intelligence received in the last couple of days since Serapin announced his big withdrawal, is that while they *have* left a lot of men and materiel scattered around the globe, the main bulk of their forces really is going home and the main thrust of their activity does seem to be to consolidate and regroup in their own backyard. And that means, it seems to me, that we inevitably return to Western Europe as the principal target because that's what they've been planning on all along. Otherwise why the SS-20 missiles, the enormous tank buildup facing Western Europe, and all the rest of it? It doesn't make sense if they're planning to strike somewhere else."

"Maybe 'strike' is the wrong word," Admiral Rydecker suggested. "Maybe 'subversion' or 'brushfire' or 'national wars of liberation' would apply better here."

"My point exactly," the President said. He turned to the Secretary of State, who was staring thoughtfully out at the Rose Garden. "What do you think, Chauncey?"

Chauncey Baron, obviously brought back from somewhere far away—probably, the President thought, one of those romantic conquests for which he was famous in the gossip columns—turned his angular frame and aquiline nose back to the room and surveyed them all thoughtfully.

"I agree with everybody," he said with a wry little chuckle. "I think the principal danger still lies in an attack on Western Europe, but I also think, Snooze, that you could be quite right that 'brushfire wars' and 'wars of national liberation' could also be launched simultaneously. I assume we would have to rely on the Navy a lot for that."

"The Navy," Admiral Rydecker said somewhat stiffly, "is ready for whatever it is called upon to do."

"Well, get you," Bart Jamison said wryly. "So is the Air Force. And I assume the Army—?"

"Certainly," Bump Smith said promptly.

"And the Marines?"

"Ab-so-lutely," Gutsy Twitchell said, shifting his stocky, still-trim little frame emphatically in his chair.

"We're all a pack of cheerful liars," General Jamison said with his customary sardonic twinkle. "We all seem to be completely prepared for everything. So what are you worried about, Mr. President?"

"This is all a lot of fun and games, gentlemen," Hamilton Delbacher said, "but the basic fact is that we've just been stretched to our utmost and we may have to be again. We can't afford to let down for so much as a minute. We've got to go right on building up just as fast as we can, and there can be no slackening anywhere. I hope that's clear enough, Roger?"

The Secretary of Defense also looked thoughtfully at the military commanders and nodded slowly.

"Yes, Mr. President," he said, "I think that's clear enough. I don't think anybody here has any disposition to 'let down.' The question is, will the Congress and the country continue to support us now that the pressure seems to be off?"

There was a stirring of agreement around the half-circle facing the President. He looked grim.

"That *is* the question," he agreed, "and that's *my* problem. I don't want to overdo the warning and the exhortation but at the same time I want to keep them aware that at this point we're a long way from being able to relax."

"They're relaxed, all right," Chauncey said with some scorn. "You can't keep Americans keyed up to sacrifice without a war, that's their nature. Which they share, I might add in fairness to them, with nine-tenths of the world. Look at the euphoria that's gripping the globe. My God, they're still dancing in the streets. The processions of thanksgiving to visit the shrine of St. Yuri arrive in Moscow on the hour every hour. The Great Letdown is everywhere. Did you see the news last night? Restaurants, hotels, nightclubs, theaters—absolutely packed in every major city of the world, all other business virtually at a standstill. People are partying like crazy; it's holiday everywhere. It's as though the world has gone mad with relief."

"It's because they think the Soviets have suddenly become peace-loving," Roger Hackett said dryly. "It's because they think *this* time the devious thugs really mean it."

"Understandably enough," the President agreed. "And you can't blame them, really. It's been a terribly tense couple of months. But still . . ."

" 'But still—' " Bart Jamison echoed. "That doesn't make our job any easier, does it."

"It makes our job," the President said grimly, "just exactly as though as Yuri knew it would when he stage-managed the whole artificial crisis. You and Roger are both testifying on the Hill tomorrow, aren't you, Chauncey?"

"Senate Foreign Relations, for me," the Secretary of State said.

"House Armed Services, for me," the Secretary of Defense said.

"I'm speaking at the Air Force Academy in Colorado Springs," Bart Jamison remarked.

"And I to the new class at West Point," Bump Smith said.

"I haven't any plans," Gutsy Twitchell said, "but I could probably find something public to do."

"I'm free also," Snooze Rydecker said. "Why don't we get the Senate Armed Services Committee to invite us up for a review of readiness? I'm sure they'd be glad to."

"Good idea," General Twitchell said. "I'll have my aid call Jim Elrod to set it up."

"Fine," Admiral Rydecker said. "Maybe we can help deflate a little of the euphoria."

"If you have any trouble arranging it," the President said, "let me know and I'll talk to him."

"With Jim?" General Twitchell said with a smile. "We won't. He's on our side. And what about you, Mr. President?"

"How about a general review of forces?" he suggested. "You'll all be getting ready for the NATO exercises and Diego Garcia. It might be a good time for me to inspect a few installations and visit a few bases."

"You'll be accused of being a warmonger," Chauncey Baron predicted dryly. Hamilton Delbacher snorted.

* * *

It was announced by the press secretary that afternoon that in the next three days he would visit the naval base at Norfolk, Virginia, the Marine base at Quantico, Virginia; Ellington Field and the Johnson Space Center in Houston; NORAD headquarters near Denver; and newly reactivated Camp Roberts near Paso Robles, California. The outcry from some members of Congress, some members of the media and some members of the public was prompt and vociferous. The first step was a demonstration in Lafayette Square across Pennsylvania Avenue from the White House. Everything else was built neatly upon that.

Its organizers remained, as always in such events wherever they occurred around the world to embarrass the United States and its allies, mysterious. Apparently it sprouted from the pavement, though there seemed to be well-printed signs, pamphlets and banners; buses to bring people from New York, Chicago, Boston and other centers of enlightened protest; food stands, mobile toilets and other amenities. Permission was secured from District of Columbia authorities by a small committee composed of five individuals, all neatly dressed and earnest of demeanor, representing something they called the Coalition Against Renewed World Tensions. The tensions, CARWT maintained, were solely and entirely the doing of the President of the United States, his sinister advisers and his nefarious nation.

Looking across the street from a second-story White House window when the demonstration began, he could see that the crowd was large: close to twenty thousand, the police estimated; probably more than fifty thousand, the Washington *Post*, the Washington *Inquirer* and the networks surmised. At first orderly, it soon became more raucous. Someone had composed the chant of the day, and as if by magic it appeared, neatly printed, from the usual nowhere. With a mocking clarity it hooted across the bright sunny day just beginning to give the first crisp hints of autumn:

> Hot damn!
> Look at Ham!
> Gonna go to war and keep us free—
> Kill us in the process, yessirree—
> But by *God*, friends, we're gonna be *free!*

> Who hates nukes?
> Only us kooks!
> Old Ham loves 'em
> And he can shove 'em!
> Hot *damn!*
> Get *you*, Ham!
> *You go to war and LEAVE—US—BE!*

Thank you, Yuri, he thought wryly. Someone in your embassy is a real poet and doesn't know it.

The chant was given great prominence on the evening news, along with many shots of banners that read: **DELBACHER SEEKS NEW WAR! . . . DELBACHER THE WARMONGER! . . . YURI THE PEACEMAKER! . . . YURI THE WORLD'S HOPE! . . . YURI SAVE US FROM U.S. MADNESS!**

Major television commentaries and newspaper editorials reflected, a trifle more subtly, similar sentiments.

"President Delbacher's decision to visit major military bases in the United States is an obvious attempt to maintain war spirit in this country," said CBS's earnest little man. "It is also a deliberate and dangerous provocation to the Soviet Union that is hard to understand. One would think that the President, having just emerged from a major confrontation with Russia, would not wish to engage in such risky antics in the face of Yuri Serapin's moves toward peace. Yet Hamilton Delbacher seems determined to provoke the Kremlin with further warlike gestures. It is hard to fathom why . . ."

Said NBC's equally earnest pontificator:

"The demonstration in Lafayette Square today is ample evidence that the American people simply *do not want* their President to indulge in new warlike gestures that could conceivably precipitate another supremely dangerous confrontation with the Soviet Union. It is difficult to understand the reasoning behind Mr. Delbacher's decision to make a highly publicized visit to half a dozen major military installations, unless it is to 'show' the Russians that he is a tough guy. If this is the reason, it indicates a dangerous inferiority complex that could impel Mr. Delbacher to still more dan-

gerous gestures. It is not an auspicious start for the new era of
peace ushered in by President Serapin's statesmanship in withdrawing his major forces from around the world.''

And ABC, equally earnest—television commentators, as Elinor
remarked wryly while they watched, were always so *dreadfully*
earnest:

''It is puzzling, to say the least, to find the President of the
United States embarking on some sort of Caesar's progress to
American military bases so soon after the Soviet Union's withdrawal of its forces has opened a new era of peace. It must seem
doubly puzzling to President Serapin, who would naturally expect
that his major gesture toward peace would be met by an equally
sincere response from President Debacher. Instead, even as President Serapin is receiving the plaudits of a relieved world in Moscow, it is announced that President Delbacher is almost literally
about to hit the warpath again. It does not make sense from any
standpoint. The rally in Lafayette Square must find its sympathetic
echoes in millions of American hearts. President Serapin's goal is
obviously peace. One wonders if even President Delbacher himself
knows what his is.''

And so, next morning, echoed all the newspaper editorialists,
commentators and columnists who believe that, together with their
colleagues of television, they run the country.

The President knew from the letters, wires and telephone calls
that were flooding into the White House that these sentiments were
not necessarily dominant in the nation; yet once again, as so often,
the Soviets had appropriated the word "peace" and were reaping
the benefits therefrom. Yuri was the peaceful one, the President
was the warmonger; Yuri had opened the door to a new era of
peace, the President was the obdurate one who sought to keep it
firmly shut. Yuri could make a hundred inspection trips within the
Soviet Union and its satellites, Yuri could send a thousand secret
orders around the world, and no one would ever report it because
no one would ever know, or be allowed to report it if he did know.
The President of the United States moved in the open for the most
part, and very seldom could he do anything secretly. And, making
it even easier for Yuri, *he* had on his side the Great Gullibles of the

West, prating of his peace-loving intentions, hailing his peace-loving gestures, giving him with their unthinking, automatic adulation a hammerlock on the word "peace."

Not on the reality of peace, of course: but who, in this age of phony symbols and empty conforting words, cared about the reality of peace? The word was enough, and if it emanated often enough from Moscow, as it did, and if it was automatically coupled everywhere with Moscow, as it was, then that posed a psychological barrier for the United States that was very hard to break. Few of his predecessors had managed, Hamilton Delbacher reflected—indeed, very few of them even seemed to have understood the significance of the semantic battle that was going on. Words *were* important, in the age of universal fear of war; and victory in the battle of words went far more consistently to those who coupled their preparations for war with steady shouts of "Peace!" than it did to those who openly indicated their belief that they must maintain readiness for war if peace was to be preserved.

So he set forth on his journey accompanied by all the panoply of press and television, criticized as warmonger and war lover by many in his entourage and portrayed as such by them to his countrymen. Yet everywhere he went he found to his pleased surprise that he was greeted by crowds who, ignoring their self-appointed instructors, hailed *him* as the peace lover, the peace leader, the world's hope for peace. His press secretary informed him with great glee that this was infuriating many of his traveling companions, who seemed frustrated and uncertain as to how they should report it. They had to picture the crowds, they had to make at least passing reference to them in their news stories, they were unable to ignore or conceal the fact that this was in many ways a genuine triumphal progress for Hamilton Delbacher. It galled them terribly, but there it was.

A certain hysterical note crept into their reportage. The few hostile banners and placards that he met were brought full front and given loving coverage by the cameras. Behind them, the cheering crowds spread out.

He began to think, as his three-day tour neared its end, that perhaps he was in better shape to withstand the Soviet Union's next onslaught than he had thought.

His gloomy forebodings were soothed a bit, and he began almost to forget that his antagonist might be preparing surprises that would very soon make of this a wan and empty hope.

4

In Moscow Yuri sat in front of his giant map, which glowed in a thousand places with the secret signals of Soviet forces still in place; watched satellite transmissions of the President's tour; and brooded.

From time to time he called in the members of the Politburo, received from them their anxious reassurances of his supreme invincibility and their own desperately devoted loyalty. Knowing it would be futile, but for the record making the gesture, he plumbed minds he had long ago concluded to be, on the average, one-sixteenth of an inch in depth; and probed imaginations bounded on one hand by the rigid rules of Marx and on the other by the ever-pressing question of how best to maintain personal privileges and luxuries while ruling the threadbare citizens of the drab gray "workers' paradise." He found neither in minds nor imaginations the inspiration he had hoped against hope might be present to assist him in his task of leading the Soviet empire to its inevitable triumph over the dying but still dangerous United States, in the final conflict that would decide the fate of all mankind.

His colleagues were convinced that he could do it, but with one or two exceptions they were devoid of helpful ideas. Their combined wisdom seemed to come down basically to suggestions for further threats, further blackmail, further intimidation, continued use of the Soviet Union's still preponderant military superiority to gain—without fighting—communisism's goal of worldwide conquest.

"Comrades!" he finally snapped, bringing an instant hush along the huge rectangular table that filled one end of his enormous office. "Do you not realize that we have *tried* threats, we have *tried* blackmail, we have *tried* intimidation, we have used the correlation of forces on a worldwide scale to seek our political goals? And despite the fact that we have successfully distributed our forces where we want them under guise of our maneuvers and my own proclaimed 'withdrawal' of them—"

"A masterpiece of statesmanship, Comrade President!" exclaimed the Minister of Defense.

"An act worthy of the genius of only one man and possible only because of him!" echoed, more loudly, the Minister of Foreign Affairs, not to be outdone.

"But not," he said coldly, and felt a contemptuous inward satisfaction at the way their eagerly ecstatic faces, and those of their timorous colleagues down the table, instantly crumbled into caution at his tone, "not sufficient, for all my great supposed statesmanship and overwhelming genius, to bring to heel that dangerous fool in the White House."

"He defied me before and he defies me still."

"He is incredible," said the Minister of Foreign Affairs.

"Monstrous!" agreed the Minister of Defense.

"He is the greatest threat to world peace that has ever drawn breath," the head of the KGB said flatly. "What will you do about him, Comrade President? Shall we begin plans to get rid of him?"

"You mean you don't have them already?" Yuri inquired dryly. "You are not doing your job, comrade!"

"They await your word, Comrade President," the head of the KGB said smoothly. "They are ready. They are always ready, for any American President."

"But not so easy to accomplish, eh?" Yuri remarked. "They protect their Presidents reasonably well—except from the unexpected. And of course they are not prepared to perform the unexpected."

"We are prepared to do whatever is necessary in the best interests of the Motherland," the head of the KGB said. Yuri uttered a sardonic little laugh.

"As long as everything is expected."

"One has to make plans, Comrade President," the head of the KGB said calmly. "One cannot take chances. One must plan on a sound and reasonable basis, according to the logic of history."

"Yes," Yuri agreed in a tone of sudden disinterest they found a little puzzling but soon forgot. "One must plan . . . Well, comrades!"

He rose briskly, forcing them to follow suit. They were surprised. His dismissal had come much sooner than they had expected. Their meetings had begun with his frank appeal for "your help and your ideas, comrade—your help and your ideas." Now he appeared impatient to have them gone. Obediently they began a hasty shuffle toward the door.

"Thank you for your worthy and valued contributions to the great cause of socialist victory on a worldwide scale," he called after them, an odd note of near-sarcasm in his voice which, again, they could not understand—but, then, who could ever really understand Yuri Pavlovich? It was possibly his greatest strength. They murmured confused rejoinders and almost pushed one another in their haste to leave his presence. They were often afraid of him, but never more so than when he appeared in a mood like this.

After the last hurrying back had disappeared through the doorway and the heavy oak panel had been closed firmly upon it by the guard outside, he turned back with a snort of disgust to his desk and resumed his contemplation of the map—not only of the map but of the entire situation that faced him now that he had achieved success in his carefully planned first stage of the final battle.

It was true, as he had indicated to them candidly, that he despised Hamilton Delbacher and felt toward him a genuine personal hatred. But it was not true, in his own mind at least, that he had failed to triumph over him in their confrontation that had brought the world so close—or so the world believed—to the universal conflict that all of ordinary mankind dreaded. (Yuri knew he was not ordinary, and did not dread it so much; an ability to be objective that he seemed to share with a good many leaders around the globe.)

As Yuri saw it, his basic purpose—to distribute Soviet forces throughout the world and leave sufficient of them in place to support the second stage in his carefully thought out plan—had been achieved.

At certain moments—as when H. Delbacher had decided to make an issue of the Soviet submarines off Cuba and had issued his ultimatum—the American President had not reacted according to Yuri's plan. But Yuri felt that with great skill he had turned that to his advantage. He had set up the world-publicized press conference with his stooge-President of Cuba. He had finally appeared to yield to the extent of withdrawing six submarines. He had then taken the matter to the United Nations, where, as he expected, most of the "Third World" and many others had condemned the American President far more vigorously than they had condemned him. And finally had come his most daring gamble—a Soviet submarine's deliberate downing of an American reconnaissance plane in the Indian Ocean, provoking the American President to the very verge of a declaration of war, only ot have Yuri rise in the General Assembly and with great dramatic flare announce that he was terminating the Soviet maneuvers and calling his forces home.

And then had come the universal relief, rejoicing, almost unanimous praise and approval for Yuri's statesmanship, his great concern for humankind, his marvelous dedication to the peaceful settlement of international disputes, his supreme greatness as the world's most charismatic and effective leader in the desperate search for a genuine and lasting peace. Since his return to Moscow four days ago, he had received a steady stream of worshipful delegations, ranging from the one led by the Supreme Hero and Eternal Guiding Light of the People's Republic of Gorotoland in Central Africa to the one led by the equivocal Prime Minister of Sweden, who could always find two bad words for the United States for every one he could find for the Soviet Union. All had been almost tearfully effusive, hysterically complimentary, humble and grateful at such great length that he soon had to restrict their visits to a two-hour period each morning and direct each delegation to hold its statement to fifteen minutes.

The world—or enough of it to increase his already profound conviction that he was its most dominant, commanding and successful figure—had flocked to his door and had almost literally fallen down and worshipped. That he had not received such tributes from the United States (at least officially, though many eager private delegations had come), Britain, France, Italy, West Germany, South Africa and a handful of holdouts in South America did not disturb him at all. He did not need the approval of those supercilious states anyway, he told himself. They would worship soon enough, once they were conquered. History's inevitable timetable was unfolding at a rapidly increasing velocity that seemed to indicate that this happy day must now be very close indeed.

Then had come the fruition of many days of intense secret bargaining in Peking—the Soviet-Sino Pact—and he had received what seemed to him the final assurance of history that he was indeed the individual chosen to become the Supreme Ruler and Arbiter of All Mankind. The treaty's successful conclusion was a tribute to him and him alone. Indirectly it was the P.R.C.'s own implicit tribute to his success with the maneuvers. He had ridden roughshod by sheer force of personality and power over the shocked and dismayed opposition of his colleagues of the Politburo and the commanders of his military forces. All had been deeply skeptical, desperately afraid. Yet as he and Ju Xing-dao were going through their charade at the United Nations, their diplomatic and military aides were desperately at work in Peking under orders to produce an agreement—or else. The "or else" in both cases was sufficiently fearsome to promote great industry and a readiness to compromise—within the limits of the knowledge that the parties to the treaty were mortal enemies only cooperating temporarily for their own purposes. That these might be mutually exclusive at any moment was implicitly acknowledged, though on the surface flowery speeches and fraternal love suffused the air.

In any event, it was put together; and its chief result, as the President had tartly told Ju Xing-dao, was to free Yuri Serapin for whatever new adventures he might have in mind. That he had already done so much without the treaty seemed an ominous indication of what he might do with it.

Seated now in front of his map at ten A.M. Moscow time on the day of decision, he was unable to suppress an audible exclamation of satisfaction as he studied the four brightly glowing new areas where he had decided to move. Nothing, he told himself, could have been more brilliantly conceived or more shrewdly launched than these new steps in the steady Soviet advance that promised soon to color the globe as widely as British imperial red ever did.

Across the desk his four military commanders appeared startled by his exuberance but refrained from comment. Their stolid faces and uncommunicative eyes stared at him without expression. As always, this made him uneasy, even though he *was* Yuri Pavlovich Serapin, in all but name Czar of All the Russias and now well on his way, he believed, to becoming Supreme Ruler and Arbiter of All Mankind.

Unlike his fearfully fawning Politburo, he could never be quite sure whether his military leaders were impressed or not. He had never trusted them and he did not trust them now. He had long ago become convinced that they did not trust him. Of course this could not be admitted on either side.

"Comrades," he said, outwardly as confident and fully at ease as he had been with the Politburo, "does it not move well on all our new battlefronts—or perhaps I should call them 'our new areas of Marxist-Lenin triumph'?"

This he said with a subtle but deliberate air of challenge, although all the commanders were in their sixties and each was a veteran of at least forty years in the armed services and the Communist Party. Despite this, their loyalty to the Party and to him seemed to him to hold a slight but unmistakable reserve: and he was always trying to break it down. As usual, he did not succeed. Their responses were quite correct.

"Marxist-Leninist triumph," Marshal Gavril Petrovich Shelikov of the Strategic Rocket Forces said solemnly, "aided, as always, by your indispensable genius, Comrade President."

"Which has never been more apparent," agreed Admiral Anastas Nikolaivich Valenko.

"Or more astute and farseeing," agreed Marshal Vladimir Alexeivich Andreyev of the Army.

"Or more necessary to the glorious cause of the Motherland," gravely affirmed Marshal Andrei Andreivich Krelenko of the Air Force.

"How will the Americans respond, do you think?" Yuri inquired.

As if rehearsed, the four commanders shrugged.

"How *can* they respond?" Admiral Valenko inquired. "Your genius has guaranteed that it is virtually impossible for them to do so in any really meaningful way. It is checkmate."

"Masterful," murmured Marshal Andreyev.

"Superb," agreed Marshal Shelikov.

"Invincible," Marshal Krelenko confirmed.

"You do not expect, then, any kind of atomic or rocket response?" he asked.

Again as if rehearsed, the four looked scornful and shook their heads vigorously.

"How could they?" Admiral Valenko inquired. "We have them outnumbered in all the oceans."

"How *dare* they?" Marshal Shelikov asked. "They realize our rockets are ready—the ones they know about. The ones they do not know about, Yuri Pavlovich, the ones your own genius has placed around the world in these recent days under the guise of 'withdrawal'—well, those will be even more decisive. No, I don't think our friends in America will dare do anything."

"H. Delbacher will undoubtedly feel that he must make some response," Yuri said. "What do you think it will be, and how will the glorious forces of the Motherland counteract it?"

"I think we should see what it is," Marshal Andreyev suggested. "We are ready, no matter what. It will not hamper us to withhold response for a time. There may, in fact, be nothing to respond to."

"Except, possibly, words at the United Nations," Marshal Krelenko said scornfully.

"More speeches to Congress," Admiral Valenko remarked with equal scorn.

"Statements to the press," Marshal Andreyev offered dryly.

They all laughed, a smug and hearty sound.

"Comrade commanders," he said sharply, "do not underestimate the President; do not underestimate the Americans. You were all skeptical when I proposed our worldwide maneuvers—"

"Oh, no , Comrade President!" Marshal Shelikov protested hastily.

"Not at all, Yuri Pavlovich!" cried Marshal Andreyev.

"Never!" exclaimed Admiral Valenko.

"Indubitably never!" insisted Marshal Krelenko.

"I am sorry," Yuri said dryly. "I received that impression. Nonetheless, they proved to be successful—"

"*Highly* successful," Marshal Shelikov said fervently, and they all nodded vigorously.

"And my decisions proved to be right. Now I have made further decisions with which you may not entirely agree—"

"Comrade President," Admiral Krelenko cried earnestly as the others nodded again with vigor, "we do, we do!"

"And I cannot conceive that Delbacher will not react in some fashion. I am glad to know you consider our forces ready—"

"*Everywhere,*" Marshal Shelikov said stoutly.

"But I would like to know specifics. How, for instance, will you respond if—" And he detailed half a dozen options which he regarded as the most likely the Americans might adopt.

To each, he was staunchly assured, there would be prompt and adequate counter. Everything was in readiness everywhere— "even, if need be," Marshal Shelikov said, "a rocket and atomic response, though that I consider most unlikely because I do not think they would dare provoke us to it. They know we have them outnumbered and outclassed in rockets and atomic warheads—"

"And naval vessels," Admiral Valenko said.

"And aircraft of all kinds," Marshal Krelenko added.

"And troops and conventional weapons," Marshal Andreyev remarked.

"There is really nothing in which they are ahead. Particularly, Comrade President"—and he bowed slightly, a gesture in which they all joined—"are they not ahead in leadership. Your are far superior to H. Delbacher in every way. He cannot begin to compete."

"He competed very well last time," Yuri Serapin said sharply, and their automatically smiling flattery turned at once to somber contemplation at his tone. "He is not a man to be bluffed easily, nor is he a man to face unprepared. He has what so many of his foolish countrymen in influential positions lack, and that is *the will to resist*. If it were left to some of his countrymen who influence public opinion, the battle would be over tomorrow morning and the Soviet conquest would be complete, with great success. But there are some who still want to stand firm, and H. Delbacher, unfortunately, is one of them—the key one. Therefore I would suggest, comrades, that you proceed with full and warranted confidence in the strength of Soviet arms *but* with considerable caution. Which we must all exercise as long as H. Delbacher is in office. Even I must be very cautious—perhaps more so than anyone, since so much depends on my understanding of this supremely dangerous and irresponsible President.''

"*All* things depend on you, Yuri Pavlovich," Marshal Shelikov said. "But the comrade who led us so brilliantly through the worldwide maneuvers, and who then conceived and brought into being with such brilliant genius the Chinese treaty—"

"A masterwork!" Admiral Valenko exclaimed.

"While it lasts, comrades." Yuri reminded, yet with a satisfaction he could not quite conceal. "While it lasts."

"It will last long enough to suit our purposes," Marshal Andreyev predicted. "And then—"

"Then what, Comrade Marshal?" Yuri asked, half-teasing, and was pleased to see all their faces turn grim and determined.

"Then," Marshal Shelikov said flatly, "we will take care of *that.*"

And with one voice his colleagues said, *"Da!"*

"Good!" Yuri said. "I see we are agreed on China."

"We are agreed on all things, Comrade President," Marshal Andreyev said quickly.

"Good!" he said again. "Then proceed with all possible speed to assist in the carrying out of the objectives established this morning with the opening of action in the designated areas."

"That is your order, Comrade President," Admiral Valenko said. "And that of the Politburo," he added almost as an afterthought. "It will be carried out."

"Thank you, comrades," Yuri said. He suddenly stared straight at them, eyes cold and commanding. "Then you will not object to signing, just as the Politburo and the Council of Ministers have signed, an affirmation of loyalty and support to me in this most crucial moment as we stand on the verge of victory in the final battle that will decide the fate of all mankind?"

Instantly a veil of caution came down.

"What is that, Comrade President?" Marshal Shelikov inquired.

In a voice suddenly harsh and emphatic that brooked no opposition, Yuri read it to them.

" 'In the view of the enormous success of the recent international moves originated and directed by the genius of Y.P. Serapin, and bearing in mind his great original contributions to the ongoing success of the Motherland and the Communist Revolution, it is the sense of the Politburo and the Council of Ministers that for a period of six months, which may be extended indefinitely by the will of the Politburo and the Council of Ministers, all authority to originate and direct further moves against the imperialist enemies of mankind is vested solely and exclusively in Y.P. Serapin, to whom we pledge our total and unwavering support.'

"This is signed by all members," he concluded crisply. "Now if you will please affix your signatures of endorsement after theirs."

And he stood up, took a pen from his desk and thrust it toward them.

For a moment their faces were a study. His was adamant and unyielding. They were staring at him intently. Taking them one by one, he stared calmly back until they could no longer meet his gaze and looked away.

Finally Admiral Valenko gave a deep sigh, quite unconsciously, and with a hand that trembled noticeably, reached for the pen and signed. Slowly the three marshals followed suit.

"Thank you, comrades," Yuri said. "You have made the victory inevitable."

He reached firmly for their hands, which, at first reluctantly, then capitulating, they yielded up to him. He shook each vigorously in turn, and then, with an air of dismissal he could now afford, said, "Thank you again, comrades," and gestured bluntly toward the door.

They could not see his expression as he watched them file stolidly out, which was just as well. He was still determined to get rid of them as soon as possible after his objectives had been achieved. He still did not trust them for a moment.

He returned to his desk, seated himself once again and on the lighted map studied with growing satisfaction the pulsating lights that marked the new advances he had ordered in the final conflict that he was supremely confident would eliminate the United States, decide the fate of all mankind and assure for the Soviet Union the final conquest of the world.

They could not have been planned more astutely, he assured himself again with great satisfaction, or have been launched with greater surprise and greater success upon his naive and unsuspecting opponent.

And with this judgment, as he faced the somber faces of the Secretary of State, the Secretary of Defense and the Joint Chiefs of Staff, the President of the United States was forced to agree.

The CIA had anticipated nothing.

The National Security Agency had received no inkling.

The various military intelligence units had drawn a blank.

And the whirling satellites had found nothing unusual, being unfortunately unable to photograph the one area that confounds all predictions and upsets all prognostications, namely the mind of man.

So four things happened. Like so many things, they were much more logical in retrospect than they were in anticipation; and so the United States, despite its President's uneasy forebodings, and just as its principal enemy had shrewdly calculated, was quite unprepared to meet them.

5

In the Kingdom, it began like any other day on which the currently ruling son of prolific Ibn Saud held public audience. In the oilfields the pumps were busily pumping. In the desert the Bedouins herded their sheep and camels along ancient trails to timeless oases. In Riyadh conscientious princes ran their government and bored princes played with their Rolls-Royces, falcons, mistresses or catamites, in that order. In Jidda bored princesses sipped sickly sweet juices, gossiped avidly, displayed for one another's benefit their fabulous jewels and latest Paris fashions. A thousand miles below, economically, the ordinary tribesmen and workers in the cities ground out their bare-subsistence livelihood building the public projects and private constructions of their fantastically wealthy masters. A dark unrest gripped many. Among their rulers a smug complacence characterized most. Only a few farsighted worried. The sands continued to yield their seemingly endless bounty, prices were rising again, the United States remained the best and most reliable of customers. All seemed quiet along the vast and ill-guarded borders. To all but the most uneasy, among whom the current ruler could not be included, all seemed going well for the House of Saud.

So the King, flanked by six of his brothers who occupied the principal ministries, held his audience in the *majlis,* or audience room of the palace.

For some minutes it proceeded like all the rest. Simple tribesmen addressed him as "my brother," clapped him familiarly on the back, were embraced in turn and voiced their complaints. He settled a dozen disputes out of hand, directed his brothers to make note of a dozen more and see to their solution, conducted himself with the jovial dignity his fellow tribesmen loved, and the quick, fair-minded wisdom they had come to expect. Tea was served. Time passed. The watching crowd of petitioners diminished slightly, but he could see there were still many left. He sighed, took more tea, shifted on his throne, prepared to receive those still remaining.

Distantly an air-raid siren sounded. It was joined immediately by more, rising within ten seconds to an ear-crippling, universal roar.

So completely was the cacophony out of place in this ritual of audience stretching back into unknown mists of ancient desert time that for a moment he did not realize what it was. Then realization dawned. He started to rise. All his brothers but one gathered instinctively around him. A wild-eyed tribesman burst into the room screaming,

"Yemeni! Yemeni! Yemeni!"

As if this were the signal—no one would ever know—some fifty of the petitioners leaped to their feet, threw open their robes, began firing with machine guns. The King, his senior brothers and their subsidiary ministers were gone in seconds. Only one brother, very much younger, huddled in a corner far to one side, still lived.

Outside the sirens continued to wail, the drumming of planes was over the capital, the crump of bombs began.

No antiaircraft fire rose to meet the attackers. No Saudi planes took off.

In the blood-drenched room the youngest brother, darling of certain military, rose slowly to his feet, raised his arms commandingly in an all-embracing gesture.

A great shout went up to greet him. His fellow tribesmen tumbled forward, slipping and slithering in the blood, scrambling headlong over the bodies, heedless of the carnage, to kiss the hem of his robe and embrace him with joyous cries of fealty and obedience.

At the airport troop plane after troop plane belonging to those with whom he had made the bargain he thought he could safely keep landed smoothly and without opposition. From accompanying helicopters all across the capital, armed soldiers parachuted down like gentle, deadly rain.

At exactly the same moment in Mexico's far south, the director of petroleum administration, like the President of the United States, was asleep. So, too, in their casual, easygoing fashion, were a good many of the soldiers along the border with Guatemala. It had been a relaxed Saturday night, there were many parties, the beer and tequila flowed, the girls were willing, the weather soft and balmy. No one expected trouble. There had been a few growls between the governments from time to time, but for all its bluster the recently established People's Republic of Guatemala seemed to have sufficient problems to keep it busy at home. Once in a while some observant oilman or journalist, usually visiting from the great republic whose opinions were automatically discounted by the proud people who lived uneasily on its southern flank, would venture to express some worry about the exposed nature of the oilfields, the casual relaxation of the border.

They were always told patronizingly by their hosts that they should not worry. "We are only afraid of *you*, amigos," they would be assured with hearty laughter and a not really very friendly dig in the ribs, "and we know *you* won't attack us." And since this was quite true, the worried ones would desist and agree to laugh it off and have another tequila. And the relaxed atmosphere along the border and in the oilfields kept right on being relaxed.

So on this particular night, at the very moment when blood was gushing over the floors and walls in Riyadh, all was even calmer than usual next door to Guatemala. Not only the director of petroleum administration, who was visiting from Mexico City and had been honored with an unusually uproarious and very late party, but most of the oil workers and most of the army were sleeping, too. The few sentries who were on duty were either playing cards, gossiping drowsily about their sexual or drinking prowess, or half-dozing; coming fully awake with a start only occasionally when the jungle night was broken by some unusually raucous scream of bird or beast. Since there were many of these, few of the soldiers managed to come fully awake on each occasion. Thus they were not aware that a certain pattern was beginning to creep into the sporadic sounds along one particularly ill guarded section of the border; nor did they really hear for quite a long time the faroff, softly approaching drone of the most versatile, and overall perhaps most deadly, toy of the twentieth century.

It was true that there was one sentry, Manuel Paloma, who would survive and who did hear something and did attempt to rouse his sergeant and, finally, in desperation, his colonel. But Manuel's sergeant had consumed just too many tequilas, and Manuel's colonel just too many tequilas and too many bouts with his local girlfriends, to pay attention. The sergeant, half-stirring, cursed Manuel, told him to shut up and went back to sleep. The colonel could not even understand Manuel's name, which Manuel considered lucky. He too cursed, slammed his door in Manuel's face and subsided mumbling back into darkness.

Manuel stood irresolute for several seconds. Then he ran back to his radar equipment, noted with a desperate worry that the blips were very many, increasing and coming swiftly closer. Now he could hear the faint drone, steadily louder. Others were beginning to hear, too. Confused voices were beginning to shout here and there in the night. No one could believe an attack was coming. The first bombs took care of that.

In desperation Manuel leaped to his radio, tried frantically to raise the defense ministry in Mexico City. He got an enlisted man, shouted that they were being attacked. The soldier yelled back that he would get word at once to the minister, yelled something more that Manuel lost in the first thump of bombs, the first strafing, the first wild shouts of surprise and agony as the whole installation came awake and began to respond with antiaircraft batteries, rifles, pistols, hand grenades, whatever came to hand. Down through the sky, as over Riyadh, came the gentle deadly rain of paratroops.

Through the jungle, now lighted brightly with flares, could be heard the steady crash of advancing troops, the steady, inexorable rumble of tanks.

Simultaneously miles away air attack began upon the installations immediately around the oilfields. The bombing was skillful and precise. The order had been absolute:

No damage was to be done to the wells.
None was.

Twelve thousand miles away a beautiful spring day was unfolding in South Africa. In Johannesburg's wealthy Parktown district James Lytton, owner of the country's largest department store
chain, was yawning and just beginning to think about getting out of
bed. In Cape Town the manager of his largest local branch, Henrik
van der Merwe, was conducting an informal survey of the store
with one of his assistant managers, Nkeze Sukuza, whom he had
asked to meet him on Sunday morning because it was a good quiet
time, with the staff out of the way, to take what he called "a quiet
ramble" just to see how things looked.

James Lytton, who had inherited his commercial interests from
English forebears who had come to South Africa in the gold-and-
diamond days of Barney Barnato, Cecil Rhodes and Sir Ernest
Oppenheimer, was in no hurry to get up, as befitted a man of forty-
seven who had taken his heritage and increased it handsomely in
the fifteen years since he had come into full control of it. He was
not given to many indulgences, but sleeping in on Sunday morn-
ings was one he cherished, and not even his wife, already out and
bustling about her dearly loved garden, could break him of it. His
family was in good shape, his stores were flourishing, his cautious
experimenting with promoting nonwhites to higher and higher
administrative positions in the company was working despite some
frowning from the government, and all in all he felt his world was
moving well. He only wished, with a sleepy morning sigh, that the
same could be said for poor old South Africa, which as always was
in the state of permanent but not uncomfortable (for those of the
right skin color) tension that held its strange society in nervous but
operative balance.

In his own way Henrik van der Merwe represented this. He was
a bright young man of thirty-three, of the good Afrikaner stock that
controlled the country with the Bible in one hand and the apartheid
laws in the other, and the chances were good that he would go far
in the organization. In fact, he was already something of a personal
protégé of Mr. Lytton's, and the difference in their ages was not
too great to preclude a real personal friendship—or at least Henrik

thought, rather nervously, that it was real. He was never entirely sure, because one couldn't quite ever be, with the English-speakers. They might have lost political control of the country decades ago when the Afrikaners' Nationalist Party won power—they might even be pushed a bit, here and there, in their control of its commercial interests—but in spite of that, there was just something about them. If they wanted to—and enough of them did so that they all got the curse of it—they could make even the most assured and secure Afrikaners feel uncomfortable at social gatherings, charity affairs, artistic events, on the streets, in shops and hotels, anywhere and everywhere. Among many other aspects of the Afrikaner burden was a permanent inferiority complex toward their English-speaking countrymen. Many of them, like Henrik van der Merwe, never felt really, completely, absolutely equal.

If South Africa's white tribes had this trouble, Nkeze Sukuza often told his wife in their little brick house in the carefully restricted black residential area on the Cape flats, they couldn't even begin to contemplate the troubles the country's majority had. Some thirteen black tribes jostled uneasily side by side. Indians and "Cape Coloreds," the mixture of white and Maly, lived scattered among them in narrowly defined areas. Hardly anyone really liked or trusted anyone else. Thus it was indeed a great step forward when Henrik van der Merwe, with the blessing of Mr. Lytton, had selected Nkeze Sukuza to be his third assistant general manager in charge of the Cape Town branch.

This had been due to Nkeze's natural intelligence and a brightly winning personality which had prompted Mr. Lytton, noting his eager willingness in the shipping and receiving department one day, to tell Mr. van der Merwe, "That lad is going to go far." "He will if we help him," Mr. van der Merwe had observed, rather daringly, he felt; but Mr. Lytton had not been offended. "Right you are," he said briskly; spoke privately to a friend of his in the government; and within a month Nkeze, rechristened Mr. Sukuza, had his new job.

Now Nkeze felt that he might possibly have a real friend in Mr. Lytton, though he was not sure of Mr. van der Merwe—a certain distance remained, as of course it did with Mr. Lytton but in a somewhat less strained way. But still, he told himself and his wife stoutly and very often, it was a big step forward and in a sense he felt he was representing many millions. He was not equal, of course; no black could ever feel that as long as whites controlled South Africa, but he suspected that not even Mr. Lytton and Mr. van der Merwe really felt equal to one another. Certainly it was obvious to Nkeze, who missed very little going on among his masters, that Mr. van der Merwe did not feel equal to Mr. Lytton.

But on this beautiful Sunday morning in the southern hemisphere's spring they were about to be, though they could not possibly have anticipated it, so suddenly did it come upon them, absolutely equal.

Their equalization took place almost simultaneously, though it was Mr. Lytton who underwent it first. He was just finally getting out of bed, had both feet on the floor, was yawning one last luxurious time and absentmindedly scratching his chest, when he heard the sound. It was a sound that did not belong over Johannesburg, and in a second Mr. Lytton, who had served his time like all white males in the Republic's armed services—in the air force, actually, which was a help, briefly, now—recognized it. It could not be, but it was: missiles were falling on Jo'burg.

Wildly Mr. Lytton sprang to his feet, wildly cried out to his wife. His voice was not destined to reach her nor hers to reach him. Instead there was a great *whoompf!* which he had one millisecond to time to recognize and then he and his beautiful house and yard in Parktown, and presumably his beautiful wife, exploded into nothingness and Mr. Lytton knew no more.

At that very instant in Cape Town Mr. van der Merwe was just saying to Nkeze Sukuza in Afrikaans, "Well, Nkeze, I think perhaps if we put the ladies' handbags over *there*—" and Nkeze was looking very serious and thinking about it—when suddenly exactly the same thing was happening to them that had just happened to Mr. Lytton. Strange heavy sounds began to reverberate through the beautiful city, recognized by Mr. van der Merwe, who had served his hitch in Angola, and instinctively understood by Nkeze, who had seen such things on the television sets in the store that he and other blacks weren't supposed to look at because they were white channels. *"Duck!"* Mr. van der Merwe yelled and threw himself beneath the nearest display table, where he found himself closer than he had ever expected to be to one of Nkeze's color, because Nkeze had reached there one split second before. But it did neither of them any good. The second missile fell squarely on the store, and Mr. Lytton, Mr. van der Merwe and Mr. Sukuza were all equal at last.

On the other side of the world and the international dateline, on the big, green, beautiful, slug-shaped island lying just off the southeast coast of the People's Republic of China, it was midafternoon of the following calendar day, Monday. The streets of Taipei were, as always, jammed with hooting, blaring, smoke-belching cars, trucks, buses, taxis, motorbikes and bicycles, each proceeding full-tilt on its individual, independent, headlong way. The sidewalks and streets were jammed with shoppers, as befitted the island's prosperity, so galling to its rival on the mainland. In the Legislative Yuan, or assembly, that maintained some semblance of democratic rule, desultory debate was proceeding on how to maintain and increase that prosperity by expanding the Republic of China's many overseas markets. In his office the President, relatively youthful heir to the two Chiangs now finally gone to their ancestors, was consulting with his closest diplomatic advisers on how best to reject, without once again widening the subtly but surely narrowing gap between them, the latest offer of reconciliation from Peking.

In the great port of Kaohsiung near the island's southern tip, shipping under a dozen different flags stretched along five miles or more of docks, symbol of trade that tied the island to half the world. On the tiny islands of Quemoy and Matsu, some 150 miles southwest, scarcely a mile and a half from the mainland at nearest point, the underground garrisons were, as always, alert. They were not quite as alert as they used to be, because it had been so long since Taiwan and the mainland had exchanged anything but propaganda balloons; but they were alert enough.

It did not, this time, do them much good, although, like Manuel Paloma in faroff nighttime Mexico, they did their best with what they had.

In the presidential palace in Taipei, at the very moment that Manuel was screaming into his transmitter to Mexico City—when the younger brother and his dangerous outside friends were taking over the Kingdom—and when Mr. Lytton, Mr. van der Merwe and Mr. Sukuza were becoming finally and irrevocably equal—the President of the Republic of China and his advisers were discussing the endlessly shifting subtleties of their persistent brethren on the mainland. They understood them well, being of the same race and heritage. The essential point of discussion centered around how far to go, without going too far, in the evolving relationship with the motherland. All but the most old-line and adamant—of whom few were left, most having by now joined the Chiangs among their ancestors—acknowledged that it *was* evolving. The question was how far it must be allowed to continue to evolve. Each time Ju Xing-dao and his colleagues in Peking decided to apply the pressure a bit more, the debate raged anew.

That there would be pressure other than diplomatic did not occur to the President and his advisers: again, it had been so long since there had been anything but words. There had been some initial concern when the new Sino-Soviet treaty had been announced, some worry that it might encourage Peking, as it might encourage Moscow, to new adventures. But this was soon dismissed with confidence. Taiwan's defenses were still in excellent shape; the armed forces of the P.R.C., while vastly superior in manpower, were still vastly inferior in technology and equipment; and there was still the occasionally equivocal but basically reliable friendship of the United States to fall back upon.

So the latest approach from Peking was in process of being dismissed. There had been a renewed offer of an "autonomous region." There had been the usual vague references to Macao and what was generally expected to be the fate of Hong Kong, namely Chinese sovereignty but quasi "free" administration (in ironic essence, a return to the "foreign concessions" of the Empress Dowager's day). Once again there was the suggestion that the "autonomous region" might continue to be called, as Taipei itself called it, the "Taiwan Province of China" (Peking wanted the added words "of the People's Republic of China" instead of "of the Republic of China"—a vast difference, as both sides well knew). And once again there were soothing words about brotherhood, national pride and unity, the gloriously ancient history from which they all derived and to which they all belonged.

The document, relatively brief compared to most such communications from the homeland, had literally been studied word by word for the past hour and a half. The placement of a comma had called forth heated disputes, the selection of one adverb or noun instead of another had prompted red-faced, loud-voiced disagreements. Once this phase had passed and general accord had been reached on the certainty that this was just one more trap like all that had gone before, there came the matter of reply. On this there was immediate and unanimous agreement.

The reply was "No," and its wording was being drafted by the President himself with all the tart directness of the late President Chiang Ching-kuo himself when Quemoy and Matsu went suddenly on the alert and word was flashed instantly to the President's desk that this time more than propaganda balloons were coming over.

Things began to happen very fast.

Within thirty seconds the clipped voice of the commanding general of Quemoy boomed into the room. A squadron of fifteen missile-carrying P.R.C. planes that had been conducting what appeared to be routine maneuvers up and down the coast just opposite for the past two weeks had suddenly veered east some distance north of Quemoy and Matsu and were heading straight for Taipei. Planes from Quemoy and Matsu were already in the air, but the chances of interception were not good at the moment. The general reported that he had already sent the long-agreed-upon signal ("Celestial Typhoon") to the airfields, missile bases and antiaircraft installations on Taipei, and he assumed the long-agreed-upon automatic responses were being put into effect. The President reported that he could already hear Taiwan's planes in the air. He and the general, reverting instinctively to tradition in the face of peril, commended one another and their people to the favorable attention of the gods and hung up. The event was now in the hands of the men, particularly the young men, who had been so assiduously trained for so many years for just such a contingency.

The first sounds of battle in the air, the first *crump* of bombs and missiles, were just beginning over Taipei when a frantic call came in from the military governor of the port of Kaohsiung. No enemy planes were attacking the harbor at the moment, and radar disclosed none coming in. However, three ships, all of Panamanian registry but for the moment unknown ownership, had just blown up in the harbor mouth. Not only were the three strung out in a line that effectively closed off the harbor, but by an unhappy coincidence their obviously deliberate destruction had caught three other ships, one from Hong Kong and two from Australia, that had been standing in a little too close. The port of Kaohsiung had been carefully left unharmed, but it was now effectively sealed by five wrecks that it would take many days to remove—if there were time and opportunity to remove them.

Within a minute the President of the Republic of China was trying frantically to get through to the White House. So were the President of Mexico, the Prime Minister of South Africa and the remaining senior brother of the House of Saud.

In four impossibly separated areas of the earth where the United States had unbreakable commitments to furnish immediate military assistance in case of need, war was under way.

On Yuri Serapin's map in Moscow four new areas of delightfully desperate trouble for the United States winked and glowed. Everything had begun exactly as planned. He could not have been happier. Quite uncharacteristically, he was even humming a quiet little tune of satisfaction to himself.

The traps were sprung.

He was confident that hated America had no choice but to fall into them.

BOOK TWO

1

No choice, Hamilton Delbacher thought grimly as he surveryed the dismayed and anxious faces of his advisers, still sleepy from their unexpected awakening, but to make good on commitments long established and often reaffirmed.

Unbreakable interests of oil and treaty tied his country to Saudi Arabia.

Geography, oil and a century and a half of uneasy but inescapable association tied her to Mexico.

Strategic raw materials, the protection of the Cape of Good Hope route and the necessity of maintaining the only stable government in southern Africa tied her to South Africa.

And decades of friendship, close economic and military ties and treaty obligations tied her to Taiwan.

Your selections, he told the Soviet President with a grim irony in his mind, are excellent. Now we must see how we can knock you out of them.

That America would have to do so he did not doubt. How she would go about it he did not at the moment know. The possibility that she might not be able to entered his mind briefly for a second and was dismissed.

"Well, gentlemen?" he said, and there was a lengthy silence broken at last by Chauncey Baron with a heavy sigh.

"What choice do we have?" he inquired of no one in particular, echoing the President's thought. The Secretary of Defense replied in a tight, clipped voice.

"None."

"But—" the national security adviser began, and stopped as they turned upon him with a concerted movement that almost seemed to startle him back in his chair.

"What's the latest?" the President inquired, more kindly.

"We are in receipt," the national security adviser said with careful dignity, "of cables from the President of Taiwan and the Prime Minister of South Africa to the effect that they will be calling you within the hour. I am also informed"—he glanced at a paper that had been handed him by a white-faced young aide as he entered the room—"that the President of Mexico will do the same. There is no word, nor is any expected," he added bleakly, "from the new King of Saudi Arabia. Nonetheless, our single largest supplier of oil is now at risk, as is indeed the entire Gulf, and something must obviously be done."

"You tell me your staff expects to have options ready by six A.M.," Hamilton Delbacher remarked. "I am not sure we can wait until 6 A.M.. What do we have so far on the progress of the fighting?"

"There seems to be a strong reaction in South Africa," the national security adviser said. "In fact, a counterattack on Angola is already underway. Damage in Johannesburg and Cape Town seems relatively light according to early reports—a few structures in the business sections of each city. Satellites disclose a very substantial pincer-shaped troop movement coming south through Botswana and Namibia, which the South African air force is already trying to interdict. Things are still too chaotic in Mexico to get any clear picture either by satellite or other intelligence. According to our ambassador in Riyadh, the Kingdom as a whole does not even know yet what has happened. He has no idea what will happen when the news spreads. The South Yemeni presence is by the moment becoming too obvious to ignore, but perhaps the old royal authority will hold despite the usurpation."

"And Taiwan?"

"First reports of damage seem very light. The President's cable says the port of Kaohsiung is blocked. Other than that, a lot of air activity and a lot of propaganda leaflets but very minor bombing over Taipei.''

"That figures," the President remarked. "That's not an invasion. They're just making a point."

"Nonetheless," General Hallowell said, "we're still obligated to help if called upon."

"Which we will be," Chauncey Baron predicted glumly. "Because I don't think it will end with just making a point. There'll be a followup in the next day or two."

"I agree," Roger Hackett said. "And I very much doubt that Mexico and South Africa are calling just to pass the time of day. And suppose some of the other Saudis decide to fight little brother—"

"Which they will," Bart Jamison said, stifling a yawn and rubbing sleep-reddened eyes. "I was stationed there as air attaché in our embassy in the dark dim past, and while transitions have all been very smooth and cordial on the surface, there are a lot of jealousies in the younger group. We're going to get an appeal from somebody for help in a counterattack within the day, I'm willing to bet. Particularly when it sinks home to the tribes that this is being staged by the South Yemenis and the Soviets, whom they hate."

"It's all being staged by the Soviets," the President said, "aside from Taiwan, which seems to be China's baby. And even there, there's enough cooperation to make the timing coincide. Friend Yuri has done his planning well."

"And we have virtually no choice but to plunge straight ahead into this trap," General Twitchell said, running a hand over his short-cropped hair. "It's a bitch."

"Yes," Ham Delbacher agreed, "it *is* a bitch. What do we have to meet it with?"

"Just what we had two weeks ago when the Soviet maneuvers were underway," General Smith said, and Admiral Rydecker snorted. "Not very damned much."

"Not enough to fight in four places at once," General Hallowell agreed.

"We may have to," the President said sharply, "so don't give up yet, please."

"Nobody's giving up," Roger Hackett responded mildly, "but there's no point in closing our eyes to the probabilities."

"I'm not," the President said, "but neither am I going to get defeatist about them. If we have to we have to, that's all. And we will." He sighed, then shook it off with a determined look. "Somehow . . . What about diplomatic options, Chauncey? Not very much, are there."

"No," the Secretary of State agreed. "I suppose we can demand a Security Council meeting, and possibly you'll want to talk to Serapin direct—"

"Oh, yes," the President said grimly. "I'll talk to him. As for the Council—" He paused, mentally reviewing his recent frustrating days with that volubly ineffective body. "I don't know. I suppose so, because it's the customary thing to do. But I don't have any faith in it."

"Who does?" Chauncey inquired dryly. "But one goes through the forms and makes the record."

"Meanwhile," the President said, "when the requests come in for aid, we move. I don't know exactly how or where, but the important thing right now, it seems to me, is that we do *something*. I think in this case the perception of action is even more important than the action itself."

"Except that we can't risk a series of regional defeats at the hands of the Soviet Union," Chauncey said. "*That* perception would not be good."

"Who said anything about the Soviet Union?" the President inquired. "They're hiding out behind their stooges in all four of these cases. They won't challenge us openly. They never have and I don't think they're about to start now."

"At least for the moment," Roger Hackett murmured.

"The moment is what we have to worry about," the President said. He nodded toward the national security adviser. "Anson here says his boys will have some options ready for me by six A.M. Why don't you all do the same?" He stood up, glanced at his watch. It was four A.M. Washington time. "You can stay here if you like, order in some coffee or breakfast or whatever you want. I'm going up to the Oval Office to take the calls and promise assistance and talk to Yuri."

"Don't promise too much," the national security adviser said hastily. An expression of impatience crossed the President's face.

"I'll promise as much as I have to to keep them fighting," he said shortly. "The one thing we can't afford is for everybody to collapse in the first ten minutes."

The first thing he did when he got to the Oval Office was ask the White House operator to get Yuri Serapin in the Kremlin. Not to his surprise, she reported back within five minutes that he was "unavoidably detained" but would be available "later."

"Yes," Hamilton Delbacher said grimly. "Well, keep after him. Meanwhile, let's talk to the others."

From the four calls he then received, though they were filled with dismay and deep concern, he did not get the impression that anyone was ready to give up anytime soon. The first to come through was the Prime Minister of South Africa, calling from Cape Town. The normally unflappable Afrikaner sounded tense but determined.

"Mr. President!" he said abruptly and without preliminary.

"What do you need?" the President inquired.

"A show of naval force," the Prime Minister said crisply. "At least a dozen ships off Cape Town—at least a hundred planes in the air—the start of an immediate airlift of ammunition and supplies, probably from Diego Garcia, if you have them there."

"We do," the President said. "What about ships off Luanda, Angola, and a show of force there?"

"Would you be prepared to go that far?" the Prime Minister inquired, sounding impressed and surprised. "We would love it."

"It could be done," Hamilton Delbacher said. "How are things going so far?"

"We've taken some hits here," the Prime Minister said, "some damage to the waterfront and business area, moderate casualties. I've just been talking to Jo'burg and they tell me the same there. More a demoralizing blow than an all-out offensive at the moment." He snorted scornfully. "*Try* to demoralize us!" he exclaimed. "Who do they think they are, these *hierdie skobbejake*?" using the Afrikaner equivalent of "these jerks" with savage sarcasm.

"Our satellites show an overland advance toward the border," the President said.

"Oh, yes, they're on their way. Your satellites must also show you that we are rushing massive troop reinforcements there, including tank forces, and are also strafing them heavily."

"Are you prepared to use the bomb?" the President inquired.

There was a silence at the other end of the line.

"If they back us to the wall," the Prime Minister said finally, "we will always use it. Surely the fools know that."

"I would rather you didn't," the President said. The Prime Minister snorted.

"Mr. President, you are talking about our life, *our national life*. If they really try to destroy us we will take them with us and half the world if necessary. Do you doubt that?"

"No," Hamilton Delbacher said, "I have never doubted that. Nevertheless, I would hope we can find some other solution—"

"Only if you help us and together we prevail against them," the Prime Minister said firmly. "I do not mean to blackmail you—"

"Which you are," the President noted dryly.

"Perhaps," the Prime Minister agreed, "but this may pass beyond controllable niceties."

"How long can you hold out before it does?"

"We are bombing Luanda at the moment," the Prime Minister said, "and have shot down at least fifteen of their planes in our skies already. Our troops should meet theirs around noon your time. We can hold out a fair amount of time, I think. I would not suggest, however," he added, "that the United States dawdle."

"A week?"

"Unless they get massive aid from outside, we can hold quite a bit longer than that. But obviously from the nature of the attacks so far, they are already proceeding on a basis of substantial outside aid. There is not much time for you to make up your minds."

"They are made up," Hamilton Delbacher said shortly. "It's a question of how best to do it."

"Give us the show of force first," the Prime Minister said. "We can stand it if the substance doesn't arrive for a few days."

"All right," the President said. "Do one thing for me—"

"Yes?"

"Collect every single piece of evidence you can get of Soviet and Cuban arms, tanks, planes, materiel and rush it to me just as fast as you can."

"Surely," the Prime Minister said. "I'm told we have some items already. They'll be on their way this afternoon. We'll send them South African Airways via Rio, disguised as freight. You should have them tomorrow morning, your time."

"Good," the President said.

"Is this for presentation to the United Nations?" the Prime Minister asked in skeptical tone. "Forgive me, Mr. President, but I think it will be a futile exercise."

"Futile or not," Hamilton Delbacher said, "the record must be made."

"For whom?" the Prime Minister inquired. "Do you think there will be anyone left to read it, the way things are going now?"

"Perhaps you can live with that feeling, Prime Minister," the President said, "but I cannot."

"Forgive me, Mr. President," the Prime Minister said, "but you have not *had* to live with that feeling. It has at times not been easy to escape it, down here."

"And yet you are fighting back," Ham Delbacher pointed out.

"Certainly," the Prime Minister said, sounding surprised. "What else would you expect us to do?"

Once again he had the operator try the Kremlin. Once again there was evasive action at the other end.

Equally determined were the Presidents of Mexico and Taiwan. Understandably, he thought, the urgency was greater in the call he received from Mexico City.

"Mr. President," the President of Mexico said, "we have a serious situation."

"I am well aware of it. What can we do to help?"

"Do you wish to help?" his fellow executive inquired, surprise entering his voice for a second in spite of himself.

"Mr. President," Hamilton Delbacher said patiently, "are you jesting? We have strong reason to believe—in fact, we know—that this invasion from Guatemala is Cuban led and is directed by Soviet advisers, under direct orders from the Kremlin. You know our two countries have had their tensions with one another in the past, but I also hope you know that the United States is not going to sit by and see a successful Soviet-backed invasion topple an independent Mexico." His tone became tougher. "We have two interests in this, and I shall be blunt about them and you can balance them in whatever way you like. One is that we honestly and sincerely like Mexico and want it to remain free to work out its own destiny. The second reason is strictly selfish and strategic and that is we cannot tolerate Soviet conquest of a nation on our border. As I say, balance these as you like in assessing our motives; it doesn't matter. The essential fact is that we are not going to let this invasion succeed. How is it doing so far?"

"Effectively," the President of Mexico said unhappily. "We were taken quite by surprise, I am afraid."

"So were we all," Hamilton Delbacher said. "Nothing to be ashamed of in that. I knew President Serapin was capable of infinite mischief but I did not expect it to break out quite so soon after our recent tussle. Have they seized the oilfields yet?"

"It is not going *that* effectively," the President of Mexico said, a slight amusement apparent despite his tension. "They have seized a portion of them—so far. We have substantial casualties and we do not know when or where there may be further attacks."

"Yes," the President said, "as long as it's confined down there it can be contained reasonably well. But you have such a long coastline . . . Well: in any event. For the reasons I state, plus the inter-American treaty and many other reasons, we are here to help. What do you need most at the moment?"

"Air support," the President of Mexico said promptly. "As much as you can send."

"I'm meeting with the Secretaries of State and Defense and the Joint Chiefs of Staff in about an hour," he said. "We should have something definite for you very soon."

"That will be most appreciated," the President of Mexico said with a relief polite formality could not quite hide. He hesitated. "Will such action be supported by public opinion in the United States?"

Hamilton Delbacher gave a grim little laugh.

"It depends on what you mean by public opinion. A lot will support it. Some major voices won't, even when it's Mexico under attack. There will be the usual attempts to undercut. I've made up my mind, however. It will be done. Meanwhile, could you instruct your people to collect as much valid evidence as they can of Soviet arms, tanks, supplies, whatever—anything they capture—and rush it to me at once?"

"For the United Nations," the President of Mexico said thoughtfully. "It will do no good, you know."

Mindful of Mexican participation in similar U.N. skepticisms in the past, the President almost made a tart rejoinder but refrained. The situation was far beyond such finger pointing, however justified.

"Perhaps not," he said, "but the evidence will be placed before them all the same."

"You will not wait for a U.N. resolution before you help us!" the President of Mexico exclaimed with alarm. "There is not time!"

"No, certainly not," he said sharply. "I promised you something very soon, and it will be delivered. However, the record will be made."

"That is probably advisable," the President of Mexico agreed, sounding mollified, "because—" He broke off suddenly, said sharply, *"No!"*; uttered an unintelligible, frantic shout. In the background the President of the United States could hear the rising sound of air-raid sirens, the heavy thump of bombs.

"My *God!*" the President of Mexico cried. "They're attacking us *here!* We're being bombed *here!*"

"Fight back and hang on!" Hamilton Delbacher shouted as the line went dead. "We'll get there! Hang on!"

He put his phone slowly down. The White House operator promptly rang it. He picked it up again.

"Yes?" he said, voice still uneven with shock and excitement, thinking the connection might have been restored. "Is that you, señor?"

"It is I," the heavy, precise voice of the President of Taiwan re-

sponded with a sharp concern prompted by his obvious agitation.
"What is happening, Mr. President? Are you all right?"

"Yes, thank you," he said, forcing himself to steady down. "I
was just talking to the President of Mexico. They are bombing
Mexico City."

"The world is falling apart," the President of Taiwan said. "Insanity is king."

"We must defeat it," he said.

"We must," the President of Taiwan agreed gravely.

"How are things going there?"

"We are under attack, but typical of our brothers on the mainland, it is so far mainly ideological attack. They have closed Kaohsiung, as you probably know—just enough to cripple it temporarily
but not to destroy it so that it cannot be speedily restored if"—his
voice turned bitter for a second—"if they come here. They have
also destroyed the Grand Hotel—"

"No!" Hamilton Delbacher said, feeling the sentimental regret
of everyone who had stayed in Taipei for the enormous ornate red-
and-gold structure, built by the Generalissimo and Madame
Chiang Kai-shek, that dominated the city skyline. "I'm sorry."

"It was a symbol," the President of Taiwan said. "So was the
home of the Generalissimo and his monument in the center of the
city, both of which have also been destroyed. For the rest, they
seem to be content for the moment to scatter propaganda. This
could change at any time. We have shot down four planes of theirs,
lost three of our own. An estimated three hundred guests and staff
died in the hotel, a handful of sightseers at the monument. Otherwise, casualties are very few. It is largely a probing action so far—
designed to indicate to us that the probe may become much more
than probe if they so desire."

"Have they withdrawn?"

"Temporarily. Fifteen planes came over, four down, eight gone
back. Three are still passing over from time to time, dropping leaflets. We have some hopes," he added grimly, "of getting all three,
if they keep it up."

"But so far no sign of an all-out invasion?"

"No. We are flying reconnaissance now over Fukien Province
opposite us on the mainland and there are no invasion flotillas or

anything of the sort visible. Our radar on Quemoy and Matsu are similarly blank. This does not mean that massive air attack may not be resumed at any moment from some other sector.''

''And from us you desire—''

''Everything you can send,'' the President of Taiwan said. ''We are aware, of course''—and again his voice turned bitter—''that we are an orphan case, and your special relationship with the mainland may preclude any action that might be considered hostile to them—''

''Our special relationship,'' he interrupted, ''is that we understand each other. We have certain obligations to you. They would respect us for carrying them out, I believe. They wouldn't like it, but they would respect our keeping our word. The possibility of this must be deterring them. How else do you account for the fact that the attack so far is mostly ideological, as you say?''

''That may have a bearing,'' the President of Taiwan conceded. ''Though we do not feel here that we can count on it for very long.''

''Nor do I,'' he agreed. ''Therefore, what do you consider necessary from us?''

''Do you have naval units in the area?''

''Yes.''

''Send them. And as many planes as you can spare from Clark Field in the Philippines.''

''You know we cannot do that,'' Hamilton Delbacher said. ''We cannot openly engage in warfare with the mainland.''

''You can establish a screen,'' the President of Taiwan insisted. ''Let *them* go to war with *you,* if they wish. They will not wish,'' he predicted flatly. ''It is a bluff. They wish to scare us into negotiating with them. Don't they know by now that we will not be scared?''

''Are you so sure of your people, Mr. President?'' Hamilton Delbacher inquired. ''You and your advisers may not be scared, but how about your people in the streets right now? Are they not scared?''

''I do not mean it in the sense of not being concerned,'' the President of Taiwan said stiffly. ''We are not fools. We are very exposed here. We are very apprehensive, all of us. But we are determined. Everything we have is in the air or on or under the sea, our troops are mobilizing throughout the island and we are adequately prepared, I think, to withstand anything but the most massive invasion. As I told you, there are no signs of it yet. By the time there are—if there are—we shall be ready for it.''

"But not for repeated attack from the air.''

"We could not sustain it indefinitely, no,'' the President of Taiwan agreed, "even though we will if necessary bomb Canton and Shanghai in retaliation and give them much to think about.''

"You will not bomb them, however,'' Hamilton said in a tone that said he did not expect yes for an answer, "with . . . what you have.''

"We will not use the bomb on them, no,'' the President of Taiwan said, sounding offended. "No more will they use it on us. After all, Mr. President, what is happening today, in *this* part of the world, at least, is a quarrel within a family. Neither of us wishes to destroy China. That has never been the issue.''

"No,'' the President said, "I realize that and I apologize for the implication. I just wanted to be sure, that's all.''

"You may be sure,'' the President of Taiwan said. "We still,'' he added, "need a screen between us, which is why I suggest you provide one. Immediately.''

"I repeat—''

"You have done it in the past,'' the President of Taiwan interrupted stubbornly. "When Quemoy and Matsu were threatened.''

"That was years ago,'' Ham Delbacher responded, "long before the mainland had built up its forces, and long before we became friendly with the mainland.''

"Yes, I knew it!'' the President of Taiwan said with renewed bitterness. "That is it, exactly! 'Friendly with the mainland!' For that, we are to be sacrificed!''

"You will not be sacrificed,'' the President said firmly. "I give you my word on that. But in recent years you have been edging closer and closer to reunification of some sort, have you not?''

"Yes,'' the President of Taiwan said, still bitterly, "but not reunification by conquest. We do not reunify at the muzzle of a gun or because of bombs or trying to destroy our island.''

"No, and it seems to me quite obvious already that there is no intention of destroying your island. I gather considerable care has been exercised at Kaohsiung, from what you say."

"They want to save the port, yes, that is obvious."

"And aside from the Grand, which I regret as a matter of sentiment because there was nothing like it, and the things pertaining to the Generalissimo, they are apparently being quite careful to refrain from destroying other things. Even the casualties, sad as they are, seem secondary to symbolism."

"So far."

"What would it profit them to destroy you? Everything they might gain from reunification would be lost if Taiwan were destroyed in the process, would it not? What good would millions of dead, a devastated island and a ruined economy do them? Your brethren on the mainland are not that stupid!"

"They are not stupid at all," the President of Taiwan said. "That is why if you provide a screen, the attacks will stop and we will all be safe."

Hamilton Delbacher sighed and in spite of the anxieties of the hour could not keep a certain amusement from his voice.

"I recognize the kinship," he said. "You are all very persistent and very tenacious. You never really yield a point even under such stress as you are under now."

"We simply like to persuade those with whom we negotiate to see things our way," the President of Taiwan said with dignity. "Because it is really the only sensible way."

"Mmmhmm. I wonder how either side can seriously imagine reaching a compromise."

"It will come," the President of Taiwan said, "but they must be made to understand that it will not come by force. That is why we need—"

"The screen," Hamilton Delbacher said with him, simultaneously. "Well, screen *as* screen you are not going to get. But let me propose something that might serve the same purpose without—"

And he did so, while the President of Taiwan listened intently.

"It would be quite unheard of," he said presently in a thoughtful tone, "but the very novelty might make it work."

"If all parties pretend together," Hamilton Delbacher said

dryly, "it might. Incidentally, if your forces find any evidence of Soviet assistance, weapons, ammunition, anything at all, send it to me immediately."

"Evidence from Taiwan?" its President inquired with a wry skepticism. "I do not see that as being admissable at the U.N."

"Nonetheless, it will be presented. If you find it. You may not, in this instance."

"I would doubt it," the President of Taiwan said. "This is going to be presented to the world as a family quarrel, I can see that. If Yuri Serapin conceived otherwise," he added spitefully, "he does not know China."

"I can see that, too," Ham Delbacher said. "Which makes it even more difficult for us. But the timing, of course, has broader implications."

"Yes," the President of Taiwan agreed somberly. "They are working together for the moment, and that *does* have broader implications. We can expect your announcement before the day is out, then?"

"You can," Ham Delbacher said. "And do not even refer to it as a 'screen,' please."

"Mr. President," the President of Taiwan said blandly, "words are such wonderful things when one wishes to make unpleasant truths palatable. I would not dream of it. All I want," he added with a sudden grimness, "is for it to get here—swiftly."

"It will," the President promised, equally grim.

And that, he told himself with a wry little smile, was typical. Ju Xing-dao and the President of Taiwan—there was a similarity of approach and method. He had traveled the Orient enough as a Senator to be able to mock the old cliché, but in one respect it was true; they didn't all *look* alike, but when it came right down to the final shove they certainly acted and thought alike. It was not the flexible, easygoing pattern of the West—and so, when dealing with the West, it often got them what they wanted.

After he and the President had exchanged pledges of constant consultation and had said good-bye, he turned back to his desk and sat for some moments reviewing what he might say in what he anticipated would be his next conversation. But when the operator interrupted his train of thought he found she still had not reached

Yuri Serapin: the deliberate evasion continued. Instead it was representative of the one country he had not expected to hear from, coming not from Riyadh, not even within the Kingdom's borders. Excited, enraged and determined, the high-pitched voice of one of the older brothers came from the French Riviera.

"Mr. President!" it exclaimed. "Do you know what has happened in my country? Do you know what the worthless, no-good dog of a baby brother has done? Is it not enough to make Allah cry? You must help us, Mr. President! Now, Mr. President! *Now!* There is no choice for you! Oil, Mr. President, oil and the Gulf! To say nothing of what is right, no?"

"Yes, Your Royal Highness," he agreed. "And what does the family intend to do?"

"Fight!" the prince exclaimed. "Fight, fight, *fight!* What else would you expect us to do?"

"I should expect that of all loyal members of the House of Saud," he said soothingly. "Is anyone else in the family involved in this dangerous adventure?"

"Some of my father's grandchildren," the prince said, "may Allah curse them. Not very many," he added hastily. "Only, I am told by my brothers—my *sane* brothers—four or five. This is what comes of sending them to the West for education. This is what comes of Harvard, the Sorbonne and Oxford! *Tcha!* Better they had been sent to live on camel's milk in the desert and never seen a book! Better for the House of Saud. And better for you."

"One cannot reverse the decisions of time," the President said philosophically, deciding he had better not get involved in that one. "It has been done and now, Allah willing, we must see what can be done to reverse the consequences. What do you suggest, Your Royal Highness?"

"Increase your naval strength in the Gulf," the prince said promptly. "Send us many more planes. Attack South Yemen."

"Yes," the President said, "I've been thinking of all of those. Meanwhile, what will the House of Saud be doing?"

"Many of my brothers are in Jidda," the prince said, "holding a family council at this moment. I am flying to join them within the hour."

"Is that safe? Isn't Jidda under attack too?"

"I will get through," the prince said, "*inshallah*. In any event, the council is meeting and I am told the decision is to fight, as I told you. So far that treacherous dog, that eater of filth, that defiler of women and boys, is temporarily in command of Riyadh. Along with his worthless friends from South Yemen. His *communist* friends from South Yemen. Abdul Aziz Ibn Saud must be spinning in his grave, may Allah rest him! But already resistance is spreading. It is one thing to bomb a city or two, and it is another to occupy a desert. The tribes are loyal to us. The Yemeni and the treacherous Soviets will have their work cut out for them. They are doomed to fail."

"In the meantime," the President remarked thoughtfully, "they hold the oilfields in hostage, or soon will. They they will have a very useful weapon to curb the West's enthusiasm to help you. Is that not correct?"

"We will destroy the oilfields," the prince said flatly. "You can always help us reopen them later."

"If you destroy them carefully," Hamilton Delbacher said, "and if your people get there before the Yemenis do."

"We are not fools," the prince said with some asperity. "We have thought of this contingency for a long time. The House of Saud did not rise to eminence without enemies, you know, Mr. President. We are surrounded by them always. Many things have occurred to us, including what to do with the oilfields in an event like this. You need not worry. It is already being done."

"I see," the President said, trying to conceal the doubt in his voice. "Well: that's good."

"It is perfect," the prince said with satisfaction. "Still we need assistance. Much assistance."

"You will get as much as we are able," the President said.

"It had best be a very great deal," the Prince said, "else we will have a long and severe battle on our hands. It were best if this were to be ended at once. We do not wish it to drag on forever, like Iran and Iraq."

"No more do we," Hamilton Delbacher said, with some asperity himself. "Much will depend on how loyal your people are and how vigorously they will fight in these opening days."

"They will fight much better," the prince said crisply, "knowing the United States is sending help."

"We will do what we can," the President said. "You don't doubt our intention, I trust."

"Will it be what I have outlined?" the prince persisted. "Will you send ships into the Gulf and planes into the air? Will you attack South Yemen and stop the evil at its source?"

"South Yemen is not the source. As you are well aware."

"But you have not been given an excuse to attack the head of evil," the prince said, "so you must attack its arms. Is that not correct? The body must be eliminated limb by limb."

"The problem is that in the time it would take to do that, the objectives may all be achieved," the President said. "It may be too late to stop them. And we would be exhausted."

"Then you must obviously find the excuse to go direct to the source," the prince said. "Immediately. Not a day is to be lost!"

"That is amazingly profound advice, Highness," the President said dryly, "and you know as well as I do how impractical it is. But if you happen to think of a good excuse for me while you are dodging Soviet missiles on your way to Jidda, be sure to let me know."

"I will," the prince said with a sudden chuckle. "We sympathize with your problem, believe me, Mr. President. Because"—his voice turned somber—"it is the problem shared by all of us who wish to remain free."

"Yes," the President said, reflecting wryly that the word "freedom" was a tent that housed many different kinds of camels. "And I really do mean that I want any suggestions you may have. Meanwhile—"

"Meanwhile, you will send ships, planes and attack the Yemenis," the prince said promptly. "What is amusing?" he demanded sharply when the President laughed.

"You remind me of someone else I just talked to," Hamilton Delbacher said. "The same unshakable grasp of fundamentals."

"Well, can I tell my brothers—?"

"You may tell them that we will give every assistance we possibly can," the President said. "And as swiftly as we can. Bearing in mind that there are several other areas equally demanding of attention.''

"Yes," the prince agreed. "We have heard. It is devilish. That's why sooner or later you must attack the head. Then the arms will die of themselves. In the meantime, we count on your aid.''

"In the meantime," the President said, "you will have it.''

But how all this was to be done, he thought gloomily as he wished the prince luck on his perilous flight to Jidda and the prince said farewell with a cheerful, "I will make it, *inshallah!*" he did not at the moment know. He looked out at the Rose Garden. Its outlines were growing steadily more distinct as the clock passed 5 A.M. Indian summer lay soft on Washington. He suspected it would be another hot day.

Hot literally and hot figuratively. In the past few minutes, with what might be considered an almost carefree hand, he had scattered firm promises of American aid across the globe from one side to the other in as grand and cavalier a manner as though he really knew how he was going to make good on them. He had done so because his callers would accept nothing less. Their morale had to be encouraged. Their hopes had to be sustained. Their belief that there was a way out had to be kept vigorously alive, else their leadership would falter, their peoples would reflect it, and inexorably at four key points around the world America and the freedom she defended would go down still further. And communism would establish ever firmer footholds. And the Soviet conquest, which had been going on steadily without letup for almost seven decades, would move still closer to achieving its final and never-changing goal of complete domination over the earth.

So there had really been no choice. He could express his concern for the difficulties, as he had: that was permissible, it was human to worry. But he could never admit to his callers that he had the slightest hesitation in pledging aid or the slightest doubt as to the ultimate outcome. To do that would be to open a psychological abyss beneath their feet from which they would not recover. The battle would be lost before it really began. Like leaders before him, he found his hand forced by his followers. His country had always held out the prize of freedom and national independence. Those who accepted its promise expected it to make good.

He was bound by their expectations. There were no means of evasion.

Nor, he found, did he want any. He entered this new phase of the Soviet conquest with no doubts that the cause he was defending was the right one, though as usual with America and the West, the areas where it was being put to the test were not exactly simon pure in their adherence to democracy, human rights and the liberties which had for so long sustained the great republic. Mexico, dominated by the often corrupt and often iron-handed rule of a single party for more than half a century; South Africa, its white natives forced by the needs of survival to dominate and control its black natives in dozens of harsh and ruthless ways ; Taiwan, also dominated by a single party, its society outwardly relaxed but underneath as rigid and as ruthless toward dissent as its fellow China on the mainland; and Saudi Arabia, prerogative of a single family whose founder had conquered the country, whose children ran it with a typically Arab combination of fulsome hospitality and brutal harshness, sitting accidentally atop a still-vast and vital pool of oil. None of the four would win the prize for the perfect, hundred percent, model democratic state.

Yet none could be abandoned; and as his mind churned and rechurned the choices before him, he reflected with some irony that the United States, as usual, was on the side of some rather imperfect angels. Their natures were such as to be welcome fuel for all those critics, foreign and domestic, who always attacked America for any forceful action she took in opposition to Soviet advance. The professional purveyors of moral purity would have their usual field day, he supposed, no matter how grave the circumstances in which the United States now found herself. It did not matter how many times the Soviet hierarchy suppressed a Hungary or a Czechoslovakia, invaded an Afghanistan, crushed freedom in a Poland, destroyed the human rights and liberties of their own helpless subject races. The United States, in the minds, writings and public utterances of these critics, remained the villain. They were so determined to keep her in that category, thereby—innocently in some cases, not so innocently in some others—aiding the Soviet conquest, that no amount of logical argument could bring them over.

Fortunately the United States was not without means to maintain her position and defend her friends—not as easily as he might wish, but sufficiently so that he had been able to stand firm in these recent weeks. Yuri had once again switched back to indirect, not open, confrontation. The Soviet Union still had nuclear superiority, but both nations were at a level where "superiority" or "inferiority" were academic terms. Soviet conventional forces were still much larger; Soviet troops and planes and tanks, surface ships and nuclear submarines outnumbered the United States and NATO; Soviet SS-22 missiles still threatened Europe and the world in predominant numbers, despite the American emplacement of cruise missiles in Western Europe and Asia. But as the President had conclusively demonstrated in the confrontation just concluded, the Soviet tactic was still "the fruits of war without the penalties of war." It made for a devilish problem when the areas of danger were as far apart as they were this day.

He, too, he supposed ironically, wanted "the fruits of war without the penalties of war"; but in his case "the fruits of war" really meant just the opposite of war: just the keeping of old-fashioned peace in which both sides respected one another's boundaries, friends and interests; refrained from aggressive adventures pushing out from the center; were content to live and let live. These were really what the United States would be fighting for, if the United States ever had to fight again; it would not be "hegemony," that favorite communist word, over anyone.

Why was it so difficult to achieve live-and-let-live? The half-formed nations of the so-called "Third World" that always screamed so frantically about "American imperialism" had not seen an example of it since 1898, when the Spanish-American War had been fought. Everything since had been a desperate attempt by America to save the world from one dictator or another and try to preserve for its people and their friends a world in which they could be left alone to live in peace. Yet the screaming went on, while all the time the Soviet Union, leading some sort of miraculous charmed life created for it by "the naifs," as Lenin called them—the Great Gullibles of the West, operating the media, the arts, academe and some in business—went right ahead with its enormous military buildup and its steadily increasing pressures upon the world. It was an irony of history so great that he found it hard not to let himself become too bitter about it at times. Bitterness was a debilitating and blinding emotion and he could not afford to let it dominate him; but sometimes, he reflected with a heavy sigh, it was hard to escape. Particularly since he fully expected the perversion of truth to be applied to the present situation, by the same people and with the same scorn for America, as it had been in the past.

It was 5:30. The Secretaries, the Joint Chiefs of Staff, ubiquitous little Anson and his "position papers" would be back in half an hour.

He had no faith whatsoever that anything constructive would come of what he was about to do, but he felt it must be done before he talked to his own people again. He lifted the phone, prepared to turn on the videotape and the Picturephone.

"Try President Serapin again, will you?" he said. "He must be in his office at the Kremlin by now."

"Yes, sir," the operator responded, sounding doubtful but willing. "I'll try."

"Stay with him this time," he said. "I've had just about enough of his damned nonsense."

They sat at the long narrow table in his office now, the dozen who made up the Politburo and the Council of Ministers; and behind their dutiful smiles and fawning attention Yuri could sense, as he had ever since coming to power three months ago, the uneasy deep-seated fear that he might once again be going too far—that those qualities of gambler that had brought him to the top and that had so successfully exposed American weakness to all the world in these recent weeks might now be carrying the Soviet Union to that disastrous point they all secretly dreaded—the point at which the grasp for "the fruits of war" might finally, at last, plunge them headlong into war itself.

It was not that they doubted their ability to win such a conflict. Many years prior to the time when some in Washington had begun to toy with the fatally intriguing idea that it might actually be possible to survive a nuclear conflict, official Soviet military doctrine had already embraced the concept of winnable nuclear war and was teaching it at the Frunze Military Academy, "West Point" of the

Soviet Union. And decades before that, running on down through all official Soviet writing and all official Soviet thought, had been the single fundamental drumbeat, the single fundamental theme that to this day underlay and underscored everything they did.

It had been expressed in infinite ways, but the theme was always the same:

"There has not been, there is not, and there cannot be, class peace between socialism and capitalism, or peaceful coexistence between the communist and bourgeois ideologies."—*Peaceful Coexistence and the Security of the People,* Colonel I. Sidelnikov.

"War between countries of the capitalist and socialist systems will have a violent and acutely defined class nature of a fight to the death.—*Military Art in the Postwar Period,* Col. A. A. Strokov.

"A new world war . . . will be a struggle for the very existence of the two opposing world-wide systems, the socialist and the capitalist. This war will decide the fate of all mankind."—*The Great Soviet Encyclopedia.*

"As long as capitalism and socialism exist we cannot live in peace. A funeral dirge will be sung either over the Soviet Republic or over world capitalism."—Joseph Stalin.

"The purpose of the Soviet state is the complete and final victory of communism on a world scale."—*Pravda.*

And along with it, the constantly reiterated corollary:

"Surprise—One of the basic conditions for achieving success in battle. Surprise is achieved by the use of various ways . . . by leading the enemy into error concerning one's own intentions, by preserving in secret the plan of battle, by speed and decisiveness of action, by hidden artificial maneuvers, by the unexpected use of the nuclear weapon and other new combat means. . . ."—*Soviet Dictionary of Basic Military Terms.*

And yet he knew, as he studied his men with an outwardly welcoming but secretly cold and appraising half-smile on his lips and a cold contempt for their basic unreliability in his heart, that the last thing they wanted, even now, was "the unexpected use of the nuclear weapon and the other new combat means." They now had in their arsenal, in addition to the enormous number of missiles and nuclear warheads that he had inherited as the result of the military buildup initiated by L. I. Brezhnev, satellite killers in orbit around the earth capable of destroying the worldwide communications system of the United States and its allies in seconds; functional laser weapons in lower orbit that could obliterate any target on earth from space in an infinitesimal fraction of time; and on earth itself not only atomic weapons and the enormous stock of poison gases accumulated after the successful testings in Afghanistan, Laos and Cambodia, but a still-preponderant arsenal of conventional weapons and the largest standing army in the history of the world . . . except possibly the People's Republic of China. And how well were *they* equipped?

It was a time to be brave, to be dynamic, to move quickly and decisively upon a world still reeling from the shocks he had administered to it with the maneuvers and the confrontation in which he had enticed America to the very edge of war and then, with a sure hand at the last moment, snatched her back and permitted the world to gasp in gratitude and relief while he secretly prepared yet another surprise, the one which was now taking place in four places around the globe.

Now the globe was hemorrhaging and America was being forced to rush relief. America could not afford to do so. Yet here were his colleagues, afraid to seize the opportunity he had so skillfully and with supreme cleverness created for them.

"Comrades," he said, so sure of their wavering that he could not altogether conceal an impatient harshness in his voice, "is this not a great day for the Motherland, when our capitalist friends find themselves scurrying from one end of the earth to the other in a futile attempt to plug up the holes we have so shrewdly dug for them—these holes in which will be buried their hopes and from which we will extract our final triumph?"

There was a hurried nodding of heads, an obsequious agreement. The Minister of Foreign Affairs even began applauding, and in a second they were all on their feet, clapping and turning to Yuri their eager, obedient faces.

"Comrades," he said, returning their applause, pleased in spite of his deep skepticism concerning their courage and ability to see the gamble through, "please be seated. You do me too much honor for what is, after all, our collective judgment."

"It was your inspiration, Yuri Pavlovich," the Foreign Minister said quickly. "We approved it, in this room, scarcely a week ago."

"You did," he said, picking up the piece of paper on which it had been duly recorded and signed, and reading it aloud once again:

"'In view of the enormous success of the recent international moves originated and directed by the genius of Y.P. Serapin, and bearing in mind his great original contributions to the ongoing success of the Motherland and the communist revolution, it is the sense of the Politburo and the Council of Ministers that for a period of six months, which may be extended indefinitely by the will of the Politburo and the Council of Ministers, all authority to originate and direct further moves against the imperialist enemies of mankind is vested solely and exclusively in Y. P. Serapin, to whom we pledge our total and unwavering support.'"

He paused and looked thoughtfully along the table at their lifted, waiting faces, each cast from the same stolid, somber, unsmiling mold that the world had come to know so well down the decades in all the many photographs of the phalanx atop Lenin's mausoleum. Individual faces had come and gone, removed by death or demotion: the phalanx went on, grim and unsmiling. There was not much to laugh about, in the jungle world of the mutually jealous and suspicious Soviet leadership. He was determined to keep it that way, knowing that his skillful manipulations of those jealousies and suspicions, aided by a few judicious murders, had opened the way for his own rise to power. Their mutual mistrust of one another—and fear of him—could give him the longest and most glorious rule in Soviet history. So he intended it to be, for he had much to accomplish, once hated America was removed as a functioning power and the world lay open to the final triumph of communism.

"Comrades," he said, "that was a most generous expression of your faith and confidence, and I can only say today, as I said on the day when you approved it, that I shall continue to accept your orders with a humble heart full of gratitude. I hope you agree on this day I have justified your faith, and that on this day we have begun the process that will finally bring America down and permit the inexorable laws of history to work their final will.''

"Your decisions this day have been superb, Comrade President,'' the Foreign Minister said. "What you have set in motion is utterly masterful!''

"America is confounded, that is certain,'' the Minister of Defense agreed with satisfaction. "The imperialists quite obviously do not know where to turn.''

"Don't be too confident, Comrade Minister,'' he said in a tone cautionary but amicable. "You know our friend H. Delbacher. He may have some surprises for us yet. He has proved to us that he is not without imagination.''

"But not such an imagination as yours, Yuri Pavlovich!'' the Minister of Industry assured him fervently. "Yours is a greater imagination than has ever been seen!''

"It is historic,'' the Minister of Agriculture agreed.

"Unheard of,'' the Minister of Development concurred.

"Monumental,'' the Minister for Minorities acknowledged.

"*And* invincible,'' the Foreign Minister summed up. "Nothing can be devised by the imperialists that will adequately rescue them from the morass you have created, into which they will deservedly sink.''

"Perhaps,'' he said slowly: and instantly their gleeful expressions changed to a grave and thoughtful look suitable to his changed tone. "Perhaps . . . we must not, however, underestimate the ability of H. Delbacher and his advisers to make some last-minute attempt to rescue their dying country. We must be ever alert until the struggle at last concludes. So I have already advised the heads of the armed services and so I must advise you. It is a time for vigilance, comrades, not yet for gloating. Once the battle ends we can gloat. Now we must bend every effort to see that all necessary aid goes to the brave fighters for freedom who have responded to our call in southern Africa, in Mexico and in Saudi Arabia—which has already, I have just learned, been rechristened not '*Saud*'s Arabia' but 'The People's Republic of Arabia.' ''

There was an excited cheer and several of them slapped each other on the back with gleeful laughter.

"And in Taiwan," he added firmly, "where our great allies of the People's Republic of China are preparing the final extirpation of imperialism in that island."

There was a sudden termination of laughter, a hasty rejuggling of expressions: despite his insistence, to which they had bowed, the new alliance was not popular with his countrymen, nor would it ever be, he knew. Yet he did not regret having forced it through. It was a great blow against the United States.

"That is not to say, comrades," he added smoothly, "that we need always consider our allies of the People's Republic of China to be 'great.' Or indeed"—he permitted himself a wintry smile— "that we need even necessarily always consider them allies."

This produced the response he expected and wanted, an immediate—and relieved—renewal of laughter.

"Your genius foresees all things, Yuri Pavlovich!" the Foreign Minister said heartily. "We know, as you told us repeatedly in these recent weeks of negotiation, that we can trust you. The treaty is temporary, only; it is a means of ridding us of America, only. It does not obligate us to anything but the immediate objective."

"That is correct," Yuri said calmly. He paused and drew a deep breath. "After that objective has been achieved, we will then consider the Eastern Problem."

"And solve it, Comrade President!" the Minister of Defense assured him.

"And solve it," he echoed with a somber force that thrilled them with its certainty. "It, like the solution of the Western problem, is inevitable. It is an imperative of history. Nothing can change it. We will let them play their games with Taiwan, as long as that assists us in destroying the imperialists. When all is accomplished and they are left alone with us, we will move."

"When they least expect it," the Foreign Minister suggested.

"Certainly," he said with a sudden sharp impatience that surprised and intimidated them. "That is obvious, Comrade Minister. When else would we do it?"

"No other time, Comrade President!" the Foreign Minister said hastily. "Certainly no other time than when the treacherous fools are deluded into thinking we have forgotten their true nature!"

"That is correct," he said, less severely. "You understand me, Vaily Georgevich."

"So do we all," they cried, and again a contempt for them swept his heart. Some of them had come very close to blocking his rise to power; some had dared place their ambitions before his, along the way. He had not forgotten who they were, and someday when other more pressing problems were solved, he would take care of them, too. For now it was enough that they were all nodding and grinning and making congratulatory noises—that they were all dutifully paying him the tribute of obedience that he knew he deserved.

"Perhaps you could tell us, Yuri Pavlovich," the Minister of Defense said cautiously when their great enthusiasm had subsided a bit, "what you think will happen next, now that the conflict has been opened in these four places of such great importance to the United States. Will they go to the aid of their friends in all the places, do you think? Will they pick one or two? And what further will be expected of us? It is not that we challenge your judgment," he added hastily as a rather odd look came into Yuri's eyes. "It is just that we wish your wise guidance so that we may better know what is to be expected of us."

"That is it, Comrade President," the Minister of Industries agreed quickly. "That is exactly it!"

They all nodded fervent acquiescence.

"What is expected of you," he said, permitting an emphatic coldness to enter his voice, "is to support me and your decision of a week ago to abide by my judgment of what is best for the Motherland and for the successful conclusion of the battle to end all threat of capitalist hegemony everywhere. You must never waver," he added, making for the first time the association he had been carefully planning for weeks. "I need your unflinching support. Mother Russia needs your unflinching support. *Do we have it?*"

Again there was a fervent chorus of agreement; but it seemed to him that this time there was a certain reservation in the responses of some. He swung abruptly upon one of them. The Defense Minister's eyes widened for a second as though he expected to be struck.

"You have thoughts, Nikolai Petrovich?" The Minister of Defense paled but did not reply. "State them!" he demanded harshly. "State them, Comrade Minister! It is your duty! State them!"

But the Minister of Defense lowered his eyes and looked away.

"Yuri Pavlovich," he said in a low voice, while they all tried not to look as tense as they obviously felt, "whatever by poor thoughts may be, they are devoted to nothing but your welfare and that of the Motherland and the revolution. An end to all hegemonists!" he cried suddenly. "Death to imperialist opportunists!"

"That," said Yuri Serapin calmly, "is more suitable, Comrade Minister. Does anyone else," he inquired with a sudden soft menace in his voice, "have thoughts they wish to express about the course I have chosen?"

But when he looked slowly along the table, no one else responded; nor did anyone else look him in the eye. For a second he was tempted to force the issue, demand that they reaffirm their loyalty, ferret out at once those who did not accept his leadership wholly with absolute abandonment of independence and will. Then common sense came to his rescue. But only just—only just.

It was not until later that night, discussing it with Ekaterina in the apartment he maintained for her near his own that he realized how close—perhaps how fatally close—he had come to letting arrogance traduce him into dangerous egomania.

"They hate you," she said calmly, playing idly with the huge diamond-and-ruby pendant he had brought her from Bulgari in Rome when he had been there on a trade mission six months ago. "They will kill you in a moment if you fail, Yuri Pavlovich. One slip," she said with a certain satisfaction, as though she relished the thought, "and they will be on you like a pack of wolves. These new adventures of yours had better succeed. You have no lovers in the Politburo."

"I have no lovers anywhere," he flared back with the bitterness she often provoked in him simply by being perhaps the only Soviet citizen who was not afraid of him.

"Possibly not," she agreed complacently, "but at least—" and she shot him a quick, appraising look—"you have someone who tells you the truth. That may be worth something, comrade."

"I am too arrogant, then," he said.

She gave him the trace of a smile.

"You are not modest, Yuri Pavlovich."

"And why should I be?" he demanded angrily. "Has not everything gone the way I have planned so far?"

She shrugged with an indifference that he knew was meant to annoy him further.

"There was a confrontation—you and the President appeared about to blow up the world together—you appeared to withdraw our forces to some degree. In one way what you did could be considered clever, in another a foolish bluff that succeeded by sheer luck. Now you say you have set traps for the Americans. It remains to be seen."

"It will be seen," he snapped. "Meanwhile I have secured the absolute power I need to direct the final battle against the imperialists."

"You gamble so," she said. "That is what worries them. They are not sure you can bring it off."

"I will bring it off," he said flatly.

"Are the Americans in retreat?" she inquired dryly; and thinking back, at that time hours later, to his conversation with Hamilton Delbacher, he was forced to scowl and admit, "No, they are not in retreat!"

Indeed, the President had sounded—when Yuri finally ended his deliberate evasions and decided to take his call—as though he were moving straight ahead without the slightest qualm or hesitation. Yuri had finally permitted his call to come through just after the members of the Politburo had left, their brief moment of open uneasiness masked by subsequent hearty assurances of confidence and victory. The tensions between them were glossed over, buried; and when he had read them the latest optimistic reports from the military chiefs, they cheered and applauded and pretended the tensions had never existed. As he had done with the military chiefs, he had watched their departing backs with an expression it was as well they did not see. He had no one in the world he could trust, save possibly Ekaterina, and her only in a context too complicated with other things for him to feel he could really take strength from it. He, Yuri Pavlovich, was alone at the pinnacle of power patiently won, bitterly bought, never to be really relaxed in and enjoyed. He must be ever on guard, not only against the enemies of the revolution, the Chinese hegemonists and the Western imperialists, but against his own colleagues and his own people.

Why should he do anything for his country? he asked himself bitterly. It returned him nothing but fear and hatred.

But of course, as he knew, it did give him power—supreme power, and the enormous historical privilege of being the leader of the Soviet Union in the climactic stages of the battle to decide the fate of all mankind. Today he was supreme over Russia; tomorrow if the inevitabilities of history were correct as Marx, Engels and Lenin had foreseen them, he would be supreme over the world. Then there would be no more trouble anywhere. All dissent would be silenced, all obstructionists would be removed, antirevolutionary thought and agitation would be forever stamped out, a firm and unchallengeable conformity would be imposed upon all mankind. Universal peace, man's dream eternal, would at last exist, never to be broken again. All whose independent thoughts and antisocial protests might disrupt it would be forever silenced.

Why was it, he often wondered, that the West and so many African and Asian nations could not see the great beneficence of this, the great boon it would be to humankind? A world with no thought save that officially approved, a world with no chance for rebellion or troublesome individuality, a world in which all humanity would be born, reared, live and die within the mold of the protective and all-knowing state—harmony and order everywhere!

Why was it necessary to argue, scheme, betray and sometimes even fight to achieve this?

Its blessing was so obvious.

Unfortunately it was not that simple: lasting solutions to the problems of humanity never are. There were still people on earth—far too many, he thought grimly—who stubbornly continued to oppose history's inevitable logic, who still thought, foolishly and impossibly, that there was a place for "freedom" as they understood it: for unruly individuality and untidy independent thought—for behavior and modes of living outside the norms of acceptable socialist conformity—for a life in which thought and action were the products of free will and were not controlled by the secret police and the iron dictatorship of the proletariat.

"The proletariat!" Yuri was product enough of his times to smile at that ancient lie, still sounded so bombastically from the phalanx at Lenin's mausoleum, from the state radio and in all speeches by the Soviet leadership. Its members might have come from "proletarian" beginnings (indeed, humble origin was always eagerly stressed by the anxious Western press every time a new man murdered his way to the top of the Kremlin), but they were far from "proletarian" once they got into power. Luxurious apartments, opulent houses, lavish country *dachas*, all the clothing, jewelry, perfumes, automobiles, stereos, color televison sets and other baubles of the West—ah, yes, proletarianism had its advantages when one became a Soviet hierarch!

His mind ran scornfully over a thousand such, each of whom saw in the Soviet state and the continued dominance of communism only the chance to get and keep the material amenities that were denied absolutely to their captive millions of countrymen. To be a ruler in Soviet Russia, while it brought many terrifying strains and tensions from one's jealous competitors, could be very pleasant in a material sense. He knew luxury came before ideology in the minds of many, though all were careful to give lip service to ideology first and foremost. There were not many, any longer, who truly believed in the socialist mission. Many still held to the great dream of Mother Russia, dominant and all-conquering, over all. But it was separate from the ideology. It was only as a guarantee of their own privilege and position.

Well: he still believed in the mission. And that, he supposed, was why he was where he was. That was why history had permitted him to rise to this place at this time, when the fate of all mankind depended on what he, almost alone, was able to accomplish. To him the dream had not meant material wealth, though he was pleased to be able to live in luxury, to give Ekaterina expensive jewels, to know that every material comfort was at his disposal . . . to literally be able to command the Czars' dinner services and attendant amenities when he wished to entertain state visitors, to literally live like the Czar, in the Czar's own palaces, when he so desired . . . to be, in effect, Czar himself, modern-day Father of All the Russias.

It was nice to be able to enjoy these things, but to him the dream meant something much more fundamental. It meant power. More specifically, it meant power for Yuri Pavlovich Serapin.

Power to control the world. Power to direct all humanity into the paths where it should go. Power to determine the fates of nations and of men; to realign trade and commerce so that the Soviet Union and all its people would be the recipients of the bounty of the earth; to dispose of political boundaries and remake the surface of the globe in such a way that all the roads of earth led to Moscow as they once had led to Rome.

This was the supreme benefit, for him. This was what *he* saw in the communist dream: he, Yuri Pavlovich Serapin, enshrined forever in some impossible mausoleum, bigger than Lenin's, bigger than Lincoln's, a leader greater than Buddha or Muhammad or Christ—the universal ruler, the universal benefactor, the universal god, Yuri the Great.

And largely because of one stubborn American and his millions of stubborn countrymen and all their simpering, obedient allies, satellites, fellow-travelers and hangers-on around the globe, the dream was in jeopardy. It was not coming to him as easily and simply as historical imperatives had always led him to believe it would. It was not within his grasp as surely as his intelligence, talents and infinite scope of mind entitled him. The United States was always in the way—not only of the Soviet conquest but of his own rising to supreme power over a humanity that so obviously, with all its chaotic uncertainties, rivalries, fears and injustices, needed one iron, inexorable, implacable hand to enforce orders no one could challenge, and establish universal rules that no one could defy.

He thought for a moment, and an expression came over his face that they would have been horrified to see, of his "friends" from his days in the Soviet embassy in Washington—all those earnest, idealistic, well-meaning, wide-eyed Americans who entertained him at cocktail parties and dinners, who arranged "little intimate gatherings" at their houses with powerful people "so that you can talk and get to know and understand one another"—all that naive, dewy-eyed, fatally good-hearted and self-defeating crew that had done so much in their innocence (and sometimes, though not so many, not in their innocence) to help his country on its way to conquering the earth. His scathingly scornful expression would have grievously shocked them all. Was this their Yuri, that amiable young man they remembered so well from the old days at the embassy? It could not be! *Oh, God, it must not be!*

But it was. And the thing they could never realize—could not afford to let themselves realize, or it might send them mad, such a light did it throw on him, on his country and on them—was that this was what he had been, right along. He had gone through one or two brief moments of questioning in his life, but almost never about the Americans. He knew them inside out. And he regarded them, as did all the top leaders in the Kremlin, with a continuing and unswerving contempt.

This did not mean, however, that he and his colleagues did not consider them dangerous, or that they did not have a healthy respect for the Americans' infinite capacity for the unexpected. Their sheer unpredictability could be at times quite frightening. Logic, facts, figures might say that the Soviet Union was indubitably the superior military power in terms of simple statistics: but with the Americans the statistics were never simple because they frequently did not forecast with any accuracy what the Americans would do in any given situation. By rights Hamilton Delbacher, confronted with such a worldwide display of Soviet might as Yuri had ordered across all the seas and continents in the maneuvers just concluded, should have abandoned his stubborn recalcitrance, pulled in his horns and retreated prudently to his own shores. Instead he had met Yuri's threatening warlike gestures as firmly and unflinchingly as though he, not Yuri, had the upper hand. And had, if truth be known, bluffed Yuri quite as successfully as Yuri had bluffed him, if not more so.

So, Yuri thought grimly as he watched the four new open wounds pulsating brightly on his map of the world, see what you will do this time, Mr. President! Bluff me again if you can, with bombs falling on Mexico City, Johannesburg, Riyadh and Taipei! Put the broken eggs back in the basket this time, if you can! And show me how invincible you are now, with all your friends in trouble and the demands for your forces worldwide and your obligations such that you must furnish them or drop still further, this time I hope fatally further, in the respect and estimation of mankind!

And it had all been so easy, once the idea had come to him and he had begun with great caution and secrecy to put it into effect. United States' eavesdropping on communications within the Soviet Union had been successfully shattered several years ago by defectors coming over to furnish Moscow with information about it, and as far as he knew, it had not been successfully reestablished. But one could never be quite sure, any more than the Americans could be quite sure that they had broken Soviet eavesdropping on them, despite the defectors who had come the other way. The game went on, advantage going now to one side, now to the other. It never ended, and one had best always be cautious, and more than cautious.

He had conceived of his plan around two A.M. one morning a week ago; had confided it to four trusted young KGB colleagues who were ostensibly being posted out to South Yemen, Angola, Cuba and Peking as "secretaries" of varying ranks in the various embassies. The postings had been duly noted by the National Security Agency and the CIA in Washington, but like the satellites above, analysts on the ground were not able to penetrate the minds of men. And so the young men had departed with their messages to Yuri's obedient allies in the Middle East, Africa and Guatemala and his new friends in Peking. And with an eager grasp of his meaning, admiration for his plan and a grateful awareness of what they themselves could gain from it, his allies had proceeded to move as he requested. They could do so with faith in his promises of assistance, because part of his shrewd planning in the maneuvers had been to leave weapons, men and materiel in place around the globe for just such a contingency.

And now all was going well, and where was proud and confident America now? Where was Hamilton Delbacher, that firm, tough, American-cliché grandfather-in-the-White House? He was shrewd, Yuri could concede him that, but Yuri was shrewder. He was tough, but Yuri was tougher. Delbacher had his vision of something America called "peace," which as Yuri saw it was simply American hegemony under the cloak of the pretense of a free and fruitful life for all humanity. But Yuri's vision was stronger. And Yuri's was winning now.

He had worked himself into a mood so savage, triumphant and carried away by his own rhetoric that he did not realize for several seconds that his secretary was buzzing him frantically on his phone.

"Yes?" he asked almost stupidly, as though he were coming out of a dream, as perhaps he was. "What is it, comrade?"

"It is the President again, Comrade President!" she said with a rush of excitement.

He hesitated a second and then decided he had played the game long enough.

"Moment," he said. He too snapped on the tape recorder, activated the Picturephone. "Now, comrade. Put him through."

There was a blurring on the screen, a little warning electronic sound; and the calm, determined face that he remembered most vividly calling him "Evil! Evil! Evil!" in Fabrizio Gulak's apartment in the River House in New York City materialized before him.

"Mr. President," Hamilton Delbacher said.

"Mr. President," Yuri Serapin replied.

2

For several seconds—half a minute, perhaps, though it seemed to both of them much longer—they stared at one another with impassive appraisal. It almost became a contest; but before it could, Yuri decided to terminate the possibility. After all, he told himself contemptuously, there *was* no contest. He held all the cards.

"You wished to speak to me, Mr. President?" he inquired in a level tone. Hamilton Delbacher permitted himself the trace of an ironic smile.

"I should think you might have wished to speak to me, Mr. President, being once again the aggressor against world peace, as you are."

"Mr. President," Yuri said calmly, "I am not going to indulge in a debate with you. The Soviet Union is at peace with her neighbors. Nothing engages us militarily at the moment. All is calm. What is to be gained by an attempt to blackguard me with false charges?"

"You play a very dangerous game," Hamilton Delbacher observed. "Once again you are gambling that you can take the world to the very edge of universal conflict and, presumably, snatch it back at the last moment. It may not work this time." He rested his chin on his folded hands and stared thoughtfully at his opponent. "This time you may have really done it."

"Done what, Mr. President?" Yuri demanded with a show of

indignation. "What am I supposed to have 'done'? I have done nothing yet. Of course it may be"—and across his broad half-Asian face there also came the trace of an ironic smile—"that I presently *may* have to do something, if certain fighters in the great cause of human freedom versus the imperialist ruling circle of the United States request my aid. I might then have to do something, Mr. President."

"Yes, that's the standard routine," the President agreed. "First you foment the trouble, then you arrange for the troublemakers to ask your help, and then you come in. If you can."

"What is to prevent us, Mr. President?" Yuri inquired blandly. "Is there some obstacle in the way, should we wish to respond to the legitimate appeals of the victims of imperialism?"

"We will be in the way," Hamilton Delbacher said calmly. "What then, Mr. President?"

"How you *do* engage in sophistries!" Yuri exclaimed. "It is impossible for you to be in the way. The areas of crisis are too far apart. And in any event, we are not there. So how can you be in our way?" He slapped the desk emphatically. "Mr. President! Please do not try to trap me with clever debating tricks! It is a waste of your time and mine. There is much business here that must be attended to. I am sure the same is true of you. If there is some purpose to this call, then please state it, let us discuss it, let us conclude it, and let us return to our duties and responsibilities, which in both cases are very great. Let us not engage in clevernesses! Life is too pressing."

"Mr. President," Hamilton Delbacher said, "as always, your effrontery is breathtaking. But it does not change the fact that in four vital areas of the earth you have launched new adventures that are inevitably going to bring you once again into direct conflict with the United States. Why, Mr. President? Haven't you had enough excitement in the past few weeks? Is life in Moscow so dull that you must keep things constantly stirred up? Don't you have enough entertainment over there?"

"Now, Mr. President," Yuri said, and a dangerous edge came into his voice, "you are ridiculing me, and you should know from experience that this does not contribute to good relations between us. I do not like to be ridiculed, particularly when the world is in such serious condition due to the imperialist adventures of the United States and your own ambitions to rule the earth.''

The President of the United States shook his head as if in wonderment.

''Mr. President,'' he said, ''Mr. President! There you go again, placing your own ambitions on the shoulders of your opponents, attributing to others what you desire yourself. You have grave responsibilities to bear, Mr. President. Four of them. Mexico—Saudi Arabia—South Africa—Taiwan. Don't you think you had better abandon them before it comes to a real contest between us?''

For a moment Yuri stated at him, a scornful twist to his lips. Then he spoke with a patient reasonableness as though to a not very intelligent child.

''Mr. President,'' he said slowly and distinctly, ''how can you hold me responsible for four such widely separate actions when the Soviet Union is not even involved in them? Soviet planes are not flying, Soviet bombs are not falling, Soviet troops are not fighting. Wherein are we involved? Furthermore, Mr. President, as I told you in our very first meeting, at the United Nations three months ago, you forces are inferior to ours. They are simply not adequate. How then can you threaten us? How can you try to exercise once again your self-appointed role of policeman to the world when you do not have the strength to back it up? And particularly when we have given you no reason? It would be absurd. The world would condemn it universally. And it would mean only disaster for you. Why would you venture such a thing?''

''Mr. President,'' Hamilton Delbacher said in much the same tone, ''you are very well aware that while you may have some advantage in some areas of major weaponry, our own forces are much more than adequate to totally destroy the Soviet Union. So why play games on that score? In fact, why play games at all? It is entirely apparent what is happening around the globe at this moment: it is entirely apparent where the inspiration comes from. Who has any doubt?''

''Ah, Mr. President!'' Yuri said triumphantly. ''There you allow hope to overcome common sense. At least two-thirds of the world has doubt—enough to provide an enormous skepticism when you charge us with it. As I assume you intend to do.''

"For the record," the President said. "For the record only. I don't expect it to do much good, even with the proof we are amassing."

"What 'proof'?" Yuri demanded scornfully. "Soviet weapons? Soviet ammunition? Scraps of this and scraps of that? You could have procured them anywhere, Mr. President, and at any time, from the Israelis or anybody. Have we thoughtfully dated them for you? What will they prove?"

"Nothing to those who do not wish to believe," Hamilton Delbacher conceded. "But the number of believers may be greater than you think."

"It will be the same old charade if you take it to the United Nations," Yuri predicted. "We will veto—you will veto—there will be talk, talk, talk and nothing done. And when it is all over, you will look at your map and you will not see your four great friends who are today going down before the anticapitalist forces."

"They will not go down," Ham Delbacher said, more stoutly than he felt, "because we will not let them go down."

"How will you prop them up from so very far away?"

"We are not far away from Mexico!" the President snapped.

"Yes, I can see that is a priority for you," Yuri said with a patronizing agreement. "But South Africa? Saudi Arabia—or, as I have been informed they call it now, the People's Republic of Arabia? And Taiwan?"

"Taiwan is a special matter," the President said, "but we intend to keep our pledges there. As we do," he added, again more emphatically than he felt, "everywhere else. I would suggest to the Soviet Union, Mr. President, that considerable thought be given to the wisdom of continuing to support these imperialistic adventures that you have launched against independent governments friendly to the United States. The gravest consequences could result if they are not halted immediately."

"Mr. President," Yuri said, leaning back in his chair, gazing with an insolent air at his antagonist, "surely you are not threatening me? Surely you are not giving me ultimatums as you did over the submarines in Cuba? What is the need for ultimatums? I can only point out again: we are not involved. No Soviet arms are engaged anywhere. Spontaneous rebellions have broken out, spontaneous attacks have been begun, simply and solely because the peoples of the earth have had enough. They have had enough imperialism! They have had enough capitalist domination! They have had enough *diktats* from Washington! They have had enough," he said, and his face and voice both became savage for a second as he spat out the words, "of the United States of America!"

"You're a liar, Mr. President," Ham Delbacher said, and it was symptomatic of the state to which relations between the powers had fallen that Yuri Serapin did nothing but smile.

"Oh, Mr. President," he exclaimed. "Such grand, awful words! Such profound, scathing denunciations! Such high, righteous moral indignation! Next you will tell me I am 'Evil! Evil! *Evil!*' Well, Mr. President," he said softly, "if I am, there really is nothing you can do about it, is there? The world will not believe you—your strength is not sufficient—your obligations are too far-flung—your commitments are impossible to keep, physically, militarily, psychologically. Nothing faces you but disaster. I must repeat what I said to you at our first meeting: why do you not give up, Mr. President? Why must you force the world into the agony of another futile confrontation between us? Why must you make threats you cannot keep and issue ultimatums you cannot enforce? What earthly good does it do you? The day of the United States is over, Mr. President: history has passed you by. It would be much easier for the world and for yourselves if you would simply admit it, accept the inevitability of historical imperatives and yield peacefully to the enlightened leadership of the Soviet Union, which wants only peace for all peoples. You would save the world—yourselves—us—so much pain and difficulty, Mr. President. You are the captives of an irreversible process of history. Accept it, Mr. President! *Accept it.*"

For several moments the President of the United States did not reply, eyes thoughtful, studying the wide-cheeked face before his as though memorizing every detail of the full, arrogant lips, the shrewd, dark eyes, the expression of calm and implacable triumph.

Finally he shook his head with a heavy sigh and shifted in his chair.

"You really mean it, don't you?" he said in a wondering tone.

"You really believe that insane crap. You *really think* that the President of the United States, and the people of the United States, would ever—*ever*—give in to such a crazy demand. How can you, Mr. President? How can you, and still hold to some shred of reason, some pretense of intelligence? It is insane. It is quite literally insane."

And he sat slowly back in his chair, eyes never leaving the dark eyes, now suffused with anger, that confronted him. Once before he had provoked the Soviet President into a fury and the explosion had been near-hysterical in its quivering rage. He braced himself for it again, and yet was not surprised when it did not come.

Instead Yuri underwent what was obviously an intense inner struggle; mastered himself with great and obvious effort; finally sat back also, eyes narrowed, lips tight but aspect outwardly calm.

"Mr. President," he said softly, "I must repeat again, the Soviet Union is not involved in these outbreaks of popular anger around the world. Democratic freedom fighters, surfeited finally with the arrogant imperialism of United States ruling circles, have struck out for their freedom, their independence, their right to determine their own destiny. The Soviet Union will not refuse any appeals they make for help—none. No matter what it takes or how long, we will assist if asked. And no one is going to stop us. *No one.*"

Again Hamilton Delbacher studied him for a long moment. Then he too spoke in a calm and unhurried voice.

"By the same token, Mr. President, the United States will be equally firm. We have already been asked for assistance, it is already on the way"—an assertion not strictly true, but it would be within the hour. "When it arrives it will be put to immediate use. If this brings clashes with the Soviet forces—"

"There *are* none!" Yuri snapped.

"If this brings clashes with Soviet forces, then so be it."

"You are risking world war. You are risking the end of civilization, the atomic destruction of the world."

"Yes," Hamilton Delbacher agreed calmly. "And you?"

For several moments his opponent simply stared at him, face once more expressionless and stolid—that stolidity so characteristic of the public appearances of Soviet leaders, compounded partly of pomposity, partly of the fear of saying or doing something that would make them vulnerable to their colleagues, partly a belief that play-acting deliberate stolidity is the way to impress and frighten the world.

"Mr. President," Yuri said finally, "I think it is you who are insane. You attempt to defy not only the Soviet Union but the inevitable forces of history. You cannot threaten or browbeat *them,* Mr. President, any more than you can the Soviet Union. Capitalism is doomed, imperialism is doomed, the United States is doomed. There is no way out. The only alternative is to take the world with you; and I do not think even the ruling circles of the United States care so little for their own skins they they would actually do that."

"Nor, I think," Hamilton Delbacher remarked dryly, "the ruling circles of the Soviet Union. Nonetheless, you have created a situation in which we have no choice but to respond as requested. If you wish to respond in kind, so be it. We are ready for you."

"That is bluff, Mr. President," Yuri Serapin said quietly.

"Try us," Hamilton Delbacher said with equal quietness: and again Yuri stared at him for a long and thoughtful moment. Then he shrugged.

"In any event, we do not have to worry about it. The world will do it for us. Your own people will do it for us. You will not be able to make a move against the public outcry. You know that."

"The moves will be made before the popular outcry can have time to begin."

"Then they had best be successful with equal speed," Yuri told him grimly, "because if you allow so much as a day without decisive victory, the howling will begin."

"Prompted by you."

"Oh, yes," the Soviet President agreed cheerfully. "At least a large portion of it. We can turn millions into the streets, Mr. President, you know that. They will be marching in Amsterdam, Paris, Rome, Athens, Tokyo—you name it. Central Park and Lafayette Square will be overflowing. We know how to get your earnest, idealistic ones moving: all we do is push certain buttons and their own fears and anxieties take over and it is all done for us. You have seen it happen many times."

"And no doubt will see it many more," the President agreed

dryly. "I shall just have to keep on going somehow. I repeat one thing, Mr. President, and then I must leave for a meeting with my advisers and the Joint Chiefs of Staff. Wherever you are fomenting trouble this day, you will be met. Wherever you are breaking the peace, you will be called to account. Wherever you threaten mankind, you will be opposed. Believe me, Mr. President," he concluded quietly. "It will be so much simpler if you do."

Yuri regarded him thoughtfully again for a moment. Then he spoke with equal quietness.

"I believe your intention, Mr. President. It is your capability that I do not believe. I would caution you that you would be wise not to believe in it either. That way could lie a fatal miscalculation for us all."

Hamilton Delbacher shook his head with a wry expression.

"I would say the chance of miscalculation is just about equal on both sides. No doubt we will be talking again."

"No doubt."

For another long moment they stared at one another, eyes steady and unflinching. Then Hamilton Delbacher reached out slowly to snap off the Picturephone. As though they had rehearsed it, Yuri did the same. At the exact same moment their somber visages faded from the screens.

3

It was on days like this, Mark Coffin thought as he kissed Linda and the kids good-bye and started driving slowly through Washington's morning rush-hour traffic from Georgetown to the Senate, that he felt again something of the excitement he had felt when he took the oath of office a year ago. He had known then that he would be a witness to great events; be part of the forces that make history advance; exercise, as one member of perhaps the world's most powerful hundred men and women, a part of the governance that guides the United States and helps decide the destiny of its people and all those other peoples whose destinies are affected by theirs.

Now, it appeared, even greater demands would be made upon the Senate, upon its co-equal branch of the Congress, upon the President and his advisers—upon all Americans.

He wondered gloomily, as he found himself momentarily stuck behind an enormous limousine owned by the embassy of one of the impoverished African nation-tribes most dependent upon American financial aid, whether the world could survive the new challenges posed by the Soviet Union. He had wondered that often in the hectic weeks of the first Serapin-Delbacher confrontation. Each time it seemed that the world was about to tip over the edge into complete disaster something had snatched it back. Possibly something would snatch it back now. At the moment he was not so sure.

The excitement with which he had set out for the Hill drained away abruptly into the state of constant nervous apprehension that he realized was coming to be characteristic of his country in these days when the Soviet Union was moving to consolidate the advantage for which it had so carefully prepared during all the deliberately deceptive years of "detente" and "peaceful coexistence."

"Peace," Lenin had said, "is a time for gathering one's forces. . . . The ultimate objective of peace is world communist control."

The forces had been gathered; America and the West had not kept up; and now the account was being rendered.

The news that had been presented to the world on morning television and radio had reached his home with an effect as devastating as he suspected it had in most homes. The formal announcement from the White House had been issued at seven A.M. It had been extremely terse but its implications were vast and beyond mistaking:

"The government of the United States has been advised by its allies in Mexico, Saudi Arabia, South Africa, and Taiwan that they are under attack by forces either directly or indirectly allied with the Soviet Union.

"All four have requested immediate assistance from this country.

"Assistance is being provided."

This had been the first definite word. A few scattered scraps of news concerning some sort of crises in the four target areas had come in to the wire services from approximately three-thirty A.M. on, but first reports were so fragmentary and disjointed that no one had really begun to put them together until almost six A.M., when it had suddenly dawned on the foreign editor of United Press International in New York that there might be a pattern here.

He had immediately tried to reach his correspondents in the four countries but had been unable to do so. He had roused his principal White House and State Department correspondents and sent them rushing, still half-asleep, to their respective beats. The State Department man had drawn a blank. "Nothing here, all's quiet," he had reported scarcely fifteen minutes ago. The White House correspondent had more luck.

"Something big is going on," she reported breathlessly ten minutes after reaching the press room. "Baron and Hackett and the Joint Chiefs are meeting with the President. A few of the staff are here but they won't say anything. But it's big—really big. I can smell it."

And since after all her years on the beat he knew he could trust her instinct, her editor said, "Send me a first lead Meeting."

"First lead Crisis," she corrected and he chuckled, the last time he was to sound so relaxed for quite some time.

"I bow to superior wisdom and experience. First lead Crisis it is."

She was well into it, writing from instinct and experienced intuition and shrewdly coming close to it as she described "an apparent worldwide crisis," when the White House press secretary rushed into the press room, already filled with alert if somewhat bleary-eyed reporters, and made his brief announcement.

"What kind of assistance?" the New York *Times* shouted.

"When will it get there?" yelled CBS.

"How do you know the Soviets are involved?" demanded the Washington *Post*.

But the press secretary only yelled back, "That's all we've got right now, see you later," and dashed away.

Within an hour most of the country's morning papers had remade their front pages and were on the streets with screaming headlines:

NEW GLOBAL CRISIS! FOUR U.S. ALLIES ATTACKED! WHITE HOUSE RUSHES AID TO MEXICO, SAUDIS, SOUTH AFRICA, TAIWAN! CLAIMS SOVIETS BEHIND WAR MOVES!

And in editorial, news commentary, official statement and public demonstration, the backlash Yuri Serapin had accurately predicted began.

"Until more details are forthcoming, or until irrefutable proof is offered by the White House," the *Times* said, "we can only caution the American public to treat with great reserve statements charging that the Soviet Union is behind what appear to be the warlike attacks upon Mexico, Saudi Arabia, South Africa and Taiwan.

"Certainly the world knows, as every thinking American knows, that there are ample reasons for popular unrest in all those countries. There are also ample reasons for their neighbors to regard them with disfavor and in several cases, such as South Africa, with open and determined hostility.

"There is also every reason to believe—lacking substantive proof, which the American Government has not yet provided—that native protest movements, thwarted in their just demands for more freedom and favorable consideration of their views, may well have requested the outside assistance which seems to be coming to them from sympathetic nearby sources.

"Therefore it would seem to appear that Washington, as so often before, is once more crying 'Wolf!' when it seeks to blame the Soviet Union. And it seems dangerously clear that the President and his advisers are apparently launching an all-out military response that is not only almost impossible to maintain, given the great distances separating the areas involved, but one which is taking this country directly into another all-out confrontation with the Soviets, who may well be entirely innocent of the charges emanating from Washington.

"This is a fearfully dangerous gamble. It must be opposed by all Americans who value the safety and future of their country and do not want to see its hopes and possibly very existence tossed away by a handful of foolishly frightened and overly reactive men in Washington. . . .

"Whom the gods would destroy they first make mad," the *Post* agreed, "and unfortunately the madness of President Delbacher and his associates can result only in the destruction of the United States of America and probably of the world itself unless it can be stopped immediately.

"The facts as of this moment are that armed attacks have been launched against the territory and governments of four 'allies' that many are convinced we would be a lot better off without. Mexico is on our border and so of some reasonable concern, but corrupt regimes in Saudi Arabia, South Africa and Taiwan appear to be reaping their deserved rewards for various kinds of oppression and mismanagement of their countries. In a typical knee-jerk reaction, Hamilton Delbacher and his war-thirsty military advisers have decided that these popular movements are instigated by 'forces either directly or indirectly allied with the Soviet Union.'

"There is no slightest acknowledgment that they might be allied with forces fighting for human rights, human decency and the establishment of genuine democracy, as distinct from the corrupt dictatorial pseudodemocracy Mr. Delbacher so prides himself on defending.

"America has had occasion several times in the past few weeks to observe with alarm the President's tendency to take his gambles with world peace to the very brink of disaster, only to be saved each time by the innate common sense and steadiness of the new Soviet President, Yuri Serapin. Apparently Mr. Delbacher did not learn his lesson. He is off on another rampage, scattering America's forces from one end of the earth to the other in an impossible attempt to stamp out the irrepressible fires of genuine democracy. Americans can only hope that once again the restraint and prudence of the Soviet leader and his associates will damp down the whirlwind that seems forever to be arising in Mr. Delbacher's naive and hysterical breast.

"If it isn't damped down with great speed, we will all be in the soup. . . ."

In the same vein the network commentators viewed with alarm, pointed with dismay, observed with horror. From Capitol Hill Senator James Monroe Madison and other loud voices trumpeted consternation. In Central Park and Lafayette Square, in all the cities Yuri had so confidently enumerated, and in many more, the protesters were out in force. As Mark passed the Capitol on his way to the Senate garage he looked along the front and saw placards and banners and a confused mass of humanity held back by Capitol police. A placard caught his eye, held by an earnest young lady hurrying up the Hill to join the crowd: *WE* DON'T WANT TO DIE!

Who the hell does? he thought dryly as he turned left down the slope to the garage. Something about the banner's assumption of exclusive concern and the young lady's rigid, superior expression as she hurried along seemed to him to define very well the situation in the country. In some minds, obviously, there was a sharp division between those who grimly didn't want to die and those who happily did . . . whereas actually, they were all one in this most mutually desired avoidance; and as one, they were going to have to agree upon a way in which to guarantee it. Or death would come, regardless, to them all.

But how to prevent it with any assurance of success, he did not know. Linda's shock and fear when she heard the White House announcement represented the feelings of many millions everywhere. Her instinctive cry had summed it up.

"I can't go through it all again!" she exclaimed in a tone near despair. "We've just been wrung dry, and now we have to do it all again! It isn't human!"

But it was, as they both knew, all too human; and with all the imperfection of humankind it had to be met.

Somehow.

After the first flurry of fright and anguish, they, like millions everywhere, returned to practicalities.

"Don't you think you should take the kids and get out of Washington?" he asked. She gave him a skeptical, impatient look.

"I'll bet I couldn't get a booking on any plane, train, bus or horse out of here already," she said. "And you heard the traffic report just now about all roads already being clogged with outgoing cars. Maybe you could get us an official priority with the military if you want to sent us to your folks in Sacramento, but what good would that do, really? Everywhere is vulnerable nowadays. Besides which," she added with a sudden tartness, "I am a United States Senator's daughter and a United States Senator's wife, and neither Daddy nor you is going to run away from here. And I'm not going to run away from *you*. So stop *that* nonsense."

"All right," he said with a relieved smile. "I just don't know."

"You don't know much," she said shortly, but softening the sharpness with an answering smile. "I do feel that we should be doing *something*. I hate to just sit around and wait while that evil little monster in Moscow pulls the strings and puts us through the hoops again. He ought to be shot," she added with a sudden flat anger, "or strangled or poisoned or electrocuted or—or—something."

"Goodness, how fierce," he said, half-joking; then sobered and agreed. "It would be a good thing for the world if he weren't around, but I'm afraid unless or until there's some sort of internal upheaval in the Kremlin, we're stuck with him. He seems to be in pretty strong control right now."

"What does your friend Valerian think?" she asked. "I'm surprised he hasn't called you already with his own analysis of the latest."

"He hasn't yet," Mark said, "but if he doesn't, I'm going to get in touch with him pretty soon. At least his views will be interesting."

"He is interesting," she said. The figure of the charming young Soviet defector, amiable, pleasant and apparently very well informed on the plans and personality of Yuri, his former chief, came into both their minds with his ususal grin. "I still wonder—"

"Don't we all," Mark said. "But so far, he seems to ring true. I doubt if he knew anything about this new adventure. I think it all sprang full-blown from Yuri's brilliant mind in one of his sudden inspirations. He gambles."

"Yes," she said grimly. "With the whole earth. Apparently Uncle Ham is gambling right back."

"Yes," he agreed, and sighed. "With what, exactly, I don't know. We certainly aren't equipped to fight on four fronts, and yet we almost have to, it seems to me."

"No 'almost' with Uncle Ham," she said with an affectionate little smile for the "uncle" she had known in the Senate for so long. "He's on his way already, apparently."

"No choice," Mark said. "No choice."

But as the morning drew on, and the crescendo of world uproar rose, and the Senate went into a hastily called session at ten A.M., it began to be apparent that on the Hill, as in the media, there were those who still believed there was a choice. The gavel had scarcely fallen when what the Senate press corps referred to as "the two Jims"—Linda's father, James Rand Elrod of North Carolina, chairman of the Senate Armed Services Committee and the new Majority Leader, and Mark's senior colleague, James Monroe Madison of California, were on their feet contending for recognition from the chair. The new Vice-President, former Senate Majority Leader Art Hampton of Nebraska, studied them for a moment and then, as expected, recognized Senator Elrod.

Senator Madison sniffed and shook his silvery head with elaborate disdain, remaining on his feet, ready to challenge. Jim Elrod surveyed him with a benign smile.

"Mr. President," he said, addressing the chair. "I seem to see a large form loomin' on the horizon. It threatens to overwhelm me. But I shall proceed."

"Mr. President," Jim Madison said. "Will the Senator yield?"

"Briefly," Jim Elrod agreed. "*Very* briefly."

"Does the Senator think this is a humorous occasion?" Senator Madison demanded with a sudden display of anger. "Does he think this is a day in our history for making jokes and making light of things?"

"No, sir," Senator Elrod said with an abrupt gravity, "I do not. I think it is a day to dedicate ourselves once again to the defense of the liberty of our own land and the freedom of the earth."

There was the start of a hiss from the public galleries. Art Hampton used his gravel.

"Very noble," Jim Madison retorted dryly. "Very noble indeed. And with what, may I ask the Senator?"

"With the conviction of right and the armed forces of the United States," Jim Elrod said dryly. "What else?"

"Very little else," Jim Madison remarked with equal dryness, "and not very much of those. How can we do it, I ask the Senator? *How can we do it?*"

"If I could spell out every detail for the Senator I would be a miracle man," Senator Elrod said, "and I'm sure he wouldn't accuse me of that. I am not sure exactly how we will do it but I am sure that we have to."

"And so millions of American money and probably thousands, maybe hundreds of thousands of American boys—"

"Oh, come now," Jim Elrod said, but was drowned out by applause from the galleries.

"The galleries will be in order," Art Hampton warned in a tone that brooked no nonsense. Silence, uneasy and protesting, ensued.

"—and not only that," Jim Madison went on, "but perhaps millions or hundreds of millions of American citizens, will be sacri-

ficed, just so Hamilton Delbacher can go sallying forth across the
world to fight impossible wars on impossible battlefronts. It is outrageous, I say to the Senator. Outrageous! And he stands up here
and defends it. For shame!''

''Senator,'' Jim Elrod said, while almost a full Senate of one
hundred sat silent and intently listening, ''stop pontificatin'.
At three A.M. our time this mornin' simultaneous attacks were
launched against four American allies by forces either supported
by, or directly allied with, the Soviet Union. How would the Senator have responded to this were he in the White House? By pratin'
of American money and American boys and tryin' to frighten the
American people with talk of 'perhaps millions or hundreds of millions' who might be 'sacrificed'? There is a need for responsibility
here, Senator, not demagoguery. We face the fact of these aggressions. It must be answered.''

''Will the Senator yield?'' Clement Chisholm of Illinois inquired, handsome black face troubled.

''Certainly,'' Jim Elrod said.

''Has the Senator been in touch with the President?''

''He talked to me a few minutes ago on the telephone, yes.''

''Did he tell the Senator any details of what military movements
are going forward, or what kind of 'assistance' is planned as outlined in the White House statement?''

''He did not,'' Jim Elrod said. Again there was a tentative hiss,
quickly stilled as Art Hampton looked up sharply.

''Then the Senator is really just arguing here on faith,'' Clem
Chisholm said. ''He really does not know how deeply we are being
involved, or what we are being committed to, or exactly what actions our thinly spread forces are being asked to undertake.''

''I know I believe in the good word and good faith of Hamilton
Delbacher,'' Senator Elrod said, ''and I believe in his patriotism
and his determination to both do the right thing *and* protect the
safety and best interests of the United States.'' There was a stirring
across the Senate this time, as well as in the galleries, and he responded to it more sharply and defensively. ''I must remind the
Senator that in these very early stages of what is apparently a well
planned and well coordinated Soviet attempt to engage and entan-
gle the United States in difficult conflicts in distant places, it would

do nobody in the democratic world any good for us to tip our hand as to exactly what is planned or underway. Obviously these matters will be public very soon, either from the White House or from the various areas of conflict, but until they are, it seems to me that silence is much the better course."

"It may be," Senator Chisholm said in a stubborn tone, "but it does not impress this Senate or the many millions of people both here and abroad who may be drawn into this conflict. They want to know, Senator. Their very lives may be at stake. If this thing spreads, as the President's announced intention to help everybody who is threatened indicates it may very well spread, then the whole earth could become involved. It's easy to start wars but it isn't so easy to tamp them down again. They never end as their planners intended. They get out of hand. Many of us are afraid that's what may happen here."

"Then I'd suggest," Senator Elrod snapped with an anger rare in him, "that the Senator take his worries to the man who started all this, the President of the Soviet Union, who sits over there in the Kremlin and gloats while his puppets do his dirty work for him."

"Mr. President," Clem Chisholm said, unmoved, "with all respect I must differ with the Senator. We don't have proof as yet that the President of the Soviet Union is involved in this. We only have the unsupported charge of the White House."

"Mr. President," Mark said, "will the distinguished Senator from North Carolina yield to me?"

"I'll be glad to," his father-in-law said in a tone which was interpreted as relief and so brought a ripple of amusement across floor and galleries. He dismissed it with a scornful look as Mark turned to Clem Chisholm.

"Mr. President," he said, "the junior Senator from Illinois and I have a lot in common, having come into this body on the same day, and for a time being members of what the media chose to term "Young Turks' in opposition to some of the defense measures proposed in our first weeks here. We are also, I'm proud to say, very close personal friends. But I can't go along with the Senator on the general tenor of his remarks today. I think the new outbreak of hostilities does come directly from Moscow, I think it was planned to a major extent by President Serapin himself, and I agree with President Delbacher that the only way to meet it is head on.''

''My friend has changed,'' Clem Chisholm said with a smile.

''I've been to the mountaintop and seen the view,'' Mark replied, ''and frankly, Senator, it scares the hell out of me. You remember I was a member of the President's delegation when he went to the United Nations in the first crisis to talk to President Serapin. I had a chance to study friend Yuri pretty closely then. He is not a nice man, though I will grant you he is a very intelligent and clever one. I am as convinced as Hamilton Delbacher that he planned this whole series of explosions around the globe today. I haven't the slightest doubt of it.''

''But again,'' Clem Chisholm said, ''like the distinguished Senator from North Carolina, you argue from faith. You don't have proof.''

''Not yet,'' Mark Coffin said, ''but proof will be forthcoming before very long.''

''Meanwhile,'' Senator Chisholm said, ''we are getting ourselves more deeply involved by the minute in four situations from which it is hard to see how we can possibly get out with any kind of success. We're heading straight for disaster, Senator, on a scale we haven't courted since World War II, probably, which was before you and I were born.''

''Well, we won it, didn't we?''

''Yes, but things were a lot different then. There wasn't the potential of sliding directly into atomic war that we have now. Particularly since there seems pretty good reason to believe that two of the nations attacked today, South Africa and Taiwan, do have the bomb and might very well use it if they felt it necessary.''

''Well,'' Mark said tartly, ''leaving aside the question as to why they shouldn't if they really find their very existence threatened by unprovoked attack, isn't that all the more reason why we should come to their assistance and provide some restraints and moderation to keep them from doing just that? It seems to me that is part of our obligation too.''

''That still begs the essential point,'' Clem said, ''and that is the justification offered by our President, namely that President Serapin and the Soviet Union are behind these attacks. And of that, so far, there is no proof.''

''I concede that,'' Mark said. ''I told you Serapin is very clever, and his predecessors have been, too. All these years they've encouraged us to develop an obsession with a Maginot Line theory about Western Europe. You know France had her useless Maginot Line against Germany prior to World War II, which the Germans turned by simply going around the end of it. *All* of Western Europe has become *our* Maginot Line against the Soviets. Now they've made four end runs around it, and we're being drawn off to meet them in areas of their own choosing. And unless we decide the issue now, Western Europe, in due course, will fall into their laps.''

''Because we have let ourselves be drawn into these hopeless adventures and will be too weakened to defend it,'' Clem said.

''Oh, no,'' Mark retorted. ''Because if some Senators have their way we *won't* have stood up to them right now and convinced them they simply can't win, no matter where they try their games.''

''Well, Senators,'' Senator Elrod said, ''I don't want to interrupt your enlightenin' discussion, but seems to me you're beginnin' to meet yourselves comin' back, so perhaps I'll reclaim the floor to introduce a resolution which the Speaker is introducin' in the House and which I am introducin' in the Senate.'' He paused and appeared to fumble for it rather haphazardly through the papers on his desk. Mark and Clem sat down after shaking their heads at one another with unconvinced smiles. Tensions in the chamber suddenly rose.

''Ah, yes,'' Jim Elrod said. ''Here we go: 'Whereas there now exists in Mexico, South Africa, Saudi Arabia and Taiwan a state of war and civil conflict brought about by unprovoked attack from outside forces directly supported by or directly allied to the Soviet Union—' '' There were boos from the galleries, restless stirring from some Senators. The Vice-President rapped his gavel sharply. Senator Elrod ignored the small disturbance and read on. '' 'And whereas all four of these nations are close friends and allies of the United States of America, now, therefore, be it resolved that the Senate and the House of Representatives pledge their full support and cooperation to the President of the United States in carryin' out provisions of treaties and other agreements made with these nations and accepted and approved by the Congress of the United States as provided by the Constitution of the United States.'

"The reasons for this resolution are obvious, Mr. President, and it seems to many of us that the sooner it is passed by the Congress, the stronger the President's hand will be and the sooner this new crisis can be terminated."

He sat down to a scattering of applause, somewhat smaller than the boos. Above in the media galleries reporters scrambled out to file their stories. Jame Monroe Madison was on his feet at once.

"Mr. President," he cried in a voice that brooked no denial. "If you *please*."

"The Senator from California," Art Hampton said in a dry tone of voice.

"Mr. President," Senator Madison said, "it has been a long time since this Congress has been asked to grant a blank check to the President in an international crisis. In fact, I for one have to go back as far as the Tonkin Gulf resolution requested by President Johnson to remember anything comparable. And we all know what that led to: Vietnam—stalemate—quagmire. Is that what we want again, Mr. President, quagmire? I don't think the American people are willing to undertake that kind of adventure again!"

There was a burst of applause from the galleries, murmuring on the floor. He looked around with a satisfied air.

"No, sir, Mr. President, I do not believe the American people want quagmire! They want to stop this thing before it gets out of hand! They want to stop it *now!* They want—"

"And how are they going to stop it?" Senator Elrod demanded in a scathing tone. "By hamstringin' their own President in the face of an entirely unprovoked, deliberately aggressive series of adventures launched by the Soviet Union all around the globe? By pouncin' on him and poundin' on him and makin' his task ten times more difficult than it is? By refusin' to pledge support of this Congress when he most desperately needs it? Why don't you do all your pouncin' and your poundin' on Yuri Serapin, I'll ask the Senator? How about damnin' *him* up and down for the international thug he is, and makin' *him* stop what *he's* doin'? How about pluggin' this thing at the source, Senator? Answer that one, if you can!"

"Well!" Jim Madison said indignantly. "Well! What the Soviet President does is not the responsibility of this Congress! *Our* responsibility is the President of the United States! He's the one we're responsible for! We can't go intervening in the affairs of the Soviet Union every time somebody in the White House gets hysterical! We can't—"

But this was a bit too much, even for the President's critics. There was some laughter from around the floor, and even a little in the public galleries. Mark was on his feet again. His father-in-law with a quick glance nodded and deferred to him.

"Mr. President," he said, "that's typical of the type of argument my colleague from California is famous for. Sure, we're responsible only for our own President. Sure, we aren't responsible for what goes on in the Soviet Union. Sure, we jump on our own because we know very well we can't jump on Yuri Serapin because he simply wouldn't listen. Sure, we know how to make headlines and get publicity and pander to all the impractical souls in the United States because we know damned well we'd be shouting down a well to demand that Yuri Serapin stop something! But, Mr. President, the issue is too important for that kind of pointless demogoging. Yuri Serapin has *got* to stop what he is doing, and the only way to stop him is to *make him stop.* How does my colleague answer that one? How does he intend to stop the Soviet President, I will ask my colleague? Forget about Hamilton Delbacher, now, who is only reacting as any responsible American President would have to react to the plight of our allies, and tell us about Yuri Serapin, Senator! How do you propose to handle *him?*"

"I don't propose to 'handle' *him*, I'll say to the Senator," Jim Madison retorted angrily. *"He is not our responsibility!"*

"He is *not* our responsibility?" Mark demanded. "When four of our allies are at this moment fighting for their lives against Soviet-inspired attacks both from within and without? Senator, if I ever heard sophistry that's it. Stop begging the question! How would *you* defend our allies? What would *you* do to save them?"

"That is not my responsibility," Senator Madison said primly, and Mark threw up his hands in disgust. "In any event, I am not at all sure that these *allies* you are so worried about are even worthy to *be* allies." A flurry of applause greeted this. He nodded grimly.

"Aside from Mexico, which is on our border and so of some importance to us—"

"I'm so glad you concede that," Mark remarked acidly.

"—I can't see that the rest matter so much. What is South Africa to us? What is Taiwan? What does it matter if there is some tribal scramble in Saudi Arabia? They still have to have a market for their oil and we're still the biggest buyer, aren't we? What does it matter?"

"If the Senator is that naive," Mark said in a disgusted tone, "then there's no point in trying to reason with him. If the Senator isn't aware of the strategic importance of the minerals of South Africa, the value of the Cape of Good Hope route and the need for a stable government in that area; if he isn't aware that the new government of Saudi Arabia, if it prevails, may very well turn off the oil spigot altogether and fall directly under the control of the Soviet Union; if he doesn't value at all our good faith and good word pledged to Taiwan over and over and over again for three decades—if all he sees is that of all those attacked, only Mexico, possibly, is of 'some importance to us,' then I wonder what the Senator is doing in this chamber purporting to live up to an oath which requires him to assist in the preservation of this republic!"

Boos and catcalls from the gallery, some restless if muted protests from the floor; Art Hampton's gavel, sternly, from the chair.

"I think the junior Senator from California goes a little far," he said. "I think he will proceed in order or be seated."

"I'm sorry, Mr. President," Mark said, flushed with anger. "I extend to my colleague such apology he deserves."

There was a muted sound of amusement from across the floor. Senator Madison with exaggerated slowness turned his back upon him.

"Mr. President," he said with an elaborately injured dignity, "this demonstrates exactly why we must stop this irresponsible adventurism emanating from the White House. It is dividing this Senate, it is dividing this country. It is doing nothing but disrupt national unity and disturb national harmony. Surely there are other ways in which President Delbacher can proceed. Surely he can take this matter to the United Nations and seek a meeting of the Security

Council, where he can present the grievances he feels he has against the Soviet Union. Surely—"

"Surely that will take forever and accomplish nothing!" Senator Elrod snapped. "Mr. President, I have presented a resolution to the Senate. Time is of the essence in this matter. I do not think we should maunder on about it any longer. I ask for yeas and nays—"

"Mr. President!" Jim Madison thundered, "I intend to offer an amendment to the resolution. I suggest the absence of a quorum!"

"The yeas and nays are ordered," Art Hampton said without expression. "The Clerk will call the roll for a quorum." Quorum-call bells rang through the Senate side of the Capitol and throughout the Senate office buildings. The clerk began a slow count.

During the interval, which lasted almost half an hour while Senators wandered on and off the floor, delaying their responses as long as possible, the galleries could see that there was intense politicking going on in the chamber. Senator Elrod stood with a set and forbidding expression on his face at the Majority Leader's desk. Behind him and ten seats over, Senator Madison stood at his desk, flushed and equally adamant.

Groups of Senators formed and reformed around each. Arguments muted but obviously heated occurred at both desks. Scraps of angry conversation floated up, making quite clear to the media that there was far more sentiment riding with Senator Madison than had been at first supposed. Finally Art Hampton turned the gavel over to Clem Chisholm and came down on the floor to argue firmly but quietly with Senator Elrod.

After a couple of minutes Senator Elrod shrugged and allowed himself to be led over to Senator Madison's desk, where the Vice-President conferred in obviously urgent tones with them both while many Senators clustered around trying to hear.

"Mr. Rasmussen!" the Clerk droned, nearing the end.

Art Hampton glanced over his shoulder quickly and lifted an eyebrow.

"Mr. Rob-ert-son!" the Clerk droned, more slowly. Again Art Hampton shot him a warning glance.

"Mr. . . . Thomp . . . son," the Clerk delayed obediently.

Art Hampton took Jim Elrod firmly by one arm, Jim Madison firmly by the other and led them up the aisle into the majority cloakroom. The glass doors swung shut. Tension mounted even higher in the buzzing chamber.

Two minutes later the three emerged, both Senators still looking flushed and upset. The Vice-President reclaimed the chair, the Clerk glanced up at him, he nodded firmly. The Clerk said, so briskly that his calls, the responses and his final words were hard to understand, "Mr. Turner! Mr. Walker! Mr. Young! Mr. Zabinovich! *NinetythreeSenatorshavinganeweredtotheirnamesaquorumispresent!*"

"Does the Senator from North Carolina wish to address the Chair before the vote on his resolution?" Art Hampton inquired.

"Not particularly," Jim Elrod said dryly. There was a chuckle of amusement from the floor, and from the media, whose members by now had figured out what was going on. "I have the floor and I don't have to yield it until the vote is taken. However, considerin' the circumstances, I am willin' to yield to the senior Senator from California for the purpose he has explained to me."

"Thank you, Senator," Jim Madison said with a huffiness that did not conceal his air of triumph. "Mr. President, I offer the following amendment to the resolution of the Senator from North Carolina, and I will read it myself as he did. At the end of the resolution add the following language:

" 'Be it additionally resolved, that whereas military steps taken by the President in international crises must always be dependent upon and subsequent to the exhaustion of all diplomatic means for peaceful resolution available to him, it is the sense of the Senate and the House of Representatives that prior to taking such military steps the President should, and he is hereby advised to, request an immediate session of the United Nations Security Council so that the good offices of that body may be employed forthwith in the peaceful resolution of the existing situation.' "

"Does the Senator from North Carolina accept the amendment?" Art Hampton inquired.

For several long moments Jim Elrod said nothing while a tensely waiting silence settled over the chamber.

"Mr. President," he said finally, "there are some aspects of this amendment which are repugnant to Senators on this side of the issue, and which I know will be repugnant to the President; basically, I think, the tone of it, which sounds as though we were addressing some recalcitrant little boy instead of the President of the United States and Commander-in-Chief who must bear the full burden of these parallel crises deliberately provoked by the Soviet Union. I am also very skeptical, as I think any rational man must be, of the ability of the Security Council of the United Nations to accomplish anything, particularly in a situation as grave as this.''

"However—" he said, raising his hand as Senator Madison appeared on the point of blurting some angry rejoinder, "however, it is obvious from the sentiments expressed to me while the Clerk was calling the quorum that there is a very substantial sentiment in this body for some such amendment as has been offered by the senior Senator from California. Therefore in order to avoid an unseemly and degradin' fight here which could only give aid and comfort to the enemy—"

Jim Madison shook his head impatiently and a hiss came from somewhere in the galleries.

"—I shall accept it as an addition to my resolution, bearin' in mind that it is only advisory upon the President and that he must, is, and will be bound by his overridin' obligation to preserve and protect the United States and the allies whose security and ability to participate in mutual assistance are so vital to that task.''

"Mr. President," Senator Madison said tartly, "extending the President's obligation to protect the United States to a general obligation to protect all of its allies is an interesting reading of the Constitution that I for one cannot go along with. In any event, it is quite clear from the Senator's own reversal of field that there is a sentiment here for a peaceful resolution of the crisis which is so strong that the President would be most unwise to ignore it. Particularly since, scarcely five minutes ago, word came to the Vice-President when we were in the cloakroom that the House has just accepted and passed an amendment very similar to this by the very substantial vote of three hundred and forty to ninety-two.''

There was a general gasp of surprise and excitement, after which he said triumphantly, "Mr. President, I too think we should now vote on the resolution of the senior Senator from North Carolina, as amended.''

"Question!" shouted several Senators.

"The yeas and nays have been ordered," Art Hampton said. "The Clerk will call the roll."

CONGRESS SUPPORTS THE PRESIDENT IN CRISIS BUT DEMANDS IMMEDIATE U.N. SECURITY COUNCIL MEETING. ADMINISTRATION OVERRIDDEN AS SENATE VOTES 79–19, HOUSE 340–92 FOR PEACE AMENDMENT.

"All we want to know," UPI said when the press secretary faced the press corps, looking harassed and upset, in the White House newsroom fifteen minutes later, "is whether he is or is not going to obey Congress and ask for a Security Council meeting. And when."

"The President doesn't have to *'obey'* Congress!" the press secretary snapped.

"Is he going to defy Congress, then?" AP inquired blandly.

The press secretary looked even more harassed.

"No, he isn't going to *'defy'* Congress," he said angrily.

"Then what *is* he going to do?" the Washington *Inquirer* asked. "He's got to do something, hasn't he?"

"He's going to do what seems best to him, given all the facts he has at his disposal," the press secretary said.

"Is he going to share them with us so we'll know what he's getting us into?" UPI inquired.

"I expect he will tell you everything he feels he safely can," the press secretary replied.

"Not good enough," she said thoughtfully. "Not good enough."

"Well," he snapped again, "it's all you're going to get right now!"

"What's the problem?" a familiar voice inquired amicably from behind them. They swung around to find him smiling pleasantly, looking a little tired but otherwise not much the worse for wear after being up since three A.M.

"Good afternoon, ladies and gentlemen," he said, coming through to the press secretary's rostrum as they made way for him. "What seems to be the problem?"

"We want to know what you're going to do about the congressional resolution," UPI said. "He says you don't have to obey it but you aren't going to defy it." She uttered a sudden little giggle. "This leaves us puzzled, Mr. President."

"Puzzled myself," he agreed promptly. "I can understand the urge in Congress for a peaceful solution to this, and I gather from the debate that at least some members of Congress understand that my urge is equal to theirs. But I face a difficult problem, as seems to be obvious to some of my fellow Americans, at least. The urge for peace is all very fine, but when there is an urge for war in Moscow, it takes a little more than a congressional resolution to damp it down."

"You persist in maintaining, then, Mr. President, that Moscow is directly responsible for these scattered little conflicts?" the Washington *Post* inquired. For a second the President studied him. Then he smiled.

"*Really* 'scattered little conflicts'? A little more than that, I think, and so do you. No, these are quite, quite serious conflicts, and yes, I do think Moscow is behind them. In fact, my conversation with President Serapin—"

"When was that?" they demanded, startled and indignant that they hadn't known.

"About five-thirty this morning. He was very defiant about it."

"Did he admit Moscow had inspired the attacks?" the New York *Times* inquired.

"Would you expect him to?" the President responded in the same tone. "No, of course he didn't. But his attitude was that there wasn't much doubt."

"How did he show this 'attitude,' Mr. President?" the *Post* asked.

"You'll just have to take my word for it," Ham Delbacher said pleasantly. "It was a private conversation."

"And what are you going to do as a result of it?" CBS wanted to know.

The President gave him a bland look.

"Proceed with whatever is necessary."

"Which is what?" UPI pressed.

"Now, you don't expect me to tip my hand, do you? What help would that be?"

"But you do intend to take some action," AP said.

"Some action is already being taken," he said, and at once they were on it with clamoring questions. But his only response was to smile and say, "Many of you have your correspondents in those places. They'll tell you in due course."

"Mr. President," the *Times* finally demanded in an exasperated tone, "will you or will you not request a Security Council meeting?"

"It won't do one damned bit of good," he replied crisply, "but yes, I shall go through the motions set forth in the congressional resolution. A request has already gone forward to the Secretary-General."

"When will the meeting be held?"

"Several days from now, I suspect."

"That won't stop the fighting *now*, will it?" the *Post* demanded sharply. "Why not sooner?"

"I'm willing," he said, "but Mr. Serapin is not. Obviously he intends to drag it out in the hope that the fighting will be concluded on his terms by then. I rather think he will be mistaken."

"Only if we manage to stop him by force," the *Post* retorted; realized what he had said and amended quickly, "Only if we are able to stop these native uprisings, that is."

Ham Delbacher gave him a wry look.

"We shall see. And now, ladies and gentlemen, I have a lot to do, so if you'll excuse me—"

And with a pleasant smile he left them puzzling and arguing over his brief remarks and returned to the Oval Office. Within half an hour he received a call from Mark Coffin. He had heard from Ivan Valerian, Mark said, and he was "curious—most curious" about what action the President was planning.

"I couldn't tell him," Mark said, "because I don't know—and wouldn't anyway. But I thought perhaps he might be worth a talk one of these days. Just for the hell of it."

"Bring him around tomorrow," the President said. "About three. By that time the general outlines of what we're doing should be public knowledge. It will be interesting to see how he assesses them."

"And how we assess him," Mark suggested.

"Yes," the President said. "That too."

He turned away from the phone and sat for a moment staring out the window. He was not content with Yuri's attempt to stall the Security Council meeting, though delay could be of some advantage to the United States also. If he had to accept it, it would give him time to gather the physical evidence of Soviet and satellite intervention that he wished to present, and it would also give him time to have his countermeasures fully in place before the issue reached the Council. In the meantime he did not intend to let Yuri's stooges win quick victories—if that was Yuri's plan.

More likely, the strategy was to prolong the conflicts with the deliberate intent of miring the United States in them. More likely, Yuri didn't want quick conclusions.

Well, the President thought tartly, quick conclusions—and quick defeats—were what Yuri was going to get if *he* had anything to say about them. Reviewing the orders he had given as Commander-in-Chief during the long, hectic day, he was satisfied that they would move things rapidly along, though he was under no illusions that war, once begun, could be swiftly and neatly terminated. The days of wars like that were long gone, unless one resorted to the ultimate weapon. And he did not really think that either he or Yuri intended to do that.

By the time of the evening news, his orders were in effect.

U.S. RUSHES SOUTH ATLANTIC FORCES TO SOUTH AFRICA. ATOMIC SUBS SURFACE OFF ANGOLAN CAPITAL. RAPID DEPLOYMENT FORCE ORDERED TO AID OF SAUDI REBELS. PLANES, SHIPS FROM PHILIPPINES START "OFFICIAL STATE VISIT" TO TAIWAN. MEXICO GETS U.S. AIR, ARMY UNITS.

The reaction from major commentators in print and television was about what he had expected.

There was much use of the word "rebels" in referring to the forces attempting to oppose the usurper in Saudi Arabia and restore the legitimate government—thereby conferring instant media recognition upon the usurper and making of his opponents a somehow sinister, illegitimate group that was daring to "rebel" against him. South Yemen's participation was considered to be "legitimate aid to a long-overdue attempt to bring true democracy to Saudi Arabia."

There were stern denunciations of aid to South Africa; much praise for "spontaneous native uprisings, a natural result of decades of frustrated impatience with the continent's most notorious racist regime"; a general excusing of the sneak attacks on Cape Town and Johannesburg, a scarcely concealed air of relish that "South Africa is getting what she deserves"; and virtually no mention of the Cuban forces leading the drive south.

There were equally strong and hostile comments about the "official state visit" of U.S. forces to Taiwan; indignant reminders that the island was, after all, by its own admission a province of China, and the United States should therefore stay out of "a family quarrel"; and the observation by many major commentators and editorialists that "even though the word of the United States may have been pledged to Taiwan many years ago, to pledge it in the first place was a mistake and to break it now would only be a long-overdue redressing of one of history's most glaring errors."

Only aid to Mexico was given a modicum of grudging support. It *was* recognized that the stability and security of Mexico were important to the United States, and that a noncommunist government (and therefore by definition, some even agreed, a nonaggressive government) was was a nice thing to have there. But there were many references to "Guatemala's attempt to aid democratic elements against a corrupt regime." And the President's assertion that this invasion, too, was led by Cuban forces was generally ridiculed when it was not altogether ignored.

So much for the major media reaction, he told Elinor after they had read the newspapers and watched the last important pontificator fade from the tube.

What he did not expect, though he had hoped for it, was the reaction from Moscow.

SERAPIN ABANDONS OPPOSITION TO EARLY U.N. SECURITY MEETING, REQUESTS IMMEDIATE SESSION. DENOUNCES "UNPROVOKED U.S. IMPERIALIST AGGRESSION ON A GLOBAL SCALE." WORLD LEADERS START FOR NEW YORK.

"We progress," the President remarked with satisfaction. "So far," Elinor reminded.

4

And now they were all arriving once more for one of their most enjoyable and fondly cherished diversions: to gather once again in glamorous, exciting New York for a meeting of the international body in which sophisticated leaders of mighty nations, colorfully robed tribal chieftains from dusty African plains and importantly strutting men from tiny bits and pieces of earth lost in the seas' immensities were able to mingle happily as equals and enjoy the delights of the big city on expense accounts that, for many of them, provided living and entertainment such as their poverty-stricken peoples never dreamed of. It was just as well they did not, or their leaders would not be there; but while it lasted, it was great. Particularly in the so-called "Third World" they loved every minute of it, since in addition to all its other charms it gave them a chance to spit once again in the face of the nation that nine-tenths of them envied and disliked but from which all of them took whatever they could get with the cynical contempt of the eternally greedy for the overly generous.

So there came the Great Guiding Light and Eternal Leader of the People's Republic of Gorotoland, with his mistresses, his limousines and his fawning entourage; and the scowling President of Cuba, carefully disheveled, grimy and macho as his worshippers loved him to be and his hairdresser and makeup man made sure he was; and the President of the newest minuscule "country," Piki-Wiki in the South Pacific, thirteen atolls, ten thousand six hundred

146

and seventy-nine coconut palms and two thousand one hundred and ten (or was it eleven as of this morning?) people; and along with such as these, the Prime Ministers of Britain and India, the Vice-Premier of the People's Republic of China, the President of the Soviet Union, the President of the United States, the President of France, the leaders of West Germany, East Germany, Italy and the rest of free and nonfree Europe; the blandly smiling Arabs, the taut, suspicious Israelis, the earnestly troubled Latin Americans, and all the rest.

Brightly the hot September sun beat down on the glass-sided monolith of the General Assembly building, the rounded dome of the Security Council building, the adjoining office buildings and the long row of colorful flags, limp and lifeless in the still-humid air, each asserting its people's claim to distinction and nationhood. Alongside, the dirty East River rushed headlong to the sea; and up beneath the portico at the Delegates' Entrance rolled the steady stream of vehicles. Many of them were as long, black, sleek and gleaming as that of the Great Guiding Light of Gorotoland. Others were more modest and businesslike. They carried the leaders of a world in desperate need of leadership—though not in all cases, perhaps, such leadership as this.

Nonetheless, they were here: and since there was nobody else, it was they who were called upon to manage the fate of the world. In some cases this was a sad commentary—quite appalling, in fact, had the world really stopped to think about it. But nonetheless, they were here; and so the world, for the most part, did not ponder the many ironies of their presence.

Inside the Security Council chamber the clerks and secretaries in their usual self-important fashion milled about the circular green baize table, carefully placing papers, pens, documents at their various masters' seats. In the small public gallery the leaders of those nations who, while not on the Security Council, still wished to attend this most vital session, took their reserved seats. The G.G.L. of Gorotoland rubbed elbows, condescendingly, with the President of Piki-Wiki. The President of Argentina carefully exchanged not a glance with the President of Chile, though they were squeezed in side by side, elbows in intimate and unavoidable contact. In the small media gallery every seat was taken and every inch of space along the sides and at the back was filled with standees. In their glassed-in booths high along the walls above, the television crews swung their cameras over the crowd.

The convening of the meeting had been scheduled for ten A.M., and somewhere around ten-thirty, maintaining the United Nations record of never starting any meeting on time, the stately, dignified, white-haired old gentleman who for three years had held the post of Secretary-General came in. His kindly black face was not wearing its normal pleasant expression. Instead he looked stern and troubled. His presence brought a sudden hush to the crowded room. Then in from right and left behind the circular table there came the permanent members of the Security Council:

The People's Republic of China
France
The United Kingdom
The United States of America
The Union of Soviet Socialist Republics

—and the ten members chosen on a geographic basis to serve two-year terms:

Cameroon
Eire
Egypt
Greece
India
Iraq
Nicaragua
Seychelles
Tanzania
Tonga

These were the same who had held their seats three weeks ago at the time of the first confrontation between the Presidents of the United States and the Soviet Union; who had gone through the long, drawn-out, hectic days of the worldwide Soviet "maneuvers"; had attempted to find a viable compromise and had finally passed the matter to the General Assembly. Only one thing had changed now: Tonga's amiable brown giant, six feet eight inches tall, three hundred pounds, face almost always wreathed in a friendly, all-embracing smile, was no longer President of the Council. Prince Kaohumahili—"Koa" to everyone at the U.N.— had yielded the seat, which rotates by lot each month, to Eire's pipe-smoking little white-haired pixie. This meant, as the London Sunday *Times* murmured to his American seat mate, the Baltimore *Sun*, "Fudge and treacle." "More likely dense fog and cotton wool," the Baltimore *Sun* responded. "Whichever," the *Guardian* said. "We know if there's any way to futz it up, he will." "Don't be so harsh," the Washington *Post* chided ironically. "*He* thinks he's a statesman."

This Eire obviously did, looking about importantly while the circle filled up, puffing with a long, philosophic draw upon his ornately carved wooden pipe. From time to time his bushy eyebrows shot up as though in startled surprise; but his colleagues and the media had learned long ago that this was simply a nervous tic and not, as they had at first supposed, an indication of thought. Indications of thought, they had concluded, were seldom to be found in that sector, though they knew they could count on him for laughs.

The only trouble now was that nobody at all was in a mood for laughs. Everybody just wanted to get it over with, since the general consensus was at one with Ham Delbacher's tart comment to his impromptu press conference: the Security Council session, they were all convinced, would not accomplish "a damned thing."

"Members of the Council," Eire said when they were all settled, leaning forward to his microphone and peering myopically around the circle, "the Council will be in order. This special meeting of the Security Council has been requested by the President of the United States and the Soviet Union, acting, as it were, jointly, or at least simultaneously. Virtually simultaneously," he amended as both Hamilton Delbacher and Yuri Serapin shifted in their seats. "Actually I believe the request came first from the President of the United States, was rejected initially by the President of the Soviet Union, and then was subsequently accepted by the President of the

Soviet Union with an appeal for haste. I am not sure," he said in a puzzled tone, "exactly why the President of the Soviet Union changed his mind so quickly, but no doubt he can enlighten us when he speaks. Meanwhile, since the request came initially from the United States, it seems only fitting that President Delbacher be heard from first. If no one objects, that is."

He paused and looked around the circle. Fourteen impassive faces looked back. He cleared his throat importantly, blew out a large puff of smoke and with a twitch of his eyebrows made a sudden jab with his pipe stem in the general direction of Hamilton Delbacher. "Mr. President?"

"Thank you, Mr. President," Ham said, leaning forward to his microphone. "I shall not take much of the Council's time. The facts are obvious on the record. We also have"—and he turned around and gestured to a couple of young State Department aides who rose obediently and went out—"certain physical evidence we wish to present, as well. While my aides are getting it, I will state our position very briefly.

"Three days ago there began four vicious and unprovoked attacks upon allies of the United States which seriously jeopardize world peace in their respective areas. These attacks were inspired by, encouraged by and are being very substantially supported by the Soviet Union. Legitimate governments of Saudi Arabia, South Africa, Taiwan and Mexico are at this moment battling for their very existence. The United States has sent"—his tone hardened—"and will continue to send, in increasing amounts as necessary, aid to these allies. On the diplomatic front, we are here to request the Security Council to condemn the Soviet Union's surrogate wars and demand a stop to this vicious undermining of the whole structure of world peace.

"The President of the Soviet Union, as we all know, is an international adventurer and gambler. He is apparently gambling that these latest adventures of his will succeed in escaping the opposition of the world community. He is hoping that victories will permit him to overcome what must be the grave doubts of his own responsible advisers." Yuri shifted angrily in his seat, but the President ignored him and went on. "His irresponsible, peace-destroying adventures will not escape the opposition of the United States of America. If the Council really wishes to preserve world peace, it will join the United States in ending these new threats to world peace. If they are not ended, and if the United States must continue to actively oppose them"—his face and tone became somber—"there is no telling how far this will spread. It may well go to the point where all the roads of earth are filled with marching men. That is not, I think, the desire of most of the world's peoples. His irresponsible adventurism must be stopped and stopped now . . ." He paused, glanced back, saw his two young aides coming in with three heavy boxes. Clerks sprang to their assistance. The boxes were carefully deposited in the center of the circle.

"Mr. President," Hamilton Delbacher said, "if the Council will bear with me a moment—" He stood up, walked around the table, proceeded to its center, opened a box. Above in their booths along the sides the television cameras zoomed in intently upon his stern, determined face.

"Here," he said, raising a rifle high, "is a Soviet rifle captured yesterday in the south of Mexico. It was taken from the body of a Cuban officer leading a detachment of Guatemalan troops. A total of sixteen such rifles were captured in this one engagement.

"This"—and he held up a clearly identifiable fragment of a missile—"fell yesterday on Mexico City. It is of Soviet manufacture. It was recovered in Chapultepec Park from the fragments of a Cuban fighter plane.

"This"—he held up another missile fragment—"fell on Riyadh in the opening stages of the attack on Saudi Arabia. It is also of Soviet manufacture and was launched from a Soviet fighter plane flying with South Yemeni forces. The plane was downed and the Soviet pilot is now in captivity in the hands of the forces of the legitmate government.

"Here"—and he held up another rifle—"is a rifle of Soviet manufacture taken from the body of a Cuban officer leading a contingent of Angolan troops moving south through Botswana to the border of South Africa. Thirty-nine such weapons were seized by South African troops in this engagement. . . .

"I do not have," he concluded dryly, "any such exhibits from Taiwan, since the People's Republic of China does not employ Soviet hardware. But the timing of the attack upon Taipei, exactly coordinated with the other three attacks and coming as it did less than a week after the signing of the Sino-Soviet treaty, is sufficient evidence of collusion for any reasonable man to accept . . ."

He closed the boxes and returned to his seat while the room remained silent and intent. When he sat down, the permanent American Ambassador to the United Nations, Ambrose Johnson, handed him a paper. He nodded thanks, glanced at a grim-faced Yuri Serapin, seated three chairs away, took up the paper and proceeded in a firm and level voice.

"Mr. President, the United States offers the following resolution:

" 'Whereas a state of war now exists in Mexico, Saudi Arabia, South Africa and Taiwan; and

" 'Whereas physical evidence and the coordinated timing of the attacks upon the legitimate governments of those countries points directly to the President of the Soviet Union as their instigator and inspirer; and

" 'Whereas neither responsible Soviet military leaders nor any responsible member of this body can possibly condone or support such unprincipled adventurism and unwarranted attacks upon the peace of the world; and,

" 'Whereas these conflicts constitute a present and immediate danger to world peace as defined in the Charter of the United Nations; now, therefore,

" 'Be it resolved, that the Security Council condemns totally the wars begun at the instigation and with the support of the President of the Soviet Union and demands that the President of the Soviet Union cease his peace-destroying adventurism in these four nations immediately and forthwith.'

"Mr. President, I ask for an immediate vote on this resolution."

("What's he trying to do?" *Newsweek* murmured to CBS, "create a military revolt against Serapin?" "He may just succeed, too," CBS replied. "Look at Yuri!")

And Yuri indeed was worth looking at, because for once he was making no attempt to dissemble his feelings. His face was livid with anger, and his voice, until he got it under control, was close to an angry croak. But his normal volubility was not affected. He spoke in his heavily accented but excellent English.

"Mr. President!" he said, so angry he at first had difficulty articulating, while Eire puffed furiously on his pipe, twitched his eyebrows and looked about with considerable agitation and an Oh-dear-what-have-I-got-myself-into? expression. "Mr. President, how many lies are permitted here?"

"As many as you like, Mr. President," Eire responded hastily—realized what he had said—gulped—blushed furiously—started to stammer as nervous laughter flicked across the room. "I mean—I mean—"

"*None* are permitted here!" the Soviet President snapped. "Absolutely *none!* Yet all we have heard from the delegate of the United States is lies, lies, lies, slander, slander, slander! Empty assertions, false charges, deliberate prevarications—deliberate, vicious, unprincipled lies! Lies, lies, lies!"

"And a certain amount of evidence," Prince Koa murmured mildly from across the circle. "Don't forget that, Mr. President."

"Evidence!" Yuri cried scornfully. "*Evidence!* What is this 'evidence'? Again it is lies, lies, lies! Have you seen the guns? Have you examined the missiles? What proof is there of authenticity, I inquire of the delegate of Tonga? It is easy to stamp "U.S.S.R.' on anything. It is easy to falsify things! It is easy to fabricate so-called 'evidence'!"

"I am sure the delegate of the Soviet Union is fully aware of how easy it is," Koa said quickly. "He ought to know." There was another spate of laughter, quickly muffled as Yuri glared up at the galleries. "But why should the President of the United States stoop to such tricks? It is not *his* country which is in the habit of resorting to such practices. Why shouldn't we believe him?"

For a moment Yuri looked at him as though about to come physically across the room and assault him, which would not have been a good idea given Koa's enormous size and his own relatively short and chunky frame. Koa stared back impassively and said, "Well?"

"Mr. President," Yuri said, "I am not going to dignify the flippant remarks of the delegate of Tonga with further response. He talks like all other stooges of the United States. And like all other stooges of the United States, he will in due time receive what he deserves."

There was a gasp from somewhere in the room, but Koa, returning stare for stare, finally waved the back of his hand toward Yuri with a gesture as though brushing off a fly and looked disgustedly away.

"Mr. President," Yuri said, more calmly, "there is one purpose behind the lies and fabricated evidence of the delegate of the United States, and that is to conceal the United States' own imperialist aggressions around the world. The delegate of the United States presents what he claims to be Soviet-made rifles and bits of missiles. Has he produced a single Soviet soldier fighting in any of the four areas now being conquered by the glorious armies of the peoples' liberation? Has he produced a single Soviet ship, plane, tank from any of those areas? No, Mr. President, he has only produced rifles which he says are Soviet made and pieces of missiles which he says are Soviet made.

"Well, Mr. President! If that is the kind of argument the delegate of the United States wants to engage in, we all know that it is possible to produce U.S. made rifles and missiles from almost anywhere in the world! We all know that it is possible to produce, right this moment, U.S. soldiers, sailors, pilots and marines who are actively fighting, or on their way to fight, in the actual areas the delegate of the United States is so worried about. Let *me* start producing evidence of imperialist U.S. intervention and adventurism in these conflicts right this minute, and there would be no end to it! We would be here all day and all the night, Mr. President, if I produced such evidence! And there would be no doubt that it was true evidence, either, because the delegate of the United States has announced so grandly to the world that he is deliberately intervening in the spontaneous peoples' revolutions now going on in Saudi Arabia, South Africa, Mexico and Taiwan. He has admitted American imperialism, Mr. President! He has ordered American adventurism and anti-peoples aggression! He is a self-proclaimed enemy of democratic revolutions everywhere in the world! He is a self-proclaimed and unabashed hegemonist whose evil plans must be defeated if the peoples' democracy and freedom are to be preserved!

"And who is he attempting to protect with his feeble forces this time?" His tone became scathing. "The corrupt racist regime of

South Africa! The corrupt antidemocratic regime of Saudi Arabia! The corrupt mandarins of Taiwan! The corrupt oligarchs of Mexico! What worthy clients, Mr. President! What worthwhile people to defend! What fools he must think the rest of us to be, if he thinks we will accept his pretense of noble motives and his lies about the Soviet Union as he tries to defend such scum of the earth!

"And, Mr. President," he said, and suddenly his voice dropped to a quieter, almost conversational tone, "he is not content with that. No, that is not brazen enough for him. Now he must attempt to intervene in the internal affairs of the Soviet Union in an attempt to conceal his own evil designs. Now he must try to drive a wedge between the President of the Soviet Union and the leaders of the glorious Soviet army, air force, navy and strategic rocket forces. He tries a bare-faced child's game, Mr. President. It will not work—it can never work! Let me read to you the special resolution passed scarcely a week ago by the politburo and signed also by our military leaders, pledging to me their unshakable support. Listen to this!"

And with a flourish he picked a paper from his desk and once more read to the silent room the resolution which had in effect made him absolute dictator of the U.S.S.R.

("My God," France *Presse* muttered to Paris *Soir*, "now he is another Hitler." "Many times over," Paris *Soir* responded somberly, "for now he has at hand means one million times more terrible.")

"So, Mr. President," Yuri said softly, "you see it does no good to make foolish attempts to divide us, or to play childish games with U.N. Security Council resolutions, because nothing—*nothing*—can break the insoluble bonds which fuse the leadership of the U.S.S.R. We are one, Mr. President. We are indivisible. It will do no one any good to try to cause trouble for me. My colleagues will not stand for it.

"Nor does it do any good to try to drive a wedge between the U.S.S.R. and the People's Republic of China. Is the delegate of the U.S. unaware that we have just signed a binding new treaty of harmony and socialist solidarity? Does he think that by trying to separate us, by trying to get the United Nations to condemn the U.S.S.R. But not the P.R.C., that he can break the invincible bonds of socialist understanding that unite us? How futile, Mr. President! How obvious, how childish and how empty! It will never succeed, Mr. President, never! Our ties are too strong, our understanding too deep. Nothing can ever separate us, Mr. President, nothing!

"So, Mr. President, let us consider this pointless resolution offered by the delegate of the United States—this lie, this lie piled upon lie, this quadruple lie! We will veto it, of course, because it is worthless and because it is an insult to the truth. Let us vote now! Let us get it over with! The Soviet Union wishes to go home and get on about its business!

"I, too, Mr. President, ask for an immediate vote on the lying resolution of the United States."

"Well," Eire said nervously, "the question before the Council is—"

"Just a moment!" the Prime Minister of Great Britain and the Prime Minister of India said almost simultaneously; and confronted by the cool determination of the one lady and the implacable insistence of the other, Eire was thrown into instant confusion.

"Well," he said hastily, trying to light his pipe, grappling with his tobacco, eyebrows twitching furiously, looking desperately around the table while Tanzania, Egypt, Nicaragua, Tonga and France all raised their hands for recognition, "perhaps a vote immediately would be premature. Perhaps there *is* a desire for further debate—"

"That would seem a safe assumption, Mr. President," Britain's lady said dryly.

"Entirely safe," India's agreed.

"Very well," Eire said, sounding suddenly quite decisive and unlike himself. "We will just go down the list. The People's Republic of China!"

For a moment Ju Xing-dao looked down at his paper-thin old hands folded neatly on the table before him. Then he looked up almost shyly.

"I do not think," he said, so softly that they could barely hear his whispery old voice, "that the People's Republic of China can contribute very much to the Council's deliberations this morning. As the President of the Soviet Union says, we are not the object of the attempt at condemnation launched by the United States; and rightly so, Mr. President, for we are engaged in what has correctly been called a family matter, a private quarrel between ourselves and the province of Taiwan. It is not a matter in which we need, or would welcome, outside intervention—even though,'' he added gently, with a reproving, almost school-teacherly look at Hamilton Delbacher—''some attempt appears underway to interpose United States forces between us and our province of Taiwan. But that is a matter to be handled between the United States and the People's Republic of China, as the President of the United States wisely recognizes when he makes no attempt to link us in his resolution with the Soviet Union.''

He paused and then added gently, ''Indeed, Mr. President, we *are* in two separate categories; and while it is quite true, as the delegate of the U.S.S.R. states, that we do have a treaty of understanding and cooperation, China is not involved with the U.S.S.R. in any activities in which it may be engaging around the globe.''

''Is the delegate implying that we *are* engaging in so-called 'activities' around the globe?'' Yuri demanded in an ominous tone. ''I thought such implications were the game of hegemonists, not of allies. What does the delegate mean?''

''Nothing at all, Mr. President,'' Ju said with an airy little wave of the hand, ''beyond the words used. We are accusing the Soviet Union of nothing. We, too, will veto the United States resolution. I am simply stating the situation as it appears to us. If our view is not satisfactory to the delegate of the Soviet Union, I can only conclude that the delegate must have some difficulty with the English language.''

(''How's that again?'' the Washington *Inquirer* murmured to the chicago *Sun-Times*. ''Seemed clear enough to me,'' the *Sun-Times* responded with a smile. ''I guess it's a matter of whether you use Chinese English or Soviet English.'' ''A fine point,'' the *Inquirer* said, ''on which the fate of the world may yet turn.'')

Apparently Yuri agreed, for he gave Ju Xing-dao a sudden appraising, skeptical look which did not seem to trouble the Chinese Vice-Premier in the least. He simply looked back with a slight but pleasant smile and after a moment turned again to address Eire in the chair.

''Mr. President,'' he said, ''we will, as I have said, veto the resolution also. I join the delegate of the U.S.S.R. in requesting that we vote at the earliest moment so that we may *all* go home to more pressing concerns.''

"Mr. President," the President of France said, not waiting to be formally called upon, "I am mystified, as always, by the distinguished delegate of China. He associates his country with the Soviet Union yet he says it is not associated with the Soviet Union. He defends armed attack upon Taiwan as a family matter in which no one should interfere. And he talks of 'more pressing concerns' while major areas of the world are at this moment bleeding with war. What does he mean, Mr. President? Are there any concerns more pressing than these? I too find the English language baffling as used by the Vice-Premier.''

"Does the distinguished delegate of France intend to veto the resolution also?'' Ju inquired.

The President of France hesitated for a second.

"We have not decided," he replied, somewhat stiffly.

"Does he believe the evidence presented by the President of the United States?''

"That, too," the President of France responded, "we wish to study further.''

"Mr. President," Hamilton Delbacher said sharply, "is the delegate of France accusing me of lying as the Soviet delegate has?''

"Never," the President of France said firmly. "It is not the President's belief in his evidence or his sincerity in presenting it that we question, but rather the sources of it. They may not be the most honest or the most objective.''

"I give you my word on the authenticity," Ham Delbacher said.

"I do not doubt you give it sincerely, Mr. President," the President of France replied, "within the limits of your knowledge in the matter.''

"You do not believe, then, that the Soviet Union has coordinated these attacks upon the four victims?''

"I believe your word is sincerely given on that, too," the French President said carefully, "but again, within the limitations of your knowledge. I yield the floor," he added smoothly before Ham could retort, "to the distinguished delegate of the United Kingdom.''

"Well, Mr. President," she said tartly, "I for one do believe the President of the United States. The United Kingdom will certainly support his resolution. It is so much hiding behind sophistry for the delegate of France and some others here to claim that the evidence produced by Mr. Delbacher may be false. He is convinced of its authenticity and so are we. And even if it were utterly false, the prima facie evidence of coordination of the attacks upon these unfortunate countries is sufficient to point in but one direction, and that is to the Soviet Union. Who else stands to profit? Who else possesses the worldwide network of contacts sufficient to plan and organize such a global onslaught? Who else but the Soviet Union has such an interest in deliberately trying to exhaust the United States in such an adventure, or series of adventures?

"No, Mr. President, we are not impressed by the denials and the personal attacks of the delegate of the Soviet Union. We have seen him in action here before. His methods are quite familiar. They are exactly the same methods followed by the Soviet Union for almost seven decades: warn of the imminence of the international crime, commit the international crime and then accuse someone else of it. It is amazing to us that to this very day, despite the long sorry record stretching back from these new attacks straight through Afghanistan, Poland, Grenada, Nicaragua, Hungary, Rumania, Czechoslovakia, Cuba, Eastern Europe and all the rest, there are still people in this body and this world who are able to rationalize and excuse the Soviet Union. This fact is a triumph of Soviet propaganda and a sorry tribute to Western self-delusion and weakness. But it does not change the fact that the Soviet Union has frequently been, and is now, an international criminal whose hands are dripping with the blood of a dozen innocent nations. Today it is adding more blood to that already spilled. Mr. President, it must be stopped. The conscience of mankind must be rallied. The safety of the world cannot be allowed to be toyed with every time the new President of the Soviet Union takes a fancy to it. His terribly dangerous adventurism must be stopped, and stopped now."

"Mr. President," Yuri said dryly, "does the delegate have some proof of the Soviet actions other than the unsupported charges of the President of the United States and his fabricated 'evidence'?"

"I have said the United Kingdom accepts those charges and believes that evidence," she snapped, "and I have said furthermore
that simple common sense points to but one culprit. If it were possible to state it more bluntly in the English language, I would do so.
As it is, the United Kingdom is quite satisfied with the case made
by the President of the United States. It is also prepared, I might
add, to assist the United States and our other allies in any way possible to restrain and thwart the President of the Soviet Union in his
adventurist actions." She paused and then added in a deliberately
skeptical tone, "Even if they should be, as he claims, supported by
the military leaders of the Soviet Union. This assertion is far harder
for us to accept than the well-grounded statements of the President
of the United States."

"I will say to the delegate of the United Kingdom," Yuri said in
a tone so vicious that it made even the sympathetic in his audience
react with indrawn breaths, "that a power as feeble and as exposed
as hers is in no position to challenge the Soviet Union. Or to question its actions. Or to attempt to divide its leadership, which is absolutely united against all imperialist schemes by Britain and the
United States. She is engaged in trying to push back the wind, I say
to the lady. It is stupid!"

"Not as stupid as the actions of the delegate of the Soviet Union,
who thinks he can obfuscate and confuse all decent people," she
responded icily. "It will not wash, President Serapin. It will not
wash!"

And she glared at him as angrily as he glared at her, while in the
galleries the watching nations whispered and in the media they exchanged wry comments and in the television booths the cameras
swung back and forth between their two flushed faces.

"Mr. President," Ju Xing-dao inquired softly, "who is next on
the agenda?"

"The United States," Eire replied. Hamilton Delbacher shook
his head.

"We have had our say for the time being. Perhaps the delegate
of the U.S.S.R. wishes to elaborate on his threats to decent nations
opposing his adventurist actions?"

("Boy, they're sure working that word 'adventurist,' aren't
they?" the Kansas City *Star* murmured to the Boston *Globe*. "It's

a buzz word in Moscow, that's why," the *Globe* responded. "Designed to upset more conservative Soviet circles. Which I don't think can be upset this time." "Serapin seems very confident," the *Star* agreed.)

Whether he was or not could not be clearly determined at the moment. In any event, he now merely shrugged and nodded toward Cameroon. Cameroon leaned forward to his microphone, colorful robes rustling.

"Cameroon has no comment at this time, Mr. President," he said, "except to say that I thought we were here for serious debate, not to chase will-o'-the-wisps and pretended 'evidence' of something that cannot be proved. Had we the veto, we should exercise it too! That is all."

"Well, thank *you*," Hamilton Delbacher murmured dryly to Ambrose Johnson, who smiled slightly and shrugged.

"They're all scared to death of Yuri," he said. "He's got most of them quite successfully cowed."

This appeared to include Eire, whose turn it now was. After hemming and hawing for several moments, again puffing furiously on his pipe and attempting to look profound, he finally said,

"Eire prefers to reserve comment at the present time."

And turned, with an obvious relief that brought a little stir of amusement, to Egypt. Egypt did not appear to be under any inhibitions. Her President, who on his last appearance at the U.N. had worn a beautifully embroidered galabaya, was dressed today in a Western business suit. His manner was equally businesslike.

"Mr. President," he said, "Egypt cannot possibly condone the actions or the position of the Soviet Union in this matter. Egypt does not need evidence or proof, though it believes the President of the United States to be acting in good faith and with great credibility in what he has offered here. Egypt has proof enough in our own house. We are familiar with communist agitators among our own Moslem people, preying upon and taking advantage of innocent believers who do not understand how they are being agitated and manipulated. We are under attack ourselves, though not as openly, yet. The evidence of Soviet intentions and Soviet actions is equally evident everywhere throughout the world. We will vote accordingly, regardless of the certain veto of the Soviet Union. Of course the criminal will vote to conceal his tracks, if given the opportunity. Unfortunately he has it here. But that will not change Egypt's position."

He started to sit back, then noted Yuri's glowering expression and leaned forward again quickly. "And do not call *us* 'feeble and exposed,' " he advised sharply. "We know we are feeble and exposed. We also know we are honest people. We cannot stomach what you are doing. *It—must—be—stopped.*"

Yuri gave him a somber look which he returned, unimpressed.

The Prime Minister of Greece leaned forward to his microphone.

"Mr. President, " he said in a thoughtful voice, "Greece wishes we could believe the unsupported word of the President of the United States, but we are unable to do so. We find the rather desperate deductions of the Prime Minister of Great Britain equally unsupportable. At the same time, we do not wish to give the appearance of condoning possible violations of world peace. We will abstain on the resolution."

"Well," the Prime Minister of India said, disposing her gorgeous blue-and-gold sari about her shoulders with a flourish and jangling her earrings as she grasped the microphone firmly with a heavily bejeweled hand, "India will not abstain. India will vote! India will do her best, as always, to cut through hypocrisy and arrive at truth! India will therefore inevitably accept the argument of the Soviet Union in this matter."

"India cares nothing for the facts then, Prime Minister?" Hamilton Delbacher demanded. She shot him a scornful glance.

"Facts! What are these 'facts'? Assertions, charges, claims—an article or two which, as the delegate of the Soviet Union says, could have been manufactured anywhere and stamped 'U.S.S.R.'—bits of metal purporting to be missiles—*'facts'!* India is not very impressed with these 'facts'! "

"What is India impressed with?" the President inquired dryly. "Soviet submarines off her own shores? An attack on her own soil? A coup in Delhi backed by the Soviet Union to overthrow you and your government? That is what is going on right now in Saudi Arabia, South Africa, Mexico and Taiwan. Would it take the same to impress India?"

"Games!" the Prime Minister said scornfully, shrewd dark eyes fixed intently on his. "Word games! Yes, I will grant you there is warfare raging in those four places, but why should it concern us, I ask the President of the United States? Why should *we* care what happens to Saudi Arabia, corrupt as it is and unworthy of our concern? Why should *we* care what happens to South Africa? Do you know how Indians are treated in South Africa? Why should *we* care about Mexico or Taiwan? What are they to us, the one a corrupt regime, the other a remnant of the past that by rights is part of China anyway, as they themselves admit. What is it to us, all this?"

"Nothing now," Ham Delbacher said dryly. "Everything, on the day the President of the Soviet Union turns loose his lackeys upon *you*."

"Ha!" she cried scornfully. "Communists try to succeed in India but they do not succeed in India. Sometimes they control a state here or a state there, they have a little success now and then in this city or that, but then they lose ground, they waste away, they disappear. Success eludes them. The timeless strength of India defeats them. We are not afraid of communists. We can afford to be patient with them. We have been on this earth a very, very long time, Mr. President. Longer than America!"

"And under far more conquerors," the President remarked. "What makes you so sure you can escape this one, Prime Minister?"

"Well!" she said, momentarily taken aback by his tone; but she recovered. "India can 'escape this one,' as you call it, because 'this one' is not directed at India, and because"—she glared at Egypt, who had permitted a small snort of derision to escape him—"because the Soviet Union would not dare attack India! The world would not permit it! The world would recognize instantly what a crime was being committed against humanity! It would rise up and condemn such unprovoked and unwarranted aggression! It would simply not be permitted!"

"Prime Minister," Hamilton Delbacher said in a tired tone, confronted once again by the ineffable Indian ability to take a high moral position completely uncomplicated by reality or responsibility, "you live in a dream world which I hope for your sake and the sake of India will not soon be shattered by another such adventure as is presently underway in the four nations at risk. If that should happen, no doubt we will meet here again to hear India's pleas, as urgent and desperate as those now reaching us from the present victims. And no doubt once again the Soviet President will exercise his veto; and events will move on their way, stopped only, if they are to be stopped, by the United States, Britain and such other allies as may still adhere to some standard of decency and consistency in the world. When that day comes, Prime Minister, you will realize what is being discussed here today. But of course," he added in the same tired tone, "you do, and you are engaging in your usual pretense that you do not. I had hoped, based upon your actions in helping to work out the compromise that ended the last crisis here, that you could be more cooperative in this new one. But you have retreated into your usual refusal to face the facts, for reasons, I suspect, of attempting to restore your standing among nations similar to yours that expect everyone to help them but will themselves help no one."

(*"Wow!"* USA Today said in a startled whisper. "That's giving it to the old girl right between the eyes!" Evidently she thought so too, for she gave Ham Delbacher an angry and indignant glare.)

"You are insulting, Mr. President!" she cried. "You are insulting to India and you are insulting to me!"

"Prime Minister," he said, "we are very fast approaching the last hour of the last day, in which it really does not matter who insults whom, because if we continue as we are, we are all doomed together." He paused and then went on quietly while the room hushed to hear him out. "Let me make one thing clear to you, and to all who doubt the purpose or the will of the United States and its present leadership: we are going to stop this thing. I do not know at this moment exactly how, or exactly at what moment it will be considered to be at an end, but it will be stopped because it has to be."

"Yes," she spat out, "by using force and possibly plunging the whole world into war before you are through!"

"Prime Minister," he said gravely, "if that is what it takes, thanks to lack of cooperation and support for what is manifestly right from yourself and other like you who in their heart of hearts know better, then that is what will be done."

And so quiet yet absolute was his voice, and so calm yet frighteningly emphatic was his manner, that a cold shiver ran through many. "Death's-head stands behind every chair around this circle," he had told them in the midst of his first great battle with the Soviet Union; and with a chilling implacability he had invoked its presence for them again.

For several moments no one moved or spoke. Then, almost as if ashamed, hurriedly and in some cases speaking so fast that it was hard to understand them, Iraq, Nicaragua, the Seychelles and Tanzania echoed India—very briefly in most cases, but the purport was the same. A scornful and unshakable skepticism, a profound and by now almost instinctive mistrust of American motives and disbelief in the American word infused them all. The Soviet Union, carrying on its unceasing conquest for many decades, had done its work well in the absence of any really energetic and determined American response. Too many Americans had themselves been bemused by the unrelenting hammers of Soviet propaganda for any such response to be mounted by administrations in Washington: they were in fact intimidated by the protests of their own people and so for far too long had let the battle go by default. Now only an automatic skepticism, expressed in his own leading media and through such means as the demonstrations in Lafayette Park and in many other places throughout the world, came back to Hamilton Delbacher from the Security Council.

Only Prince Koa, bowing low to the American President, pledged the support of tiny faroff Tonga and defied the Soviet President, who sat with a superior, complacent air, eyes never leaving the face of his antagonist, who stared impassively back. Very soon all speeches were finished and Eire, who had never made his government's position known, put the question and, mumbling something around his pipe about "reasonable differences . . . understandable uncertainties . . . difficulty in perceiving what—" voted No on the American resolution.

Both the Soviet Union and the People's Republic of China cast their vetoes. The United Kingdom, the United States and a finally emphatic France voted with Egypt and Tonga in favor.

Yuri leaned forward to his microphone and claimed the floor. The expected Soviet counterresolution spewed out.

" 'Whereas,' " he read with a slow, deliberate relish, " 'the United States of America has, without proof, provocation or warning, begun rushing troops, planes, submarines, naval vessels and other implements of war to The People's Republic of Arabia, South Africa, Mexico and Taiwan; and,

" 'Whereas, these imperialist aggressive moves have been launched by the President of the United States on the empty and untrue justification that spontaneous peoples' wars of national liberation in these four areas have been somehow "inspired" or "coordinated" or "launched" by the Soviet Union; and,

" 'Whereas, no proof of such Soviet responsibility has been offered this council by the President of the United States of America save false and fabricated "evidence" of a totally unproven and suspect nature; and,

" 'Whereas, these American attacks upon the spontaneously rising peoples' wars of national liberation now occurring in the People's Republic of Arabia, South Africa, Mexico and Taiwan are an absolute threat to world peace and are simply a screen for American imperialist aggression and desire for conquest; now, therefore,

" 'Be it resolved that the Council does completely and without reservation condemn the wars of imperialist aggression launched by the President of the United States of America upon the democratic peoples of these four areas and demands that he withdraw his aggressive forces immediately and forthwith.' "

There ensued a mirror image of the debate just preceding. At its end the vote again stood five to ten, the five this time in opposition and the three vetoes of the United Kingdom, the United States and France cast against the Soviet resolution.

During the course of the debate Taiwan tried unsuccessfully to get recognition and present arguments in its defense; was indignantly voted down as a "nonstate" when Ju Xing-dao gently remarked that any such proceeding would obviously violate the P.R.C.'s exclusive right to represent China. South Africa also sought recognition and was denied despite vigorous (and, as they knew, foredoomed) pleas for fairness by the American President and the British Prime Minister. Mexico was allowed to speak for ten minutes, during which the Soviet Union, the P.R.C., India, Iraq, Nicaragua and Tanzania ostentatiously vacated their seats, not returning until Mexico concluded. At Soviet insistence an individual who described himself as "the new and only legal delegate of the People's Republic of Arabia" was allowed to speak for half an hour, during which he heaped further scathing denunciations upon the United States and its "imperialist, interventionist, hegemonistic President," who responded with a look of contempt but did not otherwise dignify the tirade.

After the vote Yuri Serapin turned to Eire, still fiddling nervously with his pipe.

"Mr. President," he announced happily, "it is the intention of the Soviet Union to introduce this resolution tomorrow in the General Assembly."

"Feel free," Hamilton Delbacher said. "The American delegation will not attend."

And despite frantic protests and condemnations of this decision from his own major media and many demonstrators at home and abroad, he did not change this decision. He watched with the world next day while the General Assembly, after many more vituperative denunciations of the United States, voted 114 to 23 for the Soviet resolution. He then announced through the White House press secretary that:

"The President has taken note of the one-sided and totally unjustified vote in the General Assembly. The President accords to the vote the weight it deserves. United States actions in support of the legally constituted governments of Saudi Arabia, South Africa, Mexico and Taiwan will continue and will be, if necessary, increased."

And returned to the imperative and seemingly impossible task of trying to devise the means and methods with which to do so.

5

For his part, the President of the Soviet Union flew home to Moscow that night well content. He had accomplished exactly what he had set out to do, exactly what almost seven decades of constant propagandizing had made inevitable. So well trained were most of the world's peoples by this time that all that was required of a Soviet leader was that he start the tide of skepticism flowing. It moved on inexorably in ever-growing flood to overwhelm poor, futile, doomed America. No amount of protestations from Washington, no amount of evidence, no amount of truth—and in this instance, of course, he knew as Hamilton Delbacher did that what Hamilton Delbacher said was the absolute truth—could stand against the smug, automatic sarcastic disbelief of most of humankind.

He could not refrain from a little satisfied nod in the direction of all his predecessors in the Kremlin and all their eager lieutenants and willing dupes in all the lands. They had wrought long, patiently and well, prior to World War II and most particularly since, when the growing crescendo of propaganda had kept pace with the gigantic arming that had been its constant companion. Larger and larger and larger had grown the Soviet arsenal of weapons of all kinds, conventional, nuclear, chemical, bacteriological and space; more and more sophisticated, more and more effective, more and more voluminous everywhere around the globe, the propaganda offensive had kept pace.

Now America faced the four military challenges he had arranged as the opening stages in her final downfall—plus a deadweight of world scorn and disbelief that tied America's hands perhaps even more effectively than military entanglement.

He had the combination in his hands and he considered it unbeatable. The President might flounder about at the United Nations, make belligerent speeches on television, send scraps of American armed forces hastily across the globe to try to damp down the four wars—"miniwars," Yuri had noticed them described in the *Times*, which was fine with him, such derogation was a very effective part of the skepticism too—but the President's military gestures were insufficient and his response to the propaganda quite laughable.

It had been easy indeed for Yuri to dismiss the evidence of Soviet weaponry, since virtually no one wanted to believe it anyway. It had been a simple matter for him to withstand the charges of Soviet complicity, since world disbelief had already dismissed them.

He knew with a grim satisfaction the deeper cause for this, the real reason why very few wished to believe that the Soviet Union was responsible. To believe that and to accept its full implications *would mean being obligated to take a stand and do something about it*. And so frightened was the world of Soviet power now that only the foolhardy few were courageous enough to do that anymore.

He would concede, Yuri told himself as his official Aeroflot plane sped on toward his sad gray land—so forbidding outwardly, so pathetic within—that there were some few left with courage. In a grudgingly contemptuous way he had to admire them for it. The United States of course was one, the United Kingdom another, Japan usually, France sometimes, Italy sometimes, West Germany sometimes, a scattering of others now and then. But the number had dwindled rapidly and dramatically in the past decade until now there were almost too few to matter. Only the United States remained, as always, the principal obstacle; and now he had the United States where he wanted it. An overwhelming majority of the nations were now on the Soviet side. America's clumsy and inadequate attempts to meet the new crises were isolating her still further.

Once again the Soviet Union had succeeded in turning the truth on its head.

The United States was now the aggressor—at least according to the official records of the United Nations, for whatever they might be worth. And in terms of propaganda, that was considerable.

America was evidently not, however, an "aggressor" who intended to be swayed by world opinion, and for that he had to respect Hamilton Delbacher even as he despised and hated him. The American President was a stubborn man, and in Yuri's mind a dangerous one. He was so unpredictable—so stubborn—so unwilling to accept the verdict of history peaceably—so determined to continue in the hopeless pretense that his dying country was still a great nation with something to give humanity—still genuinely convinced that corrupt capitalist "democracy," "freedom," "liberty" and all his other empty catch words really meant something in a world falling ever more rapidly under control of the true people's democracy that Yuri represented.

That he also represented history's mightiest and greediest military machine, its most ruthless dictatorship, its most corrupt and secretly self-indulgent ruling class and its most pathetically misled and misruled slave peoples was something he did not wish to dwell upon too long. He knew this, as all members of the ruling class knew it, but it was imperative for the preservation of their own power and privileges that they never admit it, even to themselves, by so much as an inflection of word or lift of an eyebrow. Marx and Lenin had given them the words with which to protect themselves, and as long as they parroted them loudly enough and faithfully enough and persistently enough, they could drown out all dissident voices and feel quite safe.

Except as vis-à-vis one another: and there, he knew, he must be ever alert in the days ahead. He had been prepared for the denunciations of the American President, the British Prime Minister, even such fatuous little pinpoints as Tonga; but the words "adventurist" and "adventurism" had rankled excessively, not because he knew they were accurate but for exactly the reason his antagonists had used them—because they knew the charges would do him damage at home.

Underlying the colossus of the Soviet military and the paranoid, mutually jealous and suspicious bureaucracy of the Politburo, there was a mammoth sluggishness and unwillingness to take the risks which he knew had to be taken. There was still a great, decades-long resistance to the dramatic move, the quick, unexpected sally, the wildly exhilarating gamble of the opportunity perceived, the moment seized, the goal achieved by swift surprise and high, unmatchable daring.

Much emphasis had been laid upon surprise for many decades in Soviet military literature, where the lessons taught by Adolf Hitler had not been forgotten. Long before ill-advised blabbermouths in Washington had begun to talk indiscreetly about the possibility of "surviving" or "winning" a nuclear war, official Soviet documents used at Frunze Military Academy and in the political indoctrinations of the Soviet forces had put forward the idea of successful surprise nuclear strike and the winnability of nuclear war. As usual, however, Soviet luck had held: the world had not believed they really meant it. The come-lately Americans took all the blame. Damnation was heaped upon them for an idea that had been official Soviet doctrine for twenty years and more; and the propaganda chorus howled anew.

But actually, as he knew with a cold certainty, his comrades at the top of the Soviet empire were still the creaking, supercautious, unimaginative, plodding *apparatchiks* they had always been. Not an original idea stirred behind those medals, he told himself scornfully; not a single daring thought broke surface in those dull, comformist minds. So they had arranged the dismissal of Nikita Khrushchev, for instance, because they were afraid of his unpredictability, his "adventurism." So they had frantically, like power-mad beavers, built up the Soviet military machine to strengths unheard of in human history, unwarranted by any threat, real or imagined, to Soviet security and the safety of the ruling class.

And yet now, when *he* had finally come to power, a young, vigorous, daring man willing and able to use the monstrous power they had created in order to achieve his goals and those of Mother Russia, they were against him.

It was insane; it angered him excessively; and it made him supremely aware that his every step risked challenge, his every brilliant move, betrayal.

For this reason he had forced his military leaders to sign the Politburo's declaration of submission. They had not expected it, he had caught them by surprise—again, the gamble had carried the day. It was obvious they did not like it but he had made it impossible for them to refuse. Now they were as committed as the Politburo—on paper—to his de facto dictatorship; though he knew that words on paper meant only what he could make them mean—that he must be constantly on guard with both groups—and that only by playing skillfully upon their mistrust of one another could he maintain himself at the top of the pyramid.

Keep them divided—and put in his own men. Like his predecessor, the other Yuri, who to staff his most important offices had drawn from the little gang of murderers who had helped him run the KGB for fifteen years, this Yuri too had decided to draw heavily from the ranks of the organization in which he himself had served for six years on his way to the top. He was aware that street gossip referred to them as "the Assassins' Club," for the KGB kept as tight a check on the Soviet Union's hapless citizens as it did on any foreign enemy, and the feeble jokes with which they helped themselves get through their captive days were as faithfully recorded as any monitored telephone conversation in the White House.

So Yuri knew what his slave population thought about the men he proposed to bring into government, but that did not matter. He needed them, knowing they would be ruthless not only toward the much-feared masses but toward high-ranking enemies within the Politburo and the military as well. The rush of events in the weeks since he had taken office had prevented an earlier sorting out of his government, and the momentum of his successful rise to power was still carrying him forward without serious threat of challenge. But the day would come, and perhaps very soon, when he would need lieutenants upon whose loyalty and ruthlessness he could rely absolutely. Now that he had the United States on the run, he told himself as his secretary came in with a pot of tea, black bread and caviar, he would tend to that. And then he would indeed be impregnable, a dictator such as even Joseph Stalin had not been.

Again he reflected, as he often had before, how unfortunate it was that the bloody Georgian Josef Dzugashvili had appropriated the name "Stalin," meaning steel, because he, Yuri felt that he was even more a man of steel than that mass killer had been. Yuri had not yet been forced to liquidate his enemies by the millions as Stalin had done, and might never; but he wanted to know that he had the power. He had no doubts whatsoever but that he could exercise it with complete socialist objectivity should the need arise.

For the moment he felt the need would not be pressing as long as he could keep the United States off balance and as long as he was able to continue pushing it steadily to the wall. The United Nations had fallen in line obediently, just as he had known it would: the outcome had never been in doubt. The Soviet conquest had made sure years ago that a majority of the international organization would be as subservient as any flabby Eastern European or Caribbean satellite. Within the Kremlin, U.N. complicity had for the time being strengthened him further. There was a victory smell in the air, he thought, amused by his own romanticizing: it was like hounds when the fox is at last in view. Hated America was dying at last, and the odors of steady and inexorable putrescence filled the globe. A last spurt of life—the final pretense that America could actually defend her widely disparate and distant allies—and then collapse—surrender—carefully managed internal revolution—the installation of a "People's Republic" rigidly controlled from Moscow—and the end of the only serious obstacle still remaining to the triumphant conclusion of the long, patient Soviet conquest of the earth.

Such had been the dreams of every Soviet leader for half a century, but none had dreamed them with more certainty than he. The conquest conducted so patiently and doggedly over so many years—the Continuing Conquest that so many naive Americans could not recognize because they simply could not grasp the concept of a conquest that did not have sudden, dramatic events rising to a sudden, dramatic conclusion, but that just went patiently on hour after hour, day after day, week after week, month after month, year after year, decade after decade, wearing down and wearing down and wearing down until finally the objective disintegrated, as Yuri often expressed it to his colleagues, "like a rotten pear."

He finished his tea, directed his aides to open a line to Moscow, received from Marshal Andreyev of the Army, speaking for all the military chiefs, a report of progress.

In Riyadh, the new People's Republic of Arabia was beginning to meet some opposition but it seemed likely that American aid would fail to reach the area in time to stop the onward drive and shore up the handful of elder princes desperately trying to rally resistance from Jidda.

In South Africa, the African continent's strongest military force was recovering from initial shock and striking back hard at Angola and rebel portions of Namibia, but bombing of Pretoria, Johannesburg and Cape Town had been resumed and heavy casualties were reported both there and from the field; and there, too, the bulk of American aid was still far away, though two air raids had been launched upon Luanda, Angola, and heavy bombers were on their way from Diego Garcia and the Falklands.

In Mexico, Cuban-led Guatemalan forces had seized two major oilfields and Mexico City had been bombed again. So, too, had Guatemala City, with quite heavy casualties. But the tide was still running against Mexico despite the proximity and steadily increasing aid of her northern ally.

On Taiwan, for the moment, things were relatively quiet. The P.R.C. had not resumed bombing of Taipei, and after a single sharp, short raid on the mainland city of Amoy that had resulted in the death of several hundred, Taiwan had also refrained from further military hostilities. The battle, at least temporarily, had moved from the skies to the airwaves: both sides had begun intensive propaganda barrages. From Subic Bay in the Philippines, an American task force on its "state visit" was nearing the Taiwan Straits. Apparently both Chinas were having second thoughts at the moment, but Yuri was not concerned: that was their internal problem, in any event. The P.R.C. had cooperated with him on timing and that was the important thing. As long as the stupid Americans were moving steadily ahead straight into the middle of the quarrel, that served his purpose admirably, and he was quite content.

Not so, he suspected, his antagonist in the White House. A savage smile contorted his face at the thought of that incompetent bumbler. Very soon now, Yuri would be dictating terms to the United States, and the first of them would be the unconditional hand-over—if he was still living—of the individual who had called him with such infuriating contempt, "Evil! Evil! *Evil!*" The thought of what he would do then brought to Yuri's face an expression that might well have terrified even his toughest lieutenants. His only concern was that he might be cheated of that satisfaction; but since that eventuality, if it occured, was also part of his plan, he believed that, either way, he would be rid of Hamilton Delbacher once and for all.

Unaware of these fantasies passing pleasantly through the mind of his antagonist, but not of a temperament to be surprised or perturbed had he known of them, the President of the United States also was busy with his military chiefs. Unlike Yuri, he felt no concern about their loyalty nor did he need to. They were faithful servants, as the Founding Fathers had intended them to be when they conferred upon the office of President the further powers of Commander-in-Chief. Neither Ham Delbacher nor the Joint Chiefs had the slightest concern that either would overstep the bounds of their respective offices. He did not doubt their loyalty, nor they his, to the democratic beliefs and concepts that bound them all.

What they would have done had they been confronted by a President who in some erratic way upset the democratic balance, they would have been hard pressed to say, for they simply could not conceive of it, any more than he could conceive of a military coup in the United States. It was simply out of the question, at least in the America they had all known up to now. They were bound by an unstated, instinctive faith that it would never occur.

So he faced them now secure in the knowledge that he could rely upon them to state their misgivings, if any, candidly and without fear, as they knew he would listen to them reasonably and sensibly; and only if he considered it absolutely imperative, override them.

It was obvious that they had plenty of misgivings.

"Smidge," he said to General Hallowell on this afternoon of his return from New York, "you look unhappy. What's the problem?

Or maybe"—he smiled wryly—"I should say, what *isn't* the problem?"

The chairman of the Joint Chiefs gave him a rueful smile.

"That's more like it, Mr. President," he said. "We're getting dreadfully extended, very fast, it seems to me. And I don't quite know . . . if we're going to catch up with it in time."

"That's a thoroughly justifiable worry for everyone," the President said, "but weighing everything, I felt we had to move—even if it's only the illusion of motion, which I suppose, essentially, it is. At least it makes us unpredictable and maybe buys us a little time to bring really strong forces to bear."

"But at what cost, Mr. President?" Bart Jamison of the Air Force inquired. "And what forces? They're better than they have been for the past decade or so, true enough, but they're still not an equal match for the Soviets unless we go nuclear—and do it first— and manage to survive with the nation intact and not too many dead. Which I don't think we can."

"Nobody in Washington wants to go nuclear," Ham Delbacher said flatly. "That's one more myth they've succeeded in peddling."

"Not without some help from here," Gutsy Twitchell of the Marines remarked dryly.

"Yes, I know," the President said. "But nobody in *my* Administration has been that stupid—at least, so far. And nobody," he added grimly, "is going to be. That doesn't mean that we won't face nuclear threats from them before this is over. I fully expect it."

"And then—?" Admiral Rydecker inquired.

"Then," said Bump Smith of the Army, "we'll send the Navy out to sink Moscow and that will take care of *that*."

"The Navy is ready," Snooze Rydecker said stiffly. Both Bart Jamison and Smidge Hallowell said, "Good!" in ironic tones.

"Well," Snooze said, "at least we're as ready as any of *you* are."

"Hell, man," Bart Jamison said, "who cares how ready we are? We're on our way! It's too late to worry about 'readiness' now— whatever that is."

"It's whatever you need to meet whatever you have to face," General Hallowell said.

"It's also a state of mind," General Twitchell observed, "and I'm not too sure as a nation, that we've got it. Particularly with all the flak that's now beginning about our actions."

"*My* actions," Hamilton Delbacher said. "They're my responsibility and I accept it. The question now is, how are things going? Smidge," he addressed the chairman of the JCS, "suppose you lay it out for me."

And with a precise detail that very closely paralleled what the Soviet President had just been told in Moscow, General Hallowell did. At the conclusion of his report the President studied their somber faces for a moment, then sighed.

"Doesn't look as though we're plunging headlong into victory, does it?"

"Not at the moment," General Jamison agreed crisply. "But it can turn—as long as there's no open Soviet involvement. As long as we accept their pretense—which the U.N. has now given us official approval to do—then we're free to proceed pretty much as we want to. Give us another few days and we'll be in much better shape, I think."

"I'll give you another few days," Ham Delbacher said, "but will they? I think we're going to need more than just time."

"Such as?" Admiral Rydecker inquired.

"I think, as my Saudi friend told me when he called after the first Yemeni attack, that we must cut off the head of the beast. We can't wait to chop off the limbs one by one."

"You mean an all-out attack on *Russia*?" Bart Jamison asked in a hushed voice, and he and his colleagues looked startled, awed and dismayed.

"No, no," the President said with some impatience. "I'm not going crazy, Bart. Obviously that can never be unless we really do want to destroy the world together. They'd respond—we'd respond—they'd respond—we'd—the world would end. But there are other ways of getting at them, and I think we should. But it isn't going to be easy."

And as he outlined what he had in mind, they agreed that no, it wasn't going to be easy. In fact, they were at first much alarmed.

"It means war," General Hallowell said somberly, and at first they all agreed. But as the President presented the reasons why he did not think so, they came gradually into line with his plans.

"It's going to be one hell of a gamble," Bart Jamison said finally. "But I guess our nerves can stand it if yours can."

"We'll give it everything we've got," Smidge Hallowell finally promised for them all.

Whether that would be sufficient remained to be seen. But at least the President felt that he had proposed something definite, with some hope of ultimate success, however chancy. As he pointed out, certainly there was no chance at all if they continued to play by Yuri Serapin's rules.

When they left, instructed, and promising, to do everything possible to make ready, he watched them go with a warm, almost paternal feeling. They were good friends, and they were all in it with him together.

Ample intelligence reports were on his desk verifying the military's uneasiness in Moscow. Therein, Ham Delbacher thought, might lie Yuri's terminal sickness. He intended to do everything he could to make sure that it would rapidly metastasize and carry him away.

To that end, he met later that day with the National Security Council and then, privately, with the directors of the CIA and the National Intelligence Agency. He found them as willing and cooperative as the Joint Chiefs; filled with the same misgivings, but determined to provide all assistance their agencies could in achieving the agreed objective.

Presently, as it expanded under their intensive discussions in the next few hours, this became not only the destruction of the incumbent Soviet President but the destruction of the entire Soviet system.

As he pointed out to them with some wryness, this was a very grandiose objective. On the other hand, it was no more so than the long-held and carefully developed ambition of the Soviet Union to destroy the entire American system and along with it all of freedom in the world. Marx, Lenin, Stalin and the rest might have been right: perhaps there was no other solution possible, except the one that Soviet doctrine had so consistently and implacably demanded for almost seven decades. Perhaps they had indeed succeeded in creating at last a situation in which it was simply—one or the other.

Everything he had been brought up to believe, everything his long life in democratic public life had taught him—of the need for mutual tolerance, decency, compassion, compromise, live-and-let-live—argued against this bleak conclusion. There *must* be a way to reconcile, there *must* be a way to avoid mutual destruction, there *must* be a way to live decently and fairly together. So he had been taught by his birth into America, his upbringing, his education, his public career, his lifelong observation that this was simply the best, most rewarding and most pleasant way to live out one's life upon earth. Yet he, like all Americans and all democratic peoples everywhere, was faced with a consistently aggressive, constantly outward pushing, constantly building communist imperialism that had no wish to live and let live, only to destroy, conquer and rule.

He had always warned, in all his many speeches, writings and statements over the years, that this unrelenting pressure might finally drive America to the wall; and that when it did, America would in sheer self-defense throw everything she had against the mortal enemy who intended to destroy her.

Yet he could not seriously contemplate doing that, now that he had the power, any more than his predecessors had. They had all sought desperately for some other way out, as he was continuing to seek desperately for one now. He fully intended to take the battle directly to the heart of the Soviet hegemony, but he did not intend it to be the kind of battle Yuri and his ideological forefathers had in mind when they talked about "the final battle that will decide the fate of all mankind."

It would be a battle, or battles, principally of a military nature, true enough; but it would not be the cataclysmic, world-shattering atomic contest that the Soviets thought they could "survive" and "win." Yuri had very carefully selected his military battlegrounds in the present crisis, making sure they were far from Soviet borders, while simultaneously taking his propaganda and subversive activities directly to America. The President, as he told the Joint Chiefs during one of their many conferences over the next few days, considered that a good model.

But though he managed to project a feeling of calm and confidence, and though he usually managed to discuss it with apparent objectivity and humor, he could not conceal, at least from himself and his most intimate friends, his inner feeling that he was constantly treading the edge of the precipice. And that he indeed carried on his shoulders "the fate of all mankind."

He was always aware, and he could only hope that Yuri was, too, of the billions of fellow beings whose very lives rested in their hands. It was all very well to trade sardonic remarks with Bart Jamison, who was given to them: but they both knew that they were dealing in the lives of American boys and their parents and foreign boys and *their* parents—the whole fabric of the globe. It was possible to get so enrapt by numbers and computers (some bright brains in the Pentagon and the State Department, and certainly in the Kremlin, did) that one could talk glibly of "throw weight" and "megatonnage" and "mutually assured destruction" and forget all about the human beings involved. Fortunately, neither he nor his top advisers were of such an impervious nature. He could only hope a similar humanity imbued his antagonist, though on Yuri's record so far, he found it hard to believe. If it did not, then the roads of earth would indeed run blood and the world was surely doomed.

Challenge, however, must be met with response if there was to be any hope of stability left for mankind. The present danger must be removed, no matter that its removal would itself bring great danger and carry with it the potential for danger greater still. The Soviet Union was indeed finally pushing America to the wall. But with iron nerves and a great deal of luck the President of the United States might—just might—be able to rescue both his own country, and the world democratic freedoms that depended upon it, from the final, unthinkable catastrophe.

Worried friends, the clamor of the media—and Yuri Serapin—competed for his soul in the next few ominous days.

6

The friends, he supposed, were best symbolized by Mark Coffin and Ivan Valerian, whom he had almost come to trust during the first crisis and whose views he sought now in the thought that they might shed some light on his opponent's next moves.

He had found the stocky, good-looking Soviet major, who had defected and placed himself in Mark's hands after their meeting during the first Delbacher-Serapin confrontation in New York a month ago, an interesting study; and while he did not have time for many diversions as the world went crashing headlong toward wherever it was going in the new crisis, he did feel that Ivan was worth a little time. At least he had been one of Yuri's top aides in the Kremlin, and as such had been able to give the President and Mark very accurate advance knowledge of what Yuri had planned heretofore. The President did not know how far into the future his knowledge extended since his defection, but it seemed a good time to find out.

He asked the CIA to bring Ivan in from his safe house in the Virginia countryside. Simultaneously he summoned Mark from the Senate. He decided to see them in the small Lincoln Study on the second floor of the White House, as being more conducive to a relaxed discussion than the Oval Office. Once there he shed his shoes and suit coat and put on slippers and a favorite smoking jacket.

His young visitors arrived together, exchanging amiable greetings at the door when his secretary showed them in.

"I thought you were going to call me for a game of tennis," Mark said, shaking hands.

"My dear friend!" Ivan exclaimed, giving him a strong handshake and an affectionate hug, "I am afraid to do it! You would beat me too badly. I should never be able to lift a racket again."

"You did pretty well the first time," Mark observed. "*You* beat *me* a couple of weeks ago. Why all the false modesty now?"

"It is not false, it is sincere," Ivan said with his charming smile. "Anyway, who can play frivolous games now, when the world is in such chaos? Is that not right, Mr. President?"

"It's a point," the President said, rising and shaking hands, gesturing them to a couple of well-worn leather armchairs. "Although this may be a time to play tennis if one can. It takes the mind off things." He smiled somewhat ruefully. "I wish I had the time to do something like that. It would be a help to me, too."

"You are tired, Mr. President!" Ivan said, instantly sympathetic. He uttered a worried little sound and sighed. "It is a terrible burden."

"One which I cannot escape, however," Hamilton Delbacher said, more cheerfully. "I think I shall survive it, providing your friend in the Kremlin does not devise too many more clever pitfalls for me."

Ivan exclaimed *"Tchk!"* and shook his head sympathetically.

"He is a clever man. Yuri Pavlovich. Always spinning plots, always thinking of things to do. He has been notorious for it all his life. It is a wonder it did not get him killed long ago."

"Why didn't it?" Mark inquired. "Wasn't it that he really expressed something the Politburo wanted to encourage? Wasn't there a consensus about him long ago, a general sub rosa conclusion that, This is the kind of material we want to develop—this is the kind of man we want at the head of things—this is the type we need to get rid of the Americans?"

"Oh, my friend!" Ivan exclaimed while they watched him closely. "Like all Americans, you succumb to the myth of the all-knowing Kremlin, the endlessly weaving spiders in their web. They are not that clever. They are just a bunch of stupid old men who are not as clever as you think. Sometimes things just happen to them."

"And sometimes they don't," the President said dryly. "So out of this geriatric muddle, Yuri Pavlovich came, is that it? He was young, he was vigorous—"

"He knew how to lie and how to murder," Ivan said crisply, "and he had always made a study of the weaknesses of others. It has made him virtually invincible in our society. And above all, he has known when to gamble. Ours is not a society of gamblers. It is one of men who like to be certain, men who plan—but more often than not, plan just to *be* planning—who do not have any real plan— who can be overtaken by those who do really plan. Yuri Pavlovich has always *really* planned, from early in his life in the party. That is why he is ruler of my country."

"And still making plans," Ham Delbacher said in the same dry tone. "How far do you think he will carry them now?"

"As far as he can go until he meets real opposition from the United States," Ivan said promptly. "Only you know how far that is, Mr. President."

"Perhaps you can advise me," the President suggested. "How far should it be?"

"Mr. President!" Ivan said with his flashing smile. "It is you who must tell me that!"

"Oh, no, I mustn't," the President said with a smile. "That, I am afraid, I will have to keep secret."

"But surely you must *have* a plan, Mr. President," Ivan said, leaning forward intently while Mark studied him thoughtfully, "Surely Yuri Pavlovich cannot be permitted to simply walk away with his gamble successfully while you offer only token opposition! There must be more than that!"

"There will be," the President said. "It just takes a little time. But not really," he added thoughtfully, "very *much* time."

"But how much, Mr. President?" Ivan asked with what seemed real dismay. "How *much* time? Things are moving very fast in the four target areas."

"Is that what you call them, 'target areas'?" Mark interrupted. "Is that the official term in the Kremlin?"

"But of course," Ivan said with some surprise. "It is logical, is it not? They are targets of Yuri Pavlovich's gamble. They are targets of his clever plans. They are targets for American response.

They are everybody's targets. Poor people!'' he added with sudden pity. ''It is so sad.'' For a moment his expression became somber. Then it brightened. ''But surely, Mr. President,'' he reiterated, ''you must have plans to stop Yuri Pavlovich for once and all! Surely you are not going to be content with little puffs!''

''No,'' the President said. ''Not 'little puffs.' Big puffs. To blow the man down, I hope.''

''So you will send many, many more troops and planes and ships and bombs to the target area,'' Ivan said with satisfaction. ''That will give him something to think about!''

''Oh, yes,'' Ham Delbacher said comfortably. ''And more besides.''

''Really?'' Ivan said, and for a split second they thought he showed more than casual interest. But whatever it was flicked away as soon as it came and they thought perhaps they were mistaken. ''And what is that, Mr. President?''

The President laughed.

''That's my secret, Major. You will just have to wait and see. Like Yuri Pavlovich.''

''I hope he is surprised!'' Ivan said with what appeared to be a genuine personal dislike. ''I hope you surprise him *very* much, Mr. President. He deserves whatever bombs, yes, even atomic bombs, that you may use against him!''

''Yes,'' the President said, ''he does deserve whatever I use against him, it seems to me. Where would you say he is most vulnerable, Major?''

''To atomic bombs?'' Ivan Valerian asked. The President smiled.

''To whatever I may use against him.''

''He is vulnerable everywhere,'' Ivan said. ''But not to an indecisive response.''

''I haven't been indecisive so far,'' Ham Delbacher pointed out mildly, ''and I don't intend to be. But in what geographic areas do you think it would be most effective for the United States to respond?''

Ivan looked a little blank.

''Right where you are, I would say. Does that not seem effective to you, Mr. President?''

"As far as it goes," Hamilton Delbacher said.

"Where else would you go?" Ivan inquired, still looking and sounding puzzled. "That is where the battles are."

"Probably nowhere else," the President agreed comfortably. "And the battles are not going so badly."

"Oh?" Ivan said politely. "Your press gives the impression that American forces are in some difficulty. Perhaps the reason is that there are not enough of them."

"That isn't the reason for their complaints," Mark remarked in a disgusted tone. "Some of them would give that impression if we were winning everywhere. They'll never be convinced we're doing the right thing, no matter what."

"Why is that?" Ivan wondered. Mark snorted.

"Because your government has done its damnedest to condition them that way over the years and far too many of them have fallen for it. That's probably the principal reason."

"Yes," Ivan said thoughtfully. "We have done some rather bad things."

"Rather," Mark agreed dryly. "A river of lies without end, covering most of the twentieth century. It's no wonder the more gullible of our media are a little confused in the wrong direction."

"It has been bad," Ivan agreed again gravely. "I must apologize for my country."

Mark laughed, not too humorously.

"Oh, don't do that. It's far too late. Now we just have to go ahead as things are."

"I hope," Ivan said with some stiffness, "that you will be able to do so in spite of what you say my bad country has done. In any event, the moves do not seem to be popular with many important voices."

"Nothing strong we do is ever popular with those particular voices," the President said. "So, as Mark says, we go ahead."

"And soon we shall know," Ivan said with a more relaxed, encouraging smile, "exactly where you will strike Yuri Pavlovich to stop his evil plans."

"Yes," Hamilton Delbacher said with an answering smile. "Since you will not advise me, I must go ahead as best I can in my own blundering, inadequate way."

"By strengthening your responses in the four target areas!" Ivan said triumphantly. "It is the only way!"

"If you say so," the President agreed. "You know nothing else about his plans in this new venture, I take it?"

Again for just a second they thought they saw a tiny change in Ivan's eyes. But his expression was as open and innocently friendly as ever when he spoke.

"Mr. President," he said regretfully, "I am afraid my only knowledge was the knowledge I brought with me—that of his plans for the worldwide maneuvers, the submarines in Cuba, and so on. But I tell you what I shall do. I shall search my memory very carefully for you, and if I can find the slightest—the very slightest— hint that might indicate, I will tell you at once. Would that be of assistance?"

"Anything you indicate will be of assistance, Ivan," the President said in a tone that he could see had Ivan momentarily puzzled too. "How are your wife and children?"

"They are doing well," Ivan said, expression again eager and bland. "The children are riding horses and becoming regular little Virginians. My wife is still very homesick for her parents, but"—he shrugged—"what can you do? It is necessary to make some sacrifices if Yuri Pavlovich is to be stopped."

"Indeed," the President agreed, rising with a smile and extending his hand. "You really should continue your tennis with Mark. It is a small price to pay for the privileges of democracy."

"No price is too great to pay for the privileges of democracy!" Ivan declared grandly and shook the President's hand with great fervor as Mark also stood.

"How about tomorrow morning?" he asked. "I'll meet you at Langley at seven-thirty. I'll tell the Agency."

"Good!" Ivan said with a smile. "I shall be there! Come, I shall walk to the door with you." And he started to take Mark's arm amicably and lead him along. Mark drew back, smiling.

"Sorry," he said. "I have to have a private word with the Boss. I'll see you in the morning."

"Right!" Ivan said cheerfully. "I shall leave you to plot the downfall of Yuri Pavlovich—let us hope!"

After he had left, walking briskly along the hall to the stairs in the company of his two guards, the President turned back and gestured Mark to sit down again for a moment.

"And what do you make of that?" he asked.

"He's very curious about your plans," Mark observed.

"Perhaps I should have given him some false ones he could send back," the President said. "Although"—he frowned—"I don't quite see how he *could* send them back. He's under very tight surveillance all the time."

"Unless, of course, he has a contact within the CIA."

"A mole?" Ham Delbacher said. "It's not beyond imagining, though the director assures me practically every hour on the hour that such a thing simply could not be. I suspect it could. . . . Yes, false plans might be a good idea. Except that the real ones, if they go off as scheduled, are going to be public so fast that there won't be time for it."

"You have them, then," Mark said, and smiled at the President's expression. "I'm not your mole," he added. "Like Ivan and everyone else, I'm just curious."

"Don't be," Ham Delbacher told him with a smile. "All will be revealed in due course. In the meantime, I'm glad things are relatively calm on the Hill. One little extra headache I don't need is to have another resolution from that sector."

"I think everybody's backed away a bit, at the moment. Even my noted colleague from California is quiet for the time being."

"Keep him that way," the President ordered humorously. "And keep your Young Turks in line for me too, if you can."

"I'll do my best," Mark promised, "though Clem Chisholm and Rick Duclos and Bob Templeton are all very uneasy about what's going on."

"And I'm not?" Ham Delbacher demanded, rising again and offering his hand. "You tell 'em I'm biting my nails to the quick waiting for things to turn around."

"But they aren't turning around, are they?" Mark inquired somberly, returning his grasp and moving toward the door. "Not yet, anyway."

"Not yet," the President said. "But soon," he added grimly. Soon, I hope."

* * *

"We wish it were possible," the *Times* said next day, "to view with a calmness matching his own the far-flung and extremely dangerous adventures into which the President is leading us.

"Active fighting now rages in four widely separated areas of the globe. American aid and American forces are being dragged deeper and deeper into the conflicts. America's reputation, good faith and integrity are at stake, to say nothing of American arms and the lives of American soldiers, sailors and airmen. Plus, of course, unpredictable and unknowable amounts of American money and materiel that are being wasted at this very moment and will be wasted in ever-growing flood as the four conflicts drag on.

"We are confronted now not with one, but four, Vietnams. Four quagmires lie at our feet, four whirlpools—or cesspools—await. We have stepped deliberately into all of them, and in all we stand in risk of being swallowed up in long-range, pointless, foredoomed entanglement.

"What, then, does our Commander-in-Chief offer us, in such a time? Only the naive hope that if we come stoutly to the defense of four distant, disparate, unlikely allies who are only allies because in haphazard fashion we have allowed them to become our wards in recent decades, we will somehow emerge with our world position strengthened and our world enemy—or at least what the President considers to be our world enemy—defeated. It is a flimsy hope at best. Certainly it is not one valid enough to warrant the enormous risks he is taking with our national safety and the peace of the world.

"Mr. Delbacher seems possessed by an almost paranoid fear of the Soviet Union. We are prepared to agree that the actions of Yuri Serapin since he became President of the U.S.S.R. have not all been exactly peace-loving. However, we cannot accept the proposition that he is out to rule the world, or that the Soviet aim is to conquer mankind, or that everything Mr. Serapin does is dominated and conditioned by such sinister motivation. Sensible people simply don't operate on that basis, and anyone who has risen through the sometimes competitive ranks of the Soviet hierarchy to become supreme leader has to be surpassingly sensible and realistic. Sheer logic would seem to suggest that President Serapin is not the monomaniac would-be conqueror of humanity that President

Delbacher apparently imagines him. He is a man who, in his own way, seeks peace and security for his people as genuinely and fervently as Mr. Delbacher seems to believe that he himself does.

"Disaster rides on the Delbacher adventurism in this new crisis. It can only be stopped by the strongest and most vociferous protest both from the citizenry and from Congress. We hope such protests will have decisive effect before it is too late—before the President, in his fear and overreactive concern, his plunged us even deeper into a set of morasses from which we may be completely unable to extricate ourselves."

"Hamilton Delbacher," the *Post* agreed, "has never been the most delicate and astute of diplomats. Now that he is in the White House he has become one of the heaviest-handed—Ham-handed, we were going to say—Presidents America has ever had. He also stands in good risk of becoming the last one, unless an alarmed citizenry and the good sense of the world can pull him back from his present disastrous course.

"The President seems obsessed with the belief that the Soviet Union is somehow bent upon the conquest of the entire world—not just some little piece of it, but *the entire world*. It is perfectly true that the Soviet Union had often been difficult, intransigent, overly zealous in protecting what it sees as its own security. But to extrapolate from that an intention to conquer the whole globe is to go off into realms of fantasy that only a vastly insecure President could create for himself.

"The country must not allow him to take it along with him. It is incumbent upon all Americans to insist that their President maintain a reasonable level-headedness in what he does. Otherwise we are all at terrible risk.

"Actually, we are anyway, already. Without so much as a by-your-leave from anyone—certainly not the overwhelming majority of his countrymen, and certainly not the Congress—Mr. Delbacher has hurled us headlong into the midst of four regional conflicts that only remotely concern the United States. The excuse for this is twofold: one, he claims that these regional wars of national liberation are somehow inspired, directed and supported from Moscow; and two, he claims that the restoration of discredited, reactionary governments is somehow vital to the safety and security of the United States.

"Nothing, it seems to us, could be further from a sober appraisal of the facts. On point one, Mr. Delbacher had his chance to present his proof of Soviet complicity, if any, to the United Nations: he failed dismally. He produced a few odds and ends, some of them very odd—a fragment of a bomb here, a rifle there, the stamp of the U.S.S.R. superimposed upon them by—who knows? It could have been the CIA, it could have been anyone. Certainly the President did not prove that it was anyone in Moscow. It was fitting that Mr. Serapin should greet these so-called 'proofs' with the scorn they deserved, and it was fitting that both the Security Council and the General Assembly of the United Nations should dismiss them.

"The only truly ominous thing about the episode was that President Delbacher himself obviously genuinely believes in the validity of his 'proof,' and on that 'proof' is basing his decisions to send American men and American funds and materiel headlong into the perfectly legitimate quarrels of freedom-loving peoples with their corrupt, oppressive rulers.

"That way lies utter disaster.

"On the President's point two—that the survival of the old, corrupt regimes of South Africa, Saudi Arabia, Mexico and Taiwan is somehow vital to the safety and security of the United States— common sense can only be equally skeptical. He argues that we have treaty commitments to these regimes that override all common sense and our real legitimate interests. If we do, that is our mistake and our misfortune. The sooner we declare those commitments at an end and get out, the better for all concerned.

"United States commitments to the four challenged governments were never based upon cold appraisal of what is best for America. Instead, as in the case of South Africa and Taiwan, they developed out of a sort of sentimental wooziness extending over many years that never should have been permitted to dictate American decisions in the first place. With Saudi Arabia the motivation was oil, pure and simple. With Mexico it was oil and propinquity. None of these, it seems to us, was or is sufficient to warrant the kind of global risks the President has taken in launching his hasty and ill-planned responses to events overseas.

"Particularly when those events do not in truth bear the shape or carry the wild implications that he seeks to put upon them.

"Congress, under terrific pressure from the White House, reluctantly voted a resolution approving the President's acts. That was understandable in the first rush of apprehension and uncertainty that followed the outbreak of the new crisis. Now it is time for second thoughts, a sober and less hysterical appraisal of events. It is time, indeed, for the repeal of that resolution.

"We urge all concerned citizens to make their feelings known in every way open to them. The sooner the better, for events are rushing too fast to permit delay."

These sentiments were echoed with strong approval in half a hundred major metropolitan newspapers, television news broadcasts and commentaries and in statements issued from pulpit, campus and Hollywood sound stage. Predictably, a line of pickets was organized to keep around-the-clock vigil along the White House fence on Pennsylvania Avenue—the usual ragtag and bobtail, the usual unsightly clutter of signs and placards despoiling the beautiful prospect. IMPEACH HAM was the most succinct and popular sentiment expressed. Across the street in Lafayette Park chanting groups, replicated in parks, public squares and major thoroughfares across Europe and the world, kept up their unremitting demonstrations.

Two days later the President's plans to take the initiative were finally in place and underway. Events preempted the headlines and brought from the protesters even more frantic outcries as the chances of world conflict escalated sharply in response to the actions he felt impelled by the Soviet Union to take.

After his decisive conversation with the Joint Chiefs, he had maintained before everyone except his wife the surface aspect demanded of him—steady, determined, unflappable, calm. By some miracle, possibly because the Joint Chiefs were under strictest orders and in turn had placed their subordinates under strictest orders, his plans did not surface in advance. One reason for this was that they were not transmitted to the commanders in the field until three hours before zero. There was simply no time for disruptive speculation based upon the usual leaks from individuals in the bureaucracy who could always be counted upon to rush to the media with papers marked Top Secret and confidences entrusted to theoretically honorable men. On this occasion they did not have the opportunity: the only reason, he thought wryly, that it did not happen.

There had been air activity over Florida and some other evidence of preparation at other military areas, but these were taken to be simply routine precautions necessitated by the general condition of emergency. There was no anticipation that he would move as swiftly and forcefully to the offensive as he did. He caught everyone by surprise, not least, as he told Elinor when it was finally underway, himself—that he had actually been able to secure the cooperation and secrecy necessary to guarantee surprise.

Before the moment of commitment he went through a greater inner turmoil than he had ever experienced.

He was quite literally gambling with the future of mankind.

Yet he did not see how, under the circumstances, he could do other.

Although the clamor of rationalizing voices rose at once to even higher pitch in frantic attempts to excuse Soviet culpability and place upon him the major blame for "bringing the world closer to its final disaster than all the evil leaders in history conbined" (a bouquet from his old friend Anna Hastings in the Washington *Inquirer*, echoed with only slightly less hysterical venom by the *Times* and the *Post*), the cold-sober fact of it was that he was responding, in what he believed to be the only way he could respond effectively, to the direct challenge that was the sole and inescapable responsibility of the Soviet Union.

Of course, as he said to Elinor, there were other ways. There were scuttle-and-run ways. There were roll-over-and-play-dead ways. There were surrender-and-submit ways. But they were not ways open to an American President who wished to save his own country, and with her the chance for reasonable freedom to continue to exist and, with luck, even grow greater in the world.

Against this was ranged the implacable and never-resting determination of the Soviet Union to destroy democracy and freedom everywhere and particularly to destroy, as its chief success, shield and defender, the United States of America. Yuri Serapin, heir of the crafty old men who had deliberately brought history to its most fateful climacteric with their patient plottings over so many vicious and evil decades, had chosen his own "target areas" from which to launch the final drive. Some other Soviet leader coming to power at this moment might have chosen differently. But the basic fact was, and had always been, that *sooner or later they would have struck somewhere.* This had always been the Soviet intention, it had always been the Soviet plan, and never, despite all the hysterical defensive rationalizings of the West's naive and wishful Soviet-excusers, had it changed one single, slightest iota.

Once one was honest enough to face up to this fundamental fact of twentieth-century history, Hamilton Delbacher thought, all else fell logically and inescapably into place. But how many were that honest—and that brave? The chorus of denunciation and hatred that had descended upon him with his first decisions to come to the aid of Mexico, Saudi Arabia, South Africa and Taiwan, and was now rising to even shriller extremes, was clear enough proof that among those in influential position in America, there were not very many.

Those who were not part of the conspiracy of Soviet intention were part of the conspiracy of Western fear; and those who were not part of either belonged to the conspiracy of well-meaning, self-deluding fools.

Whichever they were, they all helped the Soviets. It was in the face of their united opposition that he must act now. If he did not seize the offensive, the Soviets would achieve their purpose by default. If he did the wrong thing, he would unleash events that could destroy the world.

On a hot and muggy September night at the end of the first week, he requested and received time from the networks to address his country and the world. The announcers' voices trembled with gravity when they informed his tensely watching, near-universal audience:

"Ladies and gentlemen, the President of the United States!"

And it was with a grave and somber expression that he looked into the cameras and prepared to seek the support of people everywhere who were reluctant and afraid to take up the burden of defending the freedom they would surely lose if they did not support him in his defense of it on their behalf.

"My countrymen," he said. "My fellow citizens of Earth wherever you see my face or hear my voice:

"A week ago, in direct violation of the United Nations charter and all established norms of peaceful behavior between nations, the present leader of the Soviet Union launched unprovoked attacks upon four innocent countries with which his government was not at war and which had no reason to suspect that they would be thus assaulted.

"It is immaterial that these attacks were launched by the present leader of the Soviet Union through satellites and stooges. The fact is that there is but one single individual responsible and that is the present leader of the Soviet Union. No amount of international subterfuge can hide this fact. The present leader of Soviet Union, and he alone, bears the heavy responsibility for plunging the world again into war—not one war but four wars, which may, if he does not immediately change his course, become one war: the one final war that all sane men and women dread.

"So far, despite the urgent protests and appeals not only of his victims thus viciously attacked, but of the United States and other peace-loving nations everywhere, the present leader of the Soviet Union has not seen fit to cease his aggressive actions and withdraw his satellites and stooges so that peace may be reestablished.

"Therefore he and he alone must bear the responsibility for the things that are now about to occur."

He paused to take a sip of water from a glass which he held with no visible trembling of the hand and added quietly, "Which are, in fact, at this very moment occurring."

Throughout the world tension rose sharply; and in the big room in the Kremlin where Yuri's map glowed and sparkled, the members of the Politburo and his military leaders, whom he had invited to listen with him, felt a visceral stirring. To them it was one of foreboding. For Yuri it was a stirring of something far deeper and more atavistically satisfying: the fearfully delightful excitement of one who senses the climactic struggle of his life at last being joined.

"What will he do, Comrade President?" the Foreign Minister inquired in a voice that, despite his best efforts, trembled a little.

"He will do nothing but bluff!" Yuri snapped. But though he

said it with all the strength and conviction in him, because he had to encourage the fools and cowards who surrounded him, he did not really believe it. Something more was coming from the gravely determined individual who looked, it seemed, directly at him. But even Yuri was not prepared for what Hamilton Delbacher said next. He had not believed that any American President, even this one, would have the guts.

"Having been denied the support of the United Nations," the President said quietly, "and having found our direct pleas rejected out of hand by the present leader of the Soviet Union [that hammering, deliberate, undermining word *present*, Yuri thought furiously], the United States is now forced to seek other means.

"We are, as you know, supporting with all possible power our allies and friends in Mexico, Saudi Arabia, South Africa and Taiwan. This aid will be maintained and increased in all ways open to us. But it is not enough. It does not reach the heart of the problem."

"Good!" exclaimed the elder brother in Jidda. "He is going to strike the heart!" And though it was not quite the heart, as the prince told his brothers an excited moment later, it was quite close enough to suit *him*.

"Therefore," the President said, and around the globe there was an almost audible in-drawing of breath as billions tensely watched. "I have this day, as Commander-in-Chief, ordered the following actions."

He paused and again took a sip of water, deliberately prolonging the moment and increasing the tension mightily.

"As of"—he glanced at his watch—"approximately ten minutes ago, a complete air and sea blockade of the island of Cuba had been established and is in effect."

"Launch the missiles!" Marshal Andreyev shouted above the fearful babble that broke out in the Kremlin. And many others shouted, "Yes, yes, Comrade President! Launch the missiles! Launch the missiles! Destroy America! Destroy America!"

"Any ship, any plane, any submarine, any missile," Hamilton Delbacher continued in the same quiet, almost conversational tone, "that attempts to enter—or to leave—the island of Cuba will be destroyed. No military supplies, no food supplies—nothing—will be allowed to enter or to leave. The blockade is total, and it will be maintained as long as necessary.''

In rage and desperation the men in the Kremlin turned to the Soviet President, who had first paled, then steadied. He would not dare, he kept saying over and over to himself, *he would not dare!* But he had, and for the moment, though Yuri managed to keep his face impassive aside from its sudden unavoidable lack of color, he did not know what to do. The only thing he knew was that he must not let them realize that he did not know. To this he bent all his massive determination and iron will as they turned again in shaken disbelief to the calm face on the screen. Simply by talking on, simply by using words, the President was upsetting all Yuri's calculations. For behind the words lay a fearful import: the President of the United States, as Yuri interpreted him, was actually prepared to destroy the world to stop the Soviets. His next words seemed to give further proof to a Yuri who could not, but evidently must, believe.

''I have said,'' Hamilton Delbacher went on, ''that the blockade will be maintained as long as necessary. How long that is depends upon the decision of the President of Cuba. Because''—and again he paused and looked squarely into the cameras—''this action is something which can be changed in an instant's time if he so desires.''

In Havana the President of Cuba shouted defiantly at the screen, ''We *will* change it in an instant's time!'' and all around him his raffish crew echoed his defiance. But Big Brother Russia was far away, and they had always been secretly aware, though they could never admit it even to one another in their most candid moments, that when Big Brother Russia's ''friends'' got into trouble it was: Good luck, it's been nice to know you.

''The ties that bind the United States and Cuba are many and strong,'' Hamilton Delbacher said, ''and it is only in recent decades that the Soviet Union has sought, with some success, to divide us. If it had not been for United States action in the war of 1898, there would have been no independent Cuba. If it had not been for United States friendship and protection over many years thereafter, Cuba would not have been able to exist as a free and sovereign nation. It is time now to reestablish our long traditional friendship with the Cuban people. I propose to do this by offering to the Cuban people—in return for renewed friendship and ties with the United States—a withdrawal of all their forces from overseas—and an end to Cuba's subservience to the Soviet Union and its tragically misguided participation in the Soviet Union's vicious schemes to dominate the world—the United States naval base at Guantánamo Bay, free and clear; together with a program of financial aid designed to restore the Cuban economy and the well-being of the Cuban people to the high standard they deserve and should have.''

"Insane!" the President of the Soviet Union exclaimed in Moscow. "Typical Yankee propaganda!" the President of Cuba cried in Havana. But from outside his heavily guarded palace there came a sudden distant shout, an ominous harbinger which his sudden shaken expression indicated he knew he would have to deal with somehow: the voice of the Cuban people, aroused from their long sleepwalking at last.

The offer of Guantánamo struck them like a thunderbolt. The huge installation, more than five hundred miles from Havana near the eastern end of the south coast of the island, had been in United States hands since the victorious conclusion of the Spanish-American War in 1898. In precommunist days it had not particularly rankled; but with the coming of the communists it had been transformed by propaganda into what it was for Cuba's leaders far more than for its people: a constant irritation and threat, a standing challenge that was incessantly used to arouse national pride and resentment. To have it thus voluntarily offered back was an event so astounding for the Cubans that their response was inevitable: a spontaneous, overwhelming demand that the offer, whatever the terms, be accepted. It could only pose, as the President had shrewdly calculated, the most enormous threat to the communist regime.

"If this offer is accepted and these conditions are met," Hamilton Delbacher resumed in the same grave, unhurried tone, "the Government of the United States is prepared to turn over Guantánamo with all possible speed, allowing for sufficient time to remove American personnel, their dependents and certain items of military equipment. My advisers tell me this can be done within one week.

"Much sooner than that—in fact, tomorrow morning—we are prepared to give to Cuba the sum of one hundred million dollars as the first installment of a regular program of aid and assistance that will continue as long as Cuba needs it.

"The President of Cuba," he said, and now it did seem that he was speaking directly to that equivocal individual, "knows very well the private channels through which our two governments have communicated on several necessary occasions in the past. Let satisfactory word come to me through those channels at any time of day or night and immediately Guantánamo will be Cuba's, the money will be Cuba's—and the blockade will be instantly ended."

He paused and took a sip of water. In the streets of Havana the shouts and celebrations began to grow to near-riot proportions. At 10 Downing Street the British Prime Minister spoke for multitudes when she kept shaking her head and saying over and over again, "How clever! How *clever!*"

"Let me turn now, once again," the President said in the same quiet tone—always in the same quiet tone—"to the Soviet Union and to those actions I have ordered this day which are the direct result of the irresponsible peace-destroying adventurism of its present leader."

Suddenly his expression turned stern and forbidding, a harsher note infused his voice.

"At this very moment," he said, "the Soviet embassy here in Washington is being secured by the armed forces of the United States and all of its records, premises and personnel are being taken into protective custody.

"At my request the Swiss Ambassador and his staff are present as witnesses for the world community to attest to the firm but humane treatment we are giving Soviet citizens, who unfortunately must pay in some measure for the misdeeds of the present leader of their unhappy land."

"Seize them!" Yuri ordered in a choked voice. "Take them *now!*" The Minister of Justice fled upon his retaliatory errand.

At the same moment from somewhere offscreen a hand was suddenly thrust into the picture, a piece of paper placed before the President: whether by design or intention was not clear, but mightily effective, whichever.

"Among the Soviet embassy records," Hamilton Delbacher said, his voice showing its first sign of open emotion, "I am advised that there has just been found an official communication to the Soviet Ambassador from the Soviet President. It refers in unmistakable language, and I quote, to 'the possibility, though remote, of vigorous response by the American Government to these coming attacks on its four allies'—and this is dated more than a week ago, *before the attacks even occurred!*"

He stopped dead for a moment and then said directly into the cameras in what was, for him, a rare moment of open personal anger, "And *this* is the liar who stands before the United Nations and the world and claims that he is innocent of all connection with the attacks on four innocent and unsuspecting nations! This is the liar whose lies are defended and accepted by some even in my own country! For shame, I say to him and to them! *For shame!*"

For a long moment he stared into the cameras with a deep and naked hostility, a personal aversion so strong as apparently to be uncontrollable. In the Kremlin, startling and disturbing all around him, the President of the Soviet Union burst into a string of obscenities so furiously violent as to be unintelligible, a series of sounds that approached animal gibberish, so swiftly and incoherently did they crowd one another from his lips.

The President of the United States squeezed his eyes and shook his head as if to clear them of some unbelievable, intolerable burden and tiredness, and returned to his text.

"I have also this day," he said, voice again unemotional and steady, "frozen all Soviet assets within reach of this Government, and have terminated all trade, of whatever kind, with the Soviet Union. I have requested all our NATO allies to do the same.

"I have also declared a state of national emergency to exist in the United States and its associated territories and dependencies, and I hereby place on full Number One war alert all United States armed forces wherever they may be on land, sea, in the air or in space. I am requesting all our NATO allies to do the same.

"And what great good *that* will do him!" Yuri Serapin cried with furious scorn. But the fawning laughter that responded contained an uneasy note that he could detect, and a sudden scowl formed on his face. This genuinely frightened many—though not all—of his colleagues.

"I turn now," Hamilton Delbacher said, "to the most vital element in ending this struggle which the present leader of the Soviet Union has precipitated.

"I call upon his own associates to repudiate and overthrow him before it is too late to save the world from the consequences of the open clash between our two countries which his wanton adventurism has precipitated.

"I give my assurance and that of the United States Government that you will receive all possible assistance in this endeavor, which is the only way to save the great Russian nation and the great Russian people from the consequences of his insane and fateful irresponsibility."

Again there burst from Yuri's lips the unintelligible obscenities; and this time as he glared about the room, none of his colleagues dared openly meet his or one another's eyes. But from marshal to marshal and admiral to admiral there passed the slightest, most fleeting, most furtive of glances, gone as quickly as it came.

Had the President been able to approach them directly at that moment, they would have united instantly and completely behind Yuri Serapin. But by offering them the option and promising aid in a speech from Washington, which they could join Yuri in denouncing while contemplating other things behind his back, the President had laid skillful foundation for much that might possibly occur later. This they knew, and this Yuri knew. A hush as of circling wolves fell on the room; and now no one at all in the Kremlin dared look at anyone else, save for their angry leader whose furious eyes challenged, without response other than a dutiful indignation, the stolid faces that looked back at him.

The President paused and took another sip of water before concluding.

"There are other measures which my advisers and I are contemplating which will presently become apparent if it is necessary to use them. All are designed to bring about a swift end to the intolerable world situation created by the irresponsible adventurism of the present leader of the Soviet Union."

He paused and again looked straight into the cameras.

"My countrymen, my fellow citizens of Earth: the steps I have outlined are not gentle measures. They are not easy or sure or safe. They carry with them great risks of violent retaliation. Yet they can be stopped in an instant if the present leader of the Soviet Union so desires, and if he will prove that desire by calling off his satellites and stooges and terminating the wars he has launched in four areas around the globe.

"The American Government stands ready on a moment's notice to cancel all the actions I have announced, saving only those relating to Guantánamo and aid to Cuba, which stand a firm and irrevocable pledge by me and my government. We will sit down with responsible leaders of the Soviet Union at the negotiating table at the earliest moment it is physically possible to get there. But we will not do so with four wars raging, each one started by lackeys of the present leader of the Soviet Union, each one planned, inaugurated and directed by him.

"He must cease his lies and duplicities. He must cease his endless attacks upon the peace of the world and upon free nations everywhere. He must prove himself to be a man of peace worthy to hold the position of power he does hold. If he wants peace, he can have it. If he wishes to go down in history as the peace-loving man he claims to be, he can do so. All he needs to do is restore the peace he has broken, negotiate the differences between us and join in leading the world to a new era of trust and mutual survival.

"Otherwise, the consequences, already very grave, can rapidly become even graver. And most of all, for him.

"The American Government and its allies await with close attention his response. We are ready to negotiate and cooperate. We are not ready to let him carry out some mad dream of world conquest by riding roughshod over all who do not agree with his ideas and his methods.

"He is as near as my telephone. Let him call me and give proof that he has ended his unprovoked aggressions around the world, and instantly American countermeasures will cease.

"I am waiting.

"The world is waiting.

"It is up to him.''

With a last steady and unwavering look his face faded slowly from the screen and a hush descended on the world.

But not, of course, for more than half a minute. Presidential speech was succeeded, as always, by instant analysis from the networks. Yet somehow this time the words were not so confident, the pontifications not so arrogant, the know-it-all airs not so sure. Too much was at stake: everyone everywhere had the feeling that disaster might come at any moment. To pontificate in the shadow of the knowledge that at any second you may be blown up along with the rest of the world makes it a little difficult to concentrate; and this was the unhappy position of the network correspondents.

Nobody knew the final part of the puzzle. Hamilton Delbacher had furnished the first part. Yuri Serapin possessed the second. What appeared to be the very real possibility of instant, overwhelming, world-destroying retaliation was so omnipresent that many millions could only sit in a sort of cataleptic trance in front of their television sets, not really hearing the nervous analyses, the uneasy attempts to tell them what they ought to think and convince them what the President had *really* said. His seizure of the offensive was too sudden and too overwhelming, almost, to grasp.

The answer lay with Yuri Serapin. It took several stunned hours in the Kremlin before its outlines began to emerge.

BOOK THREE

1

For perhaps five minutes after the President of the United States ceased speaking there was no sound of any kind from the President of the Soviet Union. He simply sat, surrounded by his colleagues who hardly dared breathe and certainly did not dare speak, and contemplated his flashing map of the world. His face, at first pale, then suffused with anger, then pale again, finally stabilized at grim impassivity: he was not going to reveal any more of the shattering turmoil which that fool of an American had succeeded in inducing by his wild, insane, imperialist adventurism. Yuri Serapin, "the present"—and, he told himself with fierce determination, the future—leader of the Soviet Union must appear to be calm.

And was, at great cost.

Somewhere in the back of his mind, even when Hamilton Delbacher had proved himself a stubborn and unimpressed opponent in their first great global confrontation a month ago, he had never quite believed that the President would, in the last analysis, do more than bluff. The bluff had been good enough to shake his certainty of his own invincibility from time to time, but it had never made him doubt its ultimate wisdom or the ultimate triumph of himself and the enormous military machine he controlled. America was dying. He had felt it to be so ever since his posting to Washington as a young KGB "diplomat" almost two decades ago, and nothing that had occurred since had really disturbed this conviction.

Every move the crepitating "giant" of the West had made in recent administrations, even those which seemed to show a reviving strength, he had convinced himself to be only the last spastic quiverings of an already irrevocably decaying corpse. It had made a few spasmodic gestures that could be taken still to indicate life, but in Yuri's mind they were simply the final automatic reactions of a no longer sentient nervous system. Every time the gestures threatened to cohere into some form that might pose a threat to the Soviet conquest, the "giant's" own media or Congress would promptly tie the hands of its President so that he could do nothing really effective. Yuri had seen this happen to them all, from the futilely floundering J. Carter to the more determined but still restricted R. Reagan; and he saw no reason to reverse his fundamental judgment that H. Delbacher was the same. Soviet strength abroad and the self-imposed destructive weakness of too many powerful forces at home made it impossible, in the collective judgment of Yuri and his colleagues, for any American President to really reverse for more than a moment, as history goes, the inexorable, inevitable triumph of the Soviet Empire. And it was as history goes that Yuri thought. Not for him the desire for ten-minute quick fixes of the world's fate that characterized the impatient, careless Americans. He was thinking in years, decades, many decades if need be: though now Hamilton Delbacher, with his mad military adventures, appeared to be forcing a solution much sooner than that.

Yuri's first instinct when the President announced the blockade of Cuba and his grotesque, insane, stick-and-carrot offer of Guantánamo was to strike the heart and eliminate the problem. But he, no more than his colleagues, was really prepared to take an action so awful and so final. He did not want America destroyed any more than he wanted the rest of the world destroyed, and no more did his fellow communists. They simply wanted America captive and intact, as they wanted the rest of the world captive and intact: to be the granary and industrial underpinning for the world communist state—the worker bees, so the queens and drones could live in luxury such as history had never seen—slaves of the new and final empire that would last forever, to the glory and material contentment of its masters.

There was no altruistic feeling, no human emotion, no care for humanity in Moscow's attitude about this, any more than there had been in any of its pretended campaigns for the "betterment of mankind," "the creation of the perfect socialist state," "the establishment of universal justice for all peoples." If there had ever been those among the leadership who had been so naive and idealistic—and from what he had read of the early days of the revolution, there actually had been a few—they had been eliminated years ago, casualties of the ruthless drive toward world domination. Few empires in history had tolerated their idealists for very long. Perhaps the British and the earlier Romans had come closest, and their records were far from perfect. The communist empire had long ago abandoned any pretense of idealism within the private confines of its power-hungry, comfort-grasping elite, though it managed to this day to persuade the idealistically naive of many other lands that this was still the major motivation. In the Kremlin and throughout their vast, suffering land, the Soviets and the Russian peoples they ruled knew better.

So there were powerful factors—the love of power and the prod of greed—that made it unlikely that Yuri and his colleagues would "launch the missiles" except in the gravest of extremities. But that still left the embarrassing and most annoying problem of how to stop Delbacher from his insane adventures before he succeeded in creating fissures in the Soviet empire which might, if allowed to run long without healing, create very grave problems for the supreme leader himself.

The President's address and his actions had been cleverly designed to do exactly that. Yuri wondered savagely for a moment who had written his speech for him, but knowing his antagonist from his own Washington days and the closest study and analysis of him since, he suspected Ham Delbacher had come up with all those bright ideas himself. Certainly he had been the one who had to make the decisions. And he, Yuri was sure, had produced the concept of the hammering, disruptive, subversive repetitions of "the present leader of the Soviet Union," and the the direct appeal to Yuri's subordinates for his overthrow. (Yuri was sure, with his wry knowledge of America, that many "advisers" around the President, particularly in the State Department, were absolutely horrified by his crude and ungentlemanly attempts to undermine the Soviet President.)

That the President's strategy had done him damage, Yuri was quite aware, though he would never admit it to anyone save perhaps Ekaterina Vasarionova when he visited her later that night. He and Hamilton Delbacher had been thinking along exactly the same lines with regard to his subordinates in the Kremlin, particularly in the military; and it had been a heavier blow than Yuri liked to concede, even to himself, to have the possibility of internal upheaval raised before the entire world. It had been intended to encourage the one thing he feared, and he knew it had succeeded in its purpose despite all the hypocritical, fawning faces that surrounded him now and appeared to wait in near-paralysis for his responses. He did not see how the President could possibly make good on his offer of assistance to subversive elements within the Kremlin and the military, but he did not doubt for a moment that the appeal had fallen on fertile ground. If it could be done, Hamilton Delbacher would manage it. If, Yuri thought, remembering a card that still remained to be played, Hamilton Delbacher himself survived for very long.

This problem, Yuri decided, he would have to meet with the obvious measures that could be taken immediately: an even tighter security around his own person, the sudden shakeup in the Politburo and the military high command that he had been contemplating, the assumption of direct control of the KGB and a strike in the night that would throw additional terror into any who might be contemplating his overthrow or any treasonous attempt to contact the Americans. Like all Soviet leaders, he lacked any base of popular support in the country, because the people had never mattered except as cannon fodder in time of war and as obedient slaves for whoever was in power in time of peace. So he must survive as he always had—by his wits, his daring and his own shrewd assessment of where to strike hard and strike first.

The seizure of the Soviet embassy and the suspension of Soviet trade were relatively simple matters, he felt. Retaliation in kind would suffice there, at least for the time being; though by now, being better forewarned than his own people in Washington, the American embassy would be busily burning and destroying, and the relatively small number of vital secrets still unknown to the Soviet government, which were not many, would escape capture. But there were other ways to use the American embassy. Yuri promised himself grimly that H. Delbacher would live to regret his insolent stunt of seizing the Soviet embassy.

As for trade, that was a gesture that would not hurt very much, or if it did, its effects would be submerged in the general nationalistic excitement he could whip up among the masses. This would suffice for the time being.

NATO, and such feeble aid as it might be able to give the United States, was equally simple. The solution to that lay easily at hand. He dismissed NATO and came to the one issue that could not be evaded or easily solved—the issue whose expansion into crisis had always been implicit between the two governments ever since Nikita Khrushchev had decided to make it a test of J. Kennedy.

Cuba at last was inescapable and had to be solved. And there, perhaps, he might need, if only temporarily, the ideas, such as they might be, of the grim-faced, ponderous figures who stood uncertainly around the room waiting for him to speak.

"Comrades," he said, "what do you think of the ridiculous address of H. Delbacher?"

"Absurd!" cried the Minister of Foreign Affairs.

"Criminal!" cried the Minister of Defense.

"An open provocation to war!" said Marshal Andreyev.

"Which will be opposed by the gallant armed forces of the Motherland," said Marshal Shelikov.

"And faced with absolute determination," promised Marshal Krelenko.

"No matter where it exists, on land or sea," assured Admiral Valenko.

"And which can only disrupt the peace of the world and make it possible to find reasonable solutions to the problems that beset mankind," elaborated the Minister of Foreign Affairs.

"That is the line I shall take when I make my own address," Yuri said, and there were immediate cries of approbation at this indication that he would carry the battle directly to the hated enemy. "Some of you," he went on, "seemed anxious a few moments ago to launch immediate war as a response to these criminal actions of the American President. I do not think this would be wise, no matter how tempting it is and how satisfying it might be. There are other ways.''

"Tell us, Comrade President," the Minister of Defense urged eagerly. But Yuri shook his head with a grim little smile.

"I need your advice," he said with a candid honesty he did not, of course, feel in the slightest. He turned to the Foreign Minister. "What do *you* think I should say and do, Georgi Leonevitch?"

As he expected, all his civilian associates took the same line— "the harshest and most immediate reprisals"—which, when he pressed them to be specific, really did seem to boil down to the awful simplicity of an immediate all-out nuclear attack.

The military were much more cautious. He could not resist taunting them with it.

"I do not agree with you, comrades," he said to the members of the Politburo, many of whom looked alarmed and crestfallen at his words. "But on the other hand," he said, and they brightened noticeably with relief, "I like your enthusiasm and your desire to take the most drastic steps to protect the Motherland and the Revolution. I am less pleased," he said thoughtfully, looking at the military leaders one by one, "with the responses of our comrades in the armed forces. There seems rather less enthusiasm there for the strong and positive action which, whatever its form, is the desirable reaction to the mad adventurism of H. Delbacher. Perhaps you would care to explain your reluctance to us, comrades?"

For a moment none replied, simply staring back at him—not with fear, he noted with an uneasiness he did not allow to show, but rather with a somber thoughtfulness more disturbing than open opposition would have been.

They were too clever for that.

"It is not that we are not wholeheartedly in support of the general idea of reacting strongly to this insolent impudence of the American President," Marshal Andreyev said slowly. "Nor that we disagree with your own glorious objectives, Yuri Pavlovich—"

"I am glad of that, comrade," Yuri said. "I was beginning to wonder."

"But," the marshal continued, ignoring this with an insolence, Yuri felt, as great, and as disturbing, as Hamilton Delbacher's, "we are responsible for the practical implementation of anything you may wish to do. For all the strength of the Motherland, which is very great, we still do not feel we are in a position to guarantee unqualified success if we should take the action urged by our colleagues. Have you thought of the terrible consequences for the Soviet Union, comrades, in any such exchange? Because it would be an exchange, you know. Do not think the Americans would not strike back. And it would be a very heavy blow."

"But our civil defense program, Comrade General," the Minister of Foreign Affairs protested, "our underground factories, our concealed bases, our worldwide deployment of forces—"

"All very fine," Admiral Valenko said sharply, "but the Americans too have worldwide forces, and while they have stupidly neglected civil defense and made little if any preparation for underground production, nonetheless they do have heavy striking forces within easy range of us. We will all do our best, of course, and if we decide to do this we will not announce it. It will of course be a surprise attack, as we have always planned—aided, we trust, by *your* pretense of diplomacy, Comrade Minister—"

"We will naturally do all we can to mislead and confuse the Americans," the Minister of Foreign Affairs said stiffly. "That has always been our purpose, and we have never failed the Motherland yet."

"See that you do not!" Admiral Valenko shot back, and for a moment it seemed that there would be an unseemly shouting match, such as often developed behind Kremlin walls, if the discussion went further. Yuri intervened firmly.

"Comrades," he said tartly, "do not forget who the enemy is. We are all devoted to the same purpose of destroying America and extending the benefits of socialist enlightenment throughout the world. It will do us little good to fight amongst ourselves. Or," he added with a glance at the Foreign Minister that made him gulp, "to launch strikes without absolute certainty of success."

"Did you have assurance of absolute success when you arranged the attacks in the areas that have aroused American response, Comrade President?" the Minister of Justice inquired, not sounding as impressed by Yuri as Yuri would have liked. He decided he must obviously take over the KGB himself at once. There perhaps was no time to be lost at all.

"I did not assume," he said sharply, "that H. Delbacher would be the fool he has turned out to be. Within all norms of rational capitalist behavior, he should have refrained from embroiling the United States directly in faraway quarrels. I assumed he would have more sense. That was my only miscalculation, and I think you will agree, comrades, that given the erratic and unpredictable nature of this individual, it was an eventuality no sane man could foresee."

He looked around the room, face suddenly stern, until, one by one, all eyes slid away from his demanding gaze and the silence was no longer broken by dissent.

"Now," he said, "there must be an hour or two of profound consideration of the most satisfactory measures to be taken. The American embassy is obvious—"

"It is already taken, Comrade President," the Minister of Justice said.

"Good," he said. "Equally obvious is the trade question, and even more obvious is NATO."

"They will go down like ninepins," Marshal Krelenko said scornfully.

"We will choke them a bit first," Yuri said with a sudden grim little smile. "It should not take anything very drastic to bring them to heel in short order. As for Cuba—" He frowned and paused.

"Yes, Comrade President?" Marshal Andreyev inquired softly, and again Yuri noted the muted but palpable disrespect in the way he said it.

"Cuba, too, is obvious," he said sharply. They looked startled, for it was not obvious to them; but he stared them down and for the moment the inescapable issue was avoided.

"And the other mysterious measures H. Delbacher says he may take?" Admiral Valenko inquired finally.

"First of all," Yuri said with continuing sharpness, "we must see if he takes them. I think they are words, nothing more. What else is left for him to attempt, in addition to his already futile gestures? I can think of nothing. I am assuming, of course"—and suddenly he seemed to forget the rest of the room and concentrate the entire force of his powerful personality upon the four officers before him—"that his appeal to my colleagues is futile. I am assuming that you will support me, comrades, and that no one will be so foolish and mistaken as to attempt counterrevolutionary measures which could only result in the complete elimination of anyone so stupid."

Again there was silence as he looked from face to face. It was broken finally by Marshal Shelikov, who said with a sudden vigor, "Long live Yuri Pavlovich, our far-seeing, perfect and all-knowing leader!"

"Long live Yuri Pavlovich!" echoed his fellow marshals and Admiral Valenko, and "Long live Yuri Pavlovich! Long live Comrade President, to whom we owe all things!" the others cried.

It took long moments before the fervent tumult died; and everyone assessed it for exactly what it was. But for the time being it profited them all to maintain the pretense, and so presently Yuri nodded and said smoothly,

"Thank you, comrades, for your undying loyalty and support, which strengthen me mightily in the great task of defeating America entirely, which I know will be achieved swiftly and completely with your brave aid. On to victory with the Motherland! Down with America! Long live the communist revolution!"

"Long live the glorious communist revolution!" they all cried excitedly, even the military men; and again someone yelled and they all took it up and shouted it fervently in the room whose occupant could never rest, "Long live Yuri Pavlovich, our great supreme leader!"

"And now," he said, tone flat and dismissive, "if you will notify the state radio, Comrade Minister, I will be pleased to deliver my reply to the American adventurer at six P.M. tomorrow. Please arrange everything for worldwide broadcast, and please, all of you, continue to advise me of your thoughts and suggestions in the next few hours. I need all your assistance in my speech if it is to place H. Delbacher properly where he belongs, which is at the head of the list of history's most dangerous and conscienceless criminals—perhaps *the* most dangerous and conscienceless of all time."

But of course he paid no further attention to their suggestions when later they dutifully telephoned and offered the products of minds obviously inferior to his. Sometimes laboriously, sometimes rapidly, he wrote out his speech in longhand as he always wrote all his speeches and indeed all else he did—by himself.

By himself: he could rely upon only one hand, one mind, one heart.

They had never failed him, and he was confident they would not do so now.

Only once during his lengthy speech-writing did he permit interruption, and that only because this was the one call he must take if H. Delbacher's subversive plans were not to start that perhaps unstoppable unraveling of the Soviet Empire that he so viciously and unjustifiably intended.

The satellite transmission was excellent, the words came clear and distinct. For this communication, too, he turned on the Picturephone. The bearded face, which even in normal times was oddly morose, stared impassively at him from Havana. But Yuri could sense that the mood was not impassive. The President of Cuba was a frightened man. Yuri could smell the fear across the seas.

"Comrade!" he said cordially in an attempt to wipe it out, for this was a time for iron will and courage, not for fear. "How are you and H. Delbacher getting along with your little games?"

"They are not games here, comrade," the President of Cuba said gloomily in the English he knew perfectly well but always pretended he did not. It was the only way he and Yuri could communicate without translators. "Here they are real."

"Why did you let them listen?" Yuri demanded sharply. "No one outside the leadership listened here."

"Who would have thought—?" the Cuban President inquired with a sad shrug. "We thought it would do no harm to let them hear one more playing of the same old record. It would have been easy to mock."

"Except that it was not the same old record," Yuri said grimly.

"And it is not easy to mock," the Cuban President observed. "For you, possibly. Not for me."

"Comrade!" Yuri said sternly, for somehow he must fire up this eternal heavy problem he had on his hands and get the man to show a little of his own unrelenting resolve. "You must not let the futile, ridiculous gestures of the ridiculous adventurer in Washington disturb you. You must remember the great triumphs of Cuban arms in Angola, Namibia, Nicaragua, El Salvador, Guatemala, Ethiopia—all the places where you have been of such inestimable help to the great socialist worldwide revolution. You must remember Mexico *right now*. You must remember that in you we have the key to the inevitable final destruction of American hegemony in the entire Western hemisphere. Without you, comrade, that glorious result cannot be. Think of the still greater glories that lie ahead in Mexico, eventually Brazil and all the rest. Think of yourself as we do—as the future leader of all the Americas! It is a glorious future, comrade!''

· ''Which I will not live to see,'' the President of Cuba said morosely, ''while this fool is subverting my people with promises of Guantánamo and money.''

''Promises he cannot possibly keep!'' Yuri said stoutly. ''His military will not permit the loss of such a base. American pride—such as remains of it—will be equally adamant. And where will he find this hundred million he promises so glibly? It will take an action of Congress, and Congress does not trust you, comrade! That is the saving irony of it. They would not trust you even if you took the bribe!''

''It is not the trust of Congress I must worry about now,'' his Cuban errand boy said glumly. ''It is the trust of my people.''

Yuri snorted.

''Why is their trust necessary to you, comrade? Why must you trust *them*? You have failed to absorb our lessons if you think you must have the trust of the *people*. What do they possibly have to say about it?''

But there, he immediately realized, he had gone too far. Cynical, ruthless and (in Western eyes, he supposed) worthless as his Cuban surrogate might be, still the pompous, self-important little man did cling to some lingering shred of something that perhaps might be called idealism—some last, almost-vanished thought that what he had done to Cuba had been done for the benefit of its people. A fleeting expression of shocked distaste came into his eyes for just a second, gone but not too soon for Yuri to catch it. He had been too frank, Yuri sensed at once. He spoke rapidly, with an amiable shrug.

"But of course, comrade, I know your relationship with your people is more personal than mine. You are always talking to them. It is a smaller country, and I must confess, comrade, though it is with some shame I say it, you are perhaps more sensitive to their feelings than I am. It is a worthy trait and I admire you for it. I only wish I could feel the same sense of responsibility toward 'the people' that you do. But the people here are a horse we ride. We feed them on the glories of Mother Russia and they forgive us all our sins. I envy you your feeling for your fellow citizens. It becomes you."

"It will be the death of me," the President of Cuba said dourly, "if you do not at once defeat that madman in Washington. You must immediately take action, Comrade President. He cannot be allowed to strangle my country. The consequences would be too terrible for you and for us. You must help us! At once! Because," he added, an ominous tone coming into his voice, "I may not be able to hold out alone for very long. This time I think he may have been too clever for us."

"Surely not," Yuri said sternly. "You give him too much credit, comrade."

"And you are too far away," the Cuban President responded, a rising combativeness in his voice. "My people want Guantánamo back. They want the money. They want an end to the blockade. He promises them all three. It is not an easy offer to laugh off, comrade."

"We are not laughing!" Yuri said angrily. "The blockade has not begun to hurt you yet. And we will end it!"

"How, comrade?" his errand boy, suddenly no longer so faithful and reliable, inquired heavily. "By bombing New York? Do you dare?"

"No!" Yuri snapped. "Not by bombing New York!"

"How then?" the Cuban President demanded, an insistence close to insolence in his voice. Thus, the Soviet President reflected bitterly, do small pensioners become dangerous antagonists. There would soon be changes in Cuba, though this proud, bedraggled peacock did not know it yet: and not of the kind he feared from his neighbor to the north.

"We shall meet them, comrade," Yuri said, voice firm and commanding. "We shall thwart their imperialist hegemonistic schemes, wherever they appear."

"How?" the Cuban President insisted. "It is vital that I know how and when, Comrade President, because my people are doing his work for him right now. Surely you must know they are in the streets! Listen!"

And he gestured offscreen—a window was apparently opened—a muted, distant roar came over. He gestured again, the window was closed, the roar died out.

"Now, comrade," he said, "how do I answer that?"

"Make a speech," Yuri suggested dryly. "You are very good at it, comrade. And meantime, *keep them down.*"

"Oh, I am," the President of Cuba said. "The armed forces are in the streets also, the barricades are everywhere. Surely your embassy has already told you this. But still they march and protest."

"Have they openly defied authority yet?"

"There have been no clashes," the Cuban President said. "But that does not mean—"

"Provoke some," Yuri interrupted. "Shoot them down. Kill a few. There are times when all the people understand is the whip. Give it to them, comrade! It is no time to be timorous."

"I am not timorous," the President of Cuba said sharply. "Neither do I wish to kill my people unnecessarily."

"I wish I were in your chair for twenty-four hours," Yuri said savagely. "There would be no more of this."

"Perhaps it is as well you are not," the Cuban President remarked in a tone Yuri had never heard before. "So what must I tell them, comrade? That their great ally in Moscow has abandoned them? That there will be no help from the Soviet Union? That it was all an empty mockery, what we have done for you for the past two decades? Is that the message I should take to the streets?"

For a moment a black anger against Hamilton Delbacher filled Yuri's heart and mind to the point where he could not think, where for a few seconds the world actually seemed to turn darker, confused, swirling, all uncertain, all unknown. It was almost as though he had suffered a seizure, he thought with a dreadful, unsettling, inward shudder as he came out of it. He could tell the Cuban President had noticed, for his expression was startled and, for a fleeting second, ominously calculating.

"No!" Yuri snapped. "That is not what you must tell them! You must tell them that the Soviet Union, now and forever, is their truest ally! You must tell them that the Soviet Union completely condemns and opposes the unprovoked imperialist hegemonist acts of the criminal in the White House, and that the Soviet Union will do all in its power to defeat that criminal and come to the assistance of its brave and loyal friends, the Cuban people!"

"How and when, comrade!" the Cuban President inquired again, and his tone was not at all supplicating or subservient now. "How and when? That is the question I must answer, right *now*, right *here*, in Havana. Not some empty promise of 'condemnation' and 'opposition,' comrade, but *how and when?*"

"Wait for my speech, comrade!" Yuri ordered. "Wait for my speech and do not be so frightened of American bluffs. Wait for my speech!"

"Speeches are easy, comrade," the Cuban President said with a dryness he would never have dared, Yuri thought, six hours ago, "when the bluff is thousands of miles away. For us it is ninety."

"And you have our missiles in place on your island as they have been for many years," Yuri said scornfully. "How could we *not* defend you, comrade? Do you think we will throw away our careful investment of so many years?"

"The weapons are not in our hands, comrade," his erstwhile slavey pointed out in the same dry tone, "nor have they ever been. If they were, we would have delivered our answer to the fool in Washington while you were still writing your speech."

"That would have solved nothing," Yuri said, "except to start the end of the world. Thank God you do not have control of the missiles, comrade, if that is how you think."

"You have better thoughts?" the President of Cuba inquired with an almost lazy contempt, (*How dare he?* Yuri asked himself; and the only satisfactory answer was that soon this irreverent pipsqueak would not be around to do anything.) "Tell me, comrade, so that I can tell my people."

"You will tell your people nothing," Yuri said flatly, "until I have spoken. Then if you wish to tell them anything, you may do so—if you think I have failed to cover the subject adequately. But I think you will find that I have provided quite a satisfactory answer to H. Delbacher and his insanity."

The Cuban President gave him a long stare from his sad, hound-dog eyes. The faintest gleam of a cold little smile crossed his face.

"I hope so, comrade. I hope so."

"I shall be speaking tomorrow," Yuri said, brushing aside the uneasiness he knew the smile was intended to provoke, "I think the world everywhere will be listening. Talk to me after that, comrade, if you are not satisfied. In the meantime, do not hesitate to shoot, comrade. It is the only language the people understand."

"I will tell them to await your speech, comrade," the President of Cuba said, "since I must say something immediately. And to have faith in our great Soviet ally. . . . Whether that will be a substitute for Guantánamo, American aid and an end to the blockade remains to be seen."

"Trust me," Yuri said grimly. "I did not begin this without knowing how to finish it." *And to finish all who are so foolish as to impede me*, he added to himself.

"I would appreciate it, comrade," the Cuban President said with a mild courtesy that sounded mocking and, Yuri was sure, was intended to be, "if you could let me know prior to launch if you intend to use the missiles."

"Is that not our agreement?" Yuri inquired sharply.

"Ah, yes," the President of Cuba conceded, "but I just wanted to remind you."

"I do not need reminders of anything, comrade!" Yuri snapped. "I remember all things necessary!"

"Good-bye for now, comrade," the Cuban President said blandly. "I thank you for permitting my call to come through."

"Never hesitate, comrade," Yuri assured him. "I do not forget the loyal friends of the Soviet Union."

"I pray not, comrade," the Cuban President said with a sudden laugh that sounded quite genuine. "I pray not!"

And his visage, not quite so morose, faded from Yuri's screen as Yuri's faded from his.

Within five minutes Yuri had ordered a scrambled message sent to his ambassador in Havana, two code words to put into effect a contingency plan made years ago.

Simultaneously the Cuban president ordered his double to take his place at his desk and was on his way, hidden in what appeared to be a battered garbage van, held always ready for such purposes, to a nondescript house in Havana's old quarter. From there in a couple of minutes he was trying to break through an excited, babbling old voice to insist that yes, it was indeed he, and please to stop talking and listen.

In the Soviet embassy the tapes began to turn and the ambassador eavesdropped with a grim smile as his most reliable squad of killers, disguised as brightly clad, camera-toting tourists, left their own nondescript house in Havana to go and mingle with the shouting crowds outside the heavily guarded presidential residence.

2

For the first couple of hours after he had completed his address, the President of the United States sat in the Oval Office and wondered if the world would blow up.

He did not really think so, but in the absence of some concrete sign from his opponent, he was, for a while, far from certain.

With him were his wife, the Secretaries of State and Defense, Vice-President Art Hampton, Senate Majority Leader Jim Elrod, Jim's son-in-law Mark Coffin and the Speaker of the House.

Their conversation, at first desultory and nervous, became a little less so as the minutes passed and it began to appear that the world would not suffer any such devastating fate, at least for the time being. But inexorably, on land, at sea, in the air, in space, on all the continents and oceans, American actions proceeded on the lines set forth by Hamilton Delbacher.

The potential for violent reaction, though they believed it diminishing, remained.

At the Pentagon the Joint Chiefs of Staff transmitted their orders. Around the world American forces were at battle stations. Converging on Cuba from all directions were units of the fleet. Regular air patrols already crisscrossed the island and adjacent areas. At the Soviet embassy in Glover Park grim-faced soldiers stood guard while CIA, FBI and military intelligence officers opened files and safes, searched desks, disconnected the elaborate mass of electronic communications on the roof and elsewhere in the coldly forbidding compound. In the fortress-enclaves of housing which the Soviets maintained for their rigidly controlled citizens in the midst of casual Washington, more soldiers supervised the frantic packing that was going forward preparatory to the removal of staff members to hastily organized quarters at Fort McNair on the spit of land south of the Capitol that juts out to divide the Potomac and Anacostia rivers. The Swiss Ambassador and his top assistants stood by as promised.

In Moscow certain officers very high in the military began the subtle process of playing upon the deep misgivings of their superiors regarding the gambler's instincts, gambler's tactics—and possible gambler's fate—of Yuri Pavlovich.

It was not until it was announced from the Kremlin, almost two hours after the conclusion of Ham's speech, that the Soviet President would reply within twenty-four hours, that in White House and Pentagon they began—a little—to relax. He could still react in many violent ways, but every moment that passed without it made it increasingly unlikely that he contemplated the sort of massive strikes the possibility of which had for so long haunted the minds of many in the West.

"He's still talking," Chauncey Baron said. "It is, as they say, better than shooting."

"We haven't heard what he has to say yet," the President noted. "I'm sure it won't be pleasant."

"He's already lost some psychological advantage by delaying," Elinor remarked. "I wonder why?"

"Lost some, gained some," her husband suggested. "On one hand he may look hesitant and uncertain, on the other he builds up enormous anticipation and tension. In a sense it may also be a curious kind of reverse pride. He's going to show me and the world that he's not to be rushed—he's going to take his time—he won't be panicked. The other side of the coin is that he's allowing ample time for all our native critics to start howling against me, which can only help his purposes. In any event, intelligence reports so far don't indicate any unusual movement anywhere. They do indicate," he added with grim satisfaction, "a lot of uproar in Cuba. Which is all to the good."

"Very 'destabilizing,' to use the Soviets' pet word," Mark observed dryly. "How dare you 'destabilize,' Mr. President? It's only legitimate when the Soviets do it."

"Nervy of me, I'll admit," Ham Delbacher said, "but apparently quite effective. I think Yuri's stooge down there has his hands full. To say nothing of Yuri himself."

"So may you, with Congress," Art Hampton said, and the Speaker nodded agreement. "I anticipate a rather lively session on both sides of the Capitol tomorrow."

"With a sizable portion of the media howlin', as you put it, Mr. President, offstage," Jim Elrod agreed.

"Can you damp it down?" the President inquired.

"We'll try," Senator Elrod said.

"And we'll succeed," the Speaker commented. "But I'm afraid the debate won't be exactly helpful."

"Why don't you just adjourn the session?" the President inquired. "Make a motion as soon as you convene, carry it by voice vote, and get out of there. There's hardly anybody on the floor in the first ten minutes or so."

"Pretty strong-arm tactics," the Speaker said doubtfully. "I'm afraid it would leave a lot of bad feeling—"

"Bill," the President said in a tired tone, "we aren't playing games in the world today, you know: this is really it. Or it could be. I'd rather have a few Congressmen and Senators mad at me, which they are already, than risk another divisive debate just before Serapin speaks. I'd appreciate it," he added, tone hardening, "if you could do this for me."

The Speaker nodded, though not happily.

"I'll try."

"Gentlemen of the Senate?"

"I'll make the motion," Jim Elrod said.

"I'll second it," Mark said.

"And I'll pass it," the Vice-President said with a smile. "Faster than you can say James Monroe Madison."

"Good," the President said. "That will remove one headache, anyway."

"But of course," Elinor said, "it will give the media even more to howl about."

"As with a lot of other things right now," her husband said grimly, "I'm afraid that can't be helped."

A buzzer sounded, he ascertained who it was for, listened for a second, handed it to Chauncey Baron. The Secretary of State said, "Yes?" sharply; listened intently, face growing increasingly somber; handed it back to the President to hang up; turned to them with a sigh.

"They've taken the embassy in Moscow," he said, "which we of course expected. Still—it's a blow."

"We're treating their people with scrupulous care," Roger Hackett said. "We hope they will do the same."

The President sighed also.

"No way of knowing. Is there any indication of observers like the Swiss?"

"In the last message received—the only message received," Chauncey Baron said, "our charge d'affaires notes that there are some. He believes them to be Cuban."

"Ham—!" Elinor exclaimed. The President sighed again but shook his head.

"I considered all that," he said, almost impatiently. "I considered it and did—what I had to do. I would give my arm not to have had to do it, but—I did. I can only pray that no harm comes to them and that they will understand and, somehow, forgive me. But whether they do or not"—he paused and looked far away, eyes somber and deeply unhappy—"it cannot be helped. He has created a situation in which I had no choice."

"What a job," Jim Elrod said softly. "What a job."

"Yes," Hamilton Delbacher said, with a distant ghost of his old humor. "Does anybody want it? It's yours for the asking."

When they had left, the Secretaries returning to their departments, the members of Congress returning to the Hill now that the announcement of Yuri's speech appeared to have removed some of the immediate pressure, he took Elinor's hand on a sudden impulse and led her over to the window looking out upon the brightly lit Rose Garden. They stood there for several minutes, silent, motionless, absorbed in thought. Finally she spoke.

"I think it will work out all right," she said firmly. "It must.

God isn't going to allow evil like that to triumph in the world. You have to believe that.''

"I believe it," he said, "but at the moment it's more faith than certainty. God may side with the man who has the biggest arsenal.''

"That didn't stop you a month ago," she said, turning to look at him earnestly.

"It hasn't stopped me now," he pointed out with a smile.

"I suppose that's what it comes down to when all's said and done," she said thoughtfully. "A matter of will.''

"I have that," he said, and sighed. "But at a fearful price.''

She examined him with the careful scrutiny of more than three decades of marriage.

"You aren't showing it yet," she decided.

"In spite of having the world collapse around me?" he asked wryly. "Well: it may come. I'm not quite Harry Truman, who could drop the bomb and sleep well at night.''

"You have done what you had to do, exactly as you said. There is simply *no point* in brooding about it now. You need all your energies for what lies ahead.''

"But I'm not 'brooding,' " he protested, though mildly. "I can't help thinking about our embassy people—and all the kids of our own around the world who stand ready—and all the other kids—and all the people everywhere who may not live to know another day if I'm miscalculating my opponent—and the things that are going on right this minute in the various war zones—and my responsibilities to the United States of America—and to the whole world—''

"I think you're discharging all your responsibilities to everybody very well," she said stoutly. "I don't know anyone who could handle things any better.''

"There are dozens," he said dryly. "The *Times*—the *Post*—Anna Hastings—CBS, NBC, ABC—National Public Radio—dozens of *concerned* and *committed* movie stars—dozens and *dozens* of concerned and committed professors—the World Council of Churches—even an enlightened rock star or two, I suspect. My poor efforts pale beside what all of them could do—as they will all be telling us very shortly, now. I figure they'll all be in full cry by the morning news programs—in fact, if you were to turn on the set right this minute, I have an idea you'd find them already starting. Meanwhile"—and he leaned down and kissed her lightly on the nose—"I have to get back to my desk and find out how things are going on the battlefronts."

"Don't worry," she said, giving him a sudden fierce hug. "*Don't worry*. It will be *all right*."

"I know it will," he said ruefully, "somewhere on the other side of this. It's only the getting there that has me concerned. But I daresay I'll manage. After all, I don't really have any choice."

After she too had left, extracting a promise that if possible he would come to bed soon, he sat at his desk for a few rare moments of silence. For perhaps fifteen minutes the phone did not ring. He was allowed the unusual privilege, for a President, of having a little time to himself—a strange little oasis, particularly at a time such as this . . . just long enough to review the hectic events of the week—just time enough to reassure himself once more that all was being done that at this moment could be done. The lull ended: his secretary was on the intercom.

Cheerful and determined, the voice of the elder brother came from Jidda.

"Mr. President!"

"You got there, obviously."

"Oh, yes. A few tense moments when we were buzzed by a couple of South Yemeni, but we shot them down and proceeded on our way, Allah being willing."

"Good," he said. "And how do things look now?"

"Difficult but not impossible. We are holding them. Your planes have arrived—some—and we are holding them. We will need more help, however. Much more!"

"Yes." he said, rather dryly, "I am sure you will. So will everybody."

"Will we get it?" the prince inquired.

"Whatever we can do, you know will be done."

"Yes. We trust you. Our congratulations, too, dear Mr. President, on Cuba. It is magnificent! *Magnificent!*"

"I hope it will be effective."

"It cannot be otherwise. You have them in a beautiful trap. It must be really annoying for the dog in Moscow."

"More than just annoying, I hope," he said with some grimness. "Absolutely crippling, I hope."

"Yes, it may solve your problems in the Caribbean once and for all. Many of us were never able to understand why the situation was permitted to exist as it did for so long."

"It isn't over yet," he pointed out, "so it may be a little early to engage in celebrations. But it's a beginning."

"A magnificent one," the prince repeated. "Magnificent! You are sending more planes to us, then?"

"Yes," he said, permitting some amusement to enter his voice. "As soon as we can."

"And as many?"

"And as many. You are positive you are holding them?"

"Positive!"

"Good," he said. "Keep me advised constantly."

"Yes, Mr. President," the elder brother promised fervently. "We would not dream otherwise."

Two calls were waiting, as he expected they might be; the third had not yet come in, though he was confident it would follow shortly.

"Mr. President," he said cordially when the voice of his colleague in Mexico City, sounding tired and tense, came through. "Things are better?"

"A little," the President of Mexico said. "We have shot down several enemy planes over the city and the fighting in the south seems to have slowed a little. We have reason to believe that Cuban assistance has been suddenly diminished—thanks, we believe, to your own demarche in that area. A brilliant move, Mr. President, though much too long delayed. Still, whatever the circumstances, it is good for them to have Guantánamo back."

"Yes," he said dryly. "Thank you for that somewhat qualified endorsement, Mr. President. Let us hope it eases the pressure still further on you as the days go by."

"You are sending us more help?" the President of Mexico inquired anxiously.

"Yes," he said, again dryly, "we are sending you more help.

We expect to begin around-the-clock bombing runs over their forces in the south in about an hour. How are the airfields in Mexico City?''

''They have refrained from bombing them, since they apparently have some dream of using them themselves. Do you wish to use them?''

''Eventually. For the time being we will be flying off-carrier. It seems important that we offer a show of strength in the capital as well as in the south.''

''Very important,'' the Mexican President said, more fervently than he was perhaps aware. ''It must be made apparent to everyone that you are supporting the national government. Otherwise there will be chaos.''

''It should be very clear by now that we *are* supporting the national government,'' Ham Delbacher said, ''*and* the President of the Republic.''

''Thank you,'' the President said with such obvious relief that this time Ham almost, but not quite, let some wry amusement show. ''Your additional actions will begin very soon then?''

''Within the hour, Mr. President.''

''That is good,'' the President of Mexico said. ''Because''—he paused and the crump of bombs could be clearly heard—''they appear to be starting another series of attacks here.''

''May your planes shoot them all down,'' Ham said. The President of Mexico permitted himself a small, rather wan chuckle.

''We will do our best, but *your* additional planes will be of great assistance.''

''Momentarily, Mr. President,'' Hamilton Delbacher said. ''As promised. . . .''

''Mr. President!'' the Prime Minister of South Africa boomed. ''Here we have the johnnies by the short hairs, you might say—though,'' he added hastily, ''we await the arrival of your planes with the greatest of interest—the *greatest* of interest, don't get me wrong, Mr. President! We can use everything you are sending and more, Mr. President! More!''

''That seems to be the universal thought,'' Ham Delbacher said.

''How are they doing elsewhere, Mr. President?'' the Prime

Minister inquired. "Mexico? Saudi? Taiwan? Truly, I mean, not just media reports."

"The media reports so far have been fairly accurate, I think. The Saudis claim to be doing well, the Mexicans perhaps less well but holding. I haven't heard from Taiwan in the last couple of days but I'm expecting something soon. And you, you say, have them by the short hairs."

"In a manner of speaking, yes. That is to say, we have known kills of forty-seven of their aircraft to fifteen of ours—three heavy raids on Luanda, Angola, and we have inflicted heavy damage from the air on their troop movements south through Botswana and Namibia. Bloody buggers don't know how to fight, that's the trouble with them. Makes it all the better for us, though. Not complaining, Mr. President, not complaining!"

"That's good," he said. "I'm glad someone isn't. Any new raids on Jo'burg and the Cape?"

"A couple on each tonight," the Prime Minister said. "Bad show in Jo'burg, several big office buildings hit, couple of theaters, casualties maybe two–three hundred. Lots of people go to the movies here. A bit of damage to the Parliament Building in Cape Town, but fortunately not much. Knocked old Victoria off her pedestal, poor thing, she's on her head in the garden but some don't mind that anyway. Otherwise, we're doing pretty well. Just don't forget to send us more, though."

"That, I won't forget," Ham Delbacher said. "You'll be interested to know we'll be in position to hit Luanda again ourselves in about another three hours. Fortunately we have the carrier *Weston* in the vicinity. This should relieve you considerably to operate farther south."

"Many thanks," the Prime Minister said. "That will be super. Just give our johnnies a hoot, though, so they'll know you're coming in. Wouldn't want to shoot down any Yanks, now, would we?"

"I rather hope not," the President said. "It might cause a few sticky moments."

"God forbid," the Prime Minister said. "All in all, Mr. President, I'd say morale is very good here, all things considered. We've always known we might be hit someday, and all it's done is to draw us closer together. Bloody fools might have known it would do that. Even our Bantu are volunteering by the thousands. They don't want any of these outside coons coming in and taking their country. Odd thing. It's because they know us, I suppose, and whatever our faults—and you know me, Mr. President, I've fought my own Afrikaner people to admit we have a few—at least our Bantu, coloreds and Indians *know* us. Better the devil you know, I guess. Not that I'm admitting for a minute that we *are* devils, you understand. But that's the principle, I guess. . . . So you'll be sending us more planes over Angola in a short while. How about supplies and ammunition?''

"You aren't telling me you don't have those!" Ham Delbacher exclaimed. "After all the years you've been expecting this and stockpiling for it? Come on, Prime Minister! Supplying South Africa is something I'm not going to worry about for quite a good while yet."

"Got me!" the Prime Minister admitted cheerfully. "Saw right through me! Thought I might give it a try, though. Nothing ventured, nothing gained. No harm in that, is there?"

"Not as long as I didn't fall for it," the President said. "Keep me advised on how things are going. Call me anytime, day or night."

"You can be sure of that," the Prime Minister said. "Cheerio!"

"Cheerio to you, too," Ham Delbacher said. "Give 'em hell."

"Nothing else but, Mr. President," the Prime Minister said with relish. "Nothing else but."

There still was no incoming call from Taiwan, which puzzled the President; and after a moment he decided to take the initiative and ask the chief White House operator to put him through if at all possible. When she did a thought that had crossed his mind fleetingly in the past twenty-four hours proved out: not to his surprise and not, in its final implications, to his regret.

"Mr. President!" he said when the President of Taiwan came on line. "I haven't heard from you. But I assume that is because you have been busy."

"I am deeply honored, Mr. President," the President of Taiwan said. "We have indeed been busy."

"I gather things are relatively quiet there at the moment," Ham

Delbacher said. "Both press reports and our own intelligence sources indicate something of a lull."

"We are mostly exchanging propaganda again," the President of Taiwan said with a small, uneasy laugh. "Fortunately this does not produce fatalities."

"Actually," Hamilton Delbacher said, "you really haven't exchanged anything but propaganda for the past few days, have you? It's all pretty much died down since the mutual bombings of Taipei, Kaohsiung and Amoy, has it not?"

"I think the presence of your fleet in the Taiwan Strait has had a soothing effect," the President of Taiwan said. "It has been very helpful, and we thank you for it."

"You sound very much more relaxed, Mr. President, than you did in our first—our only—conversation," Ham Delbacher observed, taking a long shot, and, not to his surprise, hitting the target. "Is there something you know that I don't know? Is your war over and your most reliable ally not informed of it?"

There was a silence on the other end for several seconds. Then the President of Taiwan spoke with great carefulness.

"There are—developments," he said, "which concern—which concern—China. We have not deemed—it has not been deemed—advisable at this stage to inform anyone of them, even you, our staunchest and oldest ally, as you truthfully point out. I am sorry, Mr. President, but things are of such delicacy that—that I cannot tell you—very much."

"I see," Ham Delbacher said crisply. "Then I should give orders to withdraw the fleet immediately, since you are evidently entirely able to handle the situation yourselves. I can certainly use the power elsewhere."

"No, Mr. President!" the President of Taiwan said hastily. "Oh, no! It is not—that—simple."

"Tell me," the President said in a tone that brooked no denial, "how simple it is, Mr. President. I want to understand it *and I have the right*. Now, tell me!"

"Mr. President," the President of Taiwan said, sounding strained, unhappy and stubborn, "you should not speak to me, the sovereign head of—"

"Very well!" Hamilton Delbacher snapped. "Please terminate

this conversation, Mr. President, as I am giving orders at once to withdraw the fleet and suspend all emergency assistance to Taiwan.''

"No!" the President of Taiwan cried again sharply. *"No!"*

"Why not?" Hamilton Delbacher demanded. *"Why not?"*

"Because," the President of Taiwan said, and each word seemed dragged out of him, though the President of the United States could not imagine why, for it was not as though he were confessing some horrible crime, though he appeared to think so. "Because there are—discussions.''

"Between you and Peking."

"Yes. Between us and Peking. And," the President of Taiwan said, his voice growing stronger, *"productive* discussions, Mr. President. For the first time ever, *productive* discussions. You see why they must remain confidential.''

"You think I am about to call the Associated Press?" Ham Delbacher inquired dryly. "Tell me more, Mr. President. I take it there is more than the usual promise that you will be allowed to keep your own foreign policy and defense arrangements if you rejoin the mainland.''

"Oh, *yes,*" the President of Taiwan said. *"Much* more.''

"Such as?''

"I really cannot tell you, Mr. President," the President of Taiwan said with a sudden recapturing of dignity. "Surely you understand that at this present juncture I cannot. I simply cannot.''

"Yes, I can understand that. But I would appreciate it if, when you reach an agreement—if you do—you will let me know what it is. Since the United States," he added dryly, "is bound to be somewhat involved.''

"Oh, a great deal, Mr. President!" the President of Taiwan agreed quickly. "A very great deal. In fact, you will be brought into it directly if—if all goes well. So you need not worry on that score.''

"And in the meantime, what am I to do with the fleet? You say don't withdraw it, yet you imply it is no longer necessary. I don't understand you, Mr. President.''

"It is no longer necessary in a military sense—perhaps," the President of Taiwan said cautiously. "It is certainly necessary in a

diplomatic sense. We should be most devastated if you were to
withdraw it now. It would upset everything at this juncture."

"It would not upset Peking, I take it," the President said.
"They would be delighted to have it out of there."

"That is exactly why you must not leave, Mr. President," the
President of Taiwan said. "You let *us* decide the timing on that. It
is only when we are very, very sure—*very* sure—that we will ask
you to withdraw. And that may be some days or weeks—or even
months—in the future."

"Yet you seem optimistic it will come."

"I *am* optimistic," the President of Taiwan said. "I am more
optimistic, and so are my colleagues, than we have ever been.
Thanks, in part, exactly to your fleet. If you had not sent it so
promptly we might never have begun to talk to one another seriously."

"And if they had not actually bombed you," Ham suggested.

"And if we had not bombed Amoy," the President of Taiwan
replied, not without satisfaction. "It has worked both ways, Mr.
President. At last, after all these years of dispute, the use of force
has worked both ways. And the presence of America has required
us both, perhaps, to consider many things and to realize, finally,
that force is not going to bring a solution for either of us."

"I hope you are correct, Mr. President," Hamilton Delbacher
said, and he was entirely sincere. "I hope with all my heart that
you are correct, for both your sakes. Nothing would please us
more, I think, than to have China genuinely reunited on a peaceful,
friendly basis—and by that," he added, "I mean not only peaceful
and friendly toward each other, but peaceful and friendly toward *us*
as well. We would not be able to contemplate with equanimity the
reunification of China on a basis of aggression toward us—or anyone else in Asia, for that matter."

"But in Asiatic Russia, Mr. President?" the President of Taiwan suggested softly. "That might be another matter?"

"You are leaping far ahead, Mr. President," Ham Delbacher
told him dryly. "Far, far ahead. You get your reunification settled
successfully first and then we'll see what happens. By that time Soviet Russia may no longer be a threat."

"May no longer be in existence," the President of Taiwan suggested.

"Perhaps," Ham Delbacher said. "But that is the kind of hope on which policies cannot be based. We have to proceed with what we have, which is not pleasant at the moment for us or anybody."

"I think you have begun the end with Cuba," the President of Taiwan remarked. "It is a master stroke. It will all unravel from there."

"We do not know yet how he will handle it," the President said. "Until we do it's idle to speculate or gloat. Let's say I've given him something to think about. . . . But all that, fortunately for you, is far away from Taiwan and the mainland."

"Except as stability here will assist you in meeting matters elsewhere," the President of Taiwan said. "It should be of great advantage to you, what we are doing here. That is why I suggest—I implore you—to be patient and, in the meantime, to leave your fleet exactly where it is. We are very much afraid the momentum would stop if its beneficent presence were removed."

"And what if the mainland attempts to attack it?"

"It has been there almost a week, Mr. President," the President of Taiwan pointed out. "Without harm and without incident. Nor will there be any. Peking is not so foolish. Also, Peking is finding advantages in compromise with us. Under the bluster there is reality, Mr. President. After all, we are all Chinese."

"Yes," the President agreed with a laugh, "that you are, and I suspect the rest of us had just better, as you said, be patient and let you work it out between you."

"At last," the President of Taiwan said gently, "someone in America is beginning to make sense. If you will forgive me, Mr. President."

"Oh, yes," Hamilton Delbacher said, "I'll forgive you. But do keep me advised, Mr. President. Let me know as you get nearer agreement."

"And meanwhile the fleet stays?"

"Meanwhile the fleet stays."

"Good," the President of Taiwan said with unconcealed relief and satisfaction.

"You're welcome," Ham Delbacher said dryly, "though I really don't see that I have much choice in the matter."

The call from Peking came within fifteen minutes after the President of Taiwan had hung up. Communications between the two, the President thought wryly, were indeed improving.

For this conversation he decided to use the Picturephone.

As frail yet persistent as the mists over a Yangtze gorge, the Vice-Premier materialized out of the ether to give him a misty and ethereal smile.

"Ah, Mr. President!" he said with a gentle sigh that was apparently meant to indicate relief. "How fortunate that your distinguished person is at your desk. I was afraid you might be occupied elsewhere, busy with your wars."

"They are not *my* wars, Vice-Premier," the President said sharply. "One of them is ours and the rest belong to Yuri Serapin."

"I am glad you draw the distinction," Ju Xing-dao remarked with the ghost of a chuckle. "I am glad you see our separateness."

"I see it better," the President said, "now that I have talked to President Li Yuan."

"Ah, yes, Li Yuan," Ju Xing-dao said with what appeared to be genuine admiration. "A most intelligent and capable young man. He is only forty-three, you know. We have had many interesting discussions."

"He has just told you of the one he has had with me."

"This modern age!" Ju said admiringly. "Is it not amazing how we communicate with one another? When I was a boy it took all day to walk from village to village if we wished to talk with someone. Now it is almost instantaneous. Too much for an old man. Too much!"

"I doubt if anything is too much for Ju Xing-dao. What did you think of my conversation with Li Yuan?"

"I did not approve of all aspects," Ju said thoughtfully. "But"—he gave a sudden charming smile—"youth is headstrong and impetuous and does not always foresee the consequences."

"And what might they be, Vice-Premier?" the President inquired dryly. "You will sink the fleet if we don't remove it, perhaps?"

"We do not regard its continued presence in a kindly light," Ju Xing-dao said, quite severely.

"And your official news service will say so later today, very loudly and sternly," Ham Delbacher predicted. "And *then* you will sink it."

"Oh, Mr. President!" Ju said with another soft little chuckle. "How quickly you jump to conclusions you know will never occur!"

"I just wanted to have the assurance from your own lips, Vice-Premier. Otherwise I should indeed tremble at the words coming from Peking."

"Now you jest with me," Ju said with a mock sigh. "That pernicious Western habit that confuses my colleagues so! Fortunately *I* understand it."

"Good," Hamilton Delbacher said. "I think we understand each other. On all counts."

"You really could not be persuaded to remove the fleet, then?" Ju inquired tentatively. "It would save *so* much bad feeling."

"Which you people turn on and off like a spigot," the President observed. "No, I cannot be persuaded. *That* I have left in the hands of Li Yuan."

"You are still hostage to Taiwan," Ju said sadly. "Never, *never* American independence in the Taiwan Straits! It is very sad."

"Not half as sad as the consequences of withdrawing the fleet," Ham Delbacher said crisply.

"What consequences?" Ju demanded in a voice suddenly strong and vigorous. "We are all Chinese!"

The President nodded.

"Yes, so I have been told, not half an hour ago. I believe it, I believe it. And if our presence there helps you resolve your differences, then friend Yuri may have wrought better than he knows."

"He will know it soon enough," Ju Xing-dao said with sudden spite. "And he will not like it. But what can he do?"

"Exactly. What can he do? Out of his deliberate intention to trap us, some good may yet come for China—all China. Providing, of course, the words from Peking are not too severe."

"They will be carefully spoken," Ju assured him. "The last blast of winter must not be allowed to shrivel the growing crocus."

"Oh, come now," the President said, and in spite of himself Ju could not quite control an answering amusement. "I refuse to swap aphorisms with you at this time, colorful though they may be. A great and most significant breakthrough is being made in China, I feel, and we should greet it with suitably solemn responses."

"I am solemn," Ju protested, suddenly appearing so.

"Providing it is genuine, of course," the President added, "and not just an attempt to trap Taiwan. In which case things could become solemn indeed."

"I think you can rely upon my young colleague in Taipei, and his colleagues," Ju said with some irony. "They are being very, very cautious. They will not let us fool them, Mr. President, you can be sure of that. Even if we wanted to, which we do not."

"I'm sure," the President said dryly. "However, I too have faith in the suspicions of Taiwan. They are the best guarantee of a fair and lasting solution, I believe. . . . Thus do events, once set in motion, assume command. If one had the time one could become very philosophical about the way in which the evil intentions of an evil man suddenly produced good and entirely unexpected results far from what he had in mind. Something may save the world yet, Vice-Premier, as long as there is always the possibility of the unexpected."

"The possibility exists in China," Ju observed. "We have created it."

"Li Yuan seems to think *we* have," Ham Delbacher remarked. "But no matter. It has been done."

"Let us say we have all done it together," the Vice-Premier suggested. "Then there is enough credit for everyone."

"A surprising concession, but welcome. Very welcome. How soon may we expect an official announcement of the new situation?"

"After the denunciation of your interference," Ju said with a sudden gleaming little smile. "The record must be kept straight."

"We shall ignore you," the President promised amicably. "Our record must be kept straight also."

"Everyone to his own record," Ju agreed with a twinkle. "And damnation," he added with a sudden sharp distaste, "to Yuri Pavlovich and all his schemes."

"As one who helped him launch them—" the President began and then thought better of it. "Ah, well. The result is what matters. If it contributes to his downfall, we mustn't complain."

"It is much to be desired," Ju observed. "*Much* to be desired."

"I am planning for it," the President said. "I am dreaming of it. I am praying for it. I am doing everything I can, starting with Cuba, to promote it. If you can do anything to help, do it. If you have any ideas to assist, please let me know. They will be mightily welcome."

"Cuba is a master stroke," Ju Xing-dao said thoughtfully. "We will see, with Cuba. It may be the turning point."

"I intended it to give him some trouble," Hamilton Delbacher said grimly. "It is."

"Enough, let us hope," Ju Xing-dao said, "to consign him to hell."

"Vice-Premier!" the President said with mock protest. "And you the chief signatory of the Sino-Soviet Cooperation Treaty, too!"

"There is cooperation," Ju remarked with another sudden twinkle, "and there is cooperation. I can honestly say"—the twinkle deepened—"that we value the treaty as much as he does. After all, look what it has brought us: possible reconciliation with Taiwan! As you say, how unexpected! What a pleasant surprise!"

"We have a saying, you know, about the cup and the lip," the President said. "Also about the proof of the pudding. We await the formal announcement from Peking and Taiwan. We will have to see subsequently how much *that* treaty means."

"With your fleet in the way," the Vice-Premier said with gentle wryness, "it will have to mean something. And as long as you befriend Taiwan, it will have to mean something. However, if your patience and your interest flag, then—" he shrugged, still amicably. "But I am an old man, and you soon will be. You probably will not live to see that day. Certainly I am sure I shall not. It will rest with other minds and other hearts, what happens then. But at least we will have pointed the way."

"Assuming the world survives."

"How American!" Ju Xing-dao said with a smile. "Of course it will survive. Think in centuries, Mr. President! We do."

"I wish I could," the President said ruefully. "It absolves one of so much: worry—and struggle—and guilt—and blame—and having to take responsibility for one's actions. All of which can be comfortably sloughed off to some hazy future and passed on, as you say, for someone else to contend with. We aren't trained to think in quite that fashion, in the West."

"Unfortunate for you."

"Perhaps . . . I can consider one of 'my' wars over, then?"

"For the time being," Ju Xing-dao said with a tiny chuckle. "Perhaps for my time and yours. Perhaps forever." He shrugged, still smiling. "Who can say?"

"I wouldn't try," the President said. "But thank you anyway. It will perhaps permit attention to be given elsewhere."

"Where it is needed," Ju agreed.

"Thank you for your call, Vice-Premier. It was thoughtful of you."

Ju chuckled.

"Young Li Yuan virtually demanded it, Mr. President. I had little choice, under the new agreement." He uttered a mock-rueful little laugh. "And still you will not remove your fleet!"

"Perhaps in my time and yours," the President said. "Perhaps never. Who can say? Good-bye, Vice-Premier. No doubt we will talk again."

"No doubt," Ju agreed with a ghostly little laugh. "There is always something."

And that, Ham Delbacher thought with a sigh of genuine relief as the wispy little visage faded from the screen, perhaps really did signal the end of one of "his" wars. Whether one could trust Peking at this point he did not really know: but he knew he could trust the self-preserving instincts of Taiwan, which would be ever alert to the first hint of deception or betrayal. He could not quite imagine how they had worked it out, and perhaps would never know all the secret details. But it sufficed for the purposes of the moment, and perhaps far beyond, to have it settled. Now, gradually, the "fleet"—that small task force he had rushed from Subic Bay in the Philippines to show the American presence and warn off Peking from anything too drastic—could be reduced to the point where it was simply a token and a symbol, valid for as long as there existed in Washington the patience and the interest, as Ju had said, to make it valid. Which he hoped would be—had better be—a long time.

He decided he would base it at Kaohsiung as soon as the port was reopened, which he assumed was one of the first items in the agreement. It might well have to share the harbor with units of the PRC: but, then, so would the Taiwanese. The American presence would be a barrier and a guarantee.

Thus had Yuri indeed wrought better than he knew in the Far East. In other areas Yuri had wrought, as the President expected and soon perceived, just about as effectively as Yuri had thought he would. This became clear in the hours preceding his speech.

"It is impossible to condone," the *Times* said, "the reasoning that underlies the President's address with its astounding combination of Cuban blockade and Guantánamo bluff, and its alarmingly inflammatory invitation to revolution in the Soviet Union.

"On neither gamble, we expect, can he make good. With the first he only increases already great resentments against the United States on the part of the Cuban government. With the second he attempts to intervene in the most shameless way in the internal affairs of a sovereign government.

"Surely history has shown time and time again that this is not how to make successful policy and achieve lasting diplomatic objectives. Ridding ourselves of the burden of Guantánamo may admittedly be a wise thing to do, but not in the context in which the President offers it. It should be a gift freely conferred upon Cuba by America as a long step toward those better relations with the island republic which all responsible Americans desire; but it can never work when it is part of a stick-and-carrot deal that includes the supreme danger of the blockade.

"Apparently, for the moment at least, the blockade has not brought the devastating and cataclysmic response that might have been expected from the Soviet Union whose cherished ally Cuba is. But this is likely due more to the statesmanly forebearance of Soviet President Yuri Serapin than it is to anything President Delbacher has done.

"In fact, what President Delbacher has done is provoke in the Caribbean the gravest and most dangerous challenge to the Soviet Union since the Cuban missile crisis of 1962. And he has compounded it by his extraordinary open attempt to subvert and overthrow Mr. Serapin. This ill-advised—indeed highly dangerous—proposal would at once remove from the world the stabilizing factor of a strong and steady Soviet Government. It would, if successful, greatly increase the dangers to peace and greatly destabilize the conditions under which peace can be achieved.

"Difficult as it has been to deal with on many occasions, the Soviet Government nonetheless is a known factor in world affairs. There is a great deal to be said for dealing with a system we know. In the minds of many who do not really think things through, it might be a glorious event to witness the collapse of the Soviet system. Yet in the long-range interests of a stable world and a viable peace, that system plays a recognized and indispensable part. We must not yield to the attractive but fearfully dangerous idea that if we could just topple the communists in Moscow, the world's problems would automatically vanish.

"We suspect that the overthrow of the Soviet Government would create far more problems than it would solve. Therefore we would devoutly hope that President Delbacher's crude and highly dangerous attempt to sabotage Yuri Serapin will not succeed. Mr. Serapin is a vital cog in the wheel of world peace. . . ."

"This is 'your enemy as necessity,' " Elinor remarked. "We're already past 1984, and in their minds, apparently, the world of Big Brother and the indispensable 'endless world conflict' is here."

"So it seems they would have us believe," he said. "And listen to the *Post*. They're even more alarmed by my audacity in daring to challenge Yuri the World Stabilizer."

And he read in a sarcastic tone:

" 'It is possible to dismiss the President's offer to return the Guantánamo base to Cuba as a simpleminded and totally worthless bluff. It is not so easy to dismiss his blockade of Cuba, which carries enormous dangers for world peace. But both pale to insignificance alongside the most dangerous and shortsighted of all his follies—his attempt to stir up a palace revolution in Moscow and overthrow the supreme Soviet leader, Yuri Serapin.

" 'We do not believe that the overthrow of Mr. Serapin, which the President so openly and blatantly invites, could be anything but a most devastating blow to world stability and peace.

" 'Responsible civilized nations in this day and age simply do not go around attempting to overthrow the leaders of other countries. Particularly do they not do so when the leader in this instance heads a government which, for all its faults, provides one of the few solid and predictable factors in an otherwise topsyturvy world.

" 'Even assuming there could be such an overthrow—and nothing on the public record indicates the kind of dissatisfaction with Mr. Serapin's leadership that such an upheaval would require—its end result could only be a vast and unmanageable destabilization of world peace. The Soviet Union is not perfect, God knows. But by the same token, it is reasonably predictable and its word, while shrewdly bargained, is usually kept, once it is finally pledged. We can in no way condone the President's blatant, barefaced, unjustified and inexcusable attempt to intervene in the affairs of a friendly—or, at least, reasonably compatible—government. It violates all the norms of civilized behavior between sovereign states. It is perhaps the most hostile of all the hostile actions he has taken against the Soviet Union in recent days—and the one likeliest to provoke the violent reaction from Mr. Serapin that could send the world headlong into its final, inescapable disaster.' "

And such, in general, ran the chorus from many influential elements of press and television. According to them Guantánamo was a stunt, the blockade a dangerous folly, but the really ghastly thing was the open attempt to remove the man most responsible for the threat to peace. In these broadsides, Yuri's responsibility was minimized, and the most awful thing the President had done was his proposal that Yuri be immediately and forcibly removed from the fulcrum of events. The suggestion "violated the norms," as the Soviets themselves would say, and quite horrified many of the most vocal elements in America. A flood of anonymous "high officials," mostly from the State Department, encouraged the outcry with carefully leaked expressions of dismay.

The proposal similarly horrified, or so they professed, many other influential organs of public opinion around the world, and not only that but governments and peoples as well. The KGB was able as always to turn out thousands of demonstrators from Managua to Lafayette Square to Stockholm to Amsterdam. Quite an impressive string of presidents and prime ministers, led by the prime ministers of India, Sweden and Canada and reaching geographically from Ho Chi Minh City to Buenos Aires, denounced the President's "unprincipled and highly dangerous attempt to seek the overthrow by force of the leader of a necessary, stabilizing world power."

Meanwhile things moved forward in Cuba, with Moscow not far behind.

3

At first the President had trouble recognizing the excited old voice that babbled in his ear from New York, even though he had been notified of the caller and accepted the call. Fabrizio Gulak, head of Gulak Equipment Company, which produced and sold truck (easily converted to tank) bodies to the Soviet Union, had for forty years been the Soviet's pet American millionaire. The President fully expected that Fabbie (a nickname its owner hated but whose recognition value he had long since accepted) had called to protest, as vigorously as all the rest, the President's "crude and highly dangerous" call for the overthrow of Yuri Serapin.

Fabbie could always be counted upon to support, and usually bankroll, every protest, demonstration, full-page ad in the New York *Times* or other outraged expression denouncing America and upholding the Soviet Union.

Third-generation son of a Polish father and an Italian mother, he had carried friendship with the Soviet Union to highly satisfying heights, at least as far as he was concerned. He maintained an apartment in Moscow, near the Kremlin, where he entertained the leaders of a ruthlessly oppressed nation in the capitalist luxury they secretly enjoyed. And it was in his other apartment in River House, in New York City—and at his anxious urgings—that Yuri and the President had met scarcely a month ago in their disastrous secret conference, which had ended with the President's denunciation of

244

Yuri as "Evil—evil—*evil*" and Yuri's final raging riposte: "You are determined to destroy yourselves. We shall be delighted to help. It is inevitable. History has always told us so. Now—now we know it is going to happen!"

Since that furious day Ham Delbacher had not heard from Fabbie, who normally was on the phone or writing a letter every time the United States showed the slightest sign of firmness toward the Soviet Union. He had concluded that his exchange with Yuri had been too much for the old man, revealing as it did the naked hostility between the two systems that underlay the increasingly thin pretenses of diplomacy; but now, he supposed, his unmannerly action in trying to foment the overthrow of Fabbie's friend had proved too much. He prepared himself for a string of indignant denunciations.

Fabbie, much to his surprise, was concerned about something else. For once, the President soon realized, it involved something that might conceivably be of help to Fabbie's own country.

"Mr. President!" he exclaimed. "Mr. President, I can hardly begin to tell you—I wonder if you will believe—it seems so extraordinary—I could hardly believe my ears—"

"Slow down, Fabbie," he urged. "Slow down. I'm right here and I'll wait until you compose yourself. What's happened? Have you called to tell me how awful I'm being to your friend Yuri?"

"That too," Fabbie said, tone momentarily growing frostier, "but it can wait. First I must tell you about the absolutely astounding—absolutely unbelievable!—telephone call I received a while ago. I couldn't believe it, so I asked the caller to call back later. Now he has. It is quite authentic, believe me. You seem to have done it, Mr. President! I never thought you would, but it seems you may really have done it!"

"Fabbie," the President said, "I must say you have my interest. What is it I have done?"

"You have started something in Cuba," Fabrizio Gulak said solemnly. "You have done it!"

"Yes, so you've told me," Ham Delbacher said, but in spite of his wry tone he could not escape a rising excitement. "Don't tell me your caller was—"

"The same," Fabbie said with even greater solemnity. "The President of Cuba *himself!*"

"Well," Ham said. "That *is* a development. Radio Havana has been deluging me with denunciations ever since my speech. The President wanted you to deliver more of the same?"

"Oh, no," Fabbie Gulak said, wonder in his voice. "On the contrary. He wanted me to tell you that he is prepared to negotiate on the basis of what you said."

"Everything I said?" the President demanded sharply. "Guantánamo? U.S. aid? Withdrawing troops from overseas? Breaking all ties to the Soviets?"

"And the end of the blockade," Fabbie reminded. "Don't forget that."

"It's hardly begun," the President pointed out in a deliberately skeptical tone. "You mean he's caving in already?"

"He isn't 'caving in,' " Fabbie said sharply. "He is voluntarily offering to negotiate on the basis of what he considers best for his people."

"So he told *you*."

"So he told me. And I believe him, Mr. President. He was *sincere*."

"Hmph!" Ham Delbacher said. "I wonder how you know."

"I have talked to him before," Fabrizio Gulak said with dignity. "Many times. I know when these people are being honest about things."

"Good," the President couldn't resist dryly. "Then you actually know of a few occasions when they have been."

"I can recognize it," Fabbie said. "Some of them are my personal friends. Including this one. He has been in my home in Moscow. He has been my guest here. What purpose would there be in his saying these things if he was not honest?"

"I don't know at the moment," Ham Delbacher said, "but give me a minute or two and I can probably think of a dozen devious reasons."

"He took great risks to call me," Fabrizio Gulak pointed out stiffly. "I don't think he would have done that if he wasn't being sincere."

"Unless his masters put him up to it and he is part of some tricky game they're playing."

"That is *exactly* why I knew this conversation would be difficult,'' Fabbie said sternly. ''I knew how suspicious and unreasonable you would be. This man has taken great risks to communicate with you, Mr. President. He deserves more than your mockery and scorn.''

''Fabbie,'' the President said, reflecting that the old man's turn of phrase sometimes sounded positively Victorian, ''I am afraid mockery and scorn are what have been earned and deserved by the actions of the other side.''

'' 'The other side'!'' Fabrizio Gulak echoed bitterly. ''That is so typical of you, 'the other side'! How can we ever have peace in the world if you persist in dividing us into two camps this way?''

''*I* persist!'' Hamilton Delbacher said angrily. ''*I* persist? You really are off the deep end, Fabbie, and I don't mean maybe. I am not the one who has divided this world into two camps, nor is it any of my predecessors. It is 'the other side' because they have deliberately made it the other side. And I am not arguing that with you, because it is true.''

''So you say,'' Fabrizio Gulak said in a smugly superior tone. ''I hear it differently in Moscow.''

''I'm sure you do,'' the President said grimly. ''I'm sure you do. One hears a lot of things differently in Moscow. But we're getting afield. How do I know your man is telling the truth, and if he is, where do we go from here?''

''You know it's the truth because I say it's the truth!'' Fabbie Gulak snapped. ''Also,'' he said, more mildly, ''because he is willing to meet with you personally and negotiate. He wouldn't do that if it wasn't the truth.''

''And how does he propose to do that, when he's a prisoner of the Soviets?''

''He is not 'a prisoner of the Soviets'! He is the free and independent President of Cuba, elected and reelected several times by free vote of the free people of Cuba!''

''Oh, Fabbie!'' the President said in a tone close to genuine despair. ''How can one ever penetrate minds as closed as yours?''

''Exactly what I was wondering myself,'' Fabrizio Gulak retorted.

There was a pause.

''Very well,'' the President said. ''Tell me how and under what

conditions this man intends to meet with me personally and negotiate. Am I supposed to fly down there, violating my own blockade,
and be received triumphantly as a humble supplicant coming to beg
favors? That would suit him and his captors best of all, wouldn't
it?''

"He is proposing," Fabrizio Gulak said with a measured slowness that indicated he was struggling to control his temper, "that
he enter Guantánamo disguised as a day laborer; that he then be
flown to Andrews Air Force Base; that he then be taken by helicopter to the White House; and that after you have talked, he be returned the same way.''

"How do I know it will be he? I've heard he has a double.''

"They all have," Fabrizio Gulak said. "One can't blame them,
considering how many enemies of the revolution there are. He proposes submitting to a complete examination inside Guantánamo,
and he proposes that before he is flown up here he will talk to you
on the telephone and give you the single word *volver*, which is the
verb 'to return.' ''

"Which he will have given to his double—or doubles—or whoever else suits him. And having arrived here, inside the White
House, he will shoot me down, perhaps?''

"He will talk under any conditions you impose. It is not a frivolous offer, Mr. President, even though you seem to be treating it
that way.''

"Not at all," the President said. "I like to think I am as serious
as he is.''

"But you are not," the old man said. "Not at all . . . *Mr.
President*: I cannot stress to you enough how serious the President
of Cuba is. He obviously risked a great deal to call me. He will
risk even more if he comes to see you.''

"Why *did* he call *you*, I wonder?" Ham Delbacher mused.
"And how does he know that at this moment you are not talking to
Yuri Serapin instead of to me? How do *I* know you haven't?''

"I might have expected that," Fabbie Gulak said. "It is typical
of the way you think. He called me because he felt he could trust
me not to tell anyone—*anyone*—but you. He asked me to give him
my word on that, and I did. I don't break it, Mr. President.''

"According to your lights," the President said, "I think you are an honest man, Fabbie. I mean that. So I accept that you haven't talked to Moscow about it. I still am not at all sure that Moscow didn't put him up to this, for some purpose detrimental to the United States and to me personally.''

"We will never know, will we," Fabrizio Gulak observed, "until you test him and see."

"That's right," Ham Delbacher conceded, "You are absolutely right. . . . When does he suggest this clandestine visit take place?"

"Immediately I get word to him. He dare not wait very long because he is afraid his plan will be discovered."

"You know how to reach him, then."

"Certainly."

"Perhaps I should talk to him first myself—"

"No!" Fabrizio Gulak said sharply. "That is not part of his offer. He will deal through me or nobody. And he said that while he doesn't want to impose any deadlines, it must be obvious to you why speed is necessary."

"Very well," the President agreed. "I will still need to know an approximate time so that I can notify Guantánamo."

"He has his contacts inside Guantánamo."

"Of course," the President agreed dryly. "I needn't have worried. And they will get him to a telephone to speak the magic word."

"Again I must beg you not to take it frivolously, Mr. President," Fabbie said coldly. "He is risking everything to meet with you."

"True. I still need to have some approximate time frame—"

"Oh, two or three hours, let's say," Fabrizio Gulak replied impatiently. "He has to make a speech first."

"Denouncing me."

"Naturally."

"And the United States."

"Naturally."

"For attempting to sabotage the glorious revolution."

"It is expected of him, Mr. President. It will also make it easier for him to slip away later if they—if they think—"

"All right. You can tell him I'll be glad to see him if he can manage to come. I still don't quite understand your motivations in all this, Fabbie. Don't you know I've launched a potentially very heavy blow against your friends in Moscow? I should think you'd be warning them in some way instead of helping me, even if you've given your word not to do it directly."

"You forget, Mr. President," Fabrizio Gulak said with great dignity. "I am an American."

"I'm sorry, Fabbie," Ham Delbacher said gravely. "Sometimes it does slip my mind. I appreciate it today, however."

"I should hope so!" Fabrizio Gulak said. "I should *hope* so!"

A minute later the President was on the scrambler to Guantánamo.

"If an unexpected visitor turns up," he said, "satisfy yourself he's who he says he is and then do exactly as he requests."

"Yes, sir," the commander said, puzzled but obedient.

Outside the President's house in Havana the crowd continued to grow. There had been no official announcement but it was assumed he would soon appear and address them. Many had their cameras ready. Some had zoom lenses.

And now, the President of the Soviet Union told himself as he sat in front of his map and reviewed the events of the week, it was time to take the domestic actions he had been secretly planning ever since his accession three months ago.

H. Delbacher's plea for his overthrow had been everything the American and world press were dutifully saying: shocking—awful—fantastic—frightful—crude—unmannerly—unstatesman-like—unjustified—inexcusable—violative of norms—disgraceful and disruptive to the cause of world peace—a desperate low blow against the leader of a nation which, difficult as it might sometimes be, nonetheless was an absolutely imperative element of world stability. "Your enemy as necessity," Elinor Delbacher had called the process of condemnation. Yuri, who had also read a lot of Western literature over the years, felt with grim humor that George Orwell would have felt justified.

However, within the highest echelons of the Soviet government H. Delbacher's plea had also been exactly what H. Delbacher had intended it to be: a really direct blow against his opponent, and far more effective than the blathering world could realize.

Yuri felt he had very little time to lose.

The world could not live with him—it also very obviously believed it could not live without him.

The dichotomy did not apply to his party colleagues or to the leaders of the Soviet military.

The feral silence that had crept over the room as the American President issued his call had not been lost on Yuri or any of them. For a few desperate seconds he had thought of holding them in continuing conference so that they would have to stay together and could not get out of his sight to conspire with one another. This would allow time to think of some way to get rid of them one by one. The memory of Lavrenty Beria and others killed in the Kremlin in hysterical blood-orgy by their colleagues had instantly canceled that idea. They might unite suddenly in a blind mass fury and stomp him to death. It had been done, within those bloody walls.

So he had let them go, making their hurried excuses and rushing off on various vague and unspecified tasks. He had assured some tenuous control by requesting them to call in with their ideas for his speech, and dutifully without exception they had done so. Thus it had been possible to trace their calls and learn that each was in or near his own office. There appeared to be no general gathering to conspire against him, nor did the continuing tapes reveal any conspiratorial telephone calls. But he could not escape the instinctive certainty that they fully intended conspiracy and would put it into effect at the very earliest moment they thought they safely could. And this despite the fact that on the battlefronts, while things were not proceeding with quite the blitzkrieg speed he had hoped for and intended, all was still going relatively well for his allies in the war zones.

He told himself that the momentum had not really been lost; and therefore it was imperative that if he intended to strike, he strike now while success seemed to be with him. He had no doubt of the final outcome of the four conflicts, or of the general conflict with the United States for which they were the indispensable, and final, preliminary. But even a slight lagging, a slight loss of momentum, would encourage his enemies within the government. Now was the time to deal with them—now, before his speech. It would be ten times as effective if he could deliver it as the invincible winner of an internal struggle which had threatened, but been unable to stop, the triumphant onward sweep of his grand design.

With a sudden decisive movement he selected a button on the console beside his telphone, jabbed it with an impatient finger. Dutifully General Mikhail Yarkov, head of the First Directorate of the KGB, responded with a calm and unhurried, "Yes, Comrade President?"

"I wish to speak with you," Yuri told the shrewd and highly intelligent forty-three-year-old he had helped to raise to his present fearsome eminence. "Here. At once."

"Yes, Comrade President," General Yarkov said in the same untroubled tone. "I am on the way."

Two minutes later he was seated across the desk as Yuri detailed his plans to perhaps the only other man in the Kremlin he really trusted, because that man was as cold-blooded, unemotional and ruthless as he.

COMMUNICATIONS BLACKOUT ISOLATES SOVIET UNION ON DAY OF SERAPIN SPEECH. WORLD PHONE, CABLE TIES CUT. PURGE RUMORS FLOOD SATELLITE CAPITALS. RADIO MOSCOW SAYS "PEACE AND CALM PREVAIL IN MOTHERLAND." NO CHANGE IN SPEECH PLANS.

But while potentially divisive meetings of Senate and House in Washington were headed off by astute legislative footwork on the part of the President's lieutenants on the Hill—leading to still further protests and outcries—in Moscow much darker means of avoiding dissent went secretly, swiftly and efficiently ahead. Eight ministers, among them the ministers of Defense, Foreign Affairs and Justice, were arrested in their offices. Within two hours—their torture-induced "confessions" having been recorded and printed for release to the media—all save those three officials were on their way to internal exile. Marshals Andreyev, Krelenko and Shelikov, together with Admiral Valenko, were seized in Yuri's own office where he had recalled them on the pretext of meeting to review battlefield progress. The last they saw of him was his triumphant and scornful smile as they were led, shouting and struggling, away. They too were tortured and, presently, "confessed." Then they found themselves standing (as much as they could manage to stand) side by side with the pale and trembling ministers of Defense, Foreign Affairs and Justice in a heavily soundproofed room in the basement of the Lubyanka. There was a heavy burst of gunfire that no one save themselves, General Yarkov and the members of the firing squad could hear; and presently, from several different entrances of adjoining buildings linked to the prison by underground passages, inconspicuous vans drove off in several directions and disappeared into the city, destinations and cargo unknown to the uninterested, often tipsy, citizens who saw them pass.

An hour after that—two hours before he was scheduled to address the world—the President of the Soviet Union received a unanimous pledge of support from his new colleagues of the Politburo and from the new marshals and new admiral who now headed the armed forces; and also from General Yarkov, who stood at Yuri's side and greeted them with a bland, half-amused and knowing air that guaranteed their loyalty, had there been any question of it. Yuri had them all repeat and sign the earlier resolution of the Politburo granting him supreme powers. All did so with alacrity, including General Yarkov, upon whom he conferred on the spot the newly created title of "First Assistant to the President." He then took General Yarkov aside to a far corner of the room, where the two of them carefully studied each of the new members of the government in turn, apparently discussing them with each other. By the time they returned to the group the new ministers and military chiefs appeared to be thoroughly cowed and eagerly compliant with every slightest wish their invincible leader uttered. He then dismissed them—each accompanied by his own newly appointed KGB "first assistant"—and returned to the preparation of his speech. He asked General Yarkov to remain and suggest changes. General Yarkov was suitably impressed and had many helpful ideas, one or two of which Yuri accepted.

In Cuba things also moved swiftly.

There was a sudden stir at the President's house in Havana, a setting-up of microphones, lights and cameras on the balcony, a heightening of tension in the crowd. It was obvious that he would soon appear and speak. The police lines that kept the crowd back a hundred yards were increased, and through the excited citizens and the interested tourists, skillful plainclothesmen began casually to circulate. Others, equally adept at appearing innocuous and part of the scenery, began to circulate also.

Purely by accident, though he took advantage of it with all the swiftness and skill of his KGB training, one of them found himself standing just behind an ecstatic tourist who looked, as he told his friends sardonically later, as though she were about to witness the Second Coming.

Mary Jasmine McWhorter of Berkeley, California, was in Cuba with a delicious feeling of defiance toward her own government. She had always been a great enthusiast for, and supporter of, the President of Cuba, and she was glad she was here on this day when her own stupid President was, she was certain, going to be told off in full for his brazen attempt to blockade the island and try to destroy its great alliance with the progressive forces of humanity as exemplified by the Soviet Union.

Mary Jasmine was virtually jumping up and down with excitement, which was why she had caught her neighbor's eye. He could see she was pretty, oblivious to her surroundings, obviously American and exactly the wide-eyed, earnest type he would have expected to find in such a place at such a time. It took only a glance and his plans for her were made.

Innocent and happy, she continued to bob up and down seeking a better view as the doors opened and the President stepped forward, right arm raised in his familiar, commanding gesture.

Silence fell, and he said the words they expected him to say, bringing to bear all the force of his personality in an attempt to get them to accept the position his masters, like his people, expected him to take.

"Comrades!" he cried, familiar voice clear and resonant.

"The vicious Yankee is threatening to choke Cuba! The foes of the revolution are conspiring to starve you and destroy the glorious motherland! They cry false promises and glittering gifts, but what they carry in their hands is death! *Death!* Together, my people, we must answer them!

"First, we defy the blockade! [There was a roar of approval. So far he was on safe and popular ground.] Together with our great Soviet allies, we will fight it with every means at our command, on land, on the sea, in the air, in space—*with every means.* Those who sit less than a hundred miles from our shores and seek to strangle us do not understand the inevitable risks they are taking. We and our great Soviet allies have the weapons! They are in place and we will use them! Those who take us lightly will learn that there is nothing small or puny about us! They will find we can strike and strike hard! We tell them to end the blockade at once *or take the consequences!*"

(Again the roar of approval, for on this they were all agreed.)

"Comrades!" he said. "Now the idiot in Washington talks about 'giving' us Guantánamo. There is nothing to 'give.' Guantánamo is ours, and we will have it. But not—" he shouted, as another roar of approval began to swell—"not as a patronizing gift from corrupt America! Not as a bauble to be dangled before us in an attempt to get us to abandon our alliance with our great Soviet ally, and to stop the great work of liberation on which our brave troops are engaged in so many places around the world! [A little uneasy murmur here, for this was not so popular.] No, my friends! We will *not* accept Guantánamo as a bribe! *We will take it as a right when we are ready.* Not one minute sooner, comrades—not one minute sooner! We are not fish to be played on a line with the bait of Guantánamo! It is ours! Why should we bargain for it? When the time is ripe we will take it! We will never accept it as a bribe!"

"Why won't you take it to stop the blockade?" someone shouted from the crowd, and several others shouted agreement. But they were quickly clubbed down. The President went on as though nothing had happened.

"Comrades," he said, "don't let promises of what is rightfully ours be combined with Yankee dollars to lead you astray. Don't fall for the clever words of a fool who is threatening to plunge the entire world into war in pursuit of his mad imperialist schemes! He talks of a hundred million dollars here and a hundred million dollars there. Americans *always* talk about hundreds of millions of dollars! American Presidents *always* throw around hundreds of millions of dollars! Why not? Money is easy for them and they promise it endlessly. But do they always pay it, my comrades? Are you so sure of that? No, I think not! It costs nothing for an American President to offer hundreds of millions of dollars, but he has to get Congress to agree to it, and that is another matter. Does he have Congress at his elbow when he promises you a hundred million dollars? No, it is not there yet and it may never be. It is all empty, his empty promises! As futile as Guantánamo, which he has no right to 'give' us because it is ours already—and now the money, which he has no right to promise us because he doesn't have it!

"He is a fraud, comrades, this idiot in Washington. An empty fraud! Only the Soviet Government is the true friend of Cuba! Only the Soviet Government will save Cuba! Together with the Soviet Government we will stop this idiot. We will say to him: Watch out, idiot, or you will receive our missiles on your head! Your pretty Florida, yes, even your pretty Washington, will go up in smoke before we yield! Together we will—"

But at that point, some agreed-upon signal passed between certain members of his audience. No one quite saw it, no one could quite identify those responsible, even had anyone dared come forward to try to do so; but some sign was given. He had obviously said enough: the record had been made.

What followed was virtually instantaneous.

From somewhere in the crowd one shot or several rang out—if there were several, as seemed likely from the later official examination of the body on the balcony, they were so close together as to sound as one. The President, spun almost completely around by their force, seemed to jump a couple of feet in the air before his lifeless body slumped out of sight. Screams, yells, chaos took over the area in front of the house as frantic soldiers, police and plainclothesmen, tourists and nontourists mingled in a forward rush that carried them almost to the steps before it was stopped. Frantic shouts and yells resounded and over it all could be heard the insignificant little Vice-President screaming for order in his high, almost falsetto voice.

Out in the crowd a sudden space began to grow around another body, this one shot down by the police—or someone—who now ringed it with rifles trained upon it. Its eyes were open in a dreadful startled stare and into its right hand the police—or someone—had thrust a still-smoking gun. She would never know it, but Mary Jasmine McWhorter had been selected by fate—or someone—to be, at least for the time being, the official assassin of the President of Cuba.

It was such a shame to have even a temporary misunderstanding, because no one could have admired him more.

At almost the same moment Sergeant Henry C. Pickle of Tullahoma, Tennessee, was preparing to swing open the gates of Guantánamo to permit the entry of a truckload of workers being allowed in to help clear the site for a new weapons storage facility. The driver of the truck had held his papers out the window, Sergeant Pickle had taken them and returned to his armored booth. There he had checked with security, found everything to be in order, and had started to wave the truck through. The driver was just applying his foot to the accelerator when suddenly, right before Sgt. Pickle's eyes, the truck just wasn't there anymore. There was an enormous explosion, a gush of smoke and dust, and flying fragments of men and machinery everywhere. Neither the gate nor Sergeant Pickle in his booth was damaged, but there certainly wasn't much left of the truck and its occupants.

Taken in conjunction with the news that flashed around the world—CUBAN PRESIDENT ASSASSINATED, AMERICAN BELIEVED MURDERER—the news of the truck, when it reached the White House, produced a profound feeling of gloom and dismay.

Fortunately it did not last long. Within half an hour the commander of Guantánamo, voice shaky with excitement, was put through to the President.

"We have a visitor," he said, words tumbling upon one another. "He came in a fishing boat that fortunately was intercepted, not fired upon. As per your order, I am satisfied he is who he says he is. I'll put him on the other phone."

"Volver," a voice said with a sardonic little chuckle. Ham Delbacher said, "Get him up here just as fast as you can."

It was then almost five P.M., and before long the world would be quieting down to listen to Yuri Serapin. The President decided to

invite the same group as before to listen with him. To it he added
Major Ivan Valerian, with the idea that he would like to observe
that bright young man's reactions while his former employer denounced his new one.

4

And now suddenly the screens of the world were blank, its radio channels silent. The roads of earth were still and waiting. Around the globe the sober-faced, solemn-voiced announcers made their introduction, as unadorned as the one they had used for the President of the United States the night before.

"Ladies and gentlemen, the President of the Union of Soviet Socialist Republics!"

There was a little preliminary *click!*, heard literally around the world, from Moscow; and then silence, deliberately prolonged, deliberately empty, deliberately tantalizing.

It lasted perhaps fifteen seconds, though it seemed much longer; and then, suddenly, the broad, half-Asian face with its stolid expression and its cold, cold eyes, was there. Many millions actually gasped, so completely and instantaneously was he with them.

For perhaps another fifteen seconds he simply stared at them, expression closed and impassive, revealing nothing, offering nothing, taking nothing.

Here I am, Yuri Serapin, it seemed to say; *make of me what you will. Find in me your hope or your despair as it suits you, but do not expect me to give you any hint as to which it is. I am whatever you want me to be—demon, scourge, savior, saint. Read into me what you will and conclude whatever your necessities require. You do not move me, either way.*

"How the world can *not* be afraid of that man—!" Elinor exclaimed.

"You should be more dramatic, Mr. President," Mark Coffin suggested dryly. "You miss these opportunities."

"Yuri Pavlovich loves drama," Ivan Valerian remarked. "He will be dramatic when they hang him from the highest pole in Red Square, which I hope will be soon."

The mask-face stirred, the cold eyes became animated. The stabbing, emphatic voice was added. The President of the Soviet Union began to make his case—in Russian, with English translation discreetly but clearly overriding.

"My fellow citizens of the world!" he began, much as Hamilton Delbacher had. "All of you who love peace, listen to me! Hear what I have to say and then judge. Judge between me and him who would destroy peace! Decide which of us you wish to believe and which you want to follow. Decide, decide! History cannot wait much longer for our battle to be concluded!"

"Well, well," Ham Delbacher said softly. "Would you be surprised, little man, to know that I agree with you?"

"Yesterday," Yuri said, "you heard a declaration of war against the Soviet Union. Oh, it was not stated formally as such. The President—the present President—of the United States is too clever for that. He confined himself to lies and slanders about me and my country, as he has from the moment we both took office. But he also announced a set of threats and conditions so grave that they can only be considered an act of war."

He paused and all over the world tension rose enormously.

"The Soviet Union," he said, "does so consider them."

"He is bluffing," Ivan said swiftly. "Wait and you will see."

An almost audible groan swept the globe: millions were not so confident as Ivan.

"However—" Yuri said slowly. Across the globe the groan was succeeded by a universal sigh.

"You see?" Ivan cried triumphantly. "You see?"

"However, the Soviet Union does not choose at this time to acknowledge or accept the openly provocatory remarks of the present President of the United States. Our desire and our intention is always to work for peace, despite the constant imperialist warmongering of the United States and it present leader. My fellow citizens of the world, you could not bear the burden of a fearful war that would destroy humanity. Therefore we will not be the ones responsible for inflicting it upon you.

"But if the United States wants war," he added, suddenly stern, "it can have it!"

"Now, just what does that mean?" Chauncey Baron inquired wryly. "War? Yes or no?" Jim Elrod snorted: "Double double-talk."

"Before I respond point by point to the lies and deliberately provocatory statements of the so-called leader of the world's so-called great democracy," Yuri said, tone turning heavy with sarcasm, "there is an announcement to be made. By decision of the Politburo and the Council of Ministers, and because of the enormous threat to world peace posed by the irresponsible provocations of the present President of the United States, the Soviet Government has today moved to a full war footing. This will enable us to face any challenge and overcome it successfully.

"This has necessitated"—he could not resist a triumphant little smile, swiftly controlled—"some changes in the membership of the Politburo and the Council of Ministers. It has also required the selection of new commanders of the brave armed forces of the Motherland."

"It *was* a purge, then," Roger Hackett said.

"I knew it must be," Chauncey said, "but we couldn't get through to our sources to be sure."

"These changes," Yuri said, "have been accepted eargerly by those I have asked to step down. Their patriotic love for the Motherland and their great desire to serve her in whatever capacity her peril requires have made it possible for them to go willingly and gladly to their new assignments. These are such that they will continue to be of service to the fullest extent of their ability."

"Which I will bet is not very great, at this moment," the President said grimly. Ivan Valerian nodded with equal grimness.

"They are dead," he said flatly. "Or in exile."

"Now," the Soviet President said, "I want you to meet their successors."

Suddenly the camera drew back and it became clear that he was not alone. Behind him in a double rank, grim, stolid, frozen, stood the twelve members of the Politburo. Flanking them on the right stood the new marshals of the army and the air force, on the left the new marshal of the strategic rocket forces and the new admiral of the navy.

"Ivan?" the President inquired. Instantly Ivan was up and peering closely at the screen.

"Starting on the left, first row," he said swiftly, "KGB/military, he is new—civilian, he is old—KGB, he is new—civilian, he is old—KGB, he is new—KGB, he is new—civilian, he is new—military, he is new. Second row, from left, military, he is new—civilian, he is old—KGB, he is old—KGB, he is new—KGB, he is new—civilian, he is new—civilian, he is new—KGB/military, he is new. In the military commands two regular officers, two from the KGB. In the Politburo six civilians, six from the KGB. Out of sixteen, twelve are new."

"Which gives the KGB a slight edge, doesn't it?" Art Hampton remarked dryly.

"Yuri Pavlovich likes the KGB," Ivan said. "He has always favored them. They have always favored him. I would say these changes remove the last possibility of effective opposition to Yuri Pavlovich. I do not think he will be overthrown, now."

"I have also appointed," Yuri said, as another officer in full uniform stepped forward from the left to face full into the screen, "Comrade General Yarkov to be First Assistant to the President."

"He is head of the First Directorate of the KGB," Ivan said. "We are almost of an age, I have known him all my life. There will be no further arguments with Yuri Pavlovich."

"Except from General Yarkov," the President said. Ivan shot him a sudden sharp look.

"It is possible. It is the only possibility. And I would not base my hopes or policies upon it, Mr. President."

"No," Hamilton Delbacher said. "But it is something to keep in mind."

Ivan Valerian nodded.

"Maybe someday, but not for a long time. Listen!"

"General Yarkov," Yuri said, "will now read the resolution of support first approved by the Politburo, the Council of Ministers and the military commanders a week ago and reaffirmed an hour ago by the new members. With names, comrade general, please.''

Obediently General Yarkov stepped forward, a tall, good-looking, well-built figure, poised and composed.

"Comrade President," he said, bowing, "it is my great honor and privilege to read these words of affirmation and support for your glorious leadership.''

And he proceeded to do so in an unhurried, level voice of great authority. When he concluded with the text he went down the list of names in the same unhurried, thorough manner. As he read each name its owner stepped forward, bowed, looked momentarily brightly happy, said loudly, *"Da!"* and sank back into the ranks.

"A perfect show of unity," Mark commented midway in the roster. "How could they get everyone to agree so beautifully!''

"It is very easy in my country," Ivan began with great seriousness, until Mark laughed and said, "I know, I know!" Ivan flashed him a smile but said, still seriously, "No, I do not think you do.''

"Now," Yuri said when Mikhail Yarkov had finished, bowed and stepped back a pace, though still standing conspicuously at his right shoulder. "Now, we take up one by one the insolent challenges to peace offered by the present President of the United States.'' His face became somber and forbidding once again. "Let us see how they sound when placed against the invincible determination of the Soviet Union. Let us see what we will do about them.''

He paused. Someone offscreen handed him sheets of paper; he scanned them for a moment, looked up with a somber expression.

"The first challenge he made was to Cuba. Already it has had tragic and ominous results.

"You are aware, fellow citizens of the world, of the criminal CIA plot which today resulted in the brutal murder of the President of Cuba.''

"*That's* a damned lie!" Senator Elrod exclaimed. The President shrugged.

"Surely. But it will be believed by many millions.''

"This CIA plot," Yuri went on, "used for its worthless purpose the seemingly innocent instrument of an American woman tourist.

However, this so-called tourist, it has now been established, was a secret agent of the American Government, acting under direct orders of the CIA, which in turn was acting under direct orders of the President of the United States. His order was simple: 'Murder the President of Cuba, so that I once and for all may be rid of him and his stubborn insistence on bringing peace and democracy to the Caribbean. Kill him! Shoot him down! Let us show the world how American imperialism works!'

"These were the orders of H. Delbacher, and they were carried out today in Havana by the woman agent of the CIA. And this is the nation, this is the man, who lectures the world on international morality and claims that he works for peace!''

"Shoot *him* down,'' Jim Elrod said angrily. "The unutterable bastard!''

"We'll issue denials,'' Hamilton Delbacher said, "but you know as well as I do how effective they will be.''

"There must be a more effective answer,'' Art Hampton said, and the President said, "Oh, there is.'' But he offered no enlightenment in response to their puzzled looks; and their attention swung back to the President of the Soviet Union.

"Why was the President of Cuba killed, fellow citizens? Because he was defying the illegal and impossible blockade of the President of the United States, announced yesterday. Because he was reaffirming Cuba's unbreakable allegiance to the Soviet Union, the unbreakable comradeship of two great peoples united in the world socialist revolution, fighting always for world peace. Because he was fighting for *you*, the oppressed peoples of the world everywhere! That is why the President of the United States, acting through the CIA and the so-called American woman tourist, chose to assassinate the President of Cuba.

"It was not the first such attempt by an American President,'' he added somberly, "only this time, on a sad day for freedom-loving peoples everywhere, it succeeded . . .

"But the blockade,'' he said, tone sharpening and growing stronger, "the illegal act of war that is the blockade—that will not succeed! Because with this criminal act of the hegemonistic, warmongering President of the United States the situation has changed entirely in Cuba. The Cuba which was to be the object of the criminal blockade of the imperialist President no longer exists. As a result of this dreadful crime against freedom-loving peoples everywhere, a new Cuba has been born.

"As of this moment," he said slowly, slapping his hand on the table at regular intervals for emphasis, "the President, Politburo and Council of Ministers of the Union of Soviet Socialist Republics declare the incorporation of the island of Cuba as a full and equal member of the Union of Soviet Socialist Republics, with all the rights and privileges associated with that membership. From this moment on the island of Cuba is a part of the Soviet Union as surely as though it were ten miles from Moscow. As of this moment anyone touching Cuban soil touches the Soviet Union. Anyone who seeks to blockade Cuba is blockading the Soviet Union. Anyone who wars with Cuba is warring with the Soviet Union.

"Let us see now," he said with a sudden savage scorn, "what the brave imperialist President does with that one!"

"What *will* you do, Mr. President?" Ivan Valerian demanded excitedly. "What *can* you do?"

"The first thing I can do," Hamilton Delbacher said, studying him for just a second with an appraising glance, "is keep calm. After that, we will see. But first we must hear out your friend."

"He is not my friend!" Ivan protested heatedly. "I hate him for what he has done to the world!"

The President smiled—a rather inscrutable smile, his wife thought—and without comment, nodded toward the screen.

"The hegemonist tricks of the imperialist President of the United States," Yuri said flatly, "will not be effective with Soviet Cuba. There will be no blockade of Soviet Cuba, Soviet Cuba will not accept the bribe of Guantánamo. Soviet Cuba will *take* Guantánamo when it is ready to do so, and will not break its indissoluble ties with the Motherland. And Soviet Cuba will not accept the bribe of a hundred million dollars—or two hundred million dollars—or a billion dollars! Soviet Cuba rejects all such stupid imperialist, hegemonist tricks of the American President! They are childish. They are pointless. Soviet Cuba rejects them utterly. All, all are rejected!"

He paused and took a sip of water. "Is that water or vodka?" Elinor inquired. "He's *talking* like vodka." Yuri again glanced at papers before him with a quick, disdainful air and turned back to the camera.

"There are other tricks of the imperialist President," he observed in a tone now almost conversational. "There is, for instance"—and suddenly his tone hardened, his eyes again became cold, opaque and chilling—"the seizure of the Soviet embassy and its personnel in Washington.

"The Soviet Government, as you know, has chosen—so far—not to accept this act of war *as* an act of war because we are determined to maintain world peace with every means at our command. But this does not mean that the Soviet Government will not react. We have already reacted. The United States embassy in Moscow was occupied by us within one hour after word reached us of the gross violation of diplomatic norms by the United States Government. Two hundred and one American citizens are now in our hands.

"The seizure of an embassy used to mean an act of war, but"—his tone abruptly dripped with scorn—"after the President J. Carter preferred not to regard it as such in Iran, it has become an accepted principle of diplomacy in hegemonist circles that embassies and their personnel may be seized without fear of punishment. No one need be afraid of the United States on *that* score. *That* was established years ago.

"This does not apply," he said, an ominous note coming into his voice, "to the Soviet Union. Here we do not take such things quite so lightly. To use it means something.

"Accordingly," he said, and something in his voice made millions over the globe become hushed and uneasy, "I have a proposition to put to the hegemonist President. He has two hundred and one Soviet citizens. We have two hundred and one American. We are prepared to exchange them through Switzerland. We wish to have our citizens back, at once, within twenty-four hours. If they are not returned to us not later than twenty-four hours from this moment, we shall begin executing the Americans we hold, at the rate of two a day, until all of our citizens are returned."

"Son of a bitch!" the Secretary of State said softly.

"A nice man," the First Lady said, but the irony sounded rather thin. She looked, in fact, as though she might be about to cry.

Instinctively they all looked at the President. But he was sitting staring at the screen, chin on hands, impassive and expressionless.

"What will you do, Mr. President?" Ivan asked in a hushed voice. But there was no answer and no change of expression. "You must do *something!*" Ivan exclaimed. "You cannot just—just—"

"Please," the President said, lifting a hand for silence, otherwise not responding. And after a moment they settled back, dreadfully disturbed, while Yuri, not quite managing to conceal an expression of triumph, continued.

"We will see," he said savagely, "whether the President of the United States wishes to continue this charade of bluffs that he thinks will somehow intimidate the Soviet Union . . .

"So much for Cuba and the embassies. It is a game two can play and we intend to play it to the full . . .

"The President has frozen our assets and canceled all trade. It is a good idea; we accept that. We can trade through fifty partners around the world; we do not need direct trade with the United States. As for the assets, he has frozen ours, we have frozen the little they have in the Soviet Union and in the fraternal member nations of the Warsaw Pact. It may be they have more of our money than we have of theirs. They have more money than anyone and what good does it do them? Money is not enough to deflect the Soviet Government from its unrelenting search for world peace. We will never be deflected from that search! We will never let petty gestures such as this upset us!

"Equally," he said, "we cannot be threatened by U.S. appeals to NATO to cut off trade with us, or by U.S. 'Number One war alerts' and U.S. appeals to NATO to do likewise.

"We note," he said, and his voice was again heavy with sarcasm, "that to this hour, none of the NATO nations has frozen our assets or imposed any trade embargo. And we note that none of the NATO nations has begun any military maneuvers or actions which would indicate compliance with the attempts of the President of the United States to force his allies to support his imperialist ambitions.

"If they did," he said, and his voice grew stern again, "we should instantly take appropriate measures. Not the least of these would be the closing of the gas pipeline. That would be the first step. There would be others. None of them, I can assure the members of NATO, would be to their liking. It would be wise for them not to antagonize the U.S.S.R. We are in a position to make them regret it.''

He pushed aside the papers on his desk with a contemptuous motion, scattering and knocking them to the floor. No one moved to pick them up: the stolid rank of faces behind him remained impassive. The camera came in upon him. It was obvious he would soon conclude.

"My fellow citizens of the world," he said, and now his tone was conversational, no longer harsh or stern; earnest, sincere, beseeching their attention, their belief and their support.

"The President of the United States has embarked on a mad, futile, empty course. Perhaps in the grip of some strange insanity, he has attempted to challenge all peace-loving peoples everywhere, though his immediate targets seem to be the President of Cuba and myself. I do not know why he sould have done this. He alleges it is because he believes that the Soviet Union, and specifically myself as its leader—he smiled wryly and could not resist adding—"its *present* leader—are in some way responsible for four conflicts that have broken out around the globe in recent days.

"Yet, as I have told the world, and as the United Nations has certified, there are no Soviet troops, no Soviet weapons, in these conflicts. No proof has been offered, nothing has been established. All we know is that four oppressed populations, seeking to be free as all men wish to be free, are revolting against their colonialist oppressors. Should we not give every sympathy, every support—*short* of warfare—to these freedom-loving peoples? Should we not heed their desperate cries, give ear to their fervent pleas? Should we not in all humanity respond to the universal humanity that is in everyone, and say, 'Yes, freedom-loving peoples, yes, we hear you'? "

"Oh, my God," Mark said in a tone of tired disgust. "Now play us 'Hearts and Flowers.' ''

"He'll do it," Jim Elrod predicted. "Give him a minute, and he'll do it."

"No, citizens of the world," the Soviet President said, and now his voice dropped to an even more intimate, more insistent level. "We are not engaged in fighting anyone. We are simply protecting our New Soviet Republic of Cuba—and defending our own interests, and with them those of all peace-loving peoples everywhere who seek our friendship and support.

"*We* do not want war, my friends! *We* are not engaged in war! It is not *our* ships that sit in the Taiwan Strait! It is not *our* planes that threaten Angola and *our* ships that steam toward the South Atlantic in aid of the racist government of South Africia! It is not *our* ships and planes that prop up the moldering regime in Mexico! It is not *our* ships that threaten the Strait of Hormuz and *our* planes that seek to overturn the People's Republic of Arabia! Do not look to *us* when you want to find imperialists, warmongers and hegemonists! Do not turn to *us* when you seek the enemies of peace and freedom!

"But also, my friends," he said, and his voice grew louder and more emphatic, "do not expect us to sit idly by while those who *are* enemies of peace and freedom, the imperialist, warmongering President of the United States and his stooges of NATO and other areas of the globe, attempt to impose their will on the democratic peoples of corrupt regimes as they struggle to be free! Do not expect us to let their crimes go undetected and their campaigns against human freedom go unnoted and unopposed!

"No, my friends and fellow citizens of the world, we will not stand by! We will do all we can to stop the insane headlong plunge of aggression with which the President of the United States seeks to trap us all into the final war that will destroy the world! We will not let him do it, my friends! The peace-loving peoples of the U.S.S.R. and the Warsaw Pact, together with our new Soviet Republic of Cuba, will oppose him with everything we have!

"Rally to us, my friends! Follow our lead! It is the only way to peace and justice for all mankind!"

The camera came even closer. The cold eyes, animated, insistent, hypnotic, bored into those of the watching world. Somewhere in the background the strains of the "Internationale" could faintly be heard. The Soviet flag, floating supreme over a hazy montage of what seemed to be thousands of tiny people with arms uplifted to it, drifted across his face; and the whole scene faded out.

The last thing they saw were his eyes, still focused, still intent, still seeming to pierce directly into those of each and every one of his countless millions, possibly billions, of listeners.

"The world turned topsyturvy," Chauncey Baron said softly as the whole extravaganza vanished, "the world gone mad . . . So, do we shoot the Soviet captives?"

The President gave a deeply unhappy sigh; but his tone was as implacable as Yuri's when he finally replied.

"If we must."

"But—" Art Hampton began.

"You can't!" Elinor protested.

"We *mustn't* be as bad as they are," the Speaker said earnestly.

Only Ivan Valerian nodded slowly and said,

"It is the only way."

"It is," the President said, "if he does it. I am not so sure he will. He *says* he has given us twenty-four hours. A lot can happen in twenty-four hours."

"You can send the Soviet embassy staff home," Elinor suggested hopefully. Her husband nodded.

"Yes, I can do that. I think I'd rather wait and see what he does. After all, even the Iranians didn't quite dare arouse public opinion to that extent; and I think it would be dreadfully aroused, even with all the Soviet propaganda against us, if he sets out cold-bloodedly and deliberately to exterminate helpless hostages."

"Then why not exchange them at once?" Mark asked. "Why not avoid even the possibility?"

"Because for the moment I need them as chips," the President said, "and I gamble that he will not cash in some of his and take the great risk of alienating all the world . . . plus, as I say, much can happen in twenty-four hours."

"What, Mr. President?" Ivan inquired, sounding both skeptical and frustrated. "What can possibly happen now?"

"There are things," the President said, standing and shaking hands. "And now if you will all excuse me, I had best get to work on one of them. Chauncey and Roger, you stay, if you will, please. I'll be up in an hour or so for dinner, Elinor. Art, Jim, Mark and Mr. Speaker, back to the Hill with you, and keep all incipient legislative revolts under control. Ivan, thank you for your knowledgeable comments on the new Politburo and Council of Ministers, and the military commanders; it's a big help to know where we stand, there. I'll be calling on you again . . . Have as pleasant an evening as possible under the circumstances, everyone, and"—he smiled with ironic grimness—"don't believe everything you read in the newspapers or see on the tube."

He called in the press secretary and dictated a very brief statement that was released immediately.

"I have noted the usual lies and attempts to conceal the truth of the present leader of the Soviet Union. They are as false as everything else he has said and done since he took office and began his series of deliberate crimes against peace. I see no profit in further charge and countercharge between us. From this point forward the answer of the United States will be found in action."

Then he pressed a buzzer and told his secretary to show in the CIA and his visitor. The Secretary of State and the Secretary of Defense stood up, as the President did, and turned to the door. Their mouths quite literally fell open when the visitor walked in. To them, as to the entire world at this moment, he was a dead man.

For a few minutes they watched the late television news together. "The address of President Serapin," the CBS commentator said, "is in some respects a horrifying statement. Yet the true horror would seem to lie in the fact that were it not provoked by America's violent efforts to thwart struggles for freedom and independence in four widely separated parts of the globe, there would have been no need for such an ominous message from the Soviet leader.

"It seems impossible to believe that Mr. Serapin would actually carry out his threat to eliminate some of the American embassy staff now being held in Moscow, but the only way to be sure of that, of course, is for the American Government to release at once the Soviet embassy staff it is holding in Washington. President Delbacher would stand condemned forever in the eyes of this nation and the world if he allowed his personal vendetta with President Serapin to reach a tragically awful point at which American lives were sacrificed simply to satisfy his stubborn animosity.

"Equally unforgivable would be a continuation of the blockade of Cuba, now that Mr. Serapin and his colleagues have voted to make the island an integral part of the Soviet Union—something to which they have as much right as we do, for instance, to Hawaii or Guam. The blockade is now a blockade against Russia itself; it is no longer a diplomatic stunt that Mr. Delbacher can manipulate as he pleases. The murder of the Cuban President—whether CIA-inspired, as President Serapin charges, who can say? The charge does not seem illogical—makes the situation of the highest and most dangerous gravity. With great forbearance, Mr. Serapin has not declared war upon the United States—so far. But if the blockade continues, directed as it now is against the Soviet Union itself, he will have no choice.

"It is time, and past time, for President Delbacher to call a halt. He has acted with intransigent belligerence around the world on the excuse that he is seeking to maintain world peace. Instead he has placed himself, no doubt inadvertently but nonetheless fatally, in the position of being the world's biggest destroyer of peace . . ."

So said, with thoughts equally condemnatory and words equally harsh, the others. And so agreed, virtually without exception, the editorials that were being rushed into type for the upcoming editions of the major metropolitan dailies.

Hamilton Delbacher and his visitor marveled at the upside-down nature of these comments. Together they shared a wry amusement over the reports of the murder of the President of Cuba. Ham reminded his visitor of what Mark Twain had said. His visitor said yes, he remembered reading it during his days as a graduate student at Harvard. Together they agreed that Yuri Serapin was, so far, getting away with murder himself, both figuratively and literally.

And then they got down to business.

"Mr. President," Ham Delbacher said when the CIA had withdrawn, he had introduced Chauncey Baron and Roger Hackett, and they were all seated in a comfortable circle near the windows, "I assume it was Soviet agents that killed your double, was it not, poor devil?"

The President of Cuba gave an indifferent shrug.

"He was paid for it. Yes, yes, of course they were Soviet agents, what else? Your unfortunate young countrywoman just happened to be in the wrong place at the wrong time, that is all."

"Yes," the President said. "She was *not* paid for it."

"You will never convince the world of that," his visitor observed. "You cannot even convince your own press."

"Even if they were convinced," the President said, "I suspect some of them would rather print what they would like to believe."

"You should be like Cuba," his visitor said with a sardonic little chuckle. "We have no such trouble with the media there."

"You *had* no such trouble," the President reminded. "You have plenty of trouble now. What do you intend to do about it?"

"They will announce their new President, whom they have already selected. I know who it is, his mouth has been watering for it for years. I should have had him killed years ago. They will announce his selection immediately—probably it is already out in Havana and soon will be here. And then quickly, quickly, before anyone has time to think, at noon tomorrow I am sure, they will hold a magnificent state funeral for me. And then, like a miracle from the skies, I shall descend from heaven and be reborn. With your help. First you must get me safely back to Guantánamo, and then you must send me air cover, and, from Guantánamo, as many troops as you can spare. Can you do that?"

"And what will your people be doing at that point? Will we have to fight them in order to resurrect you?"

The President of Cuba chuckled and lit a cigar.

"Oh, no," he said between draws. "They may hate me but they hate the Russians more. You will see. I am very much the lesser of two evils, and when this shoddy little plot is exposed by my miraculous rising from the dead, they will flock to me. You will see, Mr. President. They will flock."

"You seem very confident," the President observed. "I hope you're right."

"I am right," his visitor said flatly. "Now. My question to you gentlemen is, how much can I depend upon you? Will you help me with force of arms? Will you return Guantánamo and stop the blockade? Will you give me money?"

"Will you renounce the Soviets and join with us? Will you withdraw your troops from abroad?" Hamilton Delbacher inquired. "I don't want any double double-crosses. I haven't got time to play that boring game, at the moment."

"May have to," the President of Cuba said with another chuckle. Then he became serious.

"No, Mr. President, you will not have to. I give you my word.

From now on. Cuba is your friend. Cuba is the Soviets' enemy. I shall deport them all, I shall drive them from the island. I shall drive them into the sea, where they may swim like snakes or sink like stones! They will be gone from Cuba, the worthless bullies, the arrogant patronizers!'' He scowled suddenly, a ferocious expression compounded by the tone in which he spoke. ''They think I am some kind of puppet!'' he said angrily. ''They think they can do anything they please and order me around and I will do anything!''

The President refrained from pointing out that this was exactly what events of recent years had convinced them they could do.

''At this moment,'' he said, ''they think you are dead because they think they have killed you. So if they think of you at all it is in the past tense. For me you are still present and, I hope, future. With regard to that, however, ludicrous though this claim of adding Cuba to the Soviet Union may be, nonetheless it poses just enough of a juridical problem so that if I am to ignore it and continue the blockade, which of course I am going to do, I am going to have to be absolutely certain that your resurrection is going to work. We can't commit ourselves to such a direct assault on their claimed sovereignty unless we are sure there really will be a massive uprising when you reappear.''

''You leave it to me,'' the President of Cuba said grimly. ''First of all, if I am correct and my funeral is tomorrow noon, starting at about eleven forty-five, you will begin jamming Radio Cuba. Then promptly at noon you will cease and put me on Radio Martí from Florida. I will begin broadcasting on the Cuban frequency at your highest possible power, which I know from experience is very strong. I think I can persuade my people when I speak to them,'' he observed with some complacency. ''I always have. As soon as I finish speaking, but with the tape still being broadcast continuously at least for the next couple of hours over Radio Martí, you will get me back to Guantánamo. By two P.M. the revolt, if I have your backing, will be underway. You will simultaneously bombard the island with propaganda leaflets from one end to the other. Meanwhile—''

He paused and the President said, ''Yes, meanwhile?'' in a tone of rather dry inquiry.

"Meanwhile," the President of Cuba said, unabashed, "the Cuban army, whose top officers are very loyal to me and have been secretly very much prepared to take arms against the occupiers for a very long time, will be assaulting and capturing all Soviet positions."

"Which have also been very much prepared for just such an eventuality for a very long time," Hamilton Delbacher pointed out. "You make it sound easy, Mr. President."

"I do not expect it will be easy," his visitor said sharply. "But I know it can be done *providing the United States is determined that it will be done.* You cannot be halfhearted, Mr. President. You must go all out. There must be no halfhearted, Kennedy-style, dip-one-toe-in-the-water-and-take-the-other-out about it. We must not have another Bay of Pigs!"

But this was too much, and suddenly his earnest demeanor broke at the sheer historical irony of what he had just said. He began to laugh, a loud booming sound that ended in choking gasps as he got a little of his cigar smoke down the wrong way. "There!" he finally choked out between gasps, red-faced but still laughing as they all laughed with him, "How is that for turning history on its head, Mr. President?"

"Not bad," Hamilton Delbacher conceded. "Not bad . . . We are still talking, however, about a great gamble. Neither of us must permit another Bay of Pigs."

"There will be none," the President of Cuba promised, solemn again. "Nor, I think, at that point will there be any execution of American hostages in Moscow. He will probably not even remember his own deadline."

"He'll remember," the President said, "but I think at that point he will think better of it. The minute the deadline passes, I'll contact Switzerland and we'll get things set for the exchange. I don't want his people, he can have them. But not under threat."

"That is the way to handle him," the Cuban President said. "They are all like that. The minute they think they have you, they threaten and bully. You just have to stand up to them."

"I don't believe he has any doubts at this point that I will," Ham Delbacher said. "But your resurrection will help remind him."

"It will be the greatest thing since the last resurrection," the Cuban President said with another chuckle. "So! It is agreed, then?"

"It is agreed," the President said.

"And I will get all necessary aid?"

The President turned to the Secretaries of State and Defense.

"We will support you completely," Chauncey Baron said crisply.

"With everything we have," Roger Hackett agreed, "and that, in your area, is substantial, as you know."

"Yes," the Cuban President said with an ironic little smile. "All these years I have been worrying about it being turned against me. It will be good to have it on my side."

"As long as you keep your part of the bargain," Hamilton Delbacher reminded.

"I would not dare abandon it now," the Cuban President said with a wry smile. "It is my only hope of rising from the dead." He started to turn away, paused. "Has anything been received yet on my funeral arrangements?"

"Hang on," Chauncey Baron said; put through a call to Foggy Bottom, talked briefly to the Assistant Secretary of State for Inter-American Affairs. "It's been announced. Tomorrow noon, as you predicted. And Gustavo Lopez Bellamín is your successor."

"Of course," the President of Cuba said, "the filthy traitor. May he enjoy his presidency while it lasts, which will be roughly forty-eight hours, if that long. Much shorter, if all goes well."

"Make sure of it," Hamilton Delbacher advised.

"If *you* will," the President of Cuba replied.

The President turned to the Secretary of State.

"Chauncey, take His Excellency to the Department and record the tape which will begin playing over Radio Martí at noon tomorrow. As soon as he is finished recording, you see to it, Roger, that he is on a plane and back to Guantánamo. I think you had better send the Deputy Secretary of Defense and the Deputy Secretary of State with him, so that there will be no question about my orders down there. In general, follow his instructions for all actions undertaken in cooperation with Cuban forces. How many Marines and soldiers do we have down there at the moment?"

"Fifteen hundred Marines, a little over five hundred soldiers," the Secretary of Defense said.

"Quite adequate, with my own troops," the Cuban President said. "And the popular rising."

"Pray God you are right, Mr. President," Ham Delbacher said.

"I tend to be," the President of Cuba said complacently. He held out his hand. "To friendship, resumed and eternal, between the great peoples of the United States and Cuba!"

"Yes," the President said dryly. "Let us hope so." He shook hands, then turned to the Secretaries of State and Defense.

"I have further orders for your deputies, gentlemen," he said while the President of Cuba's amiable expression turned rapidly first to consternation, then to anger and finally to a sort of wryly acknowledging acceptance. "They are to tell the Marine commander at Guantánamo that this man is to be accompanied by a detachment of his most expert marksmen at all times. If there is the slightest indication that he is wavering in his purpose, if there is the slightest sign of treachery toward us, if there is the slightest hint of any kind that he is even thinking about breaking his word and cooperating again with the Soviets, he is to be shot dead on the spot. The death is to be concealed as long as possible. The pretense that he is still alive is to be continued to the last possible moment. The momentum is to be maintained until the island is taken . . . I trust, Mr. President," he said, while Chauncey Baron and Roger Hackett looked at him with a mixture of surprise and rather bemused approval, "that these orders are clear to you?"

The President of Cuba gave him an ironic little bow.

"I believe I understand you, Mr. President." He chuckled. "I would do exactly the same thing myself."

"Good," Ham Delbacher said. "Then we do understand each other. And now"—he held out his hand for a second, more cordial handshake—"God speed and good luck with your mission."

"I will see you in Havana," the President of Cuba said.

"I shall be happy to accept your invitation," Hamilton Delbacher replied. "Until then."

5

They had planned to eat in one of their favorite places, outside, hidden among the trees that concealed much of the south lawn of the White House from the public, but just as the President of Cuba left with the Secretaries one of the last crashing thunderstorms of the season deluged the District of Columbia. They found themselves back at the hastily set dining table in the family quarters on the second floor.

"Not as romantic," Elinor remarked, "but dryer."

They had their customary single cocktail, he a vodka martini on the rocks, she a Manhattan; ate reasonably ample portions of the White House chef's excellent roast beef, carrots, julienne potatoes and tossed salad, accompanied by a glass apiece of velvet California zinfandel; and sat back looking at one another with half-humorous, half-embattled expressions.

"How are you bearing up?" she inquired. "You look a little tempest tossed, at the moment."

"I am a little battered," he admitted, "but managing. I'm in the process of discovering that I'm a very ruthless man. I find this disturbing to me and doubtless astounding to others. But there it is."

"For example."

"The hostages, first of all. I find I am actually contemplating allowing our fellow citizens to be killed at regular intervals by that madman, and killing his fellow citizens in return."

"I doubt if you will," she said.

"You hope I won't, because that would destroy the kindly old grandfather image you have of me."

"You *are* a kindly old grandfather," she said, "and so you won't."

"But a kindly old grandfather under siege," he pointed out, "and so I may. At least I am seriously thinking about it—really, genuinely. Which shows you how far a man can go when he's pushed by the evil ones of this world and how he can become one of them himself."

"It would mean nothing to him," she observed. "He's ordered killings—and killed, himself—before."

"I still don't think he would dare. But if he does—"

"If he does," she said, "it will mean that the world has crossed over finally into a savagery from which it may not return—a really fundamental step back to barbarism."

"Or forward," he said gloomily. "Most people think of history as a progression, you know, but really it may only be a circle. Perhaps we're about to meet ourselves coming back. If we last long enough to find out, that is."

"No sign of bombs and missiles yet, is there?"

"A state of readiness. But we're all in that. Otherwise, nothing imminent, even though he likes to scare the world into thinking so."

"Well," she said firmly, "I don't think it's going to happen. It just can't."

"That's what we all have to cling to," he agreed. "Our belief that it just can't."

"What else makes you consider yourself a ruthless man?"

"I gave orders, in his presence, that the President of Cuba is to be shot dead on the spot if he shows the slightest signs of defecting back to the Soviets when we help him launch his drive to retake the island tomorrow."

"The President of Cuba! But I thought—"

"Oh, that's right, you don't know, do you? His double was killed. He's here. He came via Guantánamo and is going back the same way sometime in the next hour or so. Tomorrow he's going to interrupt his own funeral and start an all-out revolt to oust the

Soviets. It will be, as he remarked, the most sensational resurrection since the first one. And, let up hope, as successful.''

"Life gets stranger and stranger," she remarked. "But I'll bet your order didn't faze him in the least."

"He said he would have done exactly the same."

"You're just old-fashioned," she said with a rather grim little smile. "Everybody's doing it, these days. But"—her expression changed—"I suppose it isn't funny. It too is symptomatic. The world grows sicker and sicker."

"Unto death," he said somberly. "Unless friend Yuri gets back into his bottle."

"He can't," she predicted. "He's gone too far. And you will have to go still farther, to defeat him."

He sighed.

"Great crises make great monsters, evidently; and I must make myself into one of the worst of them, to compete . . . Well—" His face suddenly did look old and tired and grim for a moment. "I find it is in me, if I have to . . . What do you hear from the kids?''

Her face softened for a moment as they both thought of Ham Jr. and his wife Cathy; Melinda and her husband John; Debby and her husband Robert; Beth and her husband Jim; and *their* kids.

"They've all called in the last hour or so—while you were still with our new friend from Cuba, apparently. They didn't want to bother you, and couldn't have anyway, but they all wanted you to know they're with you a hundred percent, whatever happens. They all said, 'whatever happens.' I suppose the fear is universal.''

"I'm sure. But not the love for me. That's rather far from universal.''

"Does it matter?" she asked. "I know it would help and be a great strength to you, but when all is said and done, you have the job to do—and there it is—and whether they like you or not, you're it. So why worry about it?''

"I'm not worried about it," he protested mildly, "I'm just saying it would be pleasanter if people liked me than it is when they don't.''

"Millions upon millions of people like you," she said stoutly. "And they approve of what you're doing, too, even if they are scared to death. Because there are enough of them who see that the only way to do this is to stand up to the Soviets and call their bluff. The only way.''

''And if it isn't a bluff?''

''Then the world blows up,'' she said, paling slightly but tone firm.

''Then the world—blows—up,'' he repeated. ''Do you realize how glib we've all become with that phrase? It doesn't mean a thing anymore.''

''Because, again, we believe that it just can't. Surely that mass conviction has some weight in the scale of things.''

''It does as long as I'm tough and you're tough and everybody else on our side is tough. Or tougher, rather. Tougher than he is. And so far there aren't too many signs of it. We seem to be standing almost entirely alone, at the moment.''

''That will change,'' she predicted confidently.

''With the pipeline closed? Not for long, if at all.''

''I think you underestimate them.''

''Not much,'' he said dryly.

''You used to be an optimist,'' she observed. ''What's become of that?''

''That was before I started living in the Oval Office,'' he said, still dryly. ''Now I have a whole new perspective on human nature. It isn't very encouraging.''

''Then it doesn't really matter if it all blows up, does it?''

He laughed, which was what she had intended him to do.

''Got me,'' he admitted with a chuckle. ''Got me cold . . . One thing I think you should know: if it does blow up, it's been fun. I'm glad I happened to know you. Life would have been much duller without you. I've been very lucky.''

''Why, thank you,'' she said, trying to make it light but obviously touched. ''That's the nicest thing that's been said to me all crisis.''

''There's nobody I'd rather be blown up with,'' he assured her solemnly, and this time she laughed and for a moment, underneath the shrewd New England grandmother, he caught a glimpse of the delightful young Elinor Seely he had married forty years ago. Not so young now, he thought with a fleeting trace of melancholy, but still delightful, and for that he was indeed very grateful.

"I think you'd better come along to bed and try to get some rest," she suggested as they finished and left the table. "You need it."

"I do indeed," he agreed, "but first I think I'd better go back to the office and check a few things."

"They'll call you, soon enough."

"I know. But I'd still feel better if I checked."

She smiled and tapped him lightly on the cheek.

"After forty years I know enough not to argue. But do come along soon, Ham. You've got to keep your strength up. Everything depends on it."

He shrugged.

"Art Hampton's there, if I'm gone. And if Art's not there, the Speaker will be. And if not him, then somebody else. Nobody's indispensable, in a democracy. Now, with friend Yuri—"

"There are others there, too," she said. "Unfortunately. Anyway, you mustn't let him obsess you. He's only a man. And you're a better one. Which is what it all comes down to in the last analysis, isn't it?"

"It helps," he said with a smile, "though in my case I think it's a little more than just the President of the United States. It's the historical background and tradition he comes from and all the people around him who support him and assist him and give him strength. Not the least of whom, if I may say so," he added with a look that made her suddenly blush and look quite young again, "is Elinor Seely Delbacher."

"I try."

"You succeed," he assured her. "I really literally do not know what I would do without you, at this point. Or any point in the last forty years, for that matter."

"You politicians," she said lightly, but obviously pleased. "You do exaggerate so. However"—and standing on tiptoe, she kissed him—"I'll accept it in lieu of something more peaceful, such as a nice long vacation at the farm in Pennsylvania or the house on Nantucket."

He returned the kiss with an intensity almost desperate and then gently released her.

"It will be a long time," he predicted gravely, "before we see the farm in Pennsylvania or the house on Nantucket again."

"Maybe not," she said, again striving to be light, "maybe not. This may all come right before we know it. There has to be hope, after all. I can't always be denied."

"It has been in history for many people, many times," he said. "Why should we be any different?"

"I don't know," she said stoutly. "I just think we are. And so do you, obviously, or all this would have swamped you long ago."

"So you say," he remarked, half-joking but feeling a little better.

"So I say," she echoed. "You've started it in Cuba, and now you're on your way."

Back in the Oval Office, receiving the calls he did receive, he could almost think she might be right.

Because, causing a surprise he would not have admitted to them, word began to come in from NATO; and counter to what he had expected, its members were in general friendly, favorable and much firmer than he had dared hope.

Apparently the allies had not been as frightened by Yuri's threats as Yuri had intended. His blatancy had finally produced a hardening of attitudes. And Ham's firm statement after Yuri's speech had apparently had considerable effect.

Evidently there had been meetings at the highest level in most of the capitals, lasting most of the night. It was nearing midnight in Washington, approaching dawn in Europe, when the first calls began to come in. He realized with a rising tide of excitement and satisfaction that most of his fellow leaders were going to stand with him, even though some continued to express grave doubts about the ultimate consequences of his policies. He did his best to allay their fears. By the time he left the Oval Office shortly before one A.M. to go to bed he felt that things were in reasonably good shape in Europe despite the obvious worries of many. He was tired, surprised, grateful and elated.

The Prime Minister of Great Britain he had known he could count upon. Her comments had been terse and to the point.

"Mr. President!" she said. "I am glad to report that we have just concluded an emergency Cabinet meeting here at Number Ten and the consensus is that we will continue to support you firmly and without flinching. The only caveat is that we do hope you will be able to work out the hostage issue very quickly so that the world can be spared that particular horror; and we do stand ready to offer our good offices as mediator if President Serapin shows the slightest sign of wishing to enter into serious negotiation."

"The proof of which," he said, "would of course have to be termination and withdrawal of his assistance to the subversive forces in the area of conflict."

"That would be the ideal," she agreed.

"It is the absolute necessity," he said flatly. She hesitated a second and then said slowly, "That may be a difficult precondition to secure."

"Then there is no point in mediating," he said, "because there is nothing to mediate."

Again she hesitated.

"The only way to salvage this situation," he said, "is to adhere to a policy of unflinching firmness and not deviate from it one iota. Believe me, it is the only way. To permit negotiations while fighting is still going on is to open the way for the Soviets to gain at the table what they are attempting to steal in the field. I will not be party to such negotiations, which are not negotiations and do not deserve the name."

She sighed, a half-exasperated, half-humorous sound.

"I told my colleagues that you would be adamant about that. Some of them did not believe it."

"Tell them to believe it. I hope it will not weaken the resolve to support me."

"Not mine," she said with a return to cheerfulness. "Your view of course parallels exactly my own, but I felt I should express to you the feeling that seemed generally prevalent in the Cabinet, namely that we should not attach conditions to mediation. Your attitude does not disturb *me* in the slightest." She chuckled. "On the contrary."

"Good," he said. "I appreciate your support, Prime Minister. If the shoe is ever on the other foot—"

"One for all and all for one," she said crisply. "I only hope our other friends in NATO will see it the way we do."

"I hope so, too," he said in a tone which indicated that he was not too sanguine.

Yet when he heard from the others his forebodings proved surprisingly groundless.

In rapid succession he took calls from the Prime Ministers of Canada, Denmark, Norway, Luxembourg, Iceland, the Netherlands, Portugal, Spain and Belgium. Some, particularly the sometimes rather fey and elusive ally on his northern border, took occasion to express their continuing consternation and alarm at what they termed his "belligerent approach" to the problems created by the Soviet President; but when it came down to their final decision, it was the same as that of Britain's determined lady: one for all and all for one, and the devil take Yuri Serapin, who did not seem to have scared them half as much as he no doubt thought he had. His threat to close the pipeline—exactly as had been predicted when it had first been built amid much controversy between the then American administration and its European allies, particularly West Germany—had shaken but not deterred them.

"If the crisis continues into winter," the Prime Ministers of Belgium, the Netherlands and Luxembourg told him, "we may have to reappraise the situation. But for now, and perhaps even then, you may count on us."

Greece and Turkey, always jealous and suspicious of one another, were not quite so forthcoming. Both began what seemed to him a tentative sounding-out process as to what kind of quid pro quo they could get for coming to his support now. He terminated this with considerable brusqueness.

"You will get exactly what you get right now as allies within NATO," he said shortly. "American assistance and American aid in case you need it. No more and no less."

"Which," the Prime Minister of Greece pointed out blandly, "may not be so great, now that American aid and assistance are being drawn off to four other places."

"But which nonetheless," he responded with some tartness,

"will be welcomed desperately by Your Excellency *and* your government *and* your people if you should find yourselves under attack. Regardless of whether what we can give is big, little or in between. I venture to predict you will want us there under any conditions. Those most critical of America, I've found, are the first to come running, Prime Minister."

"Well!" the Prime Minister of Greece said, taken aback by his uncompromising tone and obviously upset by it. "In any event—"

"In any event," he interrupted, "we may count on your support in the present crisis?"

"I suppose so," the Greek Prime Minister said huffily. "Yes. Yes. I suppose so."

"Thank you," the President said dryly. "Such wholehearted enthusiasm makes your support doubly valuable."

And rang off before there could be a no doubt indignant and contentious rejoinder.

The Prime Minister of Turkey was not quite so snide in his approach, but their conversation was essentially the same. Not so, to the President's surprise and pleasure, his talk with the President of France, who was still maintaining his country's pose of being associated with, but not in, NATO; but eager to make clear that he considered himself as determined to thwart the Soviet leader as Hamilton Delbacher himself.

"Mr. President," he said when he came on-line shortly after midnight Washington time, "we have had a long and most interesting night here. The conclusion is that M. Serapin must not be allowed to bluff his way to world dominion."

"My sentiments exactly," Hamilton Delbacher said gratefully. "We certainly appreciate your support, Mr. President."

"You have it," the President of France said emphatically. "We are not impressed by loud noises coming out of Moscow. Nor are we overly concerned about the pipeline, although if winter comes and things are still unresolved, we may find it a bit uncomfortable. We shall have to see what time brings, there."

"We hope the crisis will be over before then."

"It must be," the President of France agreed. "But there must be no compromise with the gambler Serapin. You must remain determined in the face of his adventures.''

"I intend to," the President said. "I have received other calls from Europe tonight and I am happy to say that most of them said essentially the same thing; some more, some less, but all essentially agreed. There seems to be a turning against our friend Yuri on the part of Europe's leaders. A significant change, it seems to me.''

"Europe's leaders, yes," the President of France said. His tone became thoughtful. "But we have not yet heard from Europe's peoples. They may be less easy to convince, not having the knowledge we do upon which to base their opinions.''

"If past history is any indication," the President said with some dryness, "their reactions—or the reactions of that portion of them that can be turned into the streets by the KGB and its well-meaning dupes and stooges—may be rather violent tomorrow. They aren't accustomed to saying no to the Soviet Union. It will be a big shock for them.''

"Then it is up to us convince them," the President of France said calmly. "I myself intend to address the Republic at noon tomorrow. Possibly other leaders could do the same.''

"Several have told me they intend to," Ham Delbacher said. "It will be a great help.''

"Have you heard from Dietrich Bolle yet?" the French President inquired in a tone almost overly casual. The question reminded the President that in fact he had not heard from the Chancellor of West Germany.

"Not yet," he replied; and on a sudden hunch inquired pointedly, "Should I have?''

"It would appear to be expected," the French President said with a delicate obliqueness.

"I do expect it," the President said. "I assume the conferences in Bonn must have run a little longer than the rest. Unless there is some other—''

"He has talked to me," the President of France interrupted. "I have talked to him. Several times.''

"Then that should make his conversation with me doubly interesting," the President suggested.

"I believe it will," the French President said. His tone, having been heavily significant, turned briskly businesslike. "Perhaps I should conclude, in case he may be trying to reach you at this moment."

"That is very thoughtful of you, Mr. President," Hamilton Delbacher said gravely. "And thank you again for your help. It means a great deal to know that France supports me."

"Implacably," the French President said. "Quite implacably."

For which, Ham Delbacher thought as the conversation ended, he was indeed very grateful. Again his busy telephone buzzer sounded—he reflected that he would have to give the girls on the White House switchboard something very nice for their yeoman duty during the crisis, when it was all over—and he picked up the receiver fully expecting to hear Dietrich Bolle's heavily accented excellent English, but from a source he least expected.

"Mr. President," his caller said gravely, and introduced himself; and after a moment's stunned surprise the President responded with equal gravity, "Your Holiness."

And thought to himself, *What in the world—? Am I about to be excoriated for my sins?*

The Pope, however, had far different things in mind; and this very swiftly became apparent.

"We have watched"—he began slowly and then, with a slight chuckle, dropped the pontifical "we"—"*I* have watched with profound interest and, I might truthfully say, considerable apprehension, the course of events in the past few days. However, all in all I think I can say that I am in general sympathy with what you are trying to do and I hope profoundly that it succeeds. Are we being monitored?"

"Probably," the President said, "but no matter. It will do him good to know where you stand."

"I doubt if it will be a surprise," the Pope said dryly. "They learned long ago in that place what I think of them."

"And tried to return the compliment."

"Without success, praise God."

"You can say that again," the President said and then joined the Pontiff in laughter at his own colloquialism.

"Have you considered," the Pope asked, so casually on the

wave of their amusement that it took the President a second to realize what he was saying, "the creation of diversions much closer to home?"

"Closer to—?" the President said, and the Pope uttered an affirming sound.

"I am considering them," the President said carefully, "but there is the question of creating a unity, as a result, that perhaps does not exist at the moment."

"I am sure it does not exist," the Pontiff said. "We have our own intelligence services here, you know, and they are not without skill and resources. They inform me that unity is far from present despite recent—er—rearrangements, shall we say."

"The rearrangements in themselves may have made unity even more remote," the President said. "Though that was obviously not the intention."

"Things do not always work out according to intentions," the Pope observed. "And praise God for that, too . . . So you are thinking."

"I am thinking."

"There may be ways to achieve the objective that will not be so obvious as to provoke the reaction you fear. I am wondering if you would look kindly on such efforts."

The President hesitated, but only for a moment. "I would be forever grateful for such efforts."

"And would perhaps, at the opportune moment, do what can be done to encourage and assist them?"

"Everything possible, believe me."

"More than just words, as has sometimes been the case from Washington?"

"I was not in the White House then," the President said simply.

"Nor I on the throne of St. Peter," the Pope rejoined, again with his comfortable chuckle. "So, then—we have an agreement?"

"We have an agreement. How soon do you think—?"

"You have seen Rome," the Pope said. "Right now she is turning her characteristic lovely old burnt-umber color, touched by the rising sun. By the time the color begins to fade, you will begin to see the signs."

"Excellent," the President said. "Absolutely excellent."

"We gamble with the lives and fates of many millions," the Pontiff observed, suddenly grave.

"We did not begin the gamble," the President said. "It is our responsibility to end it in a way that is worthy of them."

"May God be with us," the Pope said.

This time the President could not resist a chuckle. "If *you* can't guarantee that, Holiness, I don't know who can."

"I can try," the Pope said, responding in kind with a lighter tone. "But He does not always listen, even to me. However, this time we must hope He does."

"He has to," the President said, abruptly grave again.

"Yes," the Pontiff agreed with equal gravity. "He must."

For several moments after his pleasantly authoritative voice had faded from the line the President sat staring out into the darkness of the dimly lit Rose Garden. What an unexpected call and what unexpected help! And how bravely they were embarking together upon a course whose consequences, like so many things in the situation precipitated by Yuri Serapin, were completely unknowable and completely uncertain. When he had been writing his speech to the world he had contemplated, along with a call for internal revolution in Russia, a call to the satellites to revolt, and a promise of all-out American aid to them if they would. He had rejected it for the very reason he had told the Pope: because he was sure that if anything would unite the Soviet military behind Yuri it would be an appeal for revolt on their very borders. But if revolt could be started with means and through channels which he was sure the Pope had secretly and very carefully cultivated over the years, then the stigma of open American incitement would be avoided and American aid could then be forthcoming to rebel forces the moment they showed the slightest signs of organized form. He knew the Pope must be sure there would be organization or he would not himself take such a gamble, even indirectly.

And now he must talk to Dietrich Bolle before going to bed: the last piece, and certainly one of the most important, must be in place before he could seek the rest he desperately needed. He checked the switchboard, but no call had come in from Bonn. He initiated one himself immediately. Within five minutes it had come through.

"I am sorry, Dietrich," he said, "if I awakened you, but—"

"Not at all," the Chancellor said, sounding tired but hearty. "We have been meeting all night—*all night*—and we are still meeting. It is good to get away from these burghers, dear friends of mine though some of them may be! How is dear Elinor?"

"How thoughtful of you to ask," the President said, reflecting that it had obviously been worthwhile when, as Vice-President a year ago, he and Elinor had carefully cultivated the Chancellor and his wife at an economic meeting in Geneva. "She, like everyone, is tired but in good spirits. And Kathe?"

"Fine, fine!" Dietrich Bolle said. "Let us hope the President of the Soviet Union is *very* tired!"

"Amen to that," the President said. "And what are you deciding, in this marathon meeting?"

"To stand with you," the Chancellor said cheerfully. "But it takes much planning and endless discussion, it would seem, of contingencies."

"I am advised from Paris that contingencies there are," the President said. "Or might be. Perhaps you could enlighten me?"

He was aware at once of a decrease in heartiness. The Chancellor's tone became noticeably more formal.

"Did Paris tell you their nature, Mr. President?"

"No. He indicated you might want to tell me."

"Hm," Dietrich Bolle said, and there was silence during which the President did a quick mental review of the situation of West Germany: the end of the "economic miracle" as the result of the OPEC oil shocks and the slowness of German industry to catch up to the new technological age that was throwing so many old assumptions and alignments askew; the deep and steadily rising unemployment; the growing flirtations with the Soviet Union, both as trading partner and as potential giver of the gift all Germans and few others desired, reunification; the anti-Americanism that seemed to have as its ultimate end an inevitable drift into the Soviet orbit. He was no longer dealing with that nice, reliable ally of the early post–World War II years. He was dealing now with an increasingly sick nation whose inner malaise had produced terrible things before and might well again.

"I gather they concern the East," the President said. "I take it your intention is to—"

"Whatever my intention is," Dietrich Bolle said sharply, "it cannot be discussed like this. Perhaps I should send you a special envoy."

"It might be a good idea," the President agreed crisply. "Whatever you can do to produce diversions will of course be very welcome here."

"If they occur," Dietrich Bolle said darkly, "and they *will* occur—they will be much more than diversions. They will be *the final correction of historic wrongs.*"

I have heard that kind of language, the President thought with a chilling sense of déjà vu, before. And this is what France intends to support? Perhaps I too should be as practical as France and accept whatever will confound the Soviets. After all, that is the immediate and imperative issue now.

Nonetheless he could not keep a certain reserve out of his voice as he asked, "How soon do you expect these—corrections to take place?"

"I would not wish to name a time," the Chancellor replied in a reproving tone, "nor should I think you would want me to, Mr. President. However, it seems safe to say it will not be in the year 2001."

And he uttered an abrupt and exaggerated snort of laughter.

"Let us hope not," the President said, echoing the amusement mildly.

"No!" the Chancellor said. "It will be soon, Mr. President. Very soon!"

"Good," the President said. "If there is anything America can do to help, don't hesitate."

"You can tell your forces here to cooperate with us to the fullest," Dietrich Bolle said and added without skipping a beat, "Under our command, of course."

"Now, just a minute! You aren't telling me the French have agreed to that? I don't believe it."

"Not exactly," the Chancellor admitted. "But they have pledged full support."

"So am I pledging full support," Ham Delbacher said tartly, "but not in any subordinate command."

"We will not accept American command," the Chancellor said with a bland arrogance that momentarily took the President's breath away. But he recovered speedily.

"You will accept what we give you on any terms on which we give it," he said sharply, "or you will not have it, and be damned to you. You are not embarked on a universally popular course, you know, Chancellor, when you set out to reunify Germany: too many people have too good memories. The fear and dislike of your country will be a long time dying and is far from over yet. If we assist in reunification, it will be on our terms and our conditions, and our aid will be under our control. So make up your mind."

There was a frigid silence for several moments; but the Chancellor, as they both knew, really had nowhere else to go unless he wished to openly embrace the Soviet Union, and this was hardly the moment for that. So presently he uttered an angry and hastily suppressed sigh and struggled, with obvious difficulty, to return to his initial heartiness.

"Mr. President!" he exclaimed. "You make it all sound so serious!"

"It is," Hamilton Delbacher said, not relenting yet.

"But, no, Mr. President!" Dietrich Bolle exclaimed. "No, it is not! At least, not *that* serious. Of *course* we want your assistance and of *course* we realize that whatever happens must be done in co-operation with you; it could not be done otherwise! Of *course* we value our association and of *course* we know you have the best interests of our country at heart. I did not mean to sound abrupt, Mr. President, but it has been a long night, you know—a long night. Tempers have grown short, you know, not only mine! If you could have heard some of the things my cabinet ministers have called me tonight—!" He attempted a jovial laugh that succeeded only in sounding forced and insincere. "It has been enough to make me want to abandon politics altogether! But I persevere, Mr. President, I persevere—and shall continue to persevere, with your help and support which means so much to the Federal Republic. Where would we be without you? You have been our greatest friend. We contemplate nothing without you! We seek your advice and encouragement always. Do you not know that to be so? . . . And of course," he added, tone suddenly much tougher, "there is another alternative, Mr. President. We do not really have to do anything at all, do we? We can quite profitably, I think, sit by and do nothing while your contest with Mr. Serapin is decided on other battlegrounds. Why bloody ourselves to help *you* unless *we* can be sure of help? Is *that* not logic? And would *that* not make matters much more difficult for the United States?"

It was time for the President to remain silent, because there, of course, the Chancellor had him. If Soviet satellites flared into rebellion but the strongest of them all, East Germany, did not follow suit because it had received no encouraging signal from its brethren across the Wall, then the Soviets' problem would be to that extent reduced. And the last thing he wanted was to have the Soviet problem reduced.

So presently he too muffled an exasperated sigh and spoke in a calmer tone. "Chancellor," he said, "we both have our problems with this, but I think if you will sleep upon it for a few hours and take note of what is happening around you, you will decide the time is ripe."

"How soon will that be?" Dietrich Bolle inquired with some skepticism.

"As soon, I am told, as the color fades from Roman walls."

There was a momentary silence and then a low whistle from the Chancellor.

He almost whispered.

"You mean—he actually—"

"Chancellor!" the President said sharply; and in a deliberately more conversational tone, "Now I must get to bed and get some rest, and so must you. Tomorrow may be a busy day."

"Very," Dietrich Bolle said softly. "No doubt we shall speak again."

"Of hopeful things, I trust."

"Oh, yes!" the Chancellor said, sounding suddenly quite confident. "Of very hopeful things."

And yet what hope was there, Hamilton Delbacher thought as he prepared to leave his desk, in a reunified and almost certainly aggressive Germany, undoubtedly the strongest force to be reborn from a sudden Soviet collapse?

He sighed again, very heavily this time.

That will have to be the next man's problem, he told himself wryly.

I can only handle one decade at a time.

He pushed back his chair and started to stand up when the phone rang again.

"This is my positively last call tonight unless it's from State or Defense," he told the operator firmly. "I must get to bed."

"Yes, Mr. President," she said, "but he is virtually screaming into the telephone."

"Who on earth is it?" he asked; and when she told him, snorted in disgust.

"It only points up the general insanity of the world we live in, he told her. "Put him on."

"Yes, sir," she said; and added grimly, "It sure does."

"Mr. President!" the new, youthful leader of Iran shouted, voice so high and tense it seemed, as always, close to breaking under the weight of its own hysteria. It was no wonder he was referred to in the Western world as "the Young Fanatic" who had succeeded the old one. "Mr. President, how dare you!"

"How dare I what!" he snapped. "And what are you bothering me for at this ungodly hour?"

"I don't believe in God," the Young Fanatic said with a chuckle in a tone that sounded for the moment perfectly sane. Which he was, the President had always suspected, in his own weird way. The rest was play-acting for the benefit of a world that was supposed to be properly fearful, and now and then was.

Except that now, he reflected with an inward groan, the jerk could really make trouble if he so desired. His oil markets were collapsing along with those of the rest of the Arab world, but he had purchased himself some pretty toys with the proceeds while the going was good. It would only take one of them, dropped or planted in the right place, and the fragile shell of the living world would be shattered as surely as though an exchange had occurred between the U.S. and the U.S.S.R.

Still, there was nothing to be gained by being diplomatic, because that had been tried many times without success with this creep. He might as well say exactly what he thought.

"I don't care who you believe in," he said, "but I do not believe in you, so why don't you go back to your desert and bury yourself under a pile of camel dung?"

"Mr. President!" the Young Fanatic said, and his tone was abruptly harsh and menacing, threatening again to spiral upward. "You will not be so disrespectful someday. When you grovel at my feet you will not be so disrespectful."

"I will grovel at the feet of a pig before I grovel at yours, and consider it an honor by comparison," Ham Delbacher said. An angry animal groan of rage came over the line.

"Ah, dog," the Young Fanatic said when he could talk, in a softly crooning voice, "Dog, dog, dog. How little do you know what the future holds, arrogant infidel. How little do you know the destruction I shall visit upon you and all your cities and all your people."

"I think," the President said in a conversational tone, "that I should tell the Navy and the Air Force to eliminate Iran from the map tomorrow morning. Then perhaps I would not be bothered by gnats and crawling things."

"You gamble with your fate!" the leader of Iran screamed with a sudden wildly exaggerated vehemence. "You fly in the face of Allah, stupid man! Your dust and the dust of your ancestors will commingle in the cloud that hides the sun. There will be nothing of you left! Nothing!"

"Is there a purpose for this call, Excellency?" Ham Delbacher inquired with an abrupt politeness he knew would probably be more disconcerting to his caller than any amount of the abuse at which he excelled. "If not, it is very late here and I am tired and wish to go to bed."

"You will be much more tired," his caller said in vicious tone, "and you will go to bed never to rise, if you do not listen to me."

"I am listening, Excellency," the President said. "But not for long. Now, what is it?"

"I shall cut off all oil to Europe and the world," the Young Fanatic said in a perfectly calm voice, "unless you at once cease your imperialist adventure overseas."

"So?" the President inquired.

"I have just sai—" the Young fanatic cried, his voice scaling up again.

"I know what you said," the President interrupted, "and I said: 'So?' That implies skepticism and disdain in the Western world."

"I know what it implies!" the Young Fanatic snapped. "I am not ignorant, even though you think I am."

"Not I," the President said. "I think you are a very intelligent, very shrewd man—a little far-out, as we say over here, but smart. Too smart, I should think, to really believe you can threaten me or deflect the United States from its purposes."

"Evil purposes!"

"We all have our estimations," Ham Delbacher said in a deliberately indifferent voice. "Mine holds here."

"Arrogant!" the Iranian exclaimed, almost strangling on the word. "Arrogant, arrogant, arrogant! How you will be humbled, how you will be humbled!"

"Perhaps," the President said, "but not by you. Is that threat all you wished to tell me?"

"It is enough, dog of an imperialist President!"

"It is enough for nothing," Ham Delbacher said. "Good-bye, Excellency."

"You will listen to me, or you will die!"

"I will not listen to you and I will not die, at least at the hands of an international bully."

"Listen to me!" the Young Fanatic screamed. *"Listen to me!"*

"Good-bye, Excellency," he repeated as to a child, and hung up on the raving voice.

He could not entirely discount the potential for trouble there, but it had existed for so long, and contingency plans for removing the Iranian problem had for so long been part of American military planning, that he did not think he should waste much time worrying about it. But he made a note to check in the morning and be sure the plan was indeed in the active file. He did not think it would be needed immediately, but it was best to be sure.

One last thing he did before turning off the lights and leaving the

Oval Office: he called fussy little Anson McUmber, the hold-over national security adviser, and told him to rouse Roger Hackett, Chauncey Baron and the head of the CIA at six A.M. and tell them that it was very likely that equally longstanding Operation Tumbledown would be needed in Eastern Europe before another twenty-four hours had elapsed. Then he went at last to the Mansion to join soundly sleeping Elinor and in ten minutes was sound asleep himself.

The immediate future still looked dark and heavy but here and there a few little gleams of light might conceivably be starting to break through.

BOOK FOUR

1

For the President of the Soviet Union also, it had been a long and sleepless night whose triumphant memories—and continuing tensions—not even his present occupation could obliterate.

He lay beside the opulent body of Ekaterina Vasarionova. They were still breathing heavily from their determined exertions—to him subtly unsatisfactory, though she had dutifully followed directions. He knew her heart was not in it: it never was. He had the sense that she was always standing somewhere alongside the bed, looking down with an amused and scornful smile—which on a few occasions he had actually seen before she quickly concealed it. Lately she seemed to be making fewer attempts to conceal it.

A furious anger began to rise: he could feel it physically, in his throat. If it were not that he was so pleased with what he had recently accomplished, so certain that events were proceeding inevitably along the path he had laid out for them, so confident in his now supreme power over the Soviet Union and all the satellite peoples it controlled within its sprawling empire, he knew he might very well be in danger of letting his anger escape. To do so would be to place himself even further in thrall to the beautiful and contemptuous woman he had convinced himself three years ago he could not live without. To do so might mean even more than that—it might open an abyss of violence from which he realized he was more and more having to restrain himself.

Not that Yuri Pavlovich Serapin shrank from violence, of

course: he had just come safely through the most violent few hours of Soviet history since Joseph Stalin's day. They had left him drained of emotion, though still filled with a great inner tension that his activities with Ekaterina had only partially assuaged.

He was still "on fire," as he expressed it to himself, even more so because of an odd little episode that had occurred just before he left his Kremlin office and, with the absolute secrecy and discretion he always exercised where she was concerned, driven himself, unaccompanied by any guards or any protection—or, he believed, any surveillance—through Moscow's bleak, deserted streets to his rendezvous.

He had been sitting at his desk, surveying as usual his enormous illuminated map of the world. His four bright conflagrations still sparkled where he had caused them to be ignited, blinking and pulsating with a reassuring, satisfying vigor. Then for an odd moment it seemed to him almost as though they were fading a little, as though they were not quite as bright as before. He shook his head, rubbing a hand across eyes that clearly showed the exhaustion of the recent hours.

He knew the fires fading was an illusion.

Nothing had dimmed the power that lighted them. They gleamed as prettily as ever, proof that his plans were advancing everywhere on schedule.

Or were they?

For the first time since he had taken office some warning instinct, some fleeting malaise, touched, for an ominous second, the edges of his mind.

Angrily he shook it off. There was no reason to feel this way for even a moment. Yuri the invincible was invincible still, never more than now when he had ruthlessly removed the last possible vestiges of opposition, the last possible impediments on his road into history.

He congratulated himself that he had done so with great skill and shrewdness. He had used superbly the weapon of surprise that had always been so dominant in Soviet thought and planning. He had struck like lightning in the night and down before him had gone all who had possessed the power to say him nay.

Now there was no one at all to thwart the will of Yuri Pavlovich;

not even the man he knew he must now begin to mistrust and, ultimately, remove as he had all the others.

Mikhail Yarkov was his only potential rival now; and since he
was Yuri's creation, assisted carefully in his rise to control of the
KGB even as Yuri himself was rising to the summit of Soviet
power, there might be sufficient loyalty there to last the little time
sufficient for Yuri to hedge him about with enough restraints so
that he could never turn upon his creator. And then, when the time
was right, there could be another lightning in the night—unless the
general proved himself indeed the loyal and subservient aide that
Yuri hoped sheer self-interest would lead him to be—the permanent, and permanently obedient, "First Assistant to the President."

For the present, at any rate, he was the man upon whom Yuri
would depend to keep the empire in order during these final stages
of the war that would decide the fate of all mankind. Without hesitation and without the slightest question General Yarkov had followed orders in the sudden purge of the Politburo and the military.
Several of the victims, Yuri knew, had been Yarkov's personal
friends—as personal and as friendly as it was possible to be in the
constantly circling, constantly suspicious upper echelons of Soviet
power. Yet as cold-bloodedly as Yuri himself, Yarkov had carried
out the orders for their arrest, torture and execution. He had acted
with merciless speed and implacable force. No cry for mercy from
men who had collaborated all their lives in the murder or elimination of opposition moved Yarkov in the slightest. He had a job to
do and he did it, as impersonally as though he were dealing with
inanimate objects instead of human beings. It was an operation as
efficient and admirable as any Yuri had seen; and he could not help
but be greatly impressed by the selfless dedication of an aide who
could move so rapidly and with such efficiency to carry out the objectives of the glorious socialist revolution.

The result had been to place Yuri at the unchallenged pinnacle of
the Soviet state, mightier than any czar, mightier than Stalin,
mightier than anyone—anyone in all history, he told himself with a
grim satisfaction, even if for a strange little moment it had seemed
as though the fires he had lit around the globe were threatening to
go out. That had been a second's delusion, a childish fancy, a trick

of the mind—meaning nothing because it could mean nothing. He had dismissed it angrily and gone to Ekaterina. Now it came back again in spite of his dismissal.

He stirred uneasily.

"What's the matter?" she inquired, raising herself on an elbow to study his face with the interested and quite objective expression that he found he was beginning to hate. "Is the world getting too heavy for Yuri Pavlovich to carry?"

"No, it is not getting too heavy!" he snapped, turning on his side so that his back was toward her. She placed a hand on his hip and massaged it gently. Even her touch was ironic.

"There!" she said. "The Little Father is concerned for his children. It is natural for one who looks after their welfare so wonderfully."

"I look after yours," he said coldly, turning back as suddenly as he had turned away. She smiled her dry, infuriating smile.

"I am honored."

"I can easily kill those I do not like," he observed in a conversational tone and thought that for a second she looked startled, if not concerned. But her tone was basically as unimpressed—and disrespectful, he told himself angrily—as ever.

"If that includes a poor farmer's daughter who never asked better than bread and potatoes and an occasional pot of tea," she said calmly, stretching with a luxurious yawn, "then so be it. Though I cannot imagine why you would want to, Yuri Pavlovich. Do I not do all you ask of me?"

"No more," he remarked, and in spite of himself he heard a note of hateful petulance in his voice.

Ekaterina laughed, a cheerful, amused sound—amused at *him,* he thought bitterly, whom no one else on this earth dared be amused by.

"Poor Yuri Pavlovich! What would they say in Washington if they knew—"

"No one in Washington will ever know!" he retorted angrily. "Or Moscow! Or anywhere! Else I shall have your head!"

"My," she said, hitching herself up a bit in the bed and studying him with an even more exaggerated attention. "My poor Yuri is positively unhappy tonight—or is it this morning? He sounds quite like Ivan the Terrible. 'Else I will have your head.' Well,'' she said, and the indifference that always infuriated him increased, ''if it suits you, Yuri Pavlovich. If it will make you more certain of your own importance.''

''I am important!'' he shouted, thinking even as he said it how ridiculous it was, the soon-to-be Supreme Ruler and Arbiter of All Mankind having to yell his importance to this woman who without him would be nothing—whom with one word he could make nothing, if he so desired.

''Quiet,'' she ordered mildly. ''I know you have had the walls made thick, Yuri Pavlovich. I know there is no one else permitted to live on this floor and no one above me or below me, but still there are dignities. They must be maintained, must they not, or even so someone might hear.''

''No one can hear,'' he said bluntly, ''as you have just pointed out. I could kill you, and no one would hear.''

''Why not, then?'' she inquired, lying back, yawning again like some sleek cat, unfortunately very beautiful in her rather heavy way. ''As I said, Yuri Pavlovich, if it suits you. Certainly,'' she added, her voice hardening to an acrid edge, ''if you did it would be simply fun, would it not? It would not be a high matter of state like your murder of the Politburo and the military. It would just be for your own enjoyment. Or was that fun too?''

''It was an inevitable development of history!''

''Yes,'' she said, increasingly acrid, increasingly dry. ''If you decided you *must* get rid of them, they of course could not be sent into internal exile. They *had* to be killed.''

''An example had to be made,'' he said stubbornly, ''in case others had the same idea.''

''And did *they?* How were you so sure, Yuri Pavlovich?''

''It was obvious,'' he said, and suddenly his tone, too, hardened. ''You know much, Ekaterina Vasarionova, but you did not grow up with these men as I did. Some of them have tried to kill me before. I have had to kill in return. It is not a pleasant world we live in, in the Kremlin. But it has to be done. One must be stronger than the rest. Otherwise one does not survive to carry out the mandate of history.''

''Who gave it to you?'' she inquired, sounding genuinely curious, though he suspected this was just another form of taunting him—she was always at such pains to show that she was probably the only Soviet citizen who did not live in desperate fear of him. "Who conferred history's mandate upon you, Yuri Pavlovich?"

"I took it," he said simply. "And now," he added with a profound satisfaction he made no attempt to conceal, "it is mine and no one anywhere on this earth—*anywhere*—can challenge me."

"I would say the American President is doing reasonably well at the moment," she observed; and added quickly before he could retort, "In any event, I still do not see why it was necessary to murder them. They could have been removed as easily."

"Not as easily," he said. "If they had lived they would have conspired against me. Conspiracies sometimes succeed. I could not take the chance."

"Comrade," she said, sitting up and shifting to rest her back against the head of the bed, arms hugging knees and eyes staring thoughtfully at him as he lay beside her, "I think you are as paranoid as Joseph Stalin. I think you may go too far one of these days. Those who kill can be killed. Sometimes a reaction is set in motion. Have you thought of that?"

"I have thought of everything!" he exclaimed angrily, rising abruptly and beginning to stride up and down the room while her eyes followed with a skeptical appraisal that suddenly made him blush furiously and grab a robe to cover his nakedness, though why he should have this reaction in front of Ekaterina Vasarionova he could not understand. It increased his already simmering rage and made his tone harsh and grating. "I have tought of what I should do with them, and I have thought of what I should do with *you* should you provoke me to it!"

"I tremble, Yuri Pavlovich," she said in a mocking tone. And suddenly he was beside her, hands furiously on her throat, forcing her head back. But she did not scream or struggle. Instead she managed to turn her head enough so that her eyes, somehow even then remaining amused, met his.

"Yes, Yuri Pavlovich?" she croaked. "And now?"

He snarled, an incoherent, meaningless sound of frustration and anger; and released her, flinging her back hard so that her head struck the headboard and for a second she was dazed and did not speak. "You are nothing to me, *nothing!* I could kill you this moment and no one would ever know!"

"And why would you kill me?" she inquired finally in a husky voice, massaging her throat. "Because I do not worship you enough, Yuri Pavlovich? Because I conspire with your enemies, Yuri Pavlovich? Because I am unfaithful to you? You know it is not true!"

"Because you laugh," he said bitterly, forced into stark confession for which he hated himself but which he seemingly could not help. "Because you are *unimpressed.*"

Then she did laugh, a sound half-strangled because of the pain in her throat, but a genuine laugh nonetheless, a laugh that clearly said what he hated to hear, that she was in command of him still.

"I do not worship you enough, poor Yuri Pavlovich!" she cried in a sarcastic voice that angered him horribly. "I laugh, I am unimpressed! And that is a fearful crime, yes, I can see that, it is a crime beyond all else, it is the ultimate treason! I laugh! Oh, yes," she repeated, now laughing hysterically and almost beyond control. "I laugh, I laugh! Oh, poor Yuri Pavlovich, if you only knew! If you only knew!"

"If I only knew *what?*" he demanded, coming closer, suddenly intent and quiet in a way that warned her so that she sobered and spoke to him more respectfully though still suppressing laughter with difficulty, as he could see.

"I adore you, Yuri Pavlovich," she assured him as solemnly as she could. "I *do* worship you, Little Father of All the Russias and everyone else in the world if you could only do it. Yes, I do, I do! If I laugh sometimes, it is only because—because—" And for a moment, long enough to interrupt her horrible voice, which he could no longer tolerate, she appeared threatened by laughter again.

"Yes?" he demanded in the same quiet, intent, furiously controlled way. "Because what, Ekaterina Vasarionova?"

"Because—because—" she said, and did give way then to her dreadful cackles which seemed to rattle through his head like rockets, "because sometimes—sometimes—you are so *serious,* Yuri Pavlovich! You are so *solemn. You* do *not* laugh, ever, and so I must. It is the only way to keep me sane, Yuri Pavlovich. It is the only way—perhaps it is the *only* way"—and abruptly she was not laughing but was looking at him in the cool, appraising fashion he abominated—"to keep *you* sane. Have you thought"—her eyes narrowed—"of what I *could* tell the world about you if I so decided? The awful things you have done, all the crimes you have committed, against Russia and against the world? What then, comrade? What then?"

Suddenly the audacity of her threat, the sheer monstrosity of her disrespect, overwhelmed him. Suddenly his control was gone completely. He hated her, hated her, *hated* her with a passion that drove all sense, all caution, all reason from his mind. He *was* the ruler, he *was* supreme, he *was* alone with this being, once loved but now so infuriating, who of all people in Russia and most on earth refused to acknowledge his all-knowing wisdom and superiority.

"I am sane!" he cried furiously, seizing her again by the throat and forcing her head down against the pillows. "I *am*, I *am*, I *am!*"

She managed to give a wild yell which seemed to him almost to form a name—*Whose? Whose?*—before he managed to force her even deeper into the pillows and finally drag one across and down upon her face. There he held it for moments beyond thought, sense, reason until finally her body, thrashing wildly beneath him, slackened and at last fell still.

Slowly he drew aside the pillow and stared down into her mottled face and staring eyes that no longer saw anything nor ever would again; and then there was a slight movement behind him. He leaped up and spun around; and realized, with an instantaneous cold, drained, completely rational return of sanity, *whose.*

"Comrade President," Mikhail Yarkov said softly, "you have had a busy night."

"She was an enemy of the people," he cried harshly. "Get rid of her!"

He turned away contemptuously—he had to act that way, he could not afford to show the slightest sign of the fear and repugnance that he felt creeping up the back of his neck. "Get rid of her, I don't care how, I don't care where, *get rid of her.*"

"It will be done, Comrade President," General Yarkov said in the same soft, polite tone. "And the apartment—?"

"What would you suggest?" he inquired again contemptuously, not looking at him as he swiftly, mechanically put on his clothes and shrugged into his coat, making it clear he intended to leave, conveying the impression he had to convey, that he trusted Yarkov implicitly to protect him.

"Leave it to me," Mikhail Yarkov said smoothly. "Within two hours no one will ever know the apartment was here. People will be living here, the floors above and below will be occupied." He smiled dryly. "There are plenty of people waiting for apartments in Moscow. We will find some to jump at the chance even if we do have to drag them out of bed at this hour. There will be nothing here to indicate she ever existed."

"Good," he said calmly. "See that it is so."

For just a second he hesitated, the questions he knew he should never ask trembling on his lips, almost forcing themselves out despite him: *Were you alone? Is there a tape? Can anything be proved?* With a great effort he forced himself to remain silent. To ask those questions would be to betray a weakness that could be fatal. He had to give the impression that *of course* he trusted Yarkov, *of course* there was no record, *of course* there was no proof. The slightest doubt and he would be in his assistant's hands forever.

But he knew he could not rest until he was sure; and he knew that Yarkov knew this.

For a long moment their eyes held, tension like a singing wire between them.

"Well!" Yuri said briskly. "Good night, comrade. I shall see you in my office"—he glanced at his Rolex, gleaming golden in the first light of dawn that was beginning to seep past the curtains—"at 0900. We have much to do in the day ahead."

"Indeed, Comrade President," Mikhail Yarkov agreed. "I hope you will be able to get a little rest between now and then."

"Oh, I will," Yuri said with an abrupt laugh. "I have no problems to disturb me, and if I did, you would handle them."

"I should hope so, Comrade President," General Yarkov said with an answering smile. "That is what I am here for."

"I am glad you realize it, comrade," Yuri said, clapping him comfortably on the back as he stepped through the door. "It relieves my mind."

"I hope so, Yuri Pavlovich," General Yarkov said; and repeated blandly: "It is what I am here for."

When he reached the street, Yuri noted, his own discreet little car had disappeared. Instead his official limousine was waiting, his chauffeur standing patiently at the open door.

He shrugged, returned the man's salute, took his seat. The door closed, the chauffeur got in, they roared away at top speed along just-stirring morning streets to the Kremlin. He had no time—had he even the inclination, which he thrust from him with a deliberate and angry impatience—to think of Ekaterina Vasarionova.

He knew he must think now, and very carefully, about Mikhail Yarkov.

In his office he left orders not to be disturbed, stripped off his outer garments and stretched out on a couch. He slept for three hours and awoke refreshed, or at least feeling so. The little lights still blinked strongly away. At 0900 his new military leaders appeared as scheduled to give him a brief summary of the battlefields which echoed those received earlier in Washington by Hamilton Delbacher. Like Ham, Yuri was puzzled by the one quiescent area of conflict; and like Ham, he initiated a telephone call to the man who had the answer. Unlike Ham, he was much displeased by what he heard. It did not help to have a subtle but consistent amusement—almost, he thought with a resurgence of anger, like Ekaterina's—running through the Vice-Chairman's outwardly polite and attentive remarks.

"Mr. President!" he exclaimed in his gentle old voice when the connection was established and his face, bland and twinkling as always, had materialized on the screen, "how gracious it is of you to seek out one whose humble knowledge is so infinitely less than your own!"

Yuri sighed. He was not sad for Ekaterina, she had deserved it; but again some sort of strange malaise seemed to be affecting his mind. Perhaps she had meant more to him than he realized. He would have to think about that later—sometime—if he had the opportunity. Right now he knew he was in no mood for Ju Xing-dao's verbal cuteness. His tone was blunt.

"That is not true, Vice-Chairman. There are no longer hostilities in the province of Taiwan. Why not?"

" 'Hostilities' is a word of many interpretations," Ju said mildly. "I would not say there is *peace* in the province of Taiwan. It is possible there are no guns shooting or bombs dropping at the moment, but of course you understand, Mr. President, they could resume at any time."

"Why have they stopped?" Yuri demanded. "I thought our agreement was—"

"No agreement," Ju interrupted with sudden vigor.

"Understanding, then!" Yuri snapped. "Undertaking. Commitment."

"And no commitment," Ju retorted with equal vigor.

"What was it, then, Vice-Premier?" Yuri asked dryly. "A dream of mine, when we signed the treaty? A casual thought only, that someday we might do something jointly to embarrass the United States and terminate once and for all her hegemonistic designs upon the world? I thought China agreed with these objectives?"

"Oh, we do, we do," Ju Xing-dao said blandly. "But we feel we must approach them in our own way. In any event," he added with a sudden bluntness to match Yuri's own, "we provided the diversion you wanted, did we not?"

"Not enough," Yuri said flatly. "Not enough. Too brief, too halfhearted, too innocuous."

"You wanted us to destroy Taiwan," Ju said with a rare sharpness. "You wanted them to do great damage to us. You wanted to divide China, as if China is not divided enough. That was your plan, Mr. President. So sorry it did not work."

"My plan," Yuri said, and it was all he could do to keep the surging anger from his voice, "was to occupy our friend in Washington so completely that he would not be able to divert any forces or energies to the other areas in which we had prepared surprises for him. That was my understanding, Vice-Premier. I am sorry China has betrayed Russia once again. I am afraid it will have to be noted in the highest circles."

For a second Ju looked quite stunned, Yuri thought. But this may have been a wishful misinterpretation, for his voice was as gently bland and unyielding as ever when he replied.

"So? And what do 'highest circles' think they can do about it, Mr. President? What do *you* contemplate, for I take it there is none higher now that you have—er"—he paused delicately—"rearranged, as it were, your government?"

"I have rid myself of traitors and saboteurs," Yuri snapped, "just as I will rid myself of international traitors and saboteurs"—he paused and then added a heavy emphasis—*"if it should become necessary."*

Again the Vice-Chairman was silent for a moment, but it was only so that he might study, most carefully, the broad, half-Slavic face before him—a face that was now suffused with a dark and ominous anger—a face whose owner, therefore, in Ju's opinion, must not be as much in control of himself as he would have his listener believe.

"Again I ask you, Mr. President," he said softly, "how will you accomplish this? I cannot believe that you really consider China to be in that category, but if you do—what will you do to us? Issue ultimatums? Drop bombs? Go to war? That would be foolish in the extreme, would it not? Are you not occupied enough as it is? Or would it, perhaps," he added with a sudden bluntness of his own, "provide distractions for your people, who perhaps do not agree with all you do?"

"There is no one," Yuri exclaimed, voice rising suddenly to an angry pitch that made Ju visibly—and ironically, Yuri felt with rising bitterness—shy back from the screen, "*no one* in the Soviet Union who does not agree with my policies!"

"It is regrettable," Ju said gently, "that such unanimity does not apply to the entire world."

"It will," Yuri promised in a voice so abruptly cold and certain that this time the Vice-Chairman did give him a quite genuinely startled glance, sudden, sharp and shrewd. But his tone remained bland.

"I do not see," he remarked, "how that can ever be. But perhaps things are known to you which are not known to us, Mr. President."

"Perhaps," Yuri agreed, and in his voice was a certain inner smugness that again made Ju study him sharply for a second. "Perhaps so, Vice-Chairman. In any event," he said with sudden impatience, "I did not call you to discuss such matters but rather to protest what appears to be a slackening of China's efforts to assist in the destruction of United States imperialist hegemony. It is not something that can be done by relaxing pressures. Tension must be maintained."

"What would you suggest, Mr. President?" Ju inquired, so politely that Yuri was convinced anew that he was mocking him.

"I would suggest that the American presence in the Taiwan Straits be eliminated," he said harshly. "At once. Their ships and planes must be totally and utterly destroyed. *Now.*"

"Why would we wish to do that?" Ju inquired, a mild surprise in his whispery old voice. "They are assisting China to become one. Their very presence is of aid to both sides. Without them we would still be far apart. With them we are coming together. Why should we attack them? Even if," he added candidly, "we could."

"You could. They are under your guns, Vice-Premier. Destroy them! Get rid of them! Drive back the imperialist aggressors! You have superiority, for the moment at least. Surprise them! Bomb them! Destroy them! *Get rid of them!*"

"And embroil ourselves," Ju said, voice suddenly stronger, and as sharp as Yuri's own, "in open warfare with the United States of America."

"You will be sooner or later," Yuri said flatly. "Why not seize the moment they do not expect, and take the advantage surprise will give you? What can they do, tied down as we have them right now around the globe?"

"Ah, but Mr. President!" Ju said softly. "*You* do not have them tied down; you have told the world so. And on the surface of things, it is largely true. *Your* forces are still not engaged, *your* hostility is not declared. You are doing it through mercenaries. Yet you would have *us* openly engage them. The risks are too great, trapped and enfeebled though you consider them. I do not think they are so, Mr. President. No, I do not think they are so."

"They are making little progress anywhere," Yuri snapped. Ju's reply was instantaneous:

"Neither are you."

And he returned Yuri's glare with a calm and impassive gaze that yielded nothing and, in fact, challenged Yuri to say more.

"Well—" Yuri began; realized that it sounded lame; and started over again.

"There is a new government in place in Saudi Arabia," he said firmly. "Mexico is tottering and South Africa is ready to fall. It is a matter of days. The only piece missing is China. We do not like it, Vice-Chairman. We do not like it at all."

"Your new government in Saudi Arabia hangs by a thread," Ju retorted with an abrupt and uncharacteristically open scorn. "Mexico is shaken but hardly 'tottering,' and South Africa will be the last, if any, to fall. Those are the realities, Mr. President. In such circumstances China feels free to do what seems best for her own interests. Our brothers in Taiwan agree. Again I ask, what will you do to us? How can you stop us?"

And his clever little face creased into a sudden all-embracing smile that made Yuri feel for a moment that he was going to shout in sheer frustration. Instead he spoke in a voice that was low, ominous and openly shaking with anger.

"Vice-Premier," he said, "you try me sorely. You ask what we will do to you, you ask how we can stop you. There are means, Vice-Premier: there are means. I have them at hand. They are on your borders, in your skies, along your shores. They await only my word. I can give it in a minute and within fifteen more you will be atomized from the Gobi to the sea. There will be nothing left of China, nothing! That is what we can do to you, Vice-Premier, if you continue your intransigent and uncooperative hostility toward the Soviet Union!"

The bland old face before him moved not a muscle.

"But what are we doing to warrant such threats?" Ju inquired gently. "Such angry, impossible threats?"

"Nothing!" Yuri shouted, provoked at last beyond endurance. "*You are doing nothing!* That is what you are doing, *nothing!* And for that"—his voice sank suddenly again to its shaken, ominous note—"you may well, when the time comes, be punished."

"Good-bye, Mr. President," Ju Xing-dao said softly. "We are doing what we can, and that is all we intend to do."

And calmly, cutting off before it could begin Yuri's furious, shouting reply, he touched the button on his machine and vanished into the mists from which he had materialized.

For some moments thereafter he sat silently staring before him, hands folded upon one another, face immobile. He could only imagine what the President of the Soviet Union must be doing: probably rolling on the rug and frothing at the mouth, he thought with a scorn surpassing hatred. There was much, now, to discuss with all who might be interested.

He raised a thin old hand and gestured his waiting aides gently forward.

He would talk first to Taipei, he told them, and then to Washington.

In the Kremlin, not rolling on the rug nor frothing at the mouth, but in the grip of a monumental rage for all that, the President of the Soviet Union also stared blankly before him for several minutes. Then he commanded the appearance of the new Minister of Justice, and when that diffident gentleman virtually tiptoed into the room, gave him terse and explicit orders which he was to carry out in the most public manner not later than noon that day. The man seemed startled by the sheer animal vengeance of it, but for Yuri it needed no other justification than his own catharsis, which he badly required.

Before then, however, the world as Yuri viewed it changed abruptly, and not for the better. Equally surprised, for different reasons, was the President of the United States.

2

It was the *Times* reporter at the State Department who got the story first—in fact, got both stories first. This often happened to the *Times* just because it *was* the *Times*, although in recent years it also happened with equal frequency to the *Post*, which was annoying to the *Times* but apparently couldn't be helped. Journalistic enterprise frequently had nothing to do with it: it was *droit de institution*. Certain high officials wouldn't dream of leaking government secrets to anyone *but* the *Times;* certain others always leaked them to the *Post*. The question of whether or not this was ethical in either case had been decided long ago: ethics was whatever you could get away with, and both leaker and leaked-to in the public disclosure of a major news story had discovered decades back that publication was nine points of the law. Get it into print, and there wasn't much a frustrated administration could do but curse and complain. And that didn't put the genie back in the bottle, nor did it deter the righteous who so often felt that their personal prejudices were sufficient reason to violate the trust placed in them by Presidents who, too late, realized their mistake.

So it was that the *Times* reporter, hanging about Foggy Bottom with a hundred or so American and foreign correspondents waiting for Chauncey Baron to put in an appearance at his office (he was already there, having come in the secret entrance, but wasn't ready to tell the press about it yet) was casually bumped into by an unobtrusive black messenger girl who murmured, "Mr. Hanson wants to see you in his office" and then slipped quickly away.

The name of the Assistant Secretary for European Affairs, another holdover from the late President whom Hamilton Delbacher had not yet had time to replace, instantly galvanized the *Times* man into action. Gary Hanson was one of those ruggedly handsome all-American types who sometimes drift into diplomacy and are ready-made for the media, particularly if they can be found bitterly opposing and sabotaging the policies of their government. The fact that he was a holdover and had made little attempt in recent days to conceal from his intimates in the media his alarmed distaste for Ham's strong stand against Yuri's policies made him a real media hero. The *Times* man was perhaps his closest pal, not only because he was the *Times* man but also because they shared an affinity of view on the desperate dangers—indeed, the sheer moral *naughtiness*—of defying the Soviets in such crude and open ways: or indeed, perhaps, of defying them at all. Thus the *Times* man knew, as he raced down the corridors (as soon as he was out of sight of his colleagues) and hurried up in the elevator, that good old Gary might well have something big for him.

Gary did; and in his headlong rush to get to Gary's office, the *Times* man, in this case inadvertently, stumbled onto story number two.

This came about when he leaped into an elevator just as the door was closing and found himself unexpectedly with the Assistant Secretary for Inter-American Affairs and the director of the office of Caribbean Affairs.

"—and should be landing at Guantánamo just about now," the Assistant Secretary was saying. He had his back turned to the *Times* man, and before he grasped the director's hasty warning signal he added with a chuckle, "We think the miracle of his resurrection is going to be so startling that there'll be a great uprising that will—"

Then he got it abruptly and stopped in mid-sentence; swung about; was confronted by the *Times* man's eager face and excited eyes; and said, "Oh, *damn*," quietly, as if to himself.

Come on, Joe," the *Times* man said urgently. "*Give*. You mean

he isn't dead, then, and he's invading—*we're* invading—and—''
He stopped abruptly and suddenly looked highly indignant. ''What
the *hell* does that stupid bastard in the White House think he's trying to start, anyway?''

''I don't have any comment—'' the Assistant Secretary began, but
the *Times* man cut him off with a manner that brooked no denial.

''Oh, yes, you *do*,'' he said loudly. ''I heard what you said
and you're not going to deny it or play coy with me, Joe. I warn
you—''

''Oh, hell,'' Joe said as the elevator stopped. ''Come into my
office for a minute and I'll tell you about it. It won't matter in a
couple of hours anyway.''

''He didn't tell the media about it in advance,'' the *Times* man
said with aggrieved indignation. ''He's going to hear about *this*.''

''No doubt,'' Joe said in a tired voice, ''but come along anyway. It won't take more than five minutes. You've got the gist of it
already. Where are you barreling off to?''

''Gary wants to see me,'' the *Times* man said. Joe, an Administration loyalist, gave him a sharp look and groaned.

''Oh, Lord,'' he said. ''You're going to hit the jackpot today,
buddy boy. Come on in.''

Ten minutes later the *Times* man, hardly able to contain his
excitement—this was the stuff of Pulitzers, and he suspected Gary
would make it even better—was on his way, humming loudly to
himself, to Gary's office. He had one exclusive and as soon as he
reached Gary's office he grabbed a phone and dictated it to the
Times bureau. This took another ten minutes, after which he was
ushered quickly into Gary's office.

Looking his most Lincolnesque, Gary proceeded to do his best
to blow the plans of his President sky-high and return to the Soviets
any advantage the President might have thought he could gain by
surprise.

Even as headlines on one story were screaming

**CUBA INVADED! LEADER ALIVE, BACKED BY U.S.
TROOPS!**

headlines on the other were shouting

U.S. STIRS SATELLITE REVOLT IN EUROPE! HIGH

STATE OFFICIAL DISCLOSES PLANS, RESIGNS IN PROTEST!

It was Ham Delbacher's turn to say, "Oh, *damn*," and even, on several occasions as the day drew on and Gary Hanson seemed to be everywhere on television, "Oh, *God* damn!"

The whole thing had happened so many times before: the noble official, repelled by the foul deeds of his President—the noble official's insufferably moral, dramatic, self-righteous resignation—the media eagerly giving him every possible access to worldwide publicity—the heavy blow to America's strengths, purposes, chances for success—the triumphant *so there!* of a disgruntled headline-seeking malcontent and a determinedly hostile media, joined together to confound what they considered to be an unrelievedly evil government.

Their own, as it happened.

It all came together for Gary Hanson, as it had for so many others in the past; and as with so many others in the past, all the President could do was try to repair the damage as best he could. As for Gary, he had a ball, aided by the fact that Washington's most prestigious law firm immediately called and offered him safe harbor at three times his government salary.

"I want to say to the American people," he declared, earnestly staring into the avid cameras of all three networks, "that it is only because I could not in good conscience condone the desperately dangerous gambles of the government post and tell the truth.

"It has not been easy.

"It has not been comfortable.

"It has not been the course I would deliberately have chosen, or the course I ever suspected I would someday have to take.

"But it must be done.

"To keep silent in the face of the President's plans to engulf Eastern Europe in war would be to betray not only my oath to my government, but a higher oath—my oath to humanity."

("Oh, Christ," Mark murmured to Linda as they watched at home. "How noble, how noble, how *noble* can you be?" "He's just getting wound up," she said dryly. "Keep listening.")

"To be true to that oath," Gary said solemnly, "is the highest duty any morally decent man can have—any man who honestly believes that peace is the only honorable goal permissible to a government.''

("And the Soviet government?" the President inquired. "Let him rave on," Elinor suggested. "I can't stop him," her husband pointed out.)

"There are those," Gary said as though he had heard him, "who will inquire, 'And what of the Soviet government?' To them I can only say: I am not responsible for the Soviet government. I am, or was, one of those responsible for the American government. As such I could not condone subversion, sabotage, the deliberate fomenting of revolution against a power with which we are not at war. The Soviet Union may not be the world's most comfortable power to live with; but that does not justify us in attempting to stir up rebellion and revolt in its own front yard.

"No!" he said, his voice rising sharply. "It does not justify the President in seeking by devious means and terribly dangerous methods the overthrow of communist regimes friendly to the Soviet Government, upon which that government relies for the security of its borders. Nothing could be more deliberately aimed at toppling a regime the President chooses to regard as hostile."

("*Chooses* to regard as hostile!" Chauncey snorted; and Roger Hackett said dryly, "Oh, there are lots who agree with him. It's so much easier than facing the truth.")

"I have here," Gary Hanson said, and he held aloft a piece of paper, "a top-secret memo I received this morning from the Secretary of State setting forth the desire and intention of the President of the United States to encourage and assist rebellions in the European satellites of the Soviet Union. The memo does not contain the names of the nations targeted for attack—"

("No?" Ham Delbacher inquired dryly. "How thoughtless of me!")

"—but it does reflect the obvious determination of the President to launch such unprovoked aggression against the friends and neighbors of the Soviet Union. I quote:

" 'It is the desire of the President that immediate steps be taken to create as many diversions for the Soviet Union as possible.

" 'The purpose of these moves is to create sufficient uncertainty within the ruling circles of the Soviet Union so that those military elements which are extremely dubious of the worldwide adventurism of the present President of the Soviet Union may be encouraged to act.' "

Gary Hanson paused and looked again straight into the cameras with an expression of distaste.

"How crude!" he exclaimed. "How obvious! And how contrary to all norms of civilized behavior between sovereign states!"

He took a sip of water and resumed his reading.

" 'It is the opinion of this government, based upon intelligence received in the past few hours, that despite President Serapin's success in purging one group of officers, there are others equally reluctant who may be awaiting the right moment to strike. It is these who must be encouraged by every possible means in every area where disturbance will result in dissension and conflict of purpose within the Soviet government.

" 'You are directed'—and this memo, remember, was sent by the Secretary of State to his senior officers, including myself—'to prepare immediately suggestions for the most effective way to implement the desire of the President. A meeting of appropriate State and Defense Department officials will be held at three P.M. this afternoon to discuss plans to this end and arrange for their immediate application . . .' It is signed 'Baron, Secretary'—Chauncey Baron, the Secretary of State.

"And *that*," he concluded, "is 'the desire of the President'—to 'create as many diversions as possible for the Soviet Union.' To subvert, sabotage, stir up rebellion, probably to seek to overthrow the satellite governments in Eastern Europe—"

("The memo doesn't say that!" Chauncey Baron said angrily, "and neither did he, you slimy, two-bit sneaking bastard!")

Gary Hanson, looking nobler by the minute, sailed on to his conclusion.

"It is true," he said, anticipating with all the skill of the experienced official, "that the memo, and possibly the President's comments to the Secretary of State from which the memo derived, does not say specifically that these things are to be done in Eastern Europe. But where else could there be more troublesome 'diversions' for the Soviet Union? And what other *kinds* of 'diversions' could there be, sufficiently unsettling to create the kind of turmoil within the Soviet government that the President apparently wants—a turmoil sufficiently great to result in the overthrow of the Soviet President?

"No, my fellow Americans! The purpose is clear, the plan is clear, the meaning is clear! *And I want none of it.* I do not wish to participate in such underhanded attempts to topple a government with which we are not at war. I do not wish to engage in such devious, underhanded methods against a power with which we must get along in the world. I will not be a party to any such blatant and inexcusable plot to thwart President Serapin in his attempts to keep the peace—this shabby plot to overthrow a man who, for all his difficult qualities, is still an indispensable factor in the ongoing struggle to achieve world peace."

("What is that again?" the President demanded, lifting a hand to his ear in mock confusion. "Did I hear that right?" "You heard that right," Elinor said. "I told you, it's *1984* exactly—one's enemy as necessity.")

"Therefore," Gary Hanson concluded, looking, if possible, even nobler than before, "I have submitted my resignation to the Secretary of State, effective at once. I will no longer be a party to such peace-destroying, subversive tactics. I urge all Americans who feel the same to make your most vigorous protest known to your government. Let us stop this insanity and return to reason, at once!"

Within the hour obedient demonstrators flocked again into Lafayette Square and other favorite shouting places across the nation and the world; major columnists and editorialists tackled their typewriters and word processors with happy fury; and on television and radio all day long the noble face of Gary Hanson and his solemn exhortations assaulted the eyes and ears of his countrymen.

It was a very helpful assist for Yuri Serapin, a difficult problem for Hamilton Delbacher.

Elsewhere in the world, the situation was reversed.

* * *

"Cubans!" the Maximum Leader's voice cried out around the globe from Radio Martí, Voice of America and Radio Free Europe.

"My brothers and sisters of the glorious revolution! Be it known to you that it is indeed I! **I AM HERE! I AM ALIVE!** The evil plans of our Soviet oppressors have failed! Their crude attempt to add us to their evil empire has failed! I, your leader, your father, your friend, am coming back to you!

"**NOW!**

"**THIS VERY MOMENT THAT I SPEAK TO YOU!**

"**I AM IN CUBA AS YOU HEAR THIS!**

"**VICTORY WILL BE OURS!**

"The poor one who died in my place," he said, voice sinking to a pious reverence, "was a true son of the revolution, sacrificing himself gladly that I might be spared to return to you and lead you out of the bondage to which the evil Soviet oppressors have subjected us all these years. In due course, when victory is ours, he will be given the hero's burial he deserves.

"*Now* we must turn to the task of throwing the oppressors off our island. You will want me to prove who I am, and rightly so. To our gallant armed forces, whom I now call upon to follow me in this great crusade, I give you the password known only to myself and your topmost officers: *Revenge.*"

And abruptly his voice rose to pounding, exhortative rhythm.

"Revenge upon the evil Soviets who have kept us in chains for so many years! Revenge upon the evil Soviets who have destroyed our liberties and tried to turn Cuba into a dog on a leash! Revenge upon the evil Soviets who now attempt to add us to their empire by declaring Cuba to be a part of the Soviet Union!

"What monstrous gall, my brothers and sisters! What evil imperialism, offered under the guise that they are protecting us! We reject it, do we not, my fellow Cubans? We reject it utterly! We will never accept it, *never.* Nothing will be allowed to destroy the freedom and independence of Cuba, *nothing!*

"My brothers and sisters, you all heard the address several days ago of the President of the United States, once our enemy, now our friend. He offered us Guantánamo. He offered us financial aid. He offered us the friendship and assistance of the United States. And now he is offering us the full assistance of the armed forces of the United States in driving the evil Soviets from our island.

"I accept this, all this, in your name.

"We will not fail, my brothers and sisters! Rise and follow me and we will have our glorious vengeance! Rise and follow me, my dear Cuban people! Follow me! Rise and kill the oppressors, wherever you find them! Give them no warning, give them no quarter, show them no mercy! Rise and *follow me!* Our victory is inevitable!"

His chanting voice ceased; the Cuban national anthem followed; there was a minute of silence; and it began all over again.

And again the demonstrators screamed, this time in opposition to the Cuban leader they had once so idolized, and in the citadels of American opinion certain columnists, commentators and editorialists, certain Senators and Congressmen, certain movie stars and churchmen, aghast at his revelation that United States forces were about to be actively engaged with those of the Soviet Union, cried their anguished apprehension wildly through the land. And on the island things began to move, very fast.

He had landed at Port-au-Prince, Haiti, been taken by helicopter to rendezvous at sea with an American nuclear submarine, been taken from there to Guantánamo, his movements screened by an autumn Caribbean day of drifting clouds and squalls of warm rain. Awaiting him were some hundred of his senior officers, gathered by the Americans who had sent word through the island's efficient anti-Soviet underground the moment news came from Washington that he was alive and on his way back.

Acting more on instinct than knowledge, for nothing had been broadcast about his whereabouts or starting point, thousands of troops and ordinary citizens from the immediate area of Guantánamo had begun to converge on the base from the first airing of his call. Uprisings had instantly begun in Havana, Santiago de Cuba, Camaguey, Sancti Spiritus, Matanzas, Pinar del Rio and many rural areas. There seemed to be no doubt anywhere that he was who he said he was; or, if there was doubt, hatred of the Soviets and the urge to escape their bondage supervened. The Soviets held Cienfuegos and its adjoining territory and were deeply entrenched there; obviously they had always planned that this was how they would hold the island, if it ever came to that. But there was such a spontaneity to the risings that there was no time for them to do much but alert their forces and dig in. It was not yet time for retaliatory action, and at the moment they were obviously unsure what it should be.

In those first hours of uncertainty, the event that history would come to call the Second Cuban Revolution made astonishingly successful advances. It was as though a great tidal wave of humanity was rolling across the island. On its forward crest rode the Maximum Leader and his triumphant troops, protected by American air cover and the numerous Cuban planes whose pilots had managed to get them into the air before their Soviet captors could prevent it.

Within six hours the island was in such a state of successful rebellion against the occupiers that it was obvious that it would take a major military effort to recapture it. The brand-new Soviet-appointed ''President of Cuba'' had been assassinated, the brand-new ''Soviet Republic of Cuba'' was in collapse and it had come down to a simple question: how much was a Cuba some five thousand miles away worth to the Soviets and how much were they willing to throw into the fight to hold it?

The question was further compounded for them when the White House issued the President's statement on Gary Hanson:

''The President has no comment on the statements of former Assistant Secretary of State Hanson except to say that anyone who disagrees with the policies of his Administration is free to leave and had better do so.

''The President has ordered a complete blockade of Cuba and has directed the armed forces of the United States to give such assistance to its people as may be necessary to rescue them from their Soviet oppressors and restore to power their legitimate government.''

It was now Yuri who had the greater problem, and in Moscow he faced it with all the force of his powerful personality; congratulating himself, presently, that he was going to survive successfully what had suddenly become a major and most serious dilemma for him.

3

"Comrades!" he said, hunching forward over his desk to stare at their stolid pudding faces, closed off and carefully—desperately—noncommittal.

"Comrades! You are so serious, so grim! The mad American has frightened you! He has succeeded in making you uncertain! How am I to restore your courage?" His voice became ironic. "*Can* it be restored? Or has he turned you into a pack of quaking women unfit to run a great country? For shame if that is so, comrades! The revolution has passed into feeble hands, if that is so! What can I do to reassure you?"

He looked slowly and deliberately from face to face. Sixteen pairs of eyes avoided his; sixteen faces remained determinedly expressionless. He snorted; his scorn became more open.

"Comrades," he said dryly, "you overwhelm me with your loquaciousness. I cannot withstand such a flood of words. I am bowled over by your enthusiasm, your courage, your willingness to back me so wholeheartedly in the great task of bringing America to her knees and removing her from the rolls of history. It is a great strength and solace to me, comrades, make no mistake of that. A *great* strength. And solace."

He paused; and for a moment there was no sound in the room save their heavy breathing, and his own. He was furiously angry at their lack of enthusiasm and they knew it. They were desperately afraid of his anger and he knew it. He cold crush them like ants and they knew that, too. The headiness of this was almost too much. Only the impassive face of Mikhail Yarkov, standing to one side at his right, reminded him sharply that it was not wise to give in to such open arrogance. His tone was suddenly much milder and more mollifying.

"Comrades," he said gently, "you really must not be so afraid of this crazy one in Washington. You must not let him disconcert you. I realize you are new to your responsibilities, that there are many things that you have not yet mastered, that there is much you must learn about the duties so suddenly—and yet so deservedly—conferred upon you. But you have known about America all your lives. You have known that the aim of destroying her has never wavered or slackened in all these years. You have known that the great goal of complete world control has never changed, no matter what outward shifts of 'peaceful co-existence' or 'detente' have been adopted now and then to confuse our foredoomed enemies. Why, then, should you let the situation trouble you now? We may suffer momentary setbacks but the onward momentum cannot be stopped. Thanks to our friend in the State Department, we learn that the crazy one is trying to divide us by threatening revolts on our borders. But what better way to bring us together, is that not right, comrades? What better way?"

His gaze traveled fiercely along their faces until one by one, as if sleepwalking, they nodded; though still no one spoke.

Since no one did, he was emboldened to speak of the one event above all others which he knew had shocked and troubled them, the one that still shocked and troubled *him* more than any other. The best way, he decided, was to scoff at it and pretend it did not trouble him and hope that he could brazen it out while he tried to decide what to do about it.

"He has even succeeded in starting a clever trick in Cuba," he said, voice heavy again with scorn. "But it will not succeed. How can it?"

And the silence held and again he challenged it with a harsh, *"How can it?"*

And finally his unwilling band of brothers stirred and came to reluctant life, looking instinctively to the new Minister of Foreign Affairs, a relatively youthful fifty-eight-year-old from Kazakhstan whom Yuri thought of contemptuously as his "pet Moslem"—one who had been willing to break away from his uneasy, nationalistic tribesmen to accept high favors from the Great Russians who controlled the Soviet state.

"Comrade President," the minister said respectfully, "we do not doubt the wisdom of your course or the certainty of ultimate victory. But it does appear to some of us—and to me," he added with a firmness that for a second caused Yuri's eyes to widen in dangerous surprise—"that the situation in Cuba has now taken a very grave turning for us. It is, after all, a distant place to protect."

"Or recapture," the new Minister of Defense remarked in a voice that was discreet but also, Yuri noted with a rising anger, surprisingly definite.

"There is also," the new marshal of the Strategic Rocket Forces observed thoughtfully, "the blockade."

"Yes, yes!" half a dozen murmured. "The blockade!"

For a moment the overriding emotion of the President of the Soviet Union was rage; but instantly he realized that this was no way to calm what could become incipient revolt if he allowed it to get out of hand. His voice must be reasonable. With an effort he made it so.

"Comrades, again I emphasize, you must not let the bluffs and gestures of the crazy one in Washington upset you. He threatens a blockade. Well, he threatened one a month ago, did he not? And it never occurred because I outsmarted him! I pushed him to the limit and then at the last moment I withdrew six submarines from Cuba and sent them to Nicaragua, and he leaped at the excuse and ended the threat of blockade. And the world applauded me, just as I had planned. Is that not true?"

And he stared up and down the line of faces, daring them to challenge him.

"You were very shrewd, Comrade President," the new admiral of the Navy said quickly. "But now he is apparently returning to his blockade, and this time he shows no signs of using it to bargain. He does not seek a quid pro quo: he tells us it is there. And he accompanies it with land and air action on the island of Cuba itself. If we wish all this ended, we must stop it. It is not such an easy task."

"For many years," Yuri snapped, "we have had atomic missiles on submarines off both coasts of America. Use them!"

There was a sharp indrawing of breath.

"Comrade President!" the new marshal of the Army said in a hushed voice. "Comrade *President!*"

"Use them!" he repeated. "Take out a city or two along the Eastern seaboard and see how he likes it!"

"B-b-b-but, Comrade President," the new marshal of the Air Force stuttered in his excitement, "that would mean war—nuclear war! We could not survive it any more than they could. Surely you do not mean—"

"Why not?" Yuri demanded harshly. *"Why not?"* He leaped to his feet and began striding up and down behind his desk while they watched him fearfully, as they might some caged and maddened animal provoked beyond reason by his tormentors.

"Listen!" he cried. "Listen to me, brave new generals and admiral, brave new leaders of the Soviet Union whom *I* created, whom *I* plucked from obscurity, whom *I* have charged with saving the Motherland and making her finally triumphant over America!

"All our lives we have been taught that nuclear war could be won; all our lives we have dreamed and schemed and planned for that victory! Our armies and air force have been trained for it; our strategic rocket forces and our navy have been trained for it; our whole thinking, our whole planning has been that we could be invincible if we struck secretly and struck first with the nuclear weapon. Why are you afraid of it now, when the moment beckons, the great opportunity lies before us, the stupid fool in Washington has given us the opening by his imperialist adventuring in Cuba? He is asking for it, comrades! We would be abysmal idiots not to seize the opportunity! Must I drag you to it?"

His voice sank suddenly to an ominous level that made them all shiver, and several turn pale.

"Must I find myself yet another set of officers, yet another Politburo? I can go on and on, comrades"—he laughed suddenly, a curious jagged sound—"but I had rather not! No, it is too much bother, I had rather not! I must content myself with you, *but I will have you do my bidding or you will suffer for it . . .* Now," he said, breathing heavily but forcing himself to speak more reasonably while they watched fascinated and terrified, not daring to glance at one another, "I do *not* mean, comrade marshal, I do *not* mean, my dear comrades and colleagues, that we will destroy *all* American cities, I do not mean that we will advertise, that we will stand up and bellow to the whole world, 'Look, we did it!' I mean that at a time and a place *to be decided by me*"—he paused and articulated it again, slowly and emphatically—*"to—be—decided—by—me*, one missile, not thousands, but *one* missile will fall out of the sky on Burlington, Vermont, or Portland, Maine, or Atlantic City, or Newport News or Charleston or Savannah or Palm Beach, or some such unlikely and unexpected place. There will be no proof at all that it came from us, no slightest warning, no advertisement . . . It will just be there, suddenly, and suddenly there will be no more city. And we will deplore it along with the rest, and be baffled along with the rest, and we will match them outraged cry for outraged cry.

"And all the time he will know, that stupid adventurer in Washington, as of course everyone will know. But he will not dare retaliate, *because there will be no proof that it came from us* and he would not dare launch a retaliatory attack without proof, he simply could not. And he will be warned, and he will draw back and we will have the advantage again. And then—then, comrades, we will have them! And the final battle to decide the fate of all mankind will be over, for they will not dare to provoke us again or ever again stand in our way . . ."

He stopped, face alight with his terrifying vision, an almost otherworldly air about him, a strange, frightening aura of absolute certainty and conviction that made them shiver.

In a small voice that quavered, for he knew he was taking his life in his hands, the new Foreign Minister ventured,

"And if they *do* retaliate, Comrade President? If they *do* strike back? Then"—his voice almost failed as Yuri turned upon him the full strength of his angry glare—*"then what?"*

"Then we destroy them," Yuri said calmly. "And though they may kill many millions of us, comrades, they will not kill you or me because we will know when it is all to begin, and we will be hidden and safe, and all those we need to help us rebuild the Motherland and take over what remains of *them* will also be safe and we will emerge ready to do the bidding of history, which will at last have given us the victory that has always been inevitable . . . But it will not be necessary to fire more than one," he said, tone suddenly conversational and seemingly quite normal again. "You will see."

"We will?" the new Defense Minister asked cautiously, and Yuri said again with absolute conviction,

"Yes. *You will.*"

"When—" the new marshal of the Strategic Rocket Forces inquired, as cautiously as the minister—"when do you think this might—might happen?"

"It will happen," Yuri said, "when I consider the time is right."

"And that will be—?" the marshal pressed, but carefully.

"When I decide it is right!" Yuri snapped; and, more reasonably, "As soon as it is clear that the blockade is really in place. As soon as America is really trapped in Cuba."

"Not—very long, then," the new marshal of the army said, in the same careful way they all seemed instinctively to be adopting. "Days, perhaps?"

"Hours, perhaps," Yuri said in an almost dreamy voice, staring now at his map with its blinking lights. "Perhaps only hours, comrades . . . and then it will all be over."

"You will give us ample warning, Comrade President?" General Yarkov asked with a respectful and obsequious air that briefly brought a smile to his leader's lips.

"Ample, dear Comrade Yarkov," he said expansively. "Ample. After all"—he looked along the line of faces, his smile now calm and confident—"I need you all. If it succeeds as I believe it will, then our sheltering will be only a temporary inconvenience that we can all laugh about later when America surrenders. If it proves to be a necessity, then it will still be only a temporary inconvenience from which we will emerge safe and unharmed to ratify history's decision. Either way, you will have warning, believe me. I would be a poor leader of socialist victory were it otherwise."

"You are a *great* leader of socialist victory!" General Yarkov said fervently, and suddenly they were all crying, "Yes, Comrade President! Yes, Yuri Pavlovich! You are the greatest leader of history, you are the savior of mankind! It is you and only you, Yuri Pavlovich! Hail, Yuri Pavlovich! Hail, humanity's deliverer!''

And ecstatically they all crowded about, to shake his hand and, in the daring exuberance of the moment, to slap him on the back.

And so, laughing and shouting, they broke up. Yuri returned to his map, the new Politburo and the new military leaders went off to their offices; and into the eyes of each as he shook hands in farewell, Mikhail Yarkov looked briefly, but enough.

An hour later in Red Square, before a huge crowd that had gathered as if by magic near the tomb of Lenin, pursuant to the order given earlier by the President of the Soviet Union to the new Minister of Justice, the first two American hostages were shot.

The news found the President of the United States in conference with the Secretaries of State and Defense and the Joint Chiefs of Staff. Chauncey Baron received the first official word and turned from the telephone with a dazed and stricken face that instantly alarmed his colleagues.

''What is it?'' the President demanded sharply.

When Chauncey told him he put his face in his hands, closed his eyes and rubbed them wearily as though trying to shut out the world.

The others responded with various imprecations, including Bart Jamison's startled and, he thought later, rather silly, ''But he's violated his own deadline!''

Then a lengthy silence fell.

Finally Roger Hackett broke it.

''He has gone mad,'' he said softly. ''Literally mad. The finger that rests on the Soviet button belongs to a madman and finally we have what the world has always been afraid of: the Soviet Hitler. What do we do now?''

''Respond in kind?'' General Hallowell inquired; and the question hung there while they all looked with deeply troubled and commiserating expressions at the President.

For what seemed a very long time but was probably only a minute or two, he appeared not even to have heard Smidge Hallowell's question. Finally he raised unhappy eyes and said slowly, ''I don't know . . . I just don't know. I said I would, earlier, but earlier

was—earlier. Now—I don't know . . ." He paused and was able
to muster a small smile even in the midst of their appalled consternation. "Would you gentlemen be very upset if I called in another
adviser? I've always found her ideas pretty levelheaded."

"Elinor?" Chauncey Baron said. "By all means." He too gave
a wry little smile. "God knows we need all the help we can get."

"That's for sure!" Bump Smith said fervently. It broke the tension a little. They all laughed, briefly.

"Good," Ham Delbacher said. "She's over in the Mansion.
Hang on."

They fell silent again while they waited, contemplating the
abyss Yuri Serapin had opened at their feet and wondering desperately what they could open at his. It was already obvious from the
President's reaction that he had abandoned even the pretense that
he might retaliate in kind. But heavy on the room lay the conviction
that something must be done to meet this newest monstrosity—a
monstrosity beyond the monstrosities of war, because this was the
slaughter of captive helpless people.

Something.

But what?

It was impossible for them to believe at that moment that the
most effective thing of all would be—nothing.

But so it turned out to be, due in large part to the First Lady.
When she heard the news she turned pale and looked for a moment
as though she might faint. Then she turned to her husband and demanded:

"And are you going to kill two Russians?"

He gave her a long look, uttered a heavy sigh and responded
with a rueful smile and a shake of the head.

"No. I don't believe any American President could do that. On
the other hand, I don't believe I can afford to do nothing."

"Why not?" she inquired, sitting down and taking out her knit-
ting as though it were suddenly the calmest of days—an aptitude
for keeping cool, he reflected, from which he had often profited
greatly in the various crises of his rise through House, Senate and
Vice-Presidency to the uneasy eminence where he now sat.

"Because—" he began, and paused.

"Well, why not?" she repeated. "He's created his horror, now let him live with it. A statement, of course; you have to do that. But nothing more. Let the world contemplate him for a while. Unless all decency is gone everywhere, the longer the world thinks about it, the more awful and despicable it is going to appear. Let it sink in. It can only damage him. Sooner or later all the damage is going to add up.''

"With all respect, Mrs. Delbacher," General Twitchell said, "I doubt if anything is going to penetrate that impervious hide. Particularly if, as Secretary Hackett says, he really has gone 'round the bend.''

"Oh, I think he has," she said. "I definitely think so. And I think the world is going to sense it. And his fellow Soviets are, too. This certainly isn't the act of a rational man—it's of one mad for revenge, striking out blindly—insane. So let it work its own retribution. It will. Even in the Kremlin.''

"And to prevent more of the same?" Chauncey Baron inquired. "Let all the Russians go?''

Elinor looked at him.

"I would. If masculine pride could permit.''

"Under pressure?" her husband asked.

"You can put it on a humanitarian place in your statement. You know how to do it, Ham. Remember you're going to be the aggrieved party in this.''

"The most cynical politician in my family," the President said, again with a ghost of a smile, "isn't sitting in this chair.''

"I'm not cynical at all," she said. "I'm going back to the house and cry for those poor people. But I'm not going to cry until you've figured out some way to get back at that worthless monster. Was it the Ambassador and his wife?''

"Oh, no," Chauncey Baron said with some bitterness. "That would be too easy for the world to adjust to, in a weird sort of way. No, it was just a couple of junior clerks. I imagine the Ambassador and his wife will come last, if we permit it to go on.''

"Which you aren't going to do," she reminded, "because you're going to return all the Russians captive here, and the sooner the better!''

The President looked quizzical for a moment, then nodded with a sudden firmness.

"They'll be on their way tonight. To the Berlin Wall, I think. The East Germans can get them home from there." He surveyed their somber faces. "I have another thought, since this is turn-the-other-cheek week. Perhaps we should make Hanson look foolish, at least for the moment."

They all looked a little blank.

"Abandon the plans?" Chauncey Baron said.

"Not create 'diversions'?" Roger Hackett echoed.

"Leave the Achilles heel untouched?" General Hallowell protested.

The President nodded.

"Too much diversion right now could be the one thing that could save him if, as we fervently hope, he is really beginning to be in trouble with his own crowd. If they get the idea that we're stirring up the satellites, they're apt to unite behind him just for the sake of dear old Mother Russia. Maybe we should cool it for a bit, and let it be known we're cooling it."

"But you told me Poland is already—" Chauncey Baron said.

"I'll have to move fast," the President conceded. "But in fact I already have. I have a call in for my principal contact. I think he'll understand if we hold off a bit."

"But will his people agree?" Elinor asked. "They're such a volatile bunch over there—"

"They'll listen to *him*," the President said.

"Well . . ." she said doubtfully.

"Trust me," he said. "If we return the Russian hostages tonight, which can be done—and will be done—and then lie low for a bit in Europe, I have a hunch that maybe—just maybe—the men around Serapin will be doing as much thinking as everyone else. We get some interesting reports on this Yarkov who seems to have moved into the picture. And the new Politburo and the new military leaders must secretly hate Yuri as much as they fear him, even if he did put them where they are. He can purge them as he did the other bunch and they know it—unless they get him first. Maybe we should be quiet for a short while and see what happens—and then move on, of course, if nothing does."

"Those two poor clerks may be the turning point," General Hallowell remarked. "The beginning of the end for Mr. Yuri."

"God, wouldn't that be wonderful?" General Jamison said. "It couldn't happen to a nicer guy."

"We hope," the President said. "We hope . . ." He sighed again. "I hope he doesn't ever come into my power. I hope his own people kill him first. I hate to think what I might order done to him if he were in my hands."

"You'd soften," Elinor predicted, but fondly. "You couldn't do it, any more than you could really kill these Russians now."

"I hope I never have to find out," her husband said grimly. "In his case, I might not be so restrained."

His secretary buzzed. He lifted the phone, listened for a second, smiled and nodded them out. After they had gone he said crisply, "Thank you for responding, Your Holiness. I have a slight change of plans to propose. . . ."

So the satellite revolt did not occur that day or the next or even the next. It was a brief lull he was to recall later as "the little cooling-off period," the only one the world was to experience for the duration of what became known in the media and, eventually, the history books, as "the Second Confrontation." Without other identification.

It really needed none.

It was quite distinct, a separate episode in time.

The "little cooling-off period" lasted, as he had suggested, slightly more than three days. The Pontiff, surprised and perhaps even, the President thought, somewhat disappointed by the delay in achieving the result he had obviously hoped and planned for over a long period, nonetheless moved promptly to cooperate. The sun went down over lovely Rome without the news they had both anticipated. Uncertain and confused, but obedient, his hidden friends in many places across the map of Europe held their fire. The President assumed he must have assured them the delay was only temporary, and perhaps it would be. He himself hoped events would move in Moscow in such a way that armed rebellion with all its consequent bloodshed and horror could be avoided. Yet he knew there would be much vengeance exacted on the occupiers and their native collaborators. No matter how it came about, the freeing of the satellites would be a business whose bloodiness could only be held down, not prevented. Slaves rising against their brutal masters would not be gentle. All over Eastern Europe they would enjoy their revenge.

The second item on his agenda was the release of the Russian hostages, and even though by conservative estimate three-fourths of them were, as with any Soviet embassy, active agents of the KGB and active enemies of their host country, he did not really begrudge them their passage home. He had only seized them in response to Yuri's provocation, had never had any real intention of ordering their deaths, and now Yuri's harsh example had given him the opportunity to make his own leniency an even greater contrast in the eyes of the world. He gave considerable care to his statement and decided to deliver it in person over suddenly commandeered television and radio networks that carried him live from the White House at noon.

"The monstrous action of the present President of the Soviet Union in ordering the execution of two helpless American captives," he said, face somber and sad, "proves again to the world the utter lack of conscience and human decency that characterize that despicable individual. He was not content to wait to ascertain whether or not this government would accept an exchange of prisoners as he had suggested. He obviously felt impelled by a sheer manic desire for blood to speed his insane move.

"He has removed himself from the ranks of civilized men and returned himself to the jungle. He has become something alien to decent people everywhere; and, I suspect, alien to all the great traditions of the long-suffering Russian people in whose name he pretends to act.

"I have considered carefully the response I should make to this act of unparalleled barbarism on the part of the present President of the Soviet Union. I, too, have the option to slaughter helpless captives. I, too, can be as barbaric as he is. But to do so would be to violate the traditions and the decency of my own great people, as well as to dishonor my own Presidency and all those that have come before it. It is not a way open to a civilized man. It is not a way open to a sane man.

"I am accordingly ordering the immediate return of all the Russian hostages. They will depart this country at six P.M. our time tonight on two special army transport planes for the city of Berlin, where they will be transferred to the custody of East German authorities for return to Moscow. They will be permitted to take with them all personal belongings.

"The Soviet embassy and all Soviet consulates to the United States will remain closed indefinitely, and all records and equipment therein will remain in the custody of this government until such time as relations between our two countries can be normalized with a different and more reliable Russian government. It is the devout hope of this government that this time will not be long delayed. In the interim any necessary diplomatic business will be conducted through the good offices of the Swiss government, whose kind offer of assistance we gratefully accept.

"I now ask the present President of the Soviet Union to return immediately the remaining American citizens he is holding. Further murders of defenseless people may be gratifying to his own blood lust but they cannot be justified on any ground known to civilized human beings. Nor can the continued detention of hostages, now that his own people are being returned to him. To play any other game would be doing just that—playing a game, with the lives of helpless people.

"This government, and the conscience of civilized humanity, await together the response of the present President of the Soviet Union. He can continue to act outside the bounds of civilization or he can bring himself once more into conformity with rational behavior. He can kill more helpless people, but he would not be harming, nor has he harmed, the United States *per se*. He has harmed only himself, and will continue to harm only himself if he continues on his present deranged, barbaric course.

"More important than that, he has brought great shame and dishonor upon the great Russian people. He will continue to bring great shame and dishonor upon them unless he returns immediately those he now holds hostage without reason or excuse. He shames and dishonors Yuri Serapin but he shames and dishonors Mother Russia more.

"Surely Mother Russia deserves better than this from the individual who presently happens to hold power in Moscow. Surely there is better representation than this of the great spirit of the great Russian people. It is up to him to prove it. Time is running out.''

His face, somber and intent, faded from the screen, lapsed into silence on the airwaves. Immediately his hammering words, deliberately subversive of Yuri Serapin, deliberately designed to weaken him as much as possible with the Russian people, were rebroadcast to the world via Radio Free Europe, the Voice of America and selected satellites permanently stationed above the Soviet Union. As with the words of the Maximum Leader to Cuba, a minute of silence followed each repetition. Then the hammering words began all over again.

Within two hours, as Ham had expected, there was response from Moscow. Again as he anticipated, the response was exactly what it had been to outcries against Czechoslovakia, Poland, Afghanistan, the South Korean airliner and all the rest. The present President of the Soviet Union was hanging tough. This suited the President of the United States just fine. ''Hang tough and hang himself,'' he remarked to Elinor as they listened to Yuri's broadcast while they lunched in the family quarters of the White House. ''Or so, at least, I hope.''

That Yuri was aware of the danger that he might do just this was apparent as soon as he began. Insane he might be—and his opponent in Washington was now convinced that, if not already there, he was well on his way—but he was still a very clever man, the cleverness heightened now by his apparent realization that he was, suddenly and contrary to all his plans, on the defensive.

''Peoples of the world!'' he said, addressing them directly, broad face scowling and intent. ''You have heard the words of the President''—his voice for a moment turned heavy with sarcasm— ''the *present* President of the United States. Aside from personal attacks on me, which will not deter in the slightest the decisions of the Soviet government, what do they really say?

''They are a confession of guilt that he has illegally seized two hundred and one Soviet citizens and is now scurrying to let them go because he knows we have discovered subversives—many subversives—among his own people now held in our hands.

''Why does he think two of his countrymen were shot today on my orders? Yes, *my* orders! Because they were spies for the CIA. It is as simple as that! One need look no further to find the reasons for their execution. One need not appeal to civilization and so-called 'sanity' to excuse their crimes, or to condemn me for performing my duty to punish them, as head of the Soviet state.

"We discovered them to be active subversives seeking by every means to overthrow the Soviet government. They were engaged in typical capitalist antirevolutionary activities. They acted on direct orders of the CIA, which sends out people pretending to be diplomats who are really spies instead. We have proof of this gross violation of international law. So the two subversives died.

"It may be," he said, and an ominous inflection came into his voice, "that there are many others like them in the group we hold. We must discover this. Therefore we totally reject the demand of the President that we release them. To do this would be counter to our own interests. The Soviet state has a right to protect itself against subversives. We could not let these go now, as the American President demands, while we are still investigating their crimes against us.

"Nor," he added with a note of triumph that alerted Ham Delbacher that trouble was coming, "can we release them while the American President is still actively trying to impose his imperialistic conquest in many places of the earth.

"It may be," he said, a gleam of satisfaction clearly visible in his eyes, "that we will have to proceed in the same fashion with the other American subversives in our hands unless the American President ceases his worldwide imperialist adventures.

"It may be we will have to shoot other American subversives unless there is an immediate withdrawal of American forces from Cuba. It may be others will have to be shot if there is not an immediate stop to American aid for the corrupt government of Mexico, the bloodthirsty racist regime in South Africa, the corrupt oppressors in Saudi Arabia. Yes, it could be we will have to execute many more American criminals if the American President does not stop his imperialist adventures!

"We will not issue ultimatums, we will not set deadlines. We will simply say this: American withdrawal must begin at once. Otherwise we shall be forced to continue, possibly over quite a long time, the regular punishment of the American subversives. It will not be our choice: the blood, as they say in America, will not be on our hands. It will rest squarely on the hands of the present President of the United States.

"Let the world look to him to put a stop to what is the true insanity—the insanity of thinking that the inevitable tides of history can be reversed by the interference of the United States.

"It cannot be done, peoples of the world. It will inevitably fail. The sooner the American President recognizes behavior, the sooner the world will know peace. And the fewer American subversives from the embassy in Moscow will die."

And with a sudden abrupt, satisfied nod of the head as if to say, "That's that!" he stared sternly into the cameras as they drew back and his picture faded away.

In many places, including the family dining room at the White House, there was a silence for a while. Then, predictably, the clamor began, in America and around the world.

"Surely *now*," cried CBS's earnest little commentator, "President Delbacher will see that he *must* reach some accommodation with President Serapin before further lives of helpless American hostages are sacrificed. Surely *now* he will understand that the Soviet Union cannot be bullied and pushed to the wall simply because someone in Washington disapproves of what it is doing. Surely nothing is worth one American life, let alone the two already lost and the others that may be sacrificed if President Delbacher continues on his stubborn and totally unproductive course.

"It is clear beyond all possible doubt that the way to bring about a change in Soviet policy, if one is deemed desirable, is not by attempting to browbeat or strong-arm the man in the Kremlin. Perhaps more than any Soviet leader since the late Joseph Stalin, Mr. Serapin has made himself the undisputed master of the Soviet state. A fierce pride and patriotism seem to be inevitable concomitants of such awesome power. They are not to be lightly thwarted or challenged.

"It would seem to be time, now, for President Delbacher to make a most careful and prayerful reappraisal of his own policies vis-à-vis the Soviet Union. He still has produced no absolute proof that Mr. Serapin is directly responsible for the four regional wars of liberation now going on around the globe. And in encouraging the invasion of Cuba by an individual who may or may not be the genuine leader of that unhappy island—in attempting to establish an illegal, warlike blockade of the island—and in seizing Soviet hostages in an attempt to discourage what he feels, without proof, to be Soviet imperialism—Mr. Delbacher has only opened the way for the sad dilemma now posed for him by Mr. Serapin's threat to execute further American hostages who may well have been, as he says, acting under orders of the CIA against Soviet interests.

"No more Americans must die to satisfy President Delbacher's old-fashioned obsession with what he sees as Soviet aggression. It is time for him to accede to Mr. Serapin's demand that he abandon his warlike responses to what he alleges—but has not proved to be—Mr. Serapin's responsibility for what is going on in the world."

And so, again, agreed many of the major media and their highly vocal think-alikes around the country. There were not very many voices raised in such circles in his defense, the President noted. If he had any defenders among the hostile chorus, they were well aware that for reasons social, political or sometimes just for the safety of their own jobs, they had better not say so. The popular thing, prompted by a genuine concern for the American hostages and a genuine fear of nuclear confrontation, plus many lifelong habits of appeasement that were as old-fashioned in their way as those who had them believed the President's to be, combined to produce what seemed to be an apparently overwhelming demand that he give in at once to Yuri's threats—abandon Cuba, abandon Mexico, Saudi Arabia, South Africa, Taiwan—stop attempting to halt the ongoing tide of Soviet imperialism—yield willingly whatever influence America had in the world.

Several prominent polls were rushed to the networks and into print with computer speed made even swifter by the desire to thwart the President. They seemed to indicate a vast popular feeling that agreed. Yet the overwhelming number of telephone calls, letters and telegrams reaching the White House urged him to stand firm. The senders requested anxiously that he somehow save the American hostages, but at the same time they did not want him to yield to Yuri's threats or knuckle under to the Soviet conquest.

While Senator James Monroe Madison and a good many of the usual statement issuers on the Hill sounded off as expected against him, many others called to tell him that their own mail was running two to one in his favor.

"Not that I need their encouragement to stand firm," he told Elinor, "but it's nice to know the doom shouters aren't the *only* people in the country, anyway."

"You know they're not," she said. "Your gut instinct for how the majority feels has always been good. I'm convinced they're with you now. The only thing I worry about," she added with a sudden frown and a desperate little gesture of the hand that appeared to be grasping for support in the air, "is what you *are* going to do about the hostages. You can't just let him kill them at will."

"I may have to," he said; and at her alarmed look said firmly, "until such time as world opinion swings against him. Which I still believe is inevitable."

"If you could only help it along," she said, and for once he looked at her with a genuine impatience.

"I'm doing all I damned well can," he said sharply. Fortunately for domestic harmony, at that moment the comments began to come in from around the world. From all those leaders whose opinions he valued and whose opinions could be of real assistance, he could not have asked for more.

The Prime Ministers of Britain, France, Italy, West Germany, the Scandinavian countries, Greece, Turkey, Egypt, Israel, Canada, Japan, the Presidents of Argentina, Brazil and even, *mirabile dictu,* the Prime Minister of India, issued the strongest possible condemnations of what Britain's lady called "the Soviet President's threat of murder on the installment plan." While some refrained from outright support of Ham Delbacher's actions, all were unanimous in denouncing Yuri.

For all of these the President was deeply grateful and said so in a brief White House statement. But the one he prized most, and felt would have the most impact worldwide, came from his potential colleague in stirring the satellite revolts. The Pope was not generally a thunderer, but this time he sounded as consumed with fire as Martin Luther.

"The world," he said solemnly in a broadcast from the Vatican—he too having decided to take to radio and television—"is come close to anti-Christ. The statement of the Soviet President is an offense to God and to mankind. It is a statement so shocking and profound in its indication not only of godlessness but of sheer inhumanity to man that it appalls the mind and devastates the heart. To know that it can come from the leader of a great nation at this late date in the twentieth century after Christ makes it even more awful.

"Nothing can excuse it," he said with a sudden and virtually unprecedented flare of anger. *"Nothing.*

"Men may have legitimate quarrel with the policies of one party or the other in the dispute that now threatens the very life of the planet. But no sane man can justify the threat of the President of the Soviet Union to deliberately destroy the lives of helpless hostages as a weapon in his quarrel with the President of the United States.

"Despicable it is and despicable it will remain. May it come back to haunt forever him who said it."

He paused, took a deep breath and stared, stern and implacable, into the eyes of the many millions, perhaps billions, who listened enrapt to his words.

"It raises questions," he said slowly, "concerning the right of such a one to administer the affairs of a great power, holding as it does such enormous influence over the fate of humanity.

"Can it be God's will that such a one is to remain where he is when he so blasphemes and violates the human spirit and the very foundations on which human society rests?

"Can it be that the world would be a better place were he not where he is?

"These are questions, my children," he concluded somberly, "which must be asked."

Again there was silence all over the globe, the silence of shock and disbelief and a sense that the world was changing so fast that mankind might not be able to hang on. It had been centuries since a Pope had attempted to intervene so openly in temporal affairs. In two minutes he had changed the entire context. The consequences could only be guessed at, were dimly seen, could not yet be comprehended. But it was clear to all who heard him, not least of them the President of the Soviet Union and the President of the United

States, that a new and enormously powerful factor had suddenly been injected into their battle.

The Church, for better or for worse, had taken sides openly at last.

The only problem, as Elinor murmured to her husband, was that it might be too late. It was three days before it became clear whether she was right.

4

$\mathbf{I}$n the interval things began slowly but definitely to stabilize in the field.

It became apparent that the Mexican government would not be overthrown. Its planes, aided by the Americans, were shooting down an increasing number of the invaders. On the ground around the oilfields the defenders were beginning to dig in with a determination and tenacity that surprised and pleased their allies from the north. Off both coasts U.S. ships were tracking the Soviet submarines that always skulked in those waters; the American vessels communicated freely with one another so that there could be no question below but that they were there and ready to respond instantly to any aggressive moves. In Mexico City and throughout the provinces a new spirit of unity seemed to be alive. The skeptical attitude of the average peon toward his government, the memory of past corruptions and the shruggingly cynical expectation of future ones, had given way to a virtually unanimous swell of genuine patriotism as the nature of the attack on the homeland penetrated even the poorest barrios, the remotest villages.

The President of Mexico called the President of the United States five times. Each time he sounded more secure, more confident and more jubilant.

"We are *holding* them!" he confided triumphantly in his most recent call. "We may even, God give us grace, begin to turn them back within the next few hours. It is a miracle!"

"A miracle of your leadership," Ham Delbacher told him. The Mexican President had the honesty to laugh and return the compliment.

"Of *yours*," he said. "We could not accomplish it without your loyal support."

"May this mark a new phase in the friendship between our two peoples," the President said.

"Let us hope so," the President of Mexico replied. He chuckled. "We will link hands and dance together on the grave of the monster in Moscow."

"Perhaps," Ham said. "We have a long way to go before that can happen."

"But it will," the President of Mexico asserted with complete confidence. "It may be yet far-off, but it is inevitable."

With equal confidence—his, indeed, had never seemed to flag for a second—the Prime Minister of South Africa reported in on several occasions. Each time he, too, seemed more certain of victory and the eventual defeat of the Soviet conquest.

"How about that Pope, laddie!" he exclaimed exuberantly after the Pontiff's brief and explosive address. "How about that Johnny in the hat! He's a bloodthirsty one, isn't he? How about that!"

"He has made his choice," the President said. "I'm glad he's on our side."

"It helps," the Prime Minister agreed, more soberly. "Very, very much indeed. That is one bitch of a situation, the hostages. But all's going well here, as I'm sure your intelligence reports tell you. We're knockin' the blighters out of the sky right, left and sideways. On the ground they're using the jungle, but so are we. We're Africans as much as they are, you know; it's our terrain, too. We've already got 'em on the run in a lot of places and it's going to be more. And I must say I think your Cuban chap is keeping his promise. We get reports the Cubans from Angola are throwing down their arms and surrendering and begging to go home. It's all they want, poor buggers. They want *out of this!*"

And he chuckled delightedly at his vision of thousands of homesick Cubans—an accurate vision, the President felt.

"I'm glad to know you feel so confident," he observed. The Prime Minister snorted.

THE ROADS OF EARTH 349

"Never a doubt of it!" he declared. "I've been confident from the moment I woke up and realized the bastards were over Jo'burg and Cape Town. We're going right on into Angola, too. No point in stoppin' now. Knock 'em right back and destroy the bloody communists, that's what we feel down here. Hope you agree, Mr. President."

"Would it matter if I didn't?" the President inquired dryly. The Prime Minister chuckled.

"Not much," he agreed. "Not much. Though we'll feel better about it if you approve. And we do thank you for all your help. It's been a great assist. Not that we couldn't have done it by ourselves, of course, I'm sure you know that."

"I'm inclined to suspect it," the President said, still dryly. "But it's nice to know you recognize we've been of *some* value, anyway."

"Seriously," the Prime Minister said, "you've been of great value. Don't you find it helps *you*, though, to have an ally who knows what he's doin' and is strong enough to do it?"

"It makes it easier," the President conceded.

"Too bad we can't help out with the rest of your wars," the Prime Minister remarked. "We'd like to but—"

"They aren't *my* wars," the President interrupted sharply. "They're Yuri Serapin's wars, and may he perish of them."

"Right you are!" the Prime Minister said stoutly. "I apologize, Mr. President. Strictly a slip of the tongue. The slimy bastard deserves whatever he gets. What do you hear about that?"

"Nothing definite. Intelligence picks up some rumors of unrest in the new Politburo and military, but that's to be expected." He chuckled, rather grimly. "The Pope and I are doing our best."

"May God speed your labors."

"I hope so," the President said. "What do you need, at the moment?"

"Nothing more right now, I'm proud to say," the Prime Minister said. "We've been waiting for something like this for a long time, after all, and once we got our feet under us from the initial surprise, we've done right well. As you know, they've knocked down a few of our planes too, with the ground-to-air missiles the Soviets put in, but we've taken out most of their installations and from here on in, it looks like clear sailing. We'll send up a shout if we need more from you. But I'd say we're o.k. until it's over down here, which won't be long. From what I read and hear, it's getting better elsewhere too.''

"I'm encouraged," the President said. "I just talked to the President of Mexico and he confirms what our own people down there have told me, that the tide is beginning to turn. China is—well, China. I think this is bringing them together at last. At any rate they aren't shooting each other anymore, which in practical effect quiets things down, there." He sounded wry. "I'm happy to settle for peace and quiet, whatever the cause.''

"And Saudi Arabia?''

"Also good, I think. Fortunately tribal loyalties, combined with hatred of the South Yemenis, seem to have created a situation confused but apparently leaning toward restoration. The younger brother holds Riyadh and a circumferential area roughly fifty miles out. But the older family has never been shaken from Jidda, and out in the desert the fighting seems to be going in their favor. The Yemenis can bomb only so much sand, and it's amazing how the tribes can find shelter in it. It's like Afghanistan—they're still holding out over much of the country after all these years, despite all the modern weapons.''

"Hatred is a pretty good weapon," the Prime Minister said with a grim little chuckle. "We know—we're hated. Fortunately we hate them more, plus weapons. So, then, it doesn't look too bad anywhere, at the moment?''

"Not *too* bad," the President said. "At the moment. It could change back, of course, at any time.''

"Not if you get him first," the Prime Minister said. "Anything *we* can do to help with *that,* let us know. We've some pretty good intelligence chappies working for us, too, you know.''

"Do they look Russian," the President inquired, "or are they all big blond blue-eyed Afrikaners?''

"You're joshing me," the Prime Minister said. "You must be feeling better. Except about the hostages, of course.''

"Yes.''

"That's all right. That will work out. You handled it just right in your little talk. Let him be the villain. I don't think he'll dare—not even he, after what you said. And then to have the Pope follow it up like that—it was a combination, I tell you. A combination!''

"I hope so," the President said grimly. "Because if it doesn't work out, then''—he sighed—''we're in for a bloody time.''

"It's got to work out," the Prime Minister said solemnly, "or there's no God in heaven. Be of good cheer, Mr. President. That, too, has got to turn.''

"I hope so," Ham Delbacher said again. "I hope so.''

His talk with the older brother in Jidda lightened his mood a little more, for that gentleman, like the Prime Minister, was his usual ebullient self. Things were going well everywhere—they were getting reports from all the tribes in the desert that the South Yemenis were making no progress—word came from the loyal underground in Riyadh that the younger brother was already neglecting his command duties in favor of those more personal pursuits to which he was addicted—so far the oilfields had not been seriously damaged because both sides wanted them preserved intact—the ''People's Republic of Arabia'' was a farce whose writ ran nowhere outside Riyadh, and there only thinly—all in all, Allah was good and the sun was shining in Jidda. But keep on sending supplies, because the battle was not over yet, good though it was in the eyes of heaven.

The prince was concerned, though, about the hostages.

"I am sorry, Mr. President," he said gravely. "We believe you should shoot all the Soviet dogs at once. It is all they deserve. It would rid you of the problem once and for all.''

"It would not rid us of the problem of the American hostages,'' the President objected. "They are *my* responsibility, after all. I can't simply invite their deaths as freely as you suggest.''

"He will kill them anyway," the prince said, and the President could envision his pragmatic shrug. "You might as well make him suffer too. But of course I agree, he would not suffer personally, he is as cold-blooded as a snake. But in a larger sense, he would suffer. In the eyes of the Russian people. In the eyes of the world.''

"I think he will suffer in both if I refrain and he does go ahead as he threatens," Ham Delbacher said. "That at least is what I'm counting on.''

"Perhaps," the prince said, sounding skeptical. "We will see

. . . In any event, Mr. President, everything indicates *we* will soon be victorious. At which time," he added with some relish, "there will be no delicacy here about what to do with little brother. He will be sliced from end to end and served to the vultures in the desert. Very slowly. Bit by bit."

"Well," the President said, shivering a little at the obvious enjoyment in his voice, "there, too, I think you must be a little aware of public opinion."

"Whose?" the prince asked blandly. "Everyone *here* will understand and approve of it. He wishes to do the same to us."

"Yes, no doubt. But a trial and a quick execution would look better. After all, there will be no doubt of the verdict. You will have your vengeance."

"We shall *enjoy* our vengeance," the prince promised in the same pleased, almost dreamy tone. The President made up his mind then and there that the younger brother must somehow be rescued and sent far, far away when the time came. Like the prince, he was beginning to be persuaded that it would not be long arriving.

"Our people in the field tell me you could use more planes," he said to divert the grisly conversation, of which he knew the prince meant every word. "Is that correct?"

"We can always use more planes. As you know, they shot down two of the AWACS yesterday, and twenty-three of our fighters were caught on the ground last week."

"Sloppy work," the President observed. The prince said calmly,

"Those responsible were dead within the hour. That is how we render justice in *our* country."

"I know," Ham Delbacher said. "There are occasional moments when I feel like applauding. The rest of the time I am not so sure. You need more fighters, then."

"All you can spare."

"But the final outcome is not in doubt, as you see it."

"Mr. President!" the prince said patiently. "How can he win, that besotted of women, that sodomizer of lovely boys from the desert? He is supported by the South Yemenis and the Soviets— and who else? The tribes despise him, his wives despise him, the oil and engineering companies to whom he now promises such extravagant things if they will only support him—they despise him. He cannot win because it would be *against the order of things*. It is not *right*. That is why he will lose, and very soon now, I think. Anyway, send planes, Mr. President. Send planes! If you do it will all be over in a week or two.''

"You're very optimistic," the President said. "I hope you're right."

"It is my nature to be optimistic," the prince said cheerfully. "Allah will preserve the rightful rulers of the patrimony of the House of Saud. He has never failed us yet."

"It *is* encouraging to be able to count on His support," the President said gravely. The prince laughed.

"Now you are mocking me. But you will see. It is inevitable."

"I believe you, I believe you," Ham Delbacher said. "I am glad to assist Allah with as many planes as I can."

"Good!" the prince said. "We will do the rest."

Some time later that day—or was it the next morning?—he spoke again to Peking and Taiwan. The situation there remained calm and appeared to be progressing. The young President of Taiwan was cautiously optimistic, Ju Xing-dao was elliptical but permitted a touch of excitement in his voice. It appeared they were coming nearer to some form of agreement. He congratulated them both and wished them luck. Both applauded his stand on the hostages and wished him well. Both were confident Yuri would not dare kill further Americans now, though both showed some of the prince's fatalism at the thought that this still might occur. The conversations ended with mutual goodwill all around. The President felt that history, in its inscrutable way, was taking a long leap forward in Asia.

With a frustrating sense of déjà vu he felt history was stalled at dead center in the United States. There after seventy-two hours the headlines conceded—

TIDE MAY BE TURNING ON WAR FRONTS

—but balanced this grudging optimism with—

U.S. LOSSES IN FOUR WARS AND CUBA NOW 43 PLANES, 287 MEN. CONGRESSIONAL PRESSURE GROWS TO AMEND WAR POWERS ACT TO BRING ALL FORCES HOME AT ONCE.

The more things change, he thought with a wry annoyance, the more they are the same.

Only the reports from Cuba burst unreservedly rosy through the reluctant media. The Maximum Leader was apparently sweeping all before him. Sizable numbers of Soviets had literally been pushed into the sea, and on the eastern approaches the blockade had stopped five Soviet "freighters," three tenders and a battleship, which were now at anchor within sight of the Americans—but, for the moment, coming no farther.

The lull ended with appearances by Gary Hanson on "Today," "Tonight," "A.M. America" and a Barbara Walters special. After the last of these, in which he warned ominously that, "The President's apparent denial of plans to inflame the satellites to revolt means nothing. He is pushing them ahead vigorously just the same," the President received a call from Mark Coffin. He had just received a call from Ivan Valerian. The young Soviet major "would like very much to talk to you, as he thinks he may have something to offer that would be of help with the satellites."

"I don't know what he can offer," Ham Delbacher said, "but you can bring him in after dinner tonight if you like and we'll see what he has to say."

"He's usually interesting to talk to," Mark observed.

And so he proved to be.

5

Mr. President!'' he exclaimed, almost literally bounding into the room in his customary exuberant fashion. ''How nice to see you again!''

Behind him Mark made an amused face and the two CIA men who had brought Ivan in from Virginia smiled too. Ivan, the President reflected, always did his best to live up to the image: the thought crossed his mind, as it always did, that perhaps he tried just a little too hard. But as always he dismissed it, momentarily engulfed in the young defector's puppy-dog welcome.

''Mr. President!'' he repeated dramatically, shaking Ham's hand vigorously in both of his and almost, it seemed, about to throw an arm around his shoulders and give him a hug—which he did not quite have the nerve to do, the President thought with wry relief. ''Mr. President, how busy you must be, and how kind of you to take the time to see my poor self!''

''Always a pleasure, Ivan,'' Ham Delbacher said, gesturing the CIA men to take a seat on a sofa near the doorway, back a bit from their conversation. They obeyed with some reluctance, which Ivan did not see. He only glanced about when they were safely seated and nodded with some satisfaction.

''We do not need *them!*'' he said, lowering his voice confidentially. ''It is good that they not listen to important matters.''

''Right,'' the President agreed solemnly, giving Mark a wink Ivan also did not see. ''Come sit by the desk, you two, and we'll talk. How are things going in Virginia? Is your wife any more reconciled to being in America?''

Ivan shrugged.

''Women! What can she do? I am here—she is here—the children are here. None of us,'' he said with a sudden sunny smile, ''is going to go back anytime soon. At least not''—the smile faded, a frown took its place—''not until Yuri Pavlovich is gone and Russia is free again.''

''I have some hopes both events will occur quite soon,'' the President said. Ivan responded with instant brightness.

''Oh, truly?''

''Yes, I think so. There are a few signs.''

''What?'' Ivan asked; and then shrugged and laughed. ''Not that I care *what*, exactly. *When* is more important to me. If Yuri Pavlovich goes, much could change.''

''Really?'' Mark said. ''I thought in your country it did not particularly matter who is in power, the communist system goes right on. Would that change too?''

''It could,'' Ivan said thoughtfully. ''It could.''

''Would you be glad to see that?'' the President inquired. Ivan flashed him a sudden broad smile.

''I would be delighted to see that! It would be my dream come true.''

''Really?'' Mark said again. ''I didn't realize you were such a revolutionary, Ivan. How does that happen?''

''Many of us are revolutionaries,'' Ivan said solemnly. ''It is difficult to express, if one wishes one's family to be safe, and to be safe one's self; but many of us have that feeling.''

''I understand quite a few do express it,'' Mark said, ''without regard to personal safety or the safety of families.''

''But it does no good,'' Ivan said patiently. ''What does it bring them? Death—or prison—internal exile—'psychiatric treatment' which may result in lobotomies—they may be transformed into vegetables—there are many weapons the state has that cannot be defied by ordinary men.''

''As Yuri Pavlovich's aide, you must have ordered many such

things," the President observed in a conversational tone. "Did it disturb you?"

For a moment Ivan looked genuinely crestfallen. He glanced away. An expression of deep regret passed across his face. Momentarily, the determined sun seemed under shadow.

"Mr. President," he said solemnly, "I would give anything—*anything*—could I call back those orders, restore those poor comrades to a healthy life. I have no excuse but youth—and enthusiasm, I suppose, for what I then believed was a valid cause, the cause of Mother Russia."

"For which the Soviet system is the best?" the President inquired.

"It may have been, at times in the past," Ivan said, "but it is not now. No, Mr. President, there are better things now! The best of them would be the removal of Yuri Pavlovich. After that, we shall see. I only hope you are right, that it will come soon. How will it come, do you think? What is going on in my counrty? Do you hear?"

"I hear," the President said with a smile, "but I cannot tell all I hear. It is enough to say that we detect signs that all is not well for Yuri Pavlovich. He faces real problems, which promise to get worse."

"And you will make them worse!" Ivan said happily. "You will overthrow the Warsaw Pact, you will start rebellions in the satellites, as your Mr. Hanson says!"

"He is not 'my' Mr. Hanson anymore," Ham Delbacher said. "And good riddance."

"But he is right, is he not?" Ivan asked. "You have plans? You will do it?"

"There are many options open to this government," Ham Delbacher said. "Events will have to decide which ones we pursue."

"But you do have plans," Ivan said earnestly. "You could not proceed without them. Which will it be first, Mr. President, Poland? It is the obvious."

Not for the first time, the thought shot across the President's mind: and if by the remotest chance I were to tell you, how soon would it take to get right back to your despised Yuri Pavlovich?

But then he thought: by what means? The embassy is closed, his countrymen have been sent home, who can he tell? Nonetheless, of course, he had absolutely no intention of satisfying Ivan's curiosity, which was, or perhaps was not, entirely natural.

"Many things are obvious in this world," he said with a smile, reflecting that he was beginning to sound like Ju Xing-dao, full of aphorisms, "but one does not always run after the obvious. We have indicated that we have no intention of stirring a satellite revolt—"

"Oh, but you do, Mr. President!" Ivan exclaimed, smiling as one knowing adult to another. "Surely you do! It is only common sense!"

"Not necessarily," the President said. "One man's common sense is another's insanity. So there you are."

"Anyway," Mark said, "even if he had plans, he couldn't tell you, Ivan, or me either. That would spoil the surprise."

"But how could it spoil the surprise?" Ivan asked, articulating the President's thought. "Surely *you* would tell no one, Mark! And I—even if I—even if I were not what I am, a fugitive from the Soviet system—who could I tell, if I did know? Even if our watchful friends back there"—he nodded over his shoulder at the two CIA men, now sitting bored and relaxed, one staring out the window at the Rose Garden, the other picking at a fingernail—"were not assigned to prevent my communication with anyone, who could I tell? I could not tell my embassy, it is closed. I could not tell my comrades—former comrades—there, they are already sent home. What will it matter if I know, or if you know, Mark? You will not tell—I cannot. What does it matter? So you see, Mr. President"—and he turned to him with a relaxed smile—"there is no point in being mysterious. I am simply curious, which I think is natural enough for me, a former aide to Yuri Pavlovich. After all, if it means the end of Yuri Pavlovich, that is all *I* care! Is that not the truth?"

"One way or another," the President said, "I think there will be an end of Yuri Pavlovich. But whether it will come through Poland or some other satellite, or several of them, or whether through something that happens in Moscow, or elsewhere, who can say?"

"*You* can, Mr. President!" Ivan said with a triumphant smile. "You can! Do not underestimate what you can put in motion. Do not underestimate the fact that in all the world, you—and America, of course—are the only things that can stop Yuri Pavlovich and change the Soviet system. And how better to do it than revolt in Eastern Europe. It is the best way of all!"

The President smiled.

"If you say so, Ivan."

"It is not I who say so!" Ivan exclaimed, and for a second there was a flash of something that could almost be called anger. "It is simple logic that says so! Is that not correct, Mr. President? It is simple logic that says a revolt in Eastern Europe is the best way to bring Soviet Russia down. And it is simple logic that says you are planning such a revolt, just as your Gary Hanson says! How can you play games with me about it? It is so logical!"

"Logic doesn't always determine history," the President said, and Mark agreed. "On the contrary."

"But it *is* logical!" Ivan said, voice emphatic but still low, glancing back at the CIA men, by now thoroughly bored and relaxed, the first still staring out into the Rose Garden, the second half-dozing, undisturbed by the muted conversation at the desk. "You cannot deny to me it *is* logical!"

"Ivan," Ham Delbacher said, voice deliberately curious and puzzled, "I thought you asked for this interview to tell *me* something about the satellites? Or was *I* to tell *you*? Possibly I misunderstood. What was your understanding, Mark?"

"The same as yours, Mr. President," Mark said, giving Ivan a quizzical look. "I thought you had something that would be of help to the President, Ivan, otherwise I wouldn't have bothered him with this. It's taking time from a lot of other important matters, you know. I think it's very kind of him, really. What *did* you want to say to him?"

For a moment Ivan appeared genuinely taken aback by their joint challenge; but he recovered, they noted, very fast. A shrug lifted his shoulders, a charming, disarming smile crossed his face; only the eyes, though they did not really see this because he

seemed to be glancing out the window, shaking his head in a bemused way, remained unchanged.

"Now it is an inquisition," he said, as if to himself. "Ivan must
be very careful, here . . . ." His expression became suddenly earnest and intent. He stared now directly into the President's eyes
with his usual straightforward and beguiling candor. "Mr. President, I simply wished to warn you that your plans to create revolt in
Eastern Europe will run into the very strongest opposition. The Soviet Union is in *absolute* control there. It is vital to our borders. We
cannot permit—you understand I say 'we' because it was my habit
for so many years—we cannot possibly permit any revolt to occur
in any of the Warsaw Pact nations. We are very heavily armed in
all of them, we have *absolute* hegemony there. Any revolt would
be *absolutely* futile and doomed to fail from the very beginning.
You know that, I suppose."

"I know you are heavily armed there and have apparent control," Ham Delbacher agreed. "I do not know how absolute your
control is, or whether it could hold for more than a few days against
a really determined revolt."

"It would have to be a suicidal revolt," Ivan said, "and not
even our noble freedom fighters in Poland"—his voice became,
for a moment, sarcastic before it swiftly smoothed out again—"are
that suicidal."

"Are you sure?" the President inquired. "That's not the information I get."

"No?" Ivan said, sounding suddenly concentrated and intent.
"And what information is that? Where did it come from?"

"From my sources. Which I think are possibly better than
yours."

"Perhaps," Ivan said, more calmly, "but I do not think so . . .
in any event, nothing could be more certain to make the men
around Yuri Pavlovich come to his side than to have revolts in
Eastern Europe. Is that your aim, to strengthen Yuri Pavlovich? I
thought we agreed it was the opposite, Mr. President."

"There, too, your information does not agree completely with
mine," the President said calmly. "We have reason to believe

there are some who would not be so quick to stand with him if they saw the opportunity a satellite revolt would produce.''

"Who are they?" Ivan demanded with the same intent, quick, concentrated air. And again the President rejected it with a calm smile.

"No one I am going to name now. But I have reason to believe they exist and that, at the proper time, they will come over.''

"Such talk is idle!" Ivan said, quite sternly. "It is a false hope. The new men are *new,* Mr. President, you must remember that. They would not have the courage or the organization to challenge Yuri Pavlovich. That too would be futile, hopeless, suicidal. You simply do not understand, Mr. President. Yuri Pavlovich *is* in control. He *is* the Soviet Union. No one is going to be able to dislodge him! No one!''

"Ivan," the President said, voice friendly, rising behind the desk and holding out his hand, "I thank you for coming because it is always pleasant to see you. But this time I'm afraid it *has* been something of a waste of time for me, because you haven't contributed very much. Nor," he added firmly, "have you said anything to make me change in the slightest what I plan to do.''

"Mr. President," Ivan said slowly, taking the President's extended hand firmly in his, looking grave and, suddenly, as implacable and determined as Yuri Pavlovich, "I thank you for seeing me, and I—am—sorry—''

And quite suddenly, so suddenly that the President had no time to do more than fling up his left arm to shield his face, Ivan yanked him sideways, pulling him off balance, leaped onto the desk and lunged for his throat, bowling him over backward and knocking over his chair. The two of them momentarily disappeared from Mark's horrified gaze and that of the two CIA men, now abruptly wide awake and running forward, guns drawn.

Before they could reach the desk, Mark, acting without thought and entirely on instinct, was over the desk and on the two struggling men on the floor, yanking desperately at Ivan's head and neck.

With an angry animal sound of rage and desperation Ivan took his hands for a second from the President's throat, leaped up, turned and gave Mark a karate chop to the side of the head that instantly knocked him unconscious. Then he swiveled back as if to leap again upon Ham Delbacher, who was gasping for breath and struggling desperately to rise.

Mark, however, had created just enough diversion and just enough time for the CIA's guns to come into play.

They fired simultaneously.

Ivan leaped a good two feet into the air, spun around and was dead, the doctors decided later, the moment his body, spurting blood from back and chest, fell upon the President.

After that for several seconds there was silence in the room save for the stentorian breathing of the President, the unconscious Senator and the two CIA men.

"Button—" Ham Delbacher croaked finally, managing to shift Ivan's body, staggering to his feet, waving his right arm at the desk just below the telephone, his left dangling uselessly at his side. "Call—"

His hectically flushed face turned suddenly pale. He seemed to raise himself partway to his full height and then fell back alongside the lifeless body of his young assailant.

After that things were very hectic in the Oval Office for quite a long time, but he was out of it. When he came to an hour later he was in his own bed upstairs in the family quarters, his left arm in a cast and strapped to his side, a pale and stricken Elinor weeping beside him.

The White House announcement half an hour after the event was terse.

"The President wishes it to be known that he tripped on a rug in the Oval Office at 9:43 tonight and fell against his desk, breaking his left arm as he tried to catch himself. Aside from minor contusions associated with the fall, he suffered no other injury. The fracture has been set and the President expects to be at his desk as usual tomorrow morning."

Of what had occurred immediately after the attack he was told in detail by the director of the Secret Service as soon as it was obvious that he was fully conscious. It was the sort of necessary cover-up that would have made the media scream in anguish had its members known. But they did not know, nor would they know until some days later at the U.N., where it became a sensation for a day, believed by some, scoffed at by more. Then it sank into the history books and was remembered only occasionally thereafter.

At the moment, however, it was so close to being an event that could have turned the whole course of history that the director of the Secret Service was literally almost shaking as he related the details to the President. The director could not conceal his anger and contempt for the CIA, an endemic dislike that went with the territory. But after he got that out of his system, his account was as passionless and straightforward as his obvious agitation would permit.

"After subject Valerian attacked your person, Mr. President," he said, and he could not suppress some sarcasm—"after it dawned on the CIA operatives present that something untoward was going on—subject Valerian was instantly killed by a total of seven shots from said CIA operatives. His body fell back upon your own. You apparently managed to dislodge his body and indicate to the CIA operatives that they must push the button by your desk which summons the Secret Service. This was done and within thirty seconds thereafter our operatives were in the Oval Office and in charge.

"The White House was immediately cleared of all personnel except the guards at the exits and exterior stations. Subject Valerian's body was then placed in blankets offered by Mrs. Delbacher, who had been immediately notified and who displayed great coolness and courage"—he bowed to her and Elinor returned a rather wan smile—"for which we thank you most profoundly, ma'am, it made everything much easier. Lights were doused at the service entrance and subject's body was then carried out that entrance by our operatives under cover of the ensuing darkness. To the best of our knowledge, this event passed unnoticed by anyone.

"Subject's body was taken at once to Bethesda Naval Hospital, where it is presently undergoing postmortem, particularly for evidence of drugs or other stimulants that might have encouraged what could have been either a spontaneous attack or one that was the result of long planning. This we do not know yet."

"I think the latter," Ham said, "and I suspect we won't ever know."

"No, sir, perhaps not," the director agreed. "In any event, the body is now there. Subject's wife and children, as you know, are in Virginia. It will be necessary to decide what should be done with them.

"All evidences of struggle have been removed from the Oval Office. Bloodstains on the rug behind your desk, on the desk, on your chair and on the flag behind you have been removed. The rug is wet at present but is being dried rapidly with the application of warm air. By morning there should be no traces of any kind remaining to indicate what happened there."

"A nonevent," the President said with a wry little smile. "By one who is now a nonperson."

His expression turned sad for a moment.

"He was a pleasant young man. Yuri must be desperate. Very, very desperate."

"In any event, sir," the head of the Secret Service said, "things are now in position so that no one but yourself, Senator Coffin, the CIA operatives and our own group of six operatives and myself need ever know what happened there. Your press secretary has already, at my suggestion, issued a statement that you broke your arm after tripping on a rug and striking your desk." He repeated it verbatim. "We have placed a couple of Oriental rugs near the desk, and if all goes well the media will not even notice that they are new additions."

"Reporters haven't been in that room for two weeks," the President said. "If anybody asks we can always say I decided I'd like a couple of Orientals a couple of days ago and just wasn't used to them, therefore I tripped and fell."

"Very good, sir," the director said with a smile. "Now all that remains is the disposition of subject Valerian's body and what to do with his wife and family, who of course do not know as yet what has happened to him."

"Poor woman," Elinor said. "She probably hadn't the slightest inkling of this."

"Or perhaps she did," Ham said. "That, too, we will never

know." He thought for a moment. "Have someone who speaks Russian tell her that the car in which Ivan was being brought here was struck by another and he was so badly disfigured that to save her anguish it has been decided to have him cremated and his ashes returned with her and their children to the Soviet Union, which will be done at once. If she is innocent she will accept this; if she isn't she will suspect that he was discovered and disposed of. I think we can count on our friends in Moscow to keep the whole thing quiet. Have him cremated tonight and have the family and the ashes on their way to Berlin as soon as possible tomorrow. I rely on you absolutely, as I do on the director of the CIA, to be sure that your men maintain absolute silence—permanently."

"You can count on my men," the director of the Secret Service said flatly, and the President could not suppress a smile.

"And on the CIA's too, I think. And ask Senator Coffin to come up here and see me right away—"

He was conscious of a change in both the director's expression and Elinor's and stopped abruptly.

"What's the matter with Mark?" he demanded sharply. "Isn't he all right? What is it, El?"

"He—he's—" she said with an anguished hesitation that wasn't like her. "He's—"

She looked helplessly at the director, who cleared his throat and spoke as dispassionately as he could.

"I am sorry to report, sir, that Senator Coffin is also in Bethesda Naval Hospital. I am afraid he is in a coma, apparently as a result of a blow to the head by Major Valerian. It was apparently a very experienced karate chop. The doctors have no way of knowing at the moment when, or whether, Senator Coffin will recover."

For several moments Ham said nothing, and when he finally spoke it was in a heavy voice.

"*That*—I didn't count on. I think even as Ivan jumped me, I was not surprised—you always expect something like that, consciously or subconsciously, in this office. But not—not attacks on other people. Not on Mark." A bitter little smile crossed his lips. "I suppose he was trying to defend me."

"Yes, sir," the director said, "I suppose he was."

"You know he was," Elinor said. "Could you doubt it?"

"No," he said, voice even heavier, and tired. "No, I couldn't doubt it. Where's Linda? At the hospital?"

Elinor nodded.

"I talked to her about an hour ago. She's bearing up."

He sat up and brushed aside the covers. The movement made him terribly dizzy for a moment, a sharp pain shot through his broken arm. But the dizziness cleared and the pain eased, even as his wife and the director started up in alarm.

"I'm going to go to her," he said. "Help me dress."

"You are *not!*" Elinor cried, and ran for the door shouting, "Doctor! Doctor!"

"Sir," the director said hurriedly. "Sir, I do think you had better not. Sir, I think you had better *not*—"

"I'm all right," he said sharply, though things were not quite steadied down completely; but they were rapidly getting better. "Stop fussing at me like a couple of old women and help me dress."

"Sir," the White House doctor said sharply from the door. "Sir, I must insist—"

"So must I," he said, a touch of his usual humor returning. "And I think you'll recognize, doctor, that I'm in a better position to be an insister than you are. Now help me up, all of you, and stop this damned nonsense."

"Ham," Elinor said sternly. "Ham, you *are* a fool!"

"Right," he said cheerfully, standing up and swaying, so that they all moved toward him hastily. "That's right, grab on and keep me steady. And you, Elinor, get my clothes out of that closet and start dressing me."

"Sir," the director of the Secret Service said desperately. "Sir, this may blow the whole thing. Someone will see you, sir, news will get out, the whole cover will be destroyed—sir—*you can't do this to us!*"

"Ha!" he said. "You're so perfect, you guys, *you* keep it quiet. That's *your* business. Mine is to be a friend and go see Mark and Linda. Now, God damn it everybody! *Get a move on!*"

For a tense moment they all stood stockstill staring at one another. Then with a resigned air the director of the Secret Service and the White House doctor turned to Elinor.

"Damn it to hell!" she said at last with quite uncharacteristic profanity, torn between rage and laughter. "Of all the stubborn old fools, Hamilton Delbacher, you take the cake! Hold him steady, doctor. I'll get his clothes."

"I'll go make the arrangements," the director said hastily, and disappeared.

"And I'll go along to make sure you don't have a relapse," the White House doctor said. "With all respects, Mr. President, this is *crazy*."

"Maybe," Ham said, feeling again a little lightheaded. "But I'm going, anyway."

Ten minutes later he was downstairs, also at the service entrance which was again blacked out. He stooped low to disguise his height as much as possible, and hurried, flanked by the director and the doctor, to an unmarked, modest car—the director's own, which he had hurriedly brought to the door. Quietly they swung out and away. Behind them at a discreet distance another unmarked Secret Service car with four operatives followed. Two more were squeezed into the director's car, one on each side of the President. He calculated with an irreverent relish that there must be seven Secret Service blood pressures that were at least 190 over 190 riding along with him.

"Good thing we're going to Bethesda," he remarked cheerily to the director, "in case any of you fellows has a heart attack."

"This is *most* irregular," the director said severely, not at all amused. "*Most* irregular, Mr. President."

"That's exactly why it's going to be perfectly safe," Ham said. "Step on it."

"I'll do this at my own pace," the director said firmly, "and I won't attract attention. So relax, Mr. President, and leave the driving to us. *You're* under *my* orders, now."

"Yes, sir," Ham said, deciding to stop teasing him about what really was, after all, a most irregular proceeding. "I'll be good."

"That's a welcome change," Elinor observed from the front

seat where she sat crowded in between the director and the doctor. "That will be something most unusual, Ham Delbacher."

"As long as I can be of some help to Linda," he remarked; and sobered by the thought, which brought back all the night's horror and tragedy, they rode in silence the rest of the way as the director casually but carefully threaded his way through traffic whose drivers never suspected that anything so zany as this dangerous ride of the President could ever occur.

At the hospital it was again a matter of back entrances, service elevators, unused stairs, hallways cleared of their usual population of nurses and doctors. Finally, unknown to everyone but the director of the hospital and a handful of his top aides, they arrived at the door he and Elinor dreaded to enter but knew they must. His arm was throbbing painfully but his head now was entirely steady and clear.

"We'll wait down the hall," the director of the Secret Service said. He nodded. They all moved off. Elinor raised a hand that trembled noticeably and knocked.

"Yes?" Linda said from inside. "Who is it?"

"It's us," Elinor said. "Can we come in?"

"Oh, Aunt Elinor!" Linda said with a half-cry. "Yes, *yes!*"

She opened the door and stood there, and for several seconds she and the President looked at one another without speaking. Then she reached out a hand, which he took gently in his.

"Oh, Uncle Ham," she said, starting to cry. "You shouldn't have done this. You're hurt."

"I'm all right," he said, leaning down to kiss her on the cheek, his own eyes filling in sympathy. "There's life in the old curmudgeon yet. And," he added gravely, "it seemed the least I could do. May we come in?"

"Oh, of course," she said, stepping aside to let them pass, exchanging kisses with Elinor as they entered. "Daddy's here too."

"Yes," the President said as Senator Elrod's white head and normally pleasant visage, now strained with shock and worry, came into view on the other side of the bed. "Jim," he said, holding out his hand. "These are tough times."

"Yes, Mr. President," Jim Elrod said, shaking hands; and then, as the President shook his head impatiently, "Yes, Ham, they are. But I didn't think they would touch our boy."

"Neither did I," Ham Delbacher said. "I would give anything if—"

"Nothing to be helped," Jim Elrod said gruffly. "You couldn't possibly have known. He was just there. He did his best."

"That he did," the President said gravely; "that he did"; and stepped up to the bed and finally looked down at the one his eyes had been avoiding since he entered.

Mark was lying on his back, his head bandaged, an intravenous tube in his arm, the impersonal bottle slowly dripping its contents as it hung from the metal rod above. Mark's eyes were closed. The little they could see of his face was very pale but composed. He might simply have been resting on some other, normal night in some other, normal place.

"They don't know—?" the President inquired. Linda, steadier now, shook her head.

"They say they have no way of knowing. We just have to wait . . . and pray."

"I'm doing that," the President said. "All the time . . . I wonder if you can ever forgive me, Linda."

"For what?" she asked blankly.

"For exposing him to this."

"But how *could* you know!" she exclaimed. "That's ridiculous, Uncle Ham. How could you possibly know?"

"Well, I should have suspected. Defectors at his level usually don't come that simply. And all that cozying up to me, those confidential tips on what was going to happen—"

"He fooled Mark, too," she said. "It was all very logical, wasn't it? Everybody was suspicious to begin with—then we all relaxed. It wasn't just you. And he did give you some good tips, too."

"Very good," the President said. "He knew what he was talking about." He gave a grim little smile. "Obviously."

"They must have planned it for a very long time," Jim Elrod said. "Then he saw Mark—and Mark became his ticket over."

"I think Mark was just the target of opportunity," the President said. "Ivan spotted him at that first summit meeting in New York—age called to age—wives, kids, tennis, interest in world politics, what have you—it was a natural, and he made the most of it. He was a very bright young man, was Ivan Valerian." He shook his head, face sad and somber. "What a waste! Not only for us"—he nodded sadly down at Mark—"but for them. Ivan could have gone far if he had stayed with us—if he had been genuine."

"He *was* genuine, as he saw it," Senator Elrod said. "But he owed allegiance to a terrible ideology, and it was too much for him—too much for us. He must really have been dedicated, to throw away his life like that, knowing he couldn't possibly survive but knowing it was the only chance to do the job his masters had sent him to do."

"He came close to doing it, too," Elinor said with a shiver. "If it hadn't been for Mark—"

"Yes," Senator Elrod said softly. "If it hadn't been for Mark . . ."

For a long moment they all stared down at the silent figure on the bed, the only sound its labored, but steady, breathing. Then Ham Delbacher straightened and looked across at his old colleague from Senate days.

"I wonder sometimes, Jim, what it's all worth," he said. "Why do we keep trying? Why do we keep working? What's the point in all the striving, if they're going to win anyway—if they are still able to hypnotize young men as fine as I think Ivan was, in his own mistaken way—if they're going to fool so many millions, destroy so much truth, persuade the world to put on blinders and think in such fatal, self-defeating ways . . . What am *I* worth, trying to stem the tide, trying to roll back the sea, trying—as they put it—to 'deny the logic of history'? Maybe they're right. Maybe they *do* have the logic on their side. Maybe it's all a mistake on our part. Maybe we should just give up, and then boys like Ivan wouldn't be dead, and boys like Mark wouldn't be—wouldn't be—"

His voice failed him, and again there was silence until Linda finally spoke.

"You don't mean that, Uncle Ham," she said quietly. "You're at your low point right now, just as I was when—when they first called me tonight from the White House. I felt that way too. And then I stopped to think. I thought of what we have here, and of what it means to be free to do what we want *as* we want and *when* we want—to be able to say what we think, do what we like, go to the next town or the next county without getting permission from the police, travel freely where we want to go, speak, think, express ourselves, be free in our homes and persons—just be free to *live*, like normal human beings. And I thought of all I've read about the prison they live in and the awful darkness they have imposed on their own land and the other nations they control, and want to impose on everybody, everywhere . . . and I came out of it. I decided that whatever—whatever happens to—to Mark, it's worth it, for us. Ivan's dead because he wanted to kill everything we value in liberty and human freedom, and you represented it for him—as you do for all of us. And Mark's going through this because he wanted to save you, and save all that. I don't think he would regret what's happened if he knew you were safe and that the hope is still there. As he *will* know," she said with a sudden fierceness, "because he's going to come out of this all right . . . So I don't want you to worry about it, Uncle Ham. It's too important that you be calm and sure in what you do. We all depend on you—the whole free world—the *whole* world, because there must be many, many millions over there who want to break out of the prison the Soviets have imposed on their own country and on all the other countries they control. You mustn't worry, Uncle Ham. It's o.k. Really it is."

And she looked at him with eyes again bright with tears; and again his own filled in sympathy.

"And supposing—" he said quietly. "Just supposing Mark—doesn't come out of it all right. Will you still feel the same way then?"

"Yes, I will!" she said with the same fierce certainty. "Because something has to mean something, in this world, and if one can't feel that there are some things worth more than life itself, then we might as well give up and surrender to them and all become slaves and prisoners like they are!"

Again there was silence, which he broke at last with a smile to Jim Elrod.

"Quite a daughter you have, Jim," he said softly.

"And quite a son-in-law, too," Jim Elrod said.

"And quite a son-in-law, too," he agreed. He straightened his shoulders, moved his left arm slightly to ease its steady throbbing and looked at Elinor, quietly wiping her eyes. "Well, El. I expect we'd better get on back to the house. I've got to get some sleep and give this arm a little rest before I get back to my desk tomorrow morning, like the statement said. Which I am going to do, of course . . ." He kissed Linda gravely, shook hands with Senator Elrod, turned as if to leave. Then he turned back and again approached the bed. He stood for several seconds looking down at Mark, whose chest rose and fell with his steady breathing but whose eyes were closed and whose mind, if it was anywhere, was far away, beyond the reach of any of them at the moment.

The President laid the back of his right hand gently against Mark's cheek and held it there for a long moment. The cheek felt flushed but not overly so; a moderate and probably normal fever, the President felt, to be expected under the circumstances.

"Good night, Mark," he said softly. "Thank you—sleep well—and come back to us."

He straightened again to his full six feet four, a big, heavy man who looked solid enough to take whatever the world might throw at him. Then he turned and walked out without a backward glance. Dutifully Elinor and his White House entourage followed. Their outwardly innocuous little caravan made its way, completely undetected, back through Washington's near-deserted nighttime streets to the Mansion.

There he was met by his press secretary.

"Mr. President," he began nervously. "I'm receiving a lot of requests from the media that you—"

"Yes," he said, "I'm way ahead of you, Bob. I think it's about time to have a press conference anyway, for a lot of reasons. Why don't you put it on the wires right now: ten A.M. tomorrow in the East Room."

"If you think you'll be feeling well enough, Mr. President—"

"I will," he said, ignoring Elinor's instinctive movement of protest. "I haven't got time to feel any other way."

Even leaving aside his injury, which he knew they would question him about at great length, and which he knew he would have to lie about as Presidents sometimes have to lie when great matters of state are involved, it was indeed about time to meet the media. So far he had deliberately refrained from speaking out because things were breaking so fast. After almost two weeks of pent-up pressure on both sides, they all needed the safety valve. He knew it would not be an amicable press conference, but by now it was certainly a necessary one.

6

It was, in fact, your typical, quintessential, vintage Late Twentieth Century Presidential Press Conference.

Its stars asked questions with one eye on the headlines and the other on the television cameras.

Its central figure tried with varying degrees of success to be patient with them.

Most of their questions were hostile.

Most of his answers were inevitably to some degree evasive.

They weren't satisfied with him.

He wasn't satisfied with them.

A majority of their countrymen came away, as always, scornful and disbelieving of a media, some of whose more prominent members had seemingly abandoned all pretense of fairness in their nakedly open quest for Pulitzers and preferment.

A minority of their countrymen came away, as always, convinced that their President was a no-good, lying, worthless son of a bitch.

Everybody performed right on schedule.

And the other nations of the world were, as always, depending upon which side they were on, either appalled or delighted by America's compulsion to rip itself to shreds in its moments of gravest crisis.

It began, inevitably, with his broken arm. This was examined, photographed and instantly immortalized as he entered the East

374

Room. That was the picture of the day on television and all the front pages—and not, perhaps, such a bad one, he thought wryly: the gallant leader, crippled but Carrying On. The first question got things off to a racing start.

"Mr. President," ABC asked, "if, as appears obvious, you were unable to avoid tripping over a rug, is it possible there could be some question of your competence in other areas as well?"

(The President reflected wryly that this was not as farfetched as it sounded. Wilder things than that have been asked at presidential press conferences in the never-ending game of Get the Guy.)

Some of his audience did have the grace to laugh. And he laughed himself, quite heartily.

"Why, Joe," he said, "if that's your criterion in judging my competence, then more power to you. I will just have to appeal to everyone who ever tripped over a rug, which I suspect is a good many millions: did you feel it disqualified you for whatever you were doing? I don't."

"What kind of rug was it, Mr. President?" UPI inquired.

"Oriental, as the statement said. Kazak, I believe."

"Have we seen the rug before? I don't recall seeing any Oriental rugs in your office."

"That was the problem," he said, marveling inwardly at how coolly a President could evade the truth when it was necessary. "It's only been there a short time." About twelve hours, he thought wryly. "I'm not too familiar with it yet."

"Where did it come from, Mr. President?" the *Post* inquired. "Was it a gift?"

"Yes."

"To the country?"

"Gifts to a President are gifts to the country, as you know," he said, making a mental note to find out sometime just who it *had* been given to before it had come to rest in White House storage, where the Secret Service, in desperate need of cover-up, had found it last night.

"Who gave it to you?"

"I'm not sure," he said. "These things come in all the time for one reason or another. Perhaps the State Department would know. You might ask them. Anyway, aside from being something of an obstacle, it's beautiful and I like it. I'll have to have you all in to see it one of these days. And its companion—the one I did *not* trip over, Joe.''

"Good," ABC said. "We want to see them."

"I'm sure you do," he said, and gestured toward another lifted hand.

"How *is* your arm, Mr. President?"

"Fine," he said. "It hurts a little still, but the cast helps a lot. I'll be out of it in no time, the doctors tell me. Fortunately it wasn't my right. I can still function."

"Are you pleased with the way you're functioning, Mr. President?" ABC inquired, and he thought: You persistent little devil, you! Aren't you the one!

"On the whole, yes," he said calmly, and decided to sail right into it. "I am *not* satisfied with the way the present President of the Soviet Union is functioning, however. President Serapin in my judgment is functioning in a way that has come perilously close to jeopardizing the peace of the whole world."

"What way is that, Mr. President?" NBC inquired, and the President deliberately looked blank.

"Where have *you* been? He is jeopardizing world peace right, left and center, as I have said everywhere I possibly could say it in the past two weeks. He is jeopardizing it most flagrantly in Mexico, in Saudi Arabia, in Southern Africa and in the Far East. He is jeopardizing it everywhere he can. For him, as for all his Soviet predecessors, that's the only game in town: jeopardizing peace. What more evidence do you need?"

"I haven't seen so much evidence," NBC said in a skeptical tone. "There have been many claims, from you and others in the Western bloc, but not so much evidence."

"I presented some evidence at the United Nations," he said, "and more accumulates every day. It is there for all those who are not totally prejudiced or totally blind to see."

"Mr. President," NBC said sharply, flustered by his uncompromising tone but not giving up, "I do not consider myself either prejudiced or blind, and while it is clear that you presented what you sincerely believed to be evidence of Soviet activity to the Security Council, a legitimate doubt seems to remain in many minds as to just how valid that evidence was.''

"Is that a question?" the President inquired dryly. "I don't think it scans or sounds like one."

"I was just asking," NBC said doggedly, "what real evidence there is of Soviet activity in these various wars in which we are engaged around the world. *Is* there any evidence, aside from your claim that it is so?"

"That wonderful word 'claim!' " Ham Delbacher exclaimed in mock admiration. "How wonderfully it dogs the heels of American Presidents, in the media. Heads of other governments, particularly the Soviet Union, 'charge' or 'assert' or 'state'. Presidents are always reported or headlined as *'claiming'*—that invidious word that creates such automatic built-in distrust. It's amazing."

"Is that an answer, Mr. President?" CBS inquired with the smooth insolence for which he was renowned and rewarded. "It doesn't scan or sound like one."

"It's a description, Henry," Ham said with an amiable smile, "which I am afraid rings a bell with a lot of your listeners and readers. If I were you I'd be disturbed by their reaction. I don't think they think too much of the media's 'claims,' either. So there we are. In any event," he said, dropping it and becoming businesslike, "there is ample evidence of the culpability of the present President of the Soviet Union in launching the four Soviet-inspired and Soviet-backed conflicts which are presently raging around the globe. I am therefore pleased to be able to state officially what your own news reports are apparently beginning to bring in from the field: all four conflicts are beginning to turn against the Soviets and their stooges and the prospects for early peace based upon the legitimate governments are apparently brightening by the hour."

"This does please you, Mr. President?" the *Post* inquired, also on the edge of insolence. Again Ham Delbacher looked deliberately blank.

"Shouldn't it please everyone who values freedom and independence? It does please me, yes. I couldn't be more delighted."

"Even though American losses are rising steadily?" the *Times* asked.

"One American serviceman lost, one American plane lost, is

too many," the President said. "But given the widespread nature of the battlefields and the ruthless help afforded illegitimate revolutionary elements by the Soviet Union, I do not think those losses are greater than was expected. The quicker the present President of the Soviet Union recognizes the futility and danger of his overseas adventurism and withdraws his support so that the conflicts can come swiftly to an end, the quicker we will get all the American forces home and stop suffering Soviet-caused losses which are absolutely vicious and inexcusable."

"You don't believe, then, Mr. President," AP said, "that there are legitimate freedom movements in the four areas where you have chosen to send troops—"

"I didn't 'choose' to send troops," the President said sharply. "The present President of the Soviet Union deliberately created four situations in which I had no choice but to send troops."

"Four situations in which American troops were sent," AP amended, not conceding much. "You don't think any of these freedom movements are legitimate, then?"

"Who says they're 'freedom movements,' " the President inquired tartly, "except the Soviet Union and"—he almost said "you folks" but thought better of it—"those over here and elsewhere in the free world who are suckers enough to swallow their propaganda? That's where we *really* need evidence, it seems to me. I haven't seen any that proved these so-called freedom movements were anything but screens for communist takeover."

"You don't believe the peoples of Saudi Arabia, Mexico and South Africa want freedom?" UPI demanded, sounding shocked.

"Certainly I believe it," Ham Delbacher said, "but they want it on their terms. They don't want it on the terms offered by the present President of the Soviet Union. They don't want it if it means striking a bargain with communism, because bargains with communism always seem to end in communist takeover. That's what we're there to prevent."

No one, apparently, cared to challenge this—or else they thought him so hopeless, he thought wryly, that they just decided there was no point in a challenge. There was a momentary pause, after which several hands shot up. He chose the Miami *Herald*. The heavily accented voice of their Cuban expert turned the discussion to the Maximum Leader's by now almost complete recapture of the island.

"Yes," the President said. "The United States is gratified indeed that the legitimate leader of Cuba has apparently met with great success in his drive to regain control of his country from its Soviet occupiers. We congratulate him on this triumph and we are pleased to have been of assistance. We look forward to a renewal of the strong Cuban-American ties which once bound our two countries in mutually helpful friendship."

"And the blockade, Mr. President?" asked the Boston *Globe*. "Are we pleased with that?"

"It is not being challenged so far," the President noted.

"But aren't Soviet ships just outside?" the *Globe* pressed. "It could be challenged at any time, could it not?"

"Oh, yes," the President said. "Certainly."

"And if it is?"

"We will have to see what happens then."

"You cannot tell us now."

"No," he said in a tone that clearly said, *What a foolish question.* "Certainly I cannot tell you now. For the moment, it holds. Our hope is that before it has to come to a real showdown, calmer heads in Moscow will prevail and it will be seen that there is now nothing to be gained by attempting to get through to a government that is no longer friendly to the Soviet Union."

"Do you think President Serapin sees it that way?" someone asked, and Ham Delbacher smiled grimly.

"I said 'calmer heads in Moscow,' did I not? I was not talking about President Serapin."

"Mr. President," the Chicago *Tribune* said, "do you think you were justified in sacrificing the lives of two American hostages, in view of the fact that you have now released all the Russian hostages and therefore have nothing with which to bargain with President Serapin to stop his threat to kill more Americans unless you withdraw our troops from the battle zones?"

"A complicated question with which to state a simplified view of things," he observed. "To begin with, *I* did not sacrifice the two American hostages. They were ruthlessly murdered on President Serapin's orders ahead of any deadline he might have set for negotiations about their release. It appears to have been a wanton, almost insane, act of revenge. Confronted by that, I decided to release the Soviet hostages because it had obviously become impossible to deal with President Serapin on this matter on any calm and rational basis.''

''And his threat to kill more Americans if we don't withdraw?'' the *Tribune* pressed. ''What will you do about that, Mr. President? Will you withdraw the troops or will you deliberately endanger the lives of captive Americans?''

He stared at his interrogator, who stared back.

''We will not withdraw,'' he said quietly, ''and I will take that risk. Because I do not think even the present President of the Soviet Union will fly in the face of world opinion to be that brutal and inhuman.''

''You initiated the hostage taking, did you not, Mr. President?'' CBS inquired. ''You took the original gamble—and lost. What makes you think this gamble will be any more successful?''

Again the President stared at his interrogator in a long look that was returned with unimpressed skepticism.

''Because I do not think Mr. Serapin's colleagues will allow him to do such a thing.''

''What proof do you have of that, Mr. President?'' CBS asked quickly.

''Sufficient,'' he said with a flat emphasis that effectively foreclosed CBS from any more questions on that subject.

A dozen hands shot up. He chose the Los Angeles *Times*.

''Mr. President, is it your intention to stir up revolts in Eastern Europe in an attempt to overthrow President Serapin, and if that is true, would that not have the effect of strengthening rather than weakening him with his own colleagues and the Russian people?''

''I believe we issued a statement on that the other day.''

''The statement implied that you were *not* trying to stir up revolts in Eastern Europe. Is that true?''

Here we go again, he thought; and said calmly, ''I rather think if we were engaged in stirring up revolts in Eastern Europe it would be clearly apparent, would it not? There wouldn't be any doubt or any need to ask questions about it.''

"I didn't say were you already *engaged,* Mr. President," the L.A. *Times* said quickly. "I said do you *intend* to stir up revolts."

"If at some future time," he said, thinking wryly to himself: *Such as twenty-four or forty-eight hours from now,* "some such action was deemed viable and could even be accomplished, which is very doubtful, then under such hypothetical circumstances possibly it might eventually be contemplated by those seeking Mr. Serapin's downfall."

"You've lost me, Mr. President," the L.A. *Times* said.

"Good!" he said with a laugh in which they all joined. "I meant to."

"But, Mr. President—" ABC protested.

"It's not contemplated now," the President said with a smile they all understood perfectly to mean: *Catch me if you can.* "We are entirely aware, incidentally, of the dangers of unifying rather than dividing the Soviet leadership by any such tactics."

"You do not yourself know, then," the *Post* said, seeking to sum it up before UPI, as senior White House correspondent, terminated the conference with the standard, "Thank you, Mr. President!"—"you do not yourself know at the present time of any immediate plans for creating revolts in Eastern Europe."

"Not at the present time," he repeated solemnly, seizing the opportunity offered. And again they all laughed, ruefully, for he and they both knew that "at the present time" was Washington's magic phrase behind which all manner of men, at all manner of times past, present and future, concealed their intentions.

The press secretary gave the high sign.

UPI obliged with, "Thank you, Mr. President!"

They streamed out, muttering discontentedly among themselves.

Two hours later events were taken out of both his hands and Yuri's by forces that were not even so uncertainly constrained by the responsibilities of power as they.

The overwhelming tensions of the world situation—the quarrel between the two superpowers that seemed to make all life at risk—the chance for a great gamble that might just possibly succeed—suddenly came together in the minds of leaders who decided, perhaps accurately, that their peoples had nothing to lose but their lives—and with infinite luck might gain the greatest prize of all, their freedom.

GERMANY RISES AGAINST SOVIETS! EAST GUARDS SLAUGHTER REDS, OPEN WALL! WEST TROOPS POUR THROUGH TO JOIN COUNTRYMEN IN BERLIN! JOINT FORCE CREATED AS CITIZENRY BATTLES OCCUPIERS!

And tumbling on the heels of that, two hours later:

POLES FOLLOW GERMANS, LAUNCH MASSIVE REVOLT AGAINST SOVIETS AS POPE FLIES TO JOIN "NEW CRUSADE FOR FREEDOM"! CZECH, HUNGARY, YUGO RISINGS BELIEVED IMMINENT! FRENCH PLEDGE HELP! WORLD LOOKS TO U.S.!

And at six P.M. Washington time, after conferring all afternoon with the National Security Council, the Joint Chiefs, his Cabinet, his wife and his friends on the Hill, Hamilton Delbacher gave the only response allowed him by events, now that the Soviets' slaves had jumped the gun and left him without any choice:

PRESIDENT PLEDGES "ALL POSSIBLE AID" TO REBELLION! COUPLES MASSIVE AIRLIFT TO STAGING AREAS IN FRANCE WITH PLEA FOR UN ACTION! NATO VOTES UNANIMOUS SUPPORT! CHINA HINTS POSSIBLE ASSIST! SECURITY COUNCIL CALLED!

The fragile fabric of international order was almost—almost—irrevocably ripped open at last, and the roads of earth appeared about to run with blood.

In the Kremlin the wolves began to circle the leader who refused to admit that he and his dreams of world conquest were dying.

BOOK FIVE

1

They had demanded the meeting, in telephone calls hesitant but persistent, for two hours, and for two hours he had refused to respond to the rising urgency in their voices. But when Mikhail Yarkov finally appeared at his door to announce, "Comrade President, the Politburo and the military leaders most urgently desire you to meet with them," he knew he must.

He felt nothing but contempt for their cowardice, nothing but scorn for their evident fear; and now as he sat at the head of the long conference table near his desk and looked along it, he could see all the evidence he needed of exactly how they felt. The faces were as always determinedly impassive, but the ever-suspicious eyes were now furtive with fear, the always tightly pursed lips were drawn even tighter with apprehension. They had thought war, planned war, dreamed war for many decades; and now that it appeared that war—the final war that would decide the fate of all mankind—was upon them, they were stinking with terror.

He could not understand it, for he controlled the mightiest military machine ever created by man. *He* was not uncertain or afraid. Why, then, should they be?

"Comrades!" he said, his voice calm and powerful as always. "We meet on a glorious occasion!"

He gave them a look challenging them to deny it, and for several moments it appeared no one would. Then the Foreign Minister spoke, in a voice nervous but determined.

"How is that, Comrade President? It seems a tense and difficult occasion to me, and I think"—he too looked up and down the table, and was met with determinedly blank expressions for it was not yet clear how the discussion would go and no one was ready to commit himself—"I *think* I speak for many of us when I say it is an occasion that presents grave challenges to the Party."

There was a murmur along the table, but it was unclear at the moment whether it represented agreement or whether his colleagues were simply making noises to indicate that they were present and listening very earnestly.

"In what way, comrade?" Yuri demanded sharply. "Are we not already engaged in a massive counterthrust all along the front in Eastern Europe? Are not our missiles ready to strike in an instant if we need them? Are not the armed forces of the Motherland overwhelming in their power? Is this not our great opportunity at last to conquer the West once and for all and send the capitalist imperialists of the United States into the dustbin of history where they belong? Why does it fill you with doubt, comrade? What are you afraid of?"

"I am not afraid, Yuri Pavlovich," the Foreign Minister said. "I am just—"

"Yes, you are!" he interrupted with a deliberate show of anger, knowing suddenly what he must do to stop what he could sense, again, might be incipient revolt. "While I and all your colleagues stand bravely and unafraid, *you* are playing the coward, Comrade Minister! *You* are abandoning the Motherland! *You* are doubting the truth and wisdom of the Party! *You* are betraying the socialist revolution! Comrade Minister!" he said, turning so suddenly to the Minister of Justice that the man jumped in his seat and turned pale. "Arrest this man! At once!"

And he turned upon the Minister of Justice the full force of his personality and the full weight of an anger that appeared to be absolutely genuine and implacable.

There was a long silence—so long that he felt the hairs begin to rise on the back of his neck. *Was this to be the ending? Was this when the great gamble would fail? Would history have no place for Yuri Pavlovich, after all?*

He willed it to be not so. He *willed* it, with all the force of his fearsome personality, which had never failed him in all his ruthless climb to the pinnacle of the Soviet state. And for the second time in all that long, ruthless history, his inner certainty wavered. He did not know whether his genius would fail him this time or not.

Nothing of this of course was visible on his fierce, implacable face.

Finally the Minister of Justice spoke; and instantly Yuri knew that he must adopt new tactics, make new plans—and find new men.

"Comrade President," the Minister of Justice said, voice at first hesitant but growing stronger as there was a rising murmur of assent along the table, "if you will excuse me—excuse us," he amended, emboldened by the response, which seemed to represent a sudden, united decision—"it does not seem that the comrade minister is guilty of socialist error when he simply raises questions concerning the nature of the conflict in which we are suddenly embroiled. It is natural for him to have misgivings." He looked along the table and was further emboldened by nods of agreement, at first hesitant, then open. "We all have misgivings, even though the response of our magnificent armed forces is of course at this very moment automatic and powerful, exactly as you, Yuri Pavlovich, have always planned. It is certain that the final outcome of the battle will be victory for the glorious forces of the Motherland. It is certain that the planning of the party and of you, Comrade President, will be invincible. But when we are extended over such a large area, engaged either openly or secretly in so many places, it is understandable that there should be some concern among us. Is that not true, comrades?"

For a moment there was still a remnant of hesitation. Then there was an audible intake of breath, a visible gathering together and closing of ranks. And a sudden loud chorus of *"Da!"* that was apparently unanimous.

At first Yuri wanted to shout, *"Are you defying my order to arrest the comrade minister?"* But caution and craft instantly stopped that fatal mistake. Instead with a great internal effort he made his expression change to a comfortable smile, his voice drop again to a calm and reasonable level.

"Why, comrades!" he said. "Why, comrades! I had no idea you had such uncertainties in your hearts. Why didn't you tell me at once, instead of waiting until I allowed my own tensions—for I have them, comrades, oh, yes, I am human, too, you know!—until I allowed my own tensions to make me say such an absurd thing as, 'Arrest the comrade minister.' That was truly foolish, comrades! That was, really, the cow in the buttermilk! It was really far from my mind, I do not know where it came from, it just blurted itself out and like a fool, I let it! It was crazy, comrades, the stupid error of an instant, gone, utterly gone! I apologize, Comrade Minister. I apologize to you all, dear colleagues of the Politburo and military. Can you accept my humble apology?"

Instantly, in apparent fawning gratitude, obviously so relieved by his change of tone that their words could hardly tumble over each other fast enough, they cried, "Oh, yes, Yuri Pavlovich! Yes, Comrade President! We forgive you, Comrade Yuri—but there is nothing to forgive! We understand! Oh, yes, we understand!"

No, you don't, you idiotic fools, he told himself with a grim humor, *but before long you will.*

"Very well, then!" he said. "Good! We go on together, then!"

"Together!" they all shouted happily; and after the tumult died, his tone became firm and businesslike, drawing them back to the matter at hand. "Comrade Marshal," he said, addressing the head of the Air Force, "perhaps on behalf of your military colleagues you can give us a brief report on how things are proceeding in Europe so far."

"Substantial advances were initially made by the rebel forces," the marshal said, "and factually are still being made, in all the nations involved. There are also many, many incidents of civilian sabotage against our armed forces, particularly in Poland and East Germany. These are being repelled with the most severe countermeasures. Orders to shoot on sight have been issued to all commanders. Meanwhile massive counterstrikes on land and in the air have been ordered and are being carried out. Warsaw, Prague, East Berlin, Budapest are at this moment being implacably bombed by the Air Force. Major tank and other armored units are fighting to join in an unbreakable front linking all battlefields. Similar units are being rushed in from here, from Bulgaria and from Rumania."

"And missiles?" Yuri inquired. The marshal of the Strategic Rocket Forces leaned forward.

"Ready to your command, Comrade President," he said, "though"—he hesitated, then went on—"in my judgment it would be best to wait until the situation becomes clearer on the battle-fields before we make use of these ultimate weapons."

"Perhaps," Yuri said, tone suddenly cold. "Perhaps. And poison gas and plague and other biological weapons?"

"Ready," the marshal of the Army said.

"Good!" Yuri said. "Use them! Without warning. As for the atomic and hydrogen weapons"—his eyes narrowed—"now also is the time to use *them.*"

There was an uneasy stirring and he repeated firmly:

"Now!"

"But, Comrade President," the marshal of the strategic rocket forces ventured. "Are you sure—is it wise—won't the Americans—?"

"The Americans!" Yuri said scornfully. "Nine-tenths of them are petrified at this very moment. We have conditioned them to think atomic war is inevitable just because fighting has broken out. Very well, let us show them they are right! I have already described how it is to be done, without warning, without mercy, with complete anonymity—suddenly, comrades, *suddenly,* with complete surprise. Always *surprise!* They will be unable to prove anything, they will be devastated by our swiftness, they will run about like chickens with their heads cut off." He uttered a sudden sharp bark of laughter. "Their heads *will* be cut off, in fact, poor, stupid Americans! They will not know what to do."

"I think, Comrade President," the marshal of the Strategic Rocket Forces said slowly, "I *think* they will know what to do and I am very much concerned that they will do it. Not *afraid,*" he added quickly in response to Yuri's scornful look, "but *concerned.* It could mean the full weight of America's autromic arsenal sud-denly used against us. Or it could mean a raid as startling, surpris-ing and totally unexpected as any you yourself might plan, Comrade President. The Americans are not without brains or re-sources. They have quite enough of each to create great damage here. And where is the game to stop?"

"We have been over this," Yuri grated out with an anger he made little attempt this time to conceal, "over and over and *over*, Comrade Marshal. All options have been considered, all possibilities explored. You do not need to lecture me about the potentials of America, I know them as fully as you do. You do not know the American will to resist, however, which does not exist except in a few old-fashioned minds like those of H. Delbacher—"

"But H. Delbacher has the power," the new Admiral of the Navy was emboldened to interrupt. "It only takes one mind like that in America if the mind is in the White House."

"Just as it only takes one mind like mine," Yuri snapped, "if that mind is in the Kremlin. So there you are, Comrade Admiral! In any case, H. Delbacher's advisers would not let him do such a thing. It would be outside the norms within which they believe it safe to operate."

There was an odd little sound, as of amusement half-strangled by apprehension. He glared at them with an anger that now was open and unrestrained.

"Are you drawing parallels, comrades?" he inquired with a furious, scathing sarcasm. "Are you trying to tell me that Y. P. Serapin is also surrounded by advisers who would not let him do such a thing? Are you telling me it would be outside the norms within which *they* believe it safe to operate? If that is what you are telling me, comrades, *tell* me! Tell me right out with socialist honesty and camaraderie! Do not hide behind snorts and snickers and secret amusements exchanged with one another! *Tell me . . . if—you—dare.*"

Now there was a very long and humming silence that was filled with many things, all unspoken but as clear and unmistakable as though their voices had uttered them aloud. Accompanying it was a tension that rose and rose, drawing tighter and tighter until at last the Foreign Minister took a very deep breath, leaned forward in his chair, looked down the table and spoke in a voice that trembled a little—a little, but not enough, Yuri thought. Not enough to indicate that he any longer feared Y. P. Serapin. It indicated, rather, that he had finally put aside fear of Y. P. Serapin. And that was greatly unpleasing to Y. P. Serapin.

"I think, Comrade President," the Foreign Minister said, "that it is not a matter of whether we *dare* to give you advice, which has always been the traditional role of the Politburo and the leaders of the military services. The question now is whether we *must* give you advice. And now, I think, there can no longer be doubt. We *must* give you advice.''

There were sounds of agreement down the table, no longer hesitant murmurs but loud comments. ''Yes, Comrade President! That is right, Comrade Minister! It is too much for one man! Advice is necessary! True socialist decisions must be made! The fate of the revolution cannot be decided by one man! Yuri Pavlovich is supreme but he must take advice! Advice is necessary!''

''Listen to me!'' he shouted, cutting across this senseless babble with a violence that momentarily shocked them into silence and brought the return of a few fearful looks down the table—again, not enough to please him, but a beginning on which he could build.

''Listen to me!'' he said more quietly. ''Comrade Foreign Minister, no doubt more frightened of the Americans than he wishes you to know, suggests that it is time for you to advise me. But comrades, have I not always taken your advice? Am I not taking it now? I have not yet given orders to use the missiles, have I? I have not yet ordered the poison gas, I have not ordered plague or anthrax or yellow rains or the other biological weapons which we have had in position for so many years in some of the smaller missiles facing Europe, I have not even ordered the deaths of more treacherous American hostages, much as they deserve it.

''I am still considering these things. You still have the opportunity to give me your thoughts. Nothing is irrevocable yet. So why not give me your advice, since many of you seem to think it so important that you do so? Let us go down the table one by one, so that everyone may know exactly where each of you stands and exactly what can be expected from each of you in the defense of the revolution and the Motherland.

''Comrade Foreign Minister, you are first!''

But if he thought this would intimidate a majority of the Politburo and the military, he was mistaken. The Foreign Minister stood his ground, as did the marshal of the Strategic Rocket Forces, the admiral of the Navy and a near-unanimous majority of the rest. They were desperately concerned about possible American response if Yuri were to order steps outside what they kept referring to as "the norms of international warfare"—even though, as he reminded them scornfully, furiously and many times, "the norms of international warfare" could now logically be expected to include exactly those atomic, biological and chemical agents in which the Soviet Union had superior strength—agents which, he insisted, needed only the added element of surprise to assure complete and final victory.

Repeatedly he reminded them of the imperatives of history, repeatedly he assured them that they need only seize the moment, take the gamble, "Strike, strike, *strike!*" in order to make victory finally, swiftly and irrevocably theirs.

And repeatedly he ran into the blank wall of their ingrained caution, their maddening stolidity, their appalling lack of imagination—their blindness, their stupidity, their massed unwillingness to grasp the opportunity which time, circumstance and the patiently plodding planning of their predecessors for sixty years had placed at last within their grasp.

Finally he had reached the end of his patience, exhausted all appeals to reason and to history. It was time to remind them now who it was they were attempting to restrain within the bounds of their doltish stupidity, their fatal self-defeating caution.

"Very well," he said at last, and there was that in his tone that quieted them instantly all down the table (they had been gabbling excitedly with one another as it became obvious, as speaker followed speaker, that he had lost his majority in the Politburo). "General Yarkov, will you please read the resolution unanimously adopted, signed and sworn to by all of you scarcely ten days ago. Read!"

Instantly a hush fell upon them; the last murmurs and rustles died away; absolute silence ensued. Above them on his map the little lights of conflagration still sparkled bravely, though through his furious eyes they did indeed seem dimmer now.

Presently General Yarkov stood, cleared his throat, gave Yuri a long look. Was it disrespect, disobedience or only confusion at his own error that suffused his usual calm expression with a slight, excited flush? No one could be sure. He spoke quite calmly.

"I regret, Comrade President, I did not think to bring it with me today."

For a good thirty seconds the President of the Soviet Union stared at him, his own expression a mixture of so many racing emotions and hurrying changes that they could not interpret it, except that it was obvious that its basic element was sheer savage anger. Finally he spoke in a sharp, staccato voice.

"Very well. How fortunate that I have my copy here."

And pulling it from the drawer at his seat, he read it through in a voice that shook, but only with a furious towering anger, not with fear—never with fear, for Yuri Serapin could never feel such an emotion for these cowardly souls who were not worthy of the great chance history had thrust upon them.

" 'In view of the enormous success of the recent international moves originated and directed by the genius of Y.P. Serapin, and bearing in mind his great original contributions to the ongoing success of the Motherland and the communist revolution, it is the sense of the Politburo and the Council of Ministers that for a period of six months, which may be extended indefinitely by the will of the Politburo and the Council of Ministers, all authority to originate and direct further moves against the imperialist enemies of mankind is vested solely and exclusively in Y.P. Serapin, to whom we pledge our total and unwavering support.'

"It is signed," he concluded in a tone so savage that for a few moments it seemed that no one would dare challenge him, "by each and all of you. I would remind you of that, comrades! You are committing treason against the revolution, against the party and against the Motherland if you *dare* to challenge my authority now!"

And he slapped his hand down hard upon the table in his favorite gesture of emphasis, while still the deathly silence gripped the room.

Now he glared slowly from face to face; and they allowed him time to study them fully, face by face, all down the table until he had completed the circuit and once more slapped the table hard again, as if to say, "That's that!"

It was only then that the Foreign Minister and General Yarkov both started to speak.

"Forgive me, comrade," General Yarkov said.

"My error. After you, comrade," the Foreign Minister said.

"No, please," Mikhail Yarkov insisted as politely as though they were in a drawing room, not in what might well become in moments an execution chamber.

"Very well," the Foreign Minister agreed; took a deep breath; and began to speak in a level voice that also shook—with the enormity of what they were doing, but not, as Yuri could perceive, with fear.

"Comrade President, we thank you for refreshing our memories on the document you required us to sign under different circumstances, at a different time. Much has happened since that time. Greatly have the circumstances changed.

"You will note that the first sentence you have read begins, 'In view of the enormous success of the recent international moves originated and directed by the genius of Y.P. Serapin.' The reference to 'recent international moves' is, as you know, a reference to the first confrontation with the United States which occurred some two months ago. It does not refer to events of recent days."

Yuri started to make an angry movement of protest, but the Foreign Minister raised his hand and said, "Please," in a firm voice. Yuri snapped, "Get on with it!" but made no further protest.

"It is only fair to state, Comrade President," the Foreign Minister went on, "that the former Politburo supported your moves at that time wholeheartedly, and so did those of us who were at that time not seated on the Politburo. Your strategy and your moves at that time were brilliant. They caught the United States unprepared, they achieved your basic aim of leaving our forces in place around the globe in readiness for the next step in your plan.

"Now, however, events do not proceed in such good order. Four conflicts were begun around the globe without the approval of the Politburo and the military."

"You signed the resolution *after* the conflicts had begun," Yuri said angrily. "They were begun already, and you approved it."

"Only because we were presented with a fait accompli," the Foreign Minister said, voice wavering momentarily under the vehemence of his attack but steadying again.

"You feel you have a choice now, comrade?" Yuri inquired

with a dangerous softness. The Foreign Minister glanced at General Yarkov.

"Proceed, Comrade Minister," Mikhail Yarkov said without inflection, and for a second the Foreign Minister looked uncertain. Then he did proceed, knowing that at this point he had gone too far to turn back, and that if he did not have Mikhail Yarkov's support he was doomed in any event.

"Four conflicts," he said, "which you, Comrade President, fomented, planned, directed through allies and surrogates. But they do not advance as brilliantly as we had thought they would. In fact, our friends are beginning to suffer defeats in the field. And now we are faced with even worse. We are faced with revolts in Poland and the German Democratic Republic. We are faced with the imminence of revolts in Czechoslovakia, and Hungary. We are faced with the direct—the fantastic—intervention of the head of the Roman Catholic Church—"

"That interfering fanatic!" Yuri snapped. The Foreign Minister nodded gravely.

"That may be, Comrade President. But a monumental problem for us, nonetheless. And we are faced with the active intervention of the French and of the President of the United States, who pledges aid to the rebels, starts an airlift, and at the same time calls for a meeting of the Security Council, so that he places himself cleverly in the rebellion but not of it. We think it is time to halt the march of events before they pass beyond our control. We think it is time for you, Yuri Pavlovich, to change your policies. It is time for us all to become cautious again. It is time to end adventurism."

There was a stirring of agreement. Several of the voices which had hailed him so ecstatically a few minutes before actually cried, "Hear, hear!" and "Bravo!"

And Mikhail Yarkov remained as impassive as ever.

"We do not wish," the Foreign Minister said, "to take any action at this time that would unnecessarily embarrass the Party or the Motherland—"

"You do not wish to depose me," Yuri spelled it out with a bitter sarcasm. The minister bowed his head gravely in acknowledgment.

"No, Yuri Pavlovich, we do not wish to depose you, because to do so would be to gravely embarrass the Motherland at a time when we must close ranks against all who would destroy the revolution. It does not seem the time for that. But we must request—''

''We must insist,'' someone said from down the table, and Yuri, swiveling furiously to ascertain who, saw with a sudden tightness in his heart that it was the heretofore timid and reluctant Minister of Justice.

''We must insist,'' the Foreign Minister amended, ''that you change those policies which are unnecessarily provocative and likely to lead to the strongest reprisals from the United States and perhaps from many others who may take advantage of the situation in Europe to move against us.''

''Who?'' Yuri asked scornfully. ''Who would dare?''

''The people of Kazakhstan, for one,'' the Foreign Minister said sharply.

''That would be civil war!'' Yuri said. ''It is impossible!''

''It would be a Moslem holy war by my people against the Soviet Union,'' the Foreign Minister corrected coldly, ''and it is not at all impossible. However, Comrade President, it is not *inevitable*. There is a difference. It is not inevitable if you will do certain things.''

''Resign?'' Yuri demanded with the same bitterness. ''I will never resign!''

''It is not suggested that you resign,'' the Foreign Minister said. ''It is suggested you be more restrained, Comrade President. For instance:

''It is suggested that you abandon any thoughts of a surprise atomic attack on the United States. It does not matter how cleverly it might be planned, its origin could not be concealed. We have great atomic power, yes, but so do they. They would respond. The result would be certain. It is pointless.

''It is suggested that you abandon dreams of launching chemical and bacteriological warfare, for the same reason.

''It is suggested that there be no more American hostages killed. There is no advantage in it. Our hostages have been returned. Returning theirs would be a gesture that would perhaps make the President more willing to negotiate. In any event, it would be better in the eyes of the world. In the estimation of the Politburo, this proposed open slaughter would be too much.

"It is suggested that you abandon your adventurism in Mexico, South Africa and Saudi Arabia. The situation in Taiwan is out of your hands. It is better that the remaining three be terminated also. We are now threatened directly by revolts in Eastern Europe. We are equipped to stop them and we will—but that is not enough. We must return to the necessities of our own security. It is time to end adventurism elsewhere. This includes Cuba, which I think we *all* agree is now hopeless.

"It is suggested that you proceed at once to New York and that you appear before the Security Council meeting requested by the President and that there you do everything possible to persuade the world that the Soviet Union has returned to a policy of detente and peaceful coexistence.

"This will of course not be true, but it is our judgment that it is imperative for the time being that the world once more be convinced that it is true. We will continue our plans for world conquest but with the traditional means of tactical indirection, disinformation and subterfuge we have always used. It is not yet time to be open about it. It is not yet time," he said, and Yuri could not tell whether he was being sardonic or not, "for your great honesty, Comrade President. We must still be subtle, we must still be devious, we must still retain the weapons of surprise and deceit we have always employed. We must move slowly again. We must reestablish ourselves once more in the minds of the world as the peace lovers. It is not yet time to tell the truth about our intentions.

"You have tried to go too fast, Comrade President. You have shocked the world by being too candid. So we must go back to being patient again."

He stopped, and Yuri, whose face during this recital had run the changes from astonishment to chagrin to scowling anger, for a few seconds said nothing. Then he spat out,

"Are you finished, comrade? Is it possible for your President to speak a word or two?"

"Proceed, comrade," Mikhail Yarkov said quietly from his chair behind Yuri, and the elimination of title was not lost upon any of them. Yuri challenged it instantly, as he knew he must or go down at once to final defeat.

"General Yarkov!" he snapped, turning in his chair to stare him full in the face. "I am the President of the Soviet Union! I have not resigned this office nor have I been deposed—nor have we yet tested," he added, voice dangerous in its softness—"whether anyone is strong enough to remove me if I do not wish to go. In fact, comrade, I do *not* wish to go, I will *not* go, and I suggest you refer to me properly by my title in respect to the office I hold *and in respect to me.*"

And he continued to glare until at last General Yarkov, his eyes never leaving Yuri's, said calmly, "Whatever pleases you, comrade."

"President!"

"Comrade President," Mikhail Yarkov amended; yet it was in a tone so devoid of inflection—so *uncaring,* Yuri told himself furiously—that it was almost meaningless.

But it was, he could tell, the best he was going to get.

"Comrades," he said swiftly, turning back to them before, he hoped, they would have time to really absorb the insult, "what is the gist of this indictment—for it is indictment—that has been rendered upon me by the Foreign Minister, I assume with your concurrence?"

There was no indication of agreement; the faces were still stolid and impassive; but there was now a united sameness about them that indicated what he already knew—that a previously tentative decision was becoming frozen into place. He knew he must speak very rapidly and be very persuasive—and deal with them all, including Yarkov—particularly Yarkov—with absolute ruthlessness the moment he was back in control.

That he would be, if not today then very soon, he did not doubt for an instant. As long as they left him in place, he would recapture full power. And when he did, he promised himself grimly, all these would be dead; and for all others, absolute loyalty to Yuri Serapin would be the only means of surviving in the Soviet Union.

Meanwhile, Yuri Serapin must survive. To this necessity he now bent all his powers of threat, reason and persuasion.

"Comrades," he said, speaking in a rapid but perfectly reasonable voice, "let me say to begin that within the narrow confines of what we have always done, there may be some merit to your complaints. It is true I have perhaps exceeded the norms of socialist regularity in what I have done, or caused to be done, in these recent days. But, comrades! Look at the prize that lies within our grasp! Look at the glory that awaits the party and the Motherland! Look at what we can gain if we remain courageous and daring and do not waver for an instant! It is unbelievable, comrades! At last our dream is coming true! The world will soon be ours! Is this the time to lose heart, abandon courage, turn our backs upon everything we have gained in recent weeks? What will history say of us, if we fail it now?

"It may be, comrades, that in my enthusiasm to complete the great task of world conquest successfully I have permitted myself to go a little too hastily or too far in some matters. You may be right in some of the things you suggest. And you may be right that I have, in my enthusiasm and eagerness to complete the great task, moved ahead without securing your advice in all instances as diligently and carefully as I should.

"For this I humbly apologize, and I give you my promise that in the future I shall not repeat this error. I shall consult with you always. Together we will go forward to win victory everywhere. Together we will triumph in the final battle that will decide the fate of all mankind. It is just ahead of us, comrades! We must not falter now!

"It may well be, as you advise me through the voice of Comrade Foreign Minister, that I am a little overenthusiastic in my recommendation that we launch a surprise nuclear attack upon the United States. I still believe this to be both feasible and advantageous; but I am willing to be persuaded otherwise. As we all know, it has been part of our official planning and thinking for many years: the advisability of such an attack has never been doubted by the leaders of the Soviet Union. It is only the timing that has ever been at issue. I am not wedded to a specific date, certainly not tomorrow or the next day. We will consult, comrades, and when it is advisable, we will act.

"The same applies to chemical and bacteriological warfare. We have practiced with yellow rain and other chemicals, as you know, in Laos and in Afghanistan. We have built up enormous stockpiles of the major poison gases and the major diseases while the West has danced around its conscience and gone ahead only in fits and starts. We have never changed, delayed or curtailed our plans in this regard; we have steadily increased our own arsenal while screaming bloody murder''—he permitted himself a small, savagely ironic smile—''screaming bloody murder against the West every time anybody there has even so much as whispered the words 'chemical' or 'biological.' This two-pronged policy has been most effective in this area, as it has been in so many others where we are in competition. We prepare, they hesitate; and every time they show signs of beginning to prepare, we make so much noise it frightens them into retreating. On *that* policy I take it we are all agreed, comrades!''

And he chuckled and smiled broadly and after a moment, reluctantly at first, then abandoning all restraint and laughing heartily with him, they joined in his merriment. *Score one,* he thought grimly. Keep laughing, comrades.

''It is suggested that we not punish H. Delbacher further by shooting more of his hostages whom we hold, and on that I must tell you that we are entirely agreed. In fact, I was about to say as much when Comrade Foreign Minister—and,'' he said with a jovial toss of the head in his direction—''Comrade Yarkov, who seems to think he has some special control over you—jumped in so hastily with their stern 'suggestions.' Certainly I have no intention of shooting more of them, comrades, and certainly they may be sent home at once. In fact, that will make a very good preliminary for my attendance at the Security Council, do you not agree? It will be an excellent introduction for my appearance there!''

At this they were suddenly quite ecstatic. Not only was he agreeing with them about the hostages but he was apparently more than willing to go to the Security Council. And he had combined the two most cleverly.

''Excellent, Comrade President!'' someone shouted, and instantly others were pounding on the table, shouting his praises, exalting his name. *And my title,* he thought with ironic satisfaction. ''Oh, splendid, Comrade President! Yes, yes, that will truly confound H. Delbacher and bring the world to our side! Marvelous, Yuri Pavlovich! Marvelous, Comrade President!''

"In fact," he said when the adulation died down, "what about this, comrades?: Why don't I myself *personally deliver* the hostages to H. Delbacher in New York? Why don't I take them with me when I go? The whole world will be watching. What a gesture, comrades! What a surprise for H. Delbacher!''

"Oh, clever Comrade President!" they cried. "Oh, marvelous Yuri Pavlovich! How brilliant! How perfect! How *amusing. Imagine* the faces of the Americans!"

"And you give me your advice on this, comrades?" he asked slyly. "You agree it is a good idea? You think I have consulted sufficiently with you, and that my idea is a good one?"

And again they laughed and shouted and congratulated him, even the Foreign Minister; even, with a vigorous, approving nod and a sudden expansive smile, General Yarkov.

"So, comrades," Yuri said, "you see, all this talk has been unnecessary. We agree on everything. I have even improved upon it for you . . .

"We will consult together if it becomes necessary to launch a nuclear attack on the United States. We will consult if it becomes necessary to use chemical and biological weapons. And we are certainly in complete agreement on return of the hostages and on my attendance at the Security Council. And I think there is one other thing on which we agree, comrades"—abruptly their cheerful expressions froze; they looked very cautious again—"and that is that we will prosecute most vigorously the wars in the satellites. We will put down with every single resource we have, possibly even including atomic weapons if you agree, the revolts in Eastern Europe. Are we one on that?"

Their expressions relaxed, they cheered and congratulated him once again; and smoothly he moved to conclude the meeting.

"And now," he said, "since we are in agreement on everything and you see your fears are groundless, perhaps it is not too much to ask that you give me a vote of confidence by reaffirming the resolution of trust and authority, so that it can be announced to the world that you are completely and wholeheartedly with me, and that there are no elements of socialist error here as we move forward. All those in favor—''

But now the Foreign Minister was once again on his feet, and behind Yuri's back, across the face of Mikhail Yarkov, there passed an expression that Yuri could not see.

"Yes?" he said, tone suddenly sharp. "What is it now, Comrade Minister?"

"We have not discussed the other conflicts in the world," the Foreign Minister said. "We have not discussed withdrawal from *them.*"

"That is right," he agreed promptly, "and it was stupid of me to forget them in the midst of so much other agreement among us. Let me say that there, too, we will consult and decide what to do—''

"We have already decided, Comrade President," the Minister of Justice interrupted. "Comrade Minister made it clear to you earlier what we wish. It is withdrawal, immediate and complete.''

"But—" he protested angrily, realizing that the ground, only seconds before so solid and sure, was suddenly quicksand beneath his feet.

"It is imperative, Comrade President," the Foreign Minister sad, "for all the reasons I made clear to you.''

For several moments a fearful scowl contorted his face. Then it vanished, to be replaced by a reasonable and placatory expression.

"It may well be that we will agree completely on that, comrades," he said, "but it is something that I should not like to have formally announced before I go to the Security Council. These are bargaining positions, you see. They are things I can use. Surely you would not wish to tie my hands by a premature announcement—surely you can understand why I need them as bargaining points. Perhaps, therefore, we can delay until my return any decision on—"

"Then we can also delay," the Foreign Minister said swiftly, "any vote on the resolution, as well.''

Again the scowl crossed Yuri's face, and for a moment they expected a major explosion. But he knew as well as they that it would be futile, given their basic mood of the moment; and so again the scowl gave way to a reasonable and placatory expression.

"Your logic is irrefutable, comrades," he said, and joined heartily in their laughter. "But," he said when it was over, "so is mine. Therefore let us agree on a compromise: you will delay your vote; together we will delay the withdrawal; and not by a single word will the world know that either is under discussion. Is that agreeable?"

"You still think the battles will turn our way," the Foreign Minister said.

"It is still entirely possible," he said firmly. "All but Cuba. We *are* all agreed on that. The Americans and the traitorous dog of a so-called 'Maximum Leader' caught us all by surprise and there is no point in trying to reverse things now. We will concede nothing, say nothing; our forces and our material now waiting outside the blockade will simply be withdrawn immediately. You will see to that, members of the military. As for our forces on the island—" He shrugged. "They will take their chances, and since the Americans are reasonably 'civilized,' which often hurts them and this time will help us, the chances are good that they will restrain the Cubans enough so that a good many of our people will survive and eventually we shall get them back. Our material and equipment I think we can forget, including the missiles: we will just have to place some more in Nicaragua and on our submarines. That will be no great loss. And we will not surrender, of course, or concede defeat. We will just go away and find some other, better place."

"You are very practical, Comrade President," the Foreign Minister said, and they all nodded approving agreement.

He was tempted to press once more for a vote, but it seemed best to leave things where they stood as long as the general mood had swung back in his direction. So he merely nodded and smiled and said, with a fulsome friendliness that was furthest from his mind,

"And you, comrades, are very astute in your arguments and sound in your judgments. Together we can work everything out, I am sure, and go on to the great victory which history says will inevitably be ours in the final battle to decide the fate of all mankind.

"Meanwhile," he said, rising with an air of dismissal which it pleased him to note they obediently accepted, "on to New York!"

* * *

Before he, too, departed for New York, the President of the United States received four encouraging phone calls that made him feel that things were now moving with some speed in his direction.

Ju Xing-dao informed him that it was about to be announced simultaneously in Peking and Taipei that a Joint Commission on the Peaceful Reunification of China had been agreed upon and would immediately begin meetings on alternate weeks in the two capitals. The meetings would continue "until such time as all major problems have been amicably settled between us and the Motherland is once more united in peace and harmony."

From Cape Town the Prime Minister informed him with glee that most of Angola was under occupation, that all resistance elsewhere had ceased and that South Africa, now holding some ten thousand woebegone Cubans, was triumphant, that the shaky new "People's Republic of Guatemala" had stopped its attacks, that the oilfields were intact, and that there were strong signs that the governments of both Guatemala and Nicaragua were about to fall as a result.

And from Riyadh the elder brother crowed in triumph that all was now over: the last few Yemenis were being driven back, the Yemeni air attacks had ceased, the palace had fallen and both the oldest brother and Allah were in their rightful places—the one supreme in heaven looking down kindly again upon the House of Saud, the other supreme on the throne of his father.

"And your younger brother?" Ham Delbacher asked, not really wanting to hear.

"Just as I told you," the prince said happily. "There are ants and fat vultures very busy at a certain place in the desert. Both women and boys are safe again. And so," he added complacently, "is the House of Saud."

A gain the leaders of the world gathered in their pomp and glory as they had on so many, many occasions in the past: the high, the mighty, the small, the insignificant, the worthwhile, the pretentious, the good, the bad, they of good faith and they of ill will—jumbled together in all their strange diversity to take their places once more on the stage of history and enact their odd charade that so often was so empty but in a few rare instances actually rose to the level of awesome responsibility that supposedly was theirs.

This time, they told one another solemnly as they moved from arrival at the Delegates' Entrance along the corridors to the Security Council chamber, it was Really Going to Mean Something.

This time it would be Truly Significant.

This time The Peace of the World was at Stake.

And so, perhaps, it was.

Indeed, it always was.

The only difference between one time and another was that usually they did not know it, and so acted with the irresponsibility that far more often than not characterized their deliberations.

This time, they told one another, would be worthy of their stated purpose.

But before Eire, still president of the Council, could suck his pipe in one last, delicious, noisy, gargling gurgle and bang down the gavel to open the session, there occurred the event that had

them all buzzing as they arrived—the event the New York *Daily
News* hailed perhaps most gleefully of all:

HOSTAGES HOME! YUMPIN' YURI, WHAT A HAPPY SURPRISE!

IT HAD BEGUN AT EIGHT A.M. when Anson McCumber had
called the President, catching him mid-breakfast in the bedroom,
where he and Elinor were enjoying a quiet meal before he was
scheduled to leave by helicopter for Andrews Air Force Base and
from there to the U.N.

"Mr. President," Anson said, breathless, "there's just been an
urgent communication from the Swiss Ambassador. You know
they're handling Soviet affairs for us at the moment—"

"Yes, Anson, I know," Ham Delbacher interrupted. "How urgent is it?"

"He said extremely and I *agree,* extremely," Anson McCumber said. "It seems you're to meet President Serapin's plane when
he arrives at J.F.K. at noon today."

"The hell you say!" the President exclaimed, almost choking
in his grapefruit. "What am I supposed to do, greet him with a
bouquet of roses?"

"Mr. President," the national security adviser said in a shocked
tone of voice. "This is a *very* serious matter."

"So am I serious,"the President said, "but sometimes I have to
laugh to keep from crying. Did the Ambassador give you any idea
what this is all about?"

"Not directly," Anson McCumber said. "I don't believe he
knows. But he did receive this communication from Moscow
which said you are to meet—"

"Was that the way it was stated, I must meet him?"

"Well, no, not exactly," Anson said hastily. "It was polite."

"You want to be careful how you paraphrase, Anson," the President said. "Wars have been started over less. What exactly did it
say?"

"It said President Serapin *hopes* you may be able to meet him
upon arrival at John F. Kennedy International Airport," the national security adviser said somewhat stiffly. "It added that 'President Serapin believes it will be both highly interesting and truly

advantageous to the President and to the United States if he does so.''

"What does he have in mind, I wonder, 'the Treaty of the Tarmac' or some such? What do you make of it, Anson?''

"I can't imagine,'' the national security adviser said frankly. "Unless he thinks you might be able to have some private talk out there, away from the U.N., that could be, as he says, 'advantageous.' ''

"To me and to the United States,'' the President repeated thoughtfully. "That sounds intriguing, anyway . . . I will have to be very sure, now,'' he added sharply, "that this is not just some propaganda trap to try to trick me into agreeing to something under pressure.''

"Oh, I don't believe he would do that!'' the national security adviser exclaimed.

"Anson,'' the President said, making a mental note to get his resignation as soon as everything else quieted down for ten minutes, "how long have you been in that job?''

"Six months,'' Anson McCumber said, his tone bristling a bit.

"My senior by three,'' the President said. "I can understand why you have such faith in the integrity and goodwill of the Soviet President.''

"Mr. President?'' Anson McCumber said, sounding puzzled. "I don't quite understand—?''

"Don't try,'' the President advised. "Just my irreverent sense of humor. You can send word back through the Swiss Ambassador that I will be there but I won't meet him at the plane. I'll be in the V.I.P. lounge and there will be no photographers, television cameramen or reporters. I will meet with him for exactly ten minutes if he has anything to impart to me, and I will then leave for the U.N. . . . Period.''

"Do you think that will be long enough, Mr. President?'' the national security adviser wondered cautiously. "Is it possible you should allow a little more—''

"Not possible,'' he said flatly. "That's it. Thank you, Anson.''

"Yes, sir,'' Anson McCumber said doubtfully. "Yes, sir.''

"Hmm,'' the President said, turning back to his wife. "The

message is that I'm to meet Serapin at J.F.K., as you gather, for something that will be 'highly advantageous' both to me and to the United States . . . I can only think of one thing that might fit that category, but I can't believe it can possibly be. That would be too much out of character, for him.''

"Oh, I don't know," Elinor said. "He's full of surprises."

And so, of course, he proved to be; and all Ham's strictures about the V.I.P. room, private talks, cameramen, reporters and TV went down the drain.

There was a small group of noisy protesters carrying signs such as FREE OUR HOSTAGES, MURDERER! HOSTAGES, YES, YURI, NO! STOP KILLING AMERICANS, MONSTER! and the like. There were also literally hundreds of newspeople, alerted by the offices of the Soviet delegation to the U.N. The sensation, as Yuri had accurately calculated, far overshadowed anything else that day, and put Ham Delbacher, as he had with annoyance guessed it might, directly behind the eight ball when it came time for him to address the Security Council.

There was only one saving consideration that shot through his mind as the doors of Yuri's plane opened and the Soviet President began to descend the steps, waving and smiling, followed by two individuals who were indubitably the American Ambassador to Russia and his wife:

This isn't in character. It isn't like you. Your colleagues must have forced you to do it. And if they did, then you're in trouble, friend—big trouble. Hallelujah!

None of this of course appeared in the Presidential face the world saw on television—either Presidential face.

The President of the United States, adjusting with split-second speed to the reality of his wildest surmise, showed to the world a face aglow with happiness and relief.

The President of the Soviet Union showed to the world a face pleased and smugly triumphant with his great surprise.

It was only when their eyes met for a moment as the American President shook hands, briefly and formally, with the Soviet President, that their true feelings appeared, and then only to one another.

I have you, you bastard, the eyes of the Soviet President said triumphantly.

And you're on the skids, aren't you, buster boy? the eyes of the American president replied with ironic amusement.

Then Yuri moved on and was immediately surrounded by Soviet delegation guards, who sped him swiftly away along the parkways and over the bridge to the U.N.; and Ham was left to the cameras, the reporters and the world's spotlight as he shook hands delightedly with his countrymen when they descended, many of them laughing and crying simultaneously, from the plane.

"Mr. President!" someone shouted from the media as he turned to rejoin his own official group and leave. "Did you have any advance warning of this?"

"Nope."

"Did you have anything to do with it?"

"Not a thing."

"It was all President Serapin's doing?"

"Yes, it was," he shot back. "And if you want to think about it, ask yourself why he did it after deliberately and cold-bloodedly ordering the murders of two of your innocent countrymen."

"Aw," somebody else said disgustedly. "Of all the poor sports!"

"Think about it," he repeated, unperturbed. "Just think about it!"

But of course few did, and in many of the headlines, news stories, editorials, and broadcasts, Yuri Serapin was for a short while the hero of the day. Of course it *was* a little difficult to explain the two dead clerks, but they were glossed over very smoothly in most accounts, placed far down in the news stories and editorials, far back in the broadcasts, not mentioned at all in the headlines. In the euphoric haze created by Yuri's noble humanitarianism, they became, for a short while, nonpersons, just as he had intended they should. It was one of the many things Hamilton Delbacher knew he must patiently and in detail correct when it came his time to speak.

This happened fairly soon after Eire, pleasures of pipe finally exhausted in one last cloacal cacophony, looked about brightly shortly after one P.M., twitched his eyebrows nervously several times, used the gavel, and proclaimed loudly, "This special session of the Security Council is now in session—or, er," he amended, suddenly remembering his position as one of his native land's leading practitioners of poesy, "has now begun!"

"Two 'sessions' in one sentence," AP murmured to UPI in the press section. "Can't have that."

"Old fraud!" UPI murmured back. "To think we have *him* presiding over a debate as hot as this one's going to be."

"It'll be sheer chaos," AP predicted cheerfully. "I can't wait."

It began with a chorus of praise for the President of the Soviet Union, so glowing that for a little while it appeared that almost no one would dare say anything critical. France, Cameroon, Greece, India, Iraq, Nicaragua (looking nervous because he soon might have no government at home, but hanging in there), Seychelles and Tanzania all were loud and lavish in their congratulations on his humanitarian action in freeing the American hostages.

"An act of the deepest and most moving generosity," France glowed, providing as usual a contrast so glaring between what its ambassador said here and what his government was at that very moment doing to fan revolts against the Soviet Union in Eastern Europe that it could only be classified by his listeners as "typically French."

"True statesmanship, shaming those who would seek to divide the world into warring camps," was Cameroon's contribution, delivered with an archly disapproving glance at the President of the United States, who ignored it.

"A *truly* democratic and most wonderfully humanitarian act," said India's lady, jangling a bangle.

"An act of such nobility and grace that one can only marvel in amazement," Iraq said, arousing some snickers in the press section but leaving the recipient of his praise convinced that he meant it.

"The strongest possible rebuke to Yankee imperialism, a ringing proof that the democratic Soviet Union is unmatched in its supreme regard for human life," Nicaragua asserted with perfect solemnity.

"A lesson to us all, a great, humbling gesture of generosity and love that can only lead us on to new heights of human understanding," averred the Seychelles.

"He has opened the way," declared Tanzania with the utmost gravity. "Let us follow where he leads."

"Well!" said Britain's lady tartly as the last rotund syllable of praise floated gently away upon the Security Council's long-suffering air. "Allow me to differ!"

"The distinguished delegate of the Soviet Union, the President of that peculiar country, having shamelessly murdered two innocent Americans"—there was a gasp, a hiss and a boo from many places around the room but she plunged on, undaunted and indignant—"now attempts to gain approval by releasing the remainder of the American hostages. And this only after the President of the United States voluntarily and willingly did the same thing with the Soviet hostages, some forty-eight hours earlier. Where is the praise for the President's humanity and generosity? Where are the glowing words for his noble character? Why is he not given credit for the same characteristics—which I gather from the distinguished delegate of Tanzania are almost Christlike in their perfection—as the President of the Soviet Union?

"And why, Mr. President of the Council," she demanded, fixing Eire with an eagle eye from whose piercing gaze he seemed almost physically to be squirming, "is the President of the Soviet Union suddenly so generous? Why is he doing this, after murdering two innocent American hostages? Why? Why? Why?"

"I—er—I don't know," Eire said hastily. "Me? No! No! I don't know!"

"I will tell you why," she said sternly as there was a titter of laughter. "It is to curry favor with this Council and with the world community. It is to draw the wool over all our eyes. It is to make us believe he actually *is* a great humanitarian, when actually he is the individual who has stirred up four conflicts around the globe and has ruthlessly attempted to overturn world peace in his ceaseless quest for empire. That is why! . . . Well!" she concluded, as abruptly as she had begun, "Her Majesty's Government will have none of it. The release of the American hostages, like the release of the Soviet hostages, is only what is right. Nobody deserves any great credit for it; they should never have been taken in the first place, on either side. Their release is only right!''

And she sat back, still indignant and breathing a bit heavily. Eire politely and nervously inquired if the distinguished delegate of the People's Republic of China wished to say anything, but Ju Xingdao only smiled one of his gently unfathomable smiles and said softly,

"Oh, no. Oh, no.''

"Mr. President,'' the President of Egypt said, "we do. We are not impressed with the so-called 'humanitarianism' of the head of the Soviet government. He is, as you say in the West, grandstanding. We have seen his grandstanding before. It does not impress us. We agree with the United Kingdom that there was no excuse for any hostages on either side. But having said that, we lay much the greater blame at the door of the Soviet President. He did not have to kill two helpless American hostages. That was murder, pure and simple. Neither did he have to incite four conflicts around the globe. That was also murder, on a larger scale. Now he is here on the defensive, let us not forget that. He is here because Eastern Europe is finally risen in revolt against his oppressive regime. That is what we should be talking about here and now, not empty gestures that cost him nothing to perform—but would have cost him universal condemnation if he did *not* perform them.

"Let us talk about Eastern Europe, Mr. President. That is why we are here, is it not? The United States requested this Security Council meeting to discuss Eastern Europe. I suggest we return to some kind of order and hear the distinguished delegate of the United States.''

"Yes, Mr. President,'' Prince Koa of Tonga said, breaking the beatific silence with which he had been enjoying Yuri's angry discomfort while Egypt's leader spoke. "Yes, I too would like to call for the regular order. If, here in the United Nations,'' he added with a sweet smile, "there is such a thing.''

"Well!'' Eire said hastily, returning to his pipe as to the teat and giving it another enormous gurgle. "Well! I will assure the distinguished delegate of Tonga that such is exactly what we are about to do! Yes, exactly what we are about to do! The United States has indeed requested this meeting of the Council, and therefore the United States is by rights the first speaker. Is it not so, everyone? Is it not?''

And he looked about the circular table as if seeking reassurance. Most nodded solemnly. There was a tightening of tension in the room. Eire cleared his throat portentously and announced,

"The distinguished delegate of the United States of America, the President of same!''

"Very gracefully done," the Baltimore *Sun* whispered to the London *Daily Telegraph,* who shrugged.

"The Celtic fringe. What can you expect?''

"Mr. President of the Council," Hamilton Delbacher began slowly, leaning forward almost casually in his chair, an evidence of ease belied by the firm expression around his mouth, "let me, too, comment briefly before I begin my principal statement, upon the public relations stunt of the President of the Soviet Union in bringing with him, and releasing, the American hostages he illegally held. It is too bad he did not also bring with him the coffins of the two Americans he ordered murdered, though I suppose that would have spoiled the image. No doubt they will be dumped on the White House lawn some night when no one is looking.''

There was a start, a gasp of breath, some boos and hisses.

"Wow!" the Boston *Globe* murmured to the *Post.* "Ham's out for blood today, all right.''

"He thinks he has Yuri on the run," the *Post* remarked with some scorn.

"Yuri *doesn't* look too good," the *Globe* admitted.

"Yuri has the right to look as good as honest reporting can make him!" the *Post* said sharply.

"Right!" the Boston *Globe* agreed hastily, for he too believed in honest reporting.

"Mr. President," Ham said, "like all Americans, I am delighted with the return of the American hostages. I do not think, however, that my thanks should be expressed to the present President of the Soviet Union. I think they should go rather to the members of the Politburo and the military leaders of that country, because I believe it was they who forced the present President, much against his will, to return the hostages. I think, left to himself, he would have kept them and made good on his threat to assassinate them on the installment plan. I think the present President of the Soviet Union is under intense pressure from his colleagues. I think he knows he may be on the very verge of dismissal as head of the Soviet Union unless he can pull something out of the hat there at the United Nations. I don't see why the decent nations of the earth should let him get away with it. The world would be better off without him at the head of Soviet affairs. I think we should do everything we can to encourage his removal."

At this direct attack, for which he had no grounds for assumption save his own hunch and the feeling that there was nothing to be lost and possibly a great deal to be gained, the gasps and excitement greatly increased.

Yuri, flushed with anger, a fearful scowl on his face, leaned forward and tapped on his microphone so hard with his pencil that he threatened to knock it over.

"The President of the Soviet Union!" Eire said hastily, almost biting his pipe stem in two in his excitement and as a result clutching a tooth in ill-concealed agony.

"Yes," Yuri snapped, "*the President of the Soviet Union* who intends to remain the President of the Soviet Union in spite of the vicious attempt by the delegate of the United States to interfere directly in the internal affairs of the Soviet Union. How *dare* the President of the United States attempt to overthrow the head of a sovereign state simply because he disagrees with his policies! What *right* does he have—"

"Mr. *President!*" Ham Delbacher cried with a sudden, deliberately calculated roar of anger that jolted Yuri and everyone else into silence. "Mr. President, let me tell you what happened to me. Let me tell you the story of this left arm of mine, which you see is in a cast. You know the official story. Now I will tell you what really happened."

And he proceeded to do so, while Yuri maintained a set, exaggerated, skeptical smile that was shaken only once, and that so briefly that very few noticed, when Ham described the death of Ivan Valerian.

"So don't talk to me with absolute evil hypocrisy about how awful it is to attempt to overthrow a President of a sovereign power!" Ham Delbacher concluded angrily. "Don't give me that evil hypocritical bull— . . . blarney. This individual wasn't content with ordering the murder of two American hostages. He ordered the murder of the President of the United States. How about that, Mr. present President of the Soviet Union?"

And he fixed Yuri with a stare as harsh and unyielding as Yuri's own, locked in an arc of hatred that no one broke until Ju Xing-dao said softly, "Mr. President, perhaps we could return to the purpose for which the United States requested this meeting?"

"Well, well," the *Times* remarked dryly to the *Wall Street Journal.* "So Ham thinks they tried to kill him, does he? Sounds like something straight out of a spy story, to me."

"Maybe they're what he reads at night before he goes to sleep," the *Journal* agreed with a chuckle.

"I'd say he's been reading too damned many of 'em," the *Times* said with an answering chuckle. A small story later appeared alongside the main account of the meeting:

President Claims Russ Defector Tried to Kill Him. Soviets Deny Claim.

"Mr. President," Ham said more quietly, "forgive me that personal digression, but the lies of the Soviet delegate made it necessary for me to speak . . . The last time we met here four conflicts had broken out around the globe, inspired, instigated and in at least three instances actively backed and supported by the present President of the Soviet Union. Today two major nations of Eastern Europe are in flames and the revolt against the Soviet Union on its own doorstep is rapidly spreading much farther.

"It is the purpose of the United States, Mr. President, to propose that the United Nations give all possible assistance to the fighters for freedom who are at this moment so gallantly battling against Soviet suppression in Poland and East Germany, and before this session is over will very likely be fighting in Czechoslovakia and Hungary as well.

"I do not think it is necessary to take time to belabor the reasons why we should give all possible moral and material aid to these brave people who are finally throwing off the forty-year oppression of the Soviet Union.

"Human beings have an inalienable right to be free—so we believe in the United States of America.

"Slavery of one human being by another, of one nation by another, is morally indefensible and completely against the laws of civilization—so we believe in the United States of America.

"All men of goodwill everywhere are automatically enlisted in the cause of freedom and should help it in every way they can—so we believe in the United States of America.

"Tyranny will inevitably fall in time because no man wants to be a slave but all men want to be free—so we believe in the United States of America.

"If the United Nations is to mean anything at all in this great test of humankind, it must help as much as it can all who attempt to keep—and increase—the flame of freedom burning throughout the globe.

"So we believe in the United States of America.

"Therefore I offer the following resolution:

" 'Whereas, there now exists a state of war between the Soviet Union and the peoples of Poland, the German Democratic Republic, Czechoslovakia and Hungary and,

" 'Whereas, the freedoms of all humankind are at stake in the favorable outcome of this battle between Soviet oppression and the freedom-seeking peoples of the former 'satellite nations' of the Soviet Union, and,

" 'Whereas, the United Nations is the vehicle the nations everywhere have chosen to express and protect the ideal and desire for freedom of all the peoples of the earth; now, therefore, be it resolved:

" 'That the United Nations hereby declares the present President of the Soviet Union to be the aggressor against the freedom-seeking peoples of Poland, the G.D.R., Czechoslovakia and Hungary; that it deplores and condemns such aggression and declares the present President of the Soviet Union to be an enemy of world peace, freedom and stability; and that it urges all member states to give all possible sympathy, aid and support to the gallant peoples who are seeking to throw off Soviet oppression and resume their rightful place in the world as completely free and independent peoples and nations.'

"Mr. President, I ask for the vote."

There were immediate protests from Nicaragua, Iraq, Greece, Tanzania, Seychelles, India. Finally Yuri banged one hand sharply on the table and raised the other.

"Yes," Eire said hastily. "Yes, yes! The distinguished delegate of the Soviet Union wishes to speak?"

"No," Yuri said with heavy sarcasm, "I just wish to go to the washroom, that is why I am raising my hand. *Of course I wish to speak!* Does the distinguished delegate of Ireland, the President of the Council, think I am here to play games? Of course I want to speak!"

"Well," Eire said, waving his pipe furiously about so that his head was wreathed in smoke from which he peered like some small, agitated pixie. "Well, my goodness, go right ahead, then, if you please, go right ahead!"

"Thank you," Yuri said shortly. "I will . . . Mr. President, I will not dignify the wild claims and statements of the delegate of the United States by response except for two things: his fantastic lies concerning some so-called Soviet 'defector' who he claims tried to murder him; and his charge that this 'present President of the Soviet Union,' as he so kindly and persistently refers to me, had anything to do with starting the four conflicts which agitate him so in various areas of the world.

"The second charge has already been considered at length by the Council in our last meeting. The President of the United States was unable to win a majority to his view. The United Nations has disposed of his charges. The matter is moot. There is no point in debating it here further. It is a waste of time.

"However," he said—and something about the sudden solemnity of his tone made them all quiet down and sit forward in their chairs—"*however*. In order to remove all possible question that the Soviet Union, or I personally, am somehow engaged in some sinister plot to stir up war in these farflung places around the globe, I am authorized by the Politburo and the military services—not *forced,* Mr. President of the United States, but *authorized*—to announce that we are withdrawing, immediately, any and all assistance we may have been furnishing to the freedom fighters in Mexico, South Africa, Saudi Arabia.

"We do so," he said, while a wave of excitement crossed the room, "not because we are ashamed of whatever small assistance we have been able to give these freedom fighters *at their request*— and not because we do not continue to look with sympathy on their cause. But since it has been made such an issue here, and since we do not wish to give even the appearance of helping to prolong peace-threatening situations that are of great concern to all democratic freedom-loving peoples everywhere, we are withdrawing even such infinitesimal aid as we have given. It has been only a gesture, in any event; it cannot have affected the course of events on the battlefields. But we do not want to give anyone an excuse for saying we are helping to prolong these situations.

"This I announce with the approval—*not the orders*—of my colleagues in Moscow. We are happy to make this contribution to world peace."

He paused to take a sip of water, and there was a loud burst of applause from the crowded galleries and from several around the table. Prince Koa looked at Hamilton Delbacher and shook his head in slow, obvious, ironic wonder. Ham Delbacher replied in the same spirit with a slow, wry, ironic smile. Yuri saw them. For a second his eyes flared with anger. Then he smiled blandly and gave them both an ironic little bow. The applause continued for almost a minute. Eire finally and reluctantly gaveled the room to silence.

"I also wish to announce," Yuri went on, "that it is with sympathy and understanding that the Soviet Union recognizes and accepts the course of events in Cuba."

There was another burst of applause, this time genuinely surprised, relieved and admiring from many delegates. They had been wondering desperately how this issue would be handled. Now it was suddenly clear that it would simply be declared a nonissue by the man who had created it in the first place. This would take everyone off the hook very nicely. An almost visible wave of relief swept across the room crowded with watching "Third World" delegates who had been wondering desperately how they should behave when the Maximum Leader came back to them, as he inevitably would, to crow in triumph.

"Yes, Mr. President," Yuri said with a grave and moving humility, "it is clear that someone in my government made a grievous error in advising me that we should oppose the legitimate aspirations of the Cuban people. It was a mistake to offer Cuba direct membership in the Soviet Union, when this was not actually the desire of the great Cuban people. Now that they have made their wishes unmistakably known, we withdraw that offer, Mr. President, and we wish them well in their newly independent course. We recognize their noble dedication to liberty and freedom, which is always the goal of the Soviet Union and of the great socialist revolution everywhere. We recognize it and we honor it!"

"Since you obviously aren't strong enough to wipe it out," a new young reporter for the St. Louis *Post-Dispatch* whispered sarcastically in the press section, "you'd damn well better make the best of it!" Several of his senior colleagues glared at him and he subsided, red-faced. There went his chance to ever work on *those* papers, he thought despairingly. Why couldn't he learn to keep his damned mouth shut?

"Now," Yuri said, "let me come to the other charge the delegate of the United States has made against me today—the charge that we somehow tried to murder him. I can only dismiss this for the utter fantasy it is. It sounds like an evil fabrication by the CIA. In fact," and he looked about with a scornful smile, "is the delegate of the United States sure the whole thing was not a plot *by* the CIA to kill him? Stranger things have happened, we understand, with that strange organization!"

There was laughter across the room, and he acknowledged it with an ironic nod of his head.

"Yes, Mr. President, maybe that is what the strange story of the President of the United States is all about! Maybe his own CIA tried to kill him! In any case, *we* did not. It is an utter fabrication. I do not believe it ever happened. It is too fantastic, even for the distinguished delegate of the United States to present to us. He has given us some tall tales, Mr. President, but this is too much. *Too much!*''

And he chuckled amiably for a moment before turning serious again.

Ham Delbacher thought about replying and then decided with a tired impatience that he would not. Those who wanted to believe would believe; those who did not want to believe would not believe. He wondered what Ivan would have made of his complete dismissal by the man who had sent him. He would not have been at all surprised, Ham thought. In fact, he would undoubtedly have been completely surprised if Yuri had done anything else.

''Mr. President,'' Yuri said, voice now somber and stern, ''fellow delegates: the one thing which should rightly concern us here today is indeed the rebellions in Eastern Europe which are threatening the peace of the entire world. On their importance to mankind I do agree completely with the delegate of the United States. He ought to be concerned, since he started them.

''Yes, Mr. President!'' he said sharply as Ham stirred in his chair. ''Oh, yes, he started them! You have all read the famous memorandum that was exposed by one American who places world peace above the selfish interests of his country, namely Mr. Gary Hanson who used to work for the State Department. 'Used to work,' yes! He was dismissed the moment he told the truth, Mr. President! He was forced to resign when he exposed the vicious warmongering plans of the government of the United States! And now those plans are being put into effect, and our guns and tanks and troops and planes are being forced to kill innocent people in Eastern Europe in simple self-defense, Mr. President, because *this evil man* has stirred them up. And he has persuaded NATO to join in, and there are even hints that the distinguished delegate of the People's Republic of China, whom I see smiling so complacently across the table there, may try to bring his people into it! Where will it end, Mr. President? *It had better end,*'' he said with a sudden coldly vicious emphasis, ''right here and now, or the Soviet Union will not be responsible for the consequences. They would be terrible, Mr. President. *Terrible!*''

"Mr. President," Ju Xing-dao said gently. "Might I speak, since I have been mentioned?"

"I object, Mr. President!" Yuri said promptly. "There is no reason for the delegate to speak on my time. Let him speak on his own."

"I will," Ju said, still gently. "Meantime I shall try not to smile. Not that I was before, but now I shall be very circumspect."

And true to his word, his face became impassive. Only his shrewd little eyes followed, and never left, Yuri's somber face as he continued.

"Mr. President, not only did the delegate of the United States and his government create these revolts in Poland and the German Democratic Republic, but they also persuaded a renegade priest—"

Again a gasp, this time from the Catholic states. Even those that were now communist appeared offended. Perceiving this he calmly revised his statement.

"They also persuaded the Pope, of all people, to violate the tradition of centuries and involve himself directly in the rebellions. We cannot be responsible for the Pope, I inform the Council. He has chosen to become in effect a combatant. He will have to take a combatant's chances. We would hope he survives, but we cannot guarantee it as long as this futile warfare against us is allowed to continue. The only way we can guarantee his safety," he said, obviously relishing the specter he was raising, "would be if he fell into our hands as a prisoner of war. We would then be able to guarantee his safety, for we would remove him far behind the lines. There he would remain until such time, perhaps, as he and his ally, the United States, could see fit to persuade the foolish peoples in revolt against us that they would be better advised to lay down their arms . . .

"Mr. President! There is indeed a place for the United Nations here. It is to stop this madness immediately! It is to use all its good offices, to exercise its influence, to use its strength ("What strength?" someone murmured dryly in the press section) as never before, to make an effort such as has never been seen! Stop the fighting in Poland and the G.D.R., Mr. President! Stop it from spreading to Czechoslovakia and Hungary! We are ready to lay down our arms the moment the attacks upon us cease, but we will not do it one moment sooner. And if we are forced to continue, then presently"—his voice became somber and emphatic—"we may find ourselves forced to use weapons exceeding in frightfulness any we have used so far . . .

"So, Mr. President, I too, as usual, have a resolution. But this time I think the response of the Security Council had better be a positive one.

"I move to substitute for the resolution of the delegate of the United States, the following language:

" 'Whereas, there now exists a state of armed rebellion against, and unprovoked attack upon, the Soviet Union by dissident elements in Eastern Europe; and,

" 'Whereas, this rebellion and attack is inspired, supported, aided and encouraged by the United States of America, the Vatican, the Republic of France, NATO and indirectly by the People's Republic of China; and

" 'Whereas, if these attacks continue it will be necessary for the Soviet Union to retaliate with the utmost vigor and strength with all means at its command; and

" 'Whereas, such retaliation could only create great devastation and havoc not only in the nations which have attacked the Soviet Union but throughout Europe and possibly the world as well; and

" 'Whereas, for this reason it is vital to the peace of the world that the wars upon the Soviet Union cease at once and that order and stability be restored to the areas where fighting is now going on; now, therefore, be it resolved:

" 'That the United Nations calls upon the peoples of Poland, the German Democratic Republic, Czechoslovakia and Hungary to lay down their arms immediately, resume allegiance to their duly constituted legal governments, and cease all resistance of any kind whatsoever to the Soviet Union; and further,

" 'That the United Nations condemns and deplores the aid given the rebellious forces by the United States of America, the Vatican, the Republic of France, NATO and indirectly the People's Republic of China, and demands that such aid cease immediately and forthwith; and further,

" 'That the Security Council approves and hereby establishes immediately a multinational peacekeeping force to be stationed in Poland, the German Democratic Republic, Czechoslovakia and Hungary for a period not exceeding three months; that this force be drawn from the armed forces of the nonpermanent members of the Security Council who are currently sitting, and that it be empowered to take all steps necessary to restore peace, maintain order and reestablish the legitimate governments of the aforesaid belligerent nations existing prior to the outbreak of hostilities against the Soviet Union.'

"Mr. President, I ask for the vote on my substitute resolution."

He sat back and looked around the circle, face still somber and unyielding, while Eire looked around it, too, anxious and uncertain.

"Mr. President," Prince Koa spoke up with a relaxed and amicable air that in no way reflected his true feelings concerning the delegate of the Soviet Union. "Now I again suggest the regular order for the debate on the Soviet resolution. If there is any."

"Oh, I think," Eire said hastily. "I rather think there will be."

And so there was, as he went in order, alphabetically, around the table. No one spoke at length, and although the media kept careful tabs and tried to predict in advance what the vote would be, it was not so easy to guess except in a few expected cases.

Ju Xing-dao was not one of these. His statement was brief, elliptical, contained three aphorisms—"Count 'em, three," the Baltimore *Sun* noted—and wound up with a sentence that left everyone, as he intended, puzzled as to how he would vote:

"Therefore it is the opinion of the People's Republic of China that the situation, while indeed fraught with difficulties for all concerned, is one which nonetheless is susceptible to swift solution, providing, of course, that solution is acceptable to all those who have an innate, or possibly universal, interest in the outcome and are accordingly inclined to act in such a way as to solve them."

"Eh?" the St. Louis *Post-Dispatch* whispered to the Miami *Daily News*. "Come again?"

"He means exactly what he said," the Miami *Daily News* replied. "Don't try to confuse the issue!"

The President of France, as usual, was almost equally obscure.

"Some may condemn this or that," he said, "but it is more than a question of this or that. *It is a question of what to do!*"

"So?" AP murmured to UPI. "And what the hell is that?"

"The more it changes," UPI said solemnly, "the more it is the same thing."

"Her Majesty's Government," the Prime Minister concluded with her most iron softness, "most certainly will *not* vote for the Soviet resolution and *will* vote for the American resolution."

"I shall make no further attempt to challenge the lies of the Soviet delegate," Hamilton Delbacher said. "They speak for themselves with complete dishonor. We ask the Council for a vote against the Soviet resolution followed by a vote for the resolution of the United States."

Of the remainder, only India's lady produced genuine surprise by coming out flatfooted for the American resolution when everyone had expected her to maintain her uneasy sentimental alliance with the Soviets.

The rest were deliberately equivocal, and when Eire finally called the vote on the Soviet resolution the result was a real surprise—not because the conclusion was foregone, given the veto—but because of the division of sentiment it revealed.

Yuri lost, eight to seven, and no one had to use the veto. China, France, Britain, the United States, Egypt, India, Tonga and, finally, at the very end, with a vast sigh and another mucocius swig at his pipe, Eire, voted No. The U.S.S.R., Cameroon, Greece, Iraq, Nicaragua, the Seychelles and Tanzania voted Yes.

"The vote now comes on the original resolution of the United States," Eire said, and this time there were a couple of switches and more surprise.

The other four permanent members, China, France, the U.K. and the U.S., were joined in support by Egypt, India, Tonga, Eire, Greece and Tanzania, for a total of ten. Only five voted against: the U.S.S.R., Cameroon, Iraq, Nicaragua and the Seychelles.

Yuri made a great show of exercising the Soviet veto, and that concluded that.

That night when he took the issue to a hastily called session of the General Assembly, where the veto did not apply, there were further surprises.

The Soviet resolution, which Yuri managed to have placed first on the agenda when Afghanistan yielded to him for the purpose, was defeated 53 to 42 with a sizable number of abstentions.

The American resolution, offered as a substitute by the President, was approved 74 to 52, with very few abstentions.

Half an hour later, while news of the vote was still being flashed around the world, Yuri received a telephone call in the Delegates' Lounge where he had gone with his delegation and the delegations of Rumania and Bulgaria, still loyal.

"Comrade President," Mikhail Yarkov's even voice came clearly from Moscow, "we think you had better come home immediately."

The delegate of Malawi, also taking a call nearby, thought for a second—though he could not really believe it of one so forceful and self-possessed—that he actually saw Yuri sway slightly and turn pale. Then Yuri seemed to recover his composure.

But he went.

3

All the way home in the plane he spoke to no one, was spoken to by no one beyond the necessities of serving food and drink, preparing his bed, and the like. He was very noticeably left alone. The infection, he thought with savage irony, was spreading. In the minds of the crew—who were now, he knew, his jailers—he could sense that he was already doomed.

He made up his mind with fierce determination that this would not be so, though he knew in his heart with chilling certainty that unless he could manage some miracle when he reached Moscow and faced his colleagues, it would be so.

He was not prepared, however, for the line of attack that Yarkov took, though he should have been, for it was obvious. Once stated, everything else unraveled from there.

At the airport his limousine was waiting. This time when he got in he found he had special company. A very obviously armed soldier sat in the front seat beside the driver. Two others equally obvious flanked him in the back. He usually had company of this nature, but this time they were excessively armed and he knew—and they knew he knew—that they were there to guard, not protect him. Yet even as he realized this it reinforced his contempt for his colleagues and his conviction that he would somehow come out of this: for they had sent guns and he was armed only with his own powerful personality and clever brain.

His colleagues obviously considered this an equal match, which in an odd way, even at this climactic moment of his career and quite likely his life, he took as tribute.

"Stop at my apartment," he ordered as the limousine raced into the center of the city. "I want to refresh myself before I go to my office."

"I am sorry, Comrade President," the officer in the front seat said evenly. "We have orders that you are to be taken directly to the Kremlin."

"I command you to stop at my apartment," he said sharply, "or I shall hold you all personally responsible."

"General Yarkov and the Politburo are responsible," the officer said in the same even voice. "Proceed, driver."

"You will be suitably rewarded if you stop," he said, making his tone matter-of-fact and as though this were a conversation held every day.

"It is not a matter of reward, Comrade President," the officer said with an impersonal insolence, and turned back to face forward without further comment.

He looked at the officer on his right, the officer on his left. They too were staring straight ahead, faces blank and brutish, it seemed to him. They did not appear to be watching him but he knew if he made the slightest move he would be shot on the spot. And even if he should be so foolish as to try to leap out, the car was speeding too fast for him to make the move; and even if the move were possible, where could he escape to anonymity? The police state he had always lived under, and as a member of the KGB had helped to make even more repressive, if that were possible, would find him immediately. And of course since his triumph in his first confrontation with the American President, his picture was everywhere, at every street corner, on all buildings of any size, wherever one looked in Moscow and throughout the whole vast, unhappy country. That had been his decision, and the Politburo, though seemingly a little doubtful, had approved. It was now one more weapon to trap him where he was.

They entered the Kremlin, drove up to the entrance of the President. He got out, the three officers walking just behind him, and hurried up the steps. The guards on the door were standing at attention but gave no other indication that they recognized his presence.

He started down the long corridor to his office, came to a rest room.

"Comrades," he said dryly, "surely you do not mind—?"

"We will go with you," the senior officer said, and so they did, standing silently behind him while he completed his business, not without some difficulty, for he was at last beginning to feel frightened. But he finished, washed his hands, moved again into the corridor and went along to his office.

Inside he found them, standing in two rows confronting his desk.

The lights on his map were out, and his four bright conflagrations pulsed no longer.

"Comrades," he said. "It is not necessary for you to stand. Please be seated."

"We had rather stand, Comrade President," Mikhail Yarkov said.

"And we prefer that you stand too, comrade," the Foreign Minister said.

"This is insane!" he snapped suddenly with a surge of anger and wonder that this could be happening. "This is socialist error, comrades! It is incomprehensible behavior which you will all regret when you think back on how foolish you were. Be seated, I command you!"

No one responded; and no one sat.

So he did.

"Comrade," the Minister of Defense said with a harshness Yuri had never thought to hear in his voice, "we have asked you to stand also. Must we 'command' too?"

He remained seated for the better part of a minute before he stood. During that time no one spoke; almost, it seemed, no one breathed.

"Very well," he said, managing to keep his voice, he felt, perfectly calm. "I am standing. Does someone wish to tell me what this nonsense is about?"

Again no one spoke for several seconds. Then General Yarkov cleared his throat.

"Comrade Minister of Justice will enlighten you, comrade. He has prepared the indictment."

" 'Indictment'?" he cried. "But I am the President of the Soviet Union!"

"First you are a citizen of the Soviet Union, comrade," General Yarkov said. "Comrade Minister?"

"Yes, Comrade General," the Minister said; and he, too, cleared his throat, took some papers from his coat pocket and began to read in a voice that trembled a little but did not otherwise reveal his perturbation at what he was doing.

"It is charged: that on the night of September twenty-seventh, at ten twenty-five P.M., Comrade Yuri Pavlovich Serapin deliberately and cold-bloodedly murdered Comrade Ekaterina Vasarionova—"

"It is a lie!" he said, his own voice harsh and angry.

"No, comrade," Mikhail Yarkov said without inflection. "It is not a lie. You and I know it is the truth."

"I defy you to prove it!" he exclaimed. "It is only your word against mine, comrade general, and I am the President of the—"

"Do you wish to see the film and the tapes, comrade?" General Yarkov inquired quietly. "They have been shown to these comrades. Tonight they will be shown on television throughout the Soviet Union."

(*Disinformation*, Yarkov thought with grim humor: there was no film and there were no tapes. But it was necessary.)

"No!" Yuri cried.

"Yes, comrade," Yarkov said. "They have already been placed in the hands of state television. There is no possible way to stop it now."

"She was an enemy of the people!" Yuri shouted, realizing that sweat was beginning to run down his back inside his shirt, that his hands were beginning to tremble. "You know what she was, comrade! She was intriguing with the West to betray me! She was seeking to overturn the revolution! *She was an enemy of the people!*"

"No, comrade," Mikhail Yarkov said. "She was a friend of the people, a friend of the revolution. She saw the dangers in your adventurism and in your cult of personality which led you into strange paths of egotism, and she warned us about you. She told us of your increasing paranoia and ego madness."

"Then I was right to kill her," he cried, "for she was an enemy of myself and since I am the President of the people—"

"That will be decided, comrade," Yarkov interrupted softly, "when the indictment is complete. Comrade Minister?"

"It is charged:" the minister said obediently. "That the murder of Ekaterina Vasarionova was an example of a dangerous unbalance of mind that evidenced itself in this violent and unprovoked act, and prior to and after the murder led you to take steps that have gravely endangered the safety and security of the Motherland."

"Everything I have done has been for the Motherland!" he protested bitterly. "Everything has been for the glory of the socialist revolution! Everything has been designed to bring us final triumph in the battle that will decide the fate of all mankind!"

No one replied. The minister looked at Mikhail Yarkov. He nodded. The minister continued in his voice which to Yuri now sounded dreadfully harsh, accusatory, monotonous. To the minister himself it seemed shaky, nervous and trembling with temerity.

"It is charged: That because of the great egotism shown by Comrade Yuri Pavlovich, a dangerous cult of personality has developed. Item: pictures of Comrade Yuri Pavlovich everywhere in the Soviet Union, suitable perhaps for a leader of the so-called Western democracies but not suitable for the Soviet people's democracy. Item: persuading under false pretense of humility the Politburo and the military leaders to sign an undemocratic resolution seeking to make Comrade Yuri Pavlovich dictator of the Soviet Union."

"No one forced you to sign the resolution!" he said angrily. "It was done of your own free will! And I am not a dictator! I have always discussed my actions with the Politburo!"

"It is charged:" the minister read on, trying to keep all emotion out of his voice. "In the so-called 'first confrontation' with the American President H. Delbacher, Comrade Yuri Pavlovich, without consultation with the Politburo, the Council of Ministers or the military leaders, gambled to the point of war by sending armed forces throughout the world, and particularly submarines to Cuba, thereby risking nuclear war with the United States."

"The United States retreated!" he shouted to the phalanx of grim, unchanging faces. "The United States retreated!"

"Item:" General Yarkov said calmly. "But only after a period in which Comrade Yuri Pavlovich had in effect lost control of events and the world was on the very brink of nuclear war. Read on, Comrade Minister.''

"It is charged:" the minister said obediently. "Without consulting the Politburo or the Council of Ministers or the military leaders, Comrade Yuri Pavlovich secretly inspired, instigated and set in motion four conflicts in widely separated areas of the earth where it was virtually impossible for the armed forces of the Soviet Union to provide adequate assistance or even maintain adequately their own safety, had they been challenged."

"But they were *not* challenged!" he cried. "Do you not see, comrades? It was a gamble! And it worked!"

"Item:" Mikhail Yarkov said. "It did *not* work. It was a gamble that has now begun to fail and cannot successfully be put back in place."

"It is charged:" the minister read. "Comrade Yuri Pavlovich lost Cuba."

" '*Lost* Cuba'?" he echoed in desperate indignation. "How did I 'lose' Cuba?"

"Item:" General Yarkov said. "Comrade Yuri Pavlovich ordered what he thought would be the assassination of the Cuban leader. The assassination failed. The Cuban leader returned. He has now retaken Cuba. None of this would have happened if Comrade Yuri Pavlovich had not ordered the assassination of the Cuban leader. Cuba is now lost. Ergo, Comrade Yuri Pavlovich lost it. Read on, Comrade Minister."

"It is charged:" the minister said. "Comrade Yuri Pavlovich on his own initiative, entirely, ordered the deaths of two American hostages and went so far as to threaten the lives of two hundred more, thereby bringing great harm and disgrace to the good name of the Motherland."

"They were spies!" he cried in a tone beginning to sound hopeless as the minister droned on and Yarkov prompted him to still further insane, unfounded charges. "They were CIA spies!"

"Item:" General Yarkov said. "There is no proof of that and Comrade Yuri Pavlovich knows that charge was only an afterthought when he realized the harm he had done."

"But I intended to use the remainder to force the Americans back!" he cried.

"Item:" Mikhail Yarkov said. "And so the American President gained worldwide sympathy and support by releasing all the Soviet hostages and placing the blame for what might happen on Comrade Yuri Pavlovich. Where," he added coldly, "it now rests. Read on, comrade minister."

"It is charged: Comrade Yuri Pavlovich, entirely on his own and without consulting anyone on so dangerous a step that could conceivably have provoked the United States to instant nuclear retaliation, sent a KGB operative disguised as a 'defector' to attempt the assassination of the President of the United States."

"It would not have caused nuclear war!" Yuri shouted. "If I had succeeded you all would have applauded me!"

"Item:" said Mikhail Yarkov. "You failed. Read on, Comrade Minister."

"It is charged: Comrade Yuri Pavlovich, obsessed by his cult of personality, blinded by his egotism and weakened in judgment and grasp of affairs by his adventurism, gravely miscalculated the sentiment in the United Nations and so misworded his resolution there as to bring a majority vote against the U.S.S.R. in both the Security Council and the General Assembly. Even though Comrade Yuri Pavlovich exercised the Soviet veto in the Security Council, nonetheless a large majority of the United Nations for the first time in many years voted against the U.S.S.R., thereby doing incalculable damage to the U.S.S.R.—"

"It is not incalculable!" he cried with some last vestige of scorn. "It is nothing, the United Nations! When have we ever paid attention to the United Nations? When has it been important to us? Its vote means nothing. Nothing!"

"Item:" General Yarkov said. "Then why has Comrade Yuri Pavlovich made such a great show of using it to inflame world opinion against the Americans? He did not consider it useless or unimportant then. Nor did he when he went to it two days ago. Item: Comrade Yuri Pavlovich is now trying to lie to the Politburo, the Council of Ministers and the military leaders concerning his motivations."

"I am not lying!" he shouted desperately. *"I am not lying!"*

"Read on, Comrade Minister," Yarkov said. "You are now at the end."

"It is charged: Comrade Yuri Pavlovich by his actions has brought upon us the catastrophe our diplomacy and military preparations have for four decades been designed to prevent, namely the revolt of Eastern Europe. It is a war we did not wish to fight and never should have had to fight. It is a war which could conceivably go against us in spite of all our long preparations. It will in any event engage the utmost efforts of the Motherland, with an uncertain outcome and the possibility of real trouble within the Soviet Union. This is highly dangerous for us, for the Party and for the Motherland. . . ."

Yuri made some muffled, incoherent outcry. The minister's voice, now flat and inexorable, overrode it.

"Conclusion: Comrade Yuri Pavlovich has shown egotism, cult of personality, adventurism, misjudgment, unbalanced mentality and stupidity. He is no longer fit to be head of the nation or of the Party. He is a traitor. He should be immediately deposed from all his rights and titles and should be executed immediately for his crimes against the Party, the Soviet state and the people."

"No!" he cried, and it was like a howl. *"NO!* I demand a vote. I DEMAND A VOTE! *I am the Supreme Ruler and Arbiter of All Mankind!"*

They looked at him strangely, as though he were insane, which by then he nearly was.

"Comrade Yuri Pavlovich desires a vote," General Yarkov said softly. "He shall have it. Comrade Minister, call the roll."

And starting with the Foreign Minister, Yuri's "pet Moslem" from Kazakhstan, he did; and one by one the implacable phalanx voted as Mikhail Yarkov had instructed them; as they knew they must if they were to save their own hides in the universal turmoil that had now reached the Kremlin.

"All yes, comrade," General Yarkov told Yuri with the nearest thing to a triumphant smile that he would permit himself; and it was not much. "All yes and not a single no."

For a long moment, then, there was absolute silence in the room, during which there shot through Yuri's mind many things. Somewhere far off down the years there was an innocent youth whose high intelligence and idealistic purpose had brought him to the attention of the Party; who had been taken from his parents and molded into an instrument of death. For a little while it could have been an instrument of death for the world; that had mercifully failed. Now, in an irony he could hardly comprehend in the darkness into which his mind was finally sinking as he stood there confronting their calm, immovable faces, it was an instrument of death for him.

And what a death! He knew, for he had ordered it, and witnessed it, many times. Not for him the quick surcease of the firing squad or the merciful oblivion of poison. For those it considered traitors the Party reserved methods much more exhaustive and much more time consuming.

Suddenly his whole being shook with a shudder of fear and revulsion.

"No!" he shouted again, as so many he had condemned had shouted hopelessly before him. *"No, no, no!"*

And, finally and irretrievably insane, he lowered his head like some cornered bull and charged full tilt into them. The nearer were taken by surprise, caught off balance, toppled into one another as they looked with frantic desperation at Mikhail Yarkov. His face remained impassive. Only his eyes commanded, *Finish him! Finish him! Finish him!*

There was a surge of heavy, sweating, grunting humanity. Arms flailed, legs kicked, feet began to stomp, repeatedly, hysterically, over and over until at last life expired, and across his beautiful Oriental rug—a Kazak, from the Foreign Minister's own village in Kazakhstan—blood began to gush in a crimson tide that it seemed would never stop.

Finally silence fell save for their heavy breathing. They looked at one another, dazed. Some were still human enough to be revolted by what they had done: both the Foreign Minister and the Minister of Justice began retching. Several others were close to it.

"Comrades," General Yarkov said from his seat behind the

desk, "return to me in an hour and we will discuss the future. You will find this mess will all have been cleaned away by then."

And so it was, in the sense that Yuri Pavlovich was cleaned away. But the mess he had created was with them still, and they knew it would be awhile, if ever, before that was cleaned away and their juggernaut put back upon its implacable, headlong course.

BOOK SIX

1

POWER SHIFT IN KREMLIN!
YARKOV IN AS SERAPIN, ILL, RESIGNS!
UNKNOWN KGB HEAD SUCCEEDS RETIRING
PRESIDENT. YURI ANNOUNCES HE'LL RECUPER-
ATE AT BLACK SEA RESORT, THEN "RETURN
TO THE LAND."
FIGHTING FLARES ALONG 600-MILE LINE AS
YUGOS JOIN "UNITED EAST EUROPE FRONT."
POPE'S WHEREABOUTS UNKNOWN, BELIEVED
IN POLAND.
YARKOV TO ADDRESS NATION AT NOON.

It was in some respects a Western-style speech, as befitted one who, like Yuri, had been stationed for several years as a
KGB agent in the Washington embassy. But the gist was pure Soviet.

He looked calm and firm—lacking his predecessor's flamboyant
bellicosity but giving an impression of absolute and unshakable
purpose.

Which after all, as the watching Hamilton Delbacher remarked,
was what he had to do.

"It is my unhappy duty," he said, "to inform you of the resignation of our beloved comrade Yuri Pavlovich Serapin as President

of the Soviet Union, chairman of the Politburo, chairman of the
Council of Ministers and head of the armed forces.

"Our beloved Comrade Yuri's health has been seriously jeopar-
dized by the enormous mental and physical strain he has been under as a result of the insufferable criminal actions of imperialist
circles of the United States and its NATO allies. Our beloved
Comrade Yuri ("How beloved can you get?" Elinor inquired
dryly) has struggled long and valiantly against the evil designs of
the American President and his companions in world crime. Our
beloved Comrade Yuri ("Apparently there's no limit," her husband replied) has devoted all his energies, all his waking thoughts,
every hour of every day, to the search for world peace. Everywhere
he has been thwarted by the hegemonistic desires of the United
States and its allies. The strain has proved too much for even his
brilliant leadership.

"His health is no longer what it was.

"He leaves office after only three months—but what a three
months! ("You can say that again," Chauncey Baron remarked.
"And again and again and again and *again*," Roger Hackett
agreed.) He takes with him the united gratitude and praise of the
party and the nation. He will remain for several weeks in Sochi, on
the Black Sea, and then will return to the soil of Central Mongolia,
home of his mother. There his colleagues and a grateful nation
wish for him a long and undisturbed retirement.

("Does that mean he's going to be a farmer?" Elinor inquired.
"I can think of something a lot grimmer than that which it might
mean," her husband said. "We may never know," Chauncey
Baron said. "That being the way they operate.")

"And now," Mikhail Yarkov said, "what of the future? I must
express first of all my enormous gratitude to my colleagues of the
Politburo who have unanimously elected me to head the nation. I
have given them my pledge of absolute fealty and support. In return they have given me theirs, and to ratify it have adopted unanimously the following resolution."

He picked up a piece of paper and read in a level voice:

" 'In view of the great emergency faced by the party and the
Motherland, it is the sense of the Politburo and the Council of Ministers, approved unanimously by the military leaders, that for a pe-

riod of two years, which may be extended indefinitely by the will of the Politburo and Council of Ministers with the concurrence of the military leaders, all authority to originate and direct moves against the imperialist enemies of mankind is vested solely and exclusively in M. S. Yarkov, to whom we pledge our total unwavering support.'

("He isn't going to get rid of *that* legacy from Y. P. Serapin, anyway," Roger Hackett observed. "Not on your tintype," Elinor agreed. "He's also upped the ante by a year and a half." "Confident man," Chauncey Baron said. "Or, on the contrary—" the President remarked.)

"This resolution," General Yarkov said, "was also signed by the heads of all the military services. In fact, they signed it prior to the Politburo and the Council of Ministers."

("He's taking no chances," the President said. "A cautious man and a tough one. At least I'm beginning to see what I have to deal with." "Don't worry too much," Chauncey said. "He has his hands full.")

And this Mikhail Yarkov obviously realized as he prepared to conclude his brief statement. He took a sip from a glass of water at his elbow, smoothed back with a long-fingered right hand the thick dark hair just beginning to fleck with gray, cleared his throat and stared straight into the cameras.

"I have been honored with leadership of the Soviet Union at a time of very grave consequence. Through no fault of our own, we are confronted with difficult situations both abroad and nearer home. We are taking these steps to meet them:

"As our beloved former leader Y. P. Serapin announced at the United Nations two days ago, all Soviet assistance, aid or other form of participation in the local disturbances in Mexico, Saudi Arabia, South Africa, the Taiwan Straits—*and Cuba*—is being immediately and completely terminated.

"That leaves the conflicts inspired by the imperialist capitalist leadership circles of the United States, France, the Vatican, the United Kingdom and NATO.

"These conflicts are directly on our borders and we cannot ignore them. Neither can we in any way disengage ourselves from our present efforts to bring them to a swift and satisfactory conclusion. That would be completely irresponsible.

"Those efforts," he said, and his tone hardened and became much more like Yuri's, "will continue undiminished until such swift and satisfactory conclusion has been reached. In fact, the efforts will not only be undiminished, they will be increased. And they will be increased immediately, unless there is an immediate cessation of hostilities by the imperialist-backed elements that are seeking to overturn the legitimate governments of our neighbors and establish bandit governments there.

"Unless there is a cessation of hostilities within the very near future"—his tone hardened ever further, became cold, emphatic and devoid of the air of reason that had surrounded his delivery so far—"the full power of the Soviet Union *in all its aspects* will be unleashed against the peoples of Poland, the German Democratic Republic, Czechoslovakia, Hungary and Yugoslavia. It will rain from the skies, it will strike from the earth, it will fill the atmosphere. Nothing will escape it, no thing, no living being, no person, however exalted, who attempts to meddle in affairs where he does not belong.

"Nothing will escape us—nothing!

"Eastern Europe will be a moonscape within an hour.

"Do not believe this, peoples of the world," he said, very softly, "*at your peril . . .*

"That is all I have to say to you now," he concluded, tone quite calm and conversational again. "We shall see what there is to say in the very near future."

And with a grim little smile he nodded his head abruptly as if in salute. His handsome, unyielding visage, looking thoroughly Soviet now, faded from the world's screens.

"Is he bluffing?" Elinor inquired.

Her husband shook his head.

"God knows," he said, "but whatever he's doing, *I* am moving fast."

His conversation with the Young Fanatic was terse and explicit. Millions of dollars were tossed about, certain promises of assistance were given, certain specific items mentioned, certain plans agreed upon.

"You will see that this reaches the Minister," he said.

"We have our ways," the Young Fanatic responded with a resentful sarcasm.

"And you really think you can succeed," he said.

"We are not fools, President!" the Young Fanatic snapped.

"And you are not women," he said in a deliberately mocking tone, "so you will be brave enough to assist him when the time comes."

"We are not women!" the Young Fanatic cried, in a rage to prove it, just as Ham Delbacher had planned he should. "We will do it!"

"Good for you," the President said dryly. "Thank you, dear friend and ally."

Something vicious in Arabic slithered liquidly past his ear. He put down the receiver and chuckled quietly to himself.

His conversation with the Pope was equally brief but much more pleasant.

The Pontiff spoke from somewhere in Poland, he said.

There, too, plans were proceeding posthaste.

"The threat of nuclear retaliation hangs over us, of course," the Pope said, "as well as all the other horrors he mentioned. Still, we progress."

"You are brave men," the President said gravely. "All, all brave men."

"We believe we have no choice," the Pope said with equal gravity. "And now, if ever, is the time to strike."

"Yes," Ham Delbacher agreed. "When will you reveal yourself to the nations? Or do they know already that you are there?"

"The word is spread. I believe the password is, 'The Light is come.' And so," he added gravely, "I intend for It to be."

"Good luck," the President said. "May God attend you."

"He will," the Pontiff said. "He can permit evil to endure only so long. Then He grows tired of it."

"But at such a cost," the President said aloud to himself when he hung up. "At such a cost."

And again he thought: *All, all brave men.*

"Mr. President!" Dietrich Bolle hailed him from Bonn. "We can report good progress here!"

"You sound very cheerful," the President said.

"I am!" the West German Prime Minister exclaimed. "I am! Action! *Action!* It is good for the soul to have it, after all these long, dreary, frustrating years. It is good to be one nation, one people again."

"You feel you are already that?" Hamilton Delbacher inquired. "And your peoples both agree?"

"Everything is favorable," Dietrich Bolle said. *"Everything."*

"And the other nations likewise?"

"How can they object?" the Prime Minister inquired blankly. "It is done. It is ratified by force, by unity of arms. What does it matter now what the other nations think?"

Exactly so, the President thought with a weary foreboding. Indeed it made no difference now . . . Exactly so.

"You are not afraid of Yarkov's threats?"

"His threats!" the West German Prime Minister said scornfully. "He had to make them, but let me tell you what we hear, Mr. President. We hear they murdered Serapin, we hear there has been great turmoil in the Kremlin, we hear Yarkov seized power. If he seized it, others can seize it. Everything is chaos there, inside, though of course as always they want you to think they are one united phalanx. Nonsense! *Dummköpfe!* They will crumble fast now, you wait and see."

"God knows I hope you're right," Ham Delbacher said grimly.

"I am always right," Dietrich Bolle said. "That is why I am where I am. And do you know what I am going to do now?"

"I can't imagine," the President said; and added with a chuckle to soften it somewhat, "I'm not really sure I want to know."

"I am going to call in our peaceniks over here, these great, nobel antinuclears, and I am going to say to them: Look, *Schwein!* You heard your big friend in Moscow. So now, how about a peace demonstration against him, eh? How about a new Children's Crusade, eh? How about getting up your hundred thousand, your two hundred thousand, your whatever, and staging a peace march across the Soviet border, eh? How about going unarmed straight over the border, eh, and see if they will dare, *if they will dare,* shoot you down when you come defenseless in the name of peace? How about that, eh? How about that?"

"That's a fantastic idea, Dietrich," the President said, and so it was. "Only why didn't you think of it years ago?"

The Prime Minister gave a disgusted snort.

"They never would have done it then, they're such one-sided donkeys with blinders on. But now they've heard the threats from his own lips maybe they will, maybe they will. It will be a nice diversion for Moscow. That is all I am thinking about now, providing diversions for Moscow."

"More power to you," the President said, thinking: that man really *enjoys* war. "Diversions are what we need."

Next morning the Great Peace March began; and far to the southeast amid the barren mountains and desolate deserts the Young Fanatic cooperated by launching the biggest diversion of all—considerably more drastic than a much shocked and alarmed President had intended. He had only wanted to encourage Moslem revolt, not Moslem insanity. But there was no doubt the Young Fanatic's move was effective.

ATOMIC BOMB DESTROYS BAKU!

HUGE SOVIET OIL PORT ON CASPIAN SEA BLASTED BY "ISLAMIC BOMB"!

IRANIAN LEADER JOINS PAKISTAN TO FAN FLAME OF MOSLEM REVOLT!

PROCLAIMS HOLY WAR TO SEPARATE ALL RUSSIAN MOSLEMS FROM MOSCOW!

"Get me the Foreign Minister," Mikhail Yarkov directed his secretary, his voice calm despite the inner tensions that were rapidly building, despite the hours without sleep, the enormous pressures, the sparkling lights on the wall across from his desk that now were beginning to move closer to, rather than away from, the Soviet Union. And now the awful news from Baku.

But there was no Foreign Minister.

"Where is he?" he demanded sharply, voice rising in anger and the first eroding notes of fear despite his best efforts to hold it steady. "Where is he? Get him!"

"He—" the terrified girl began. "Comrade President, he—"

"Well, *what?*" he demanded, too loudly, he knew, but he could not help himself. *"Where is the Foreign Minister?"*

"He—he—has left," she said. "He is no longer in Moscow."

"Where did he go?" he shouted.

"I—they—they say he went to the airport and took a plane—and—and left."

"Get me the commandant of the airport!" he snapped, and when the idiot came on the line he shouted:

"Why did you permit the Foreign Minister to leave, idiot?"

"But Comrade President," the man objected, alarmed but reasonable. "He asked for a plane—he is a licensed pilot—he is the Foreign Minister—what right did I have to say no to him?"

Mikhail Yarkov had the airport commandant shot on the spot.

But that did not bring back the Foreign Minister.

KAZAKHSTAN REVOLTS! FOREIGN MINISTER LEADS TRIBES TOWARD LINK WITH PAKS, IRANIANS! SOUTHERN RUSSIA IN FLAMES!
LITHUANIANS, LATS JOIN EAST EUROPE REBELLION AS ATOMIC CLOUD DRIFTS NORTH!
SUPREME SOVIET CALLED TO SPECIAL SESSION!
SOVIET GOVERNMENT MAY DISINTEGRATE!

The fabric frays, Ham Delbacher thought exultantly. The fabric frays at last.

"The President," the White House announced at six P.M., "will address the brave Russian people at noon tomorrow."

Before that, however, he had the two conversations that were to set the tone of his speech.

The first was an opening talk with Mikhail Yarkov.

The second was a final talk with Ju Xing-dao—final for the current unpleasantness, he thought wryly. He suspected that the representative of China and the representative of the United States, whoever they might be as leaders retired or were replaced, would have many, many more as the months and years went by.

He initiated the call to the Soviet President because he felt things were now at a stage at which it was both psychologically and militarily practical for him to do so. The action of the Young Fanatic had precipitated the situation the superpowers had secretly dreaded for years—that in the shadow of their ponderous jockeying for position someone smaller, less responsible, driven by ancient fears and hatreds and mad ambition, would use without warning the nuclear weapon. Now Iran and Pakistan had done so. It could mean the end of the world or the hope of the world. If it meant the latter, then the two million dead of Baku and the smoking desert where the oilfields used to be would stand as harbingers of the new world—ghastly now but perhaps ultimately to be perceived as the necessary prelude to the salvation of humankind.

If the great powers could not together seize the opportunity, if things unfrayed still further now that they were spinning almost—not quite, but almost—completely out of control, then—he shuddered at the abyss that now threatened to open at their feet.

So he called Mikhail Yarkov; and after half an hour of what was apparently face-saving delay in Moscow, made contact.

"Mr. President," he said without other preliminary, "I am going to turn on my Picturephone, as I think we should talk face to face. You may do as you please, of course."

He turned it on and waited. One minute passed while he sat back staring patiently into the little viewer; two minutes; three minutes—there was a little click! on the line and the stern but handsome face of the new Soviet leader appeared before him.

His expression was set and unyielding. It seemed to the President that he had aged noticeably since a few days ago when Yuri had first introduced him with the new Politburo. It might be imagination or hope, the President told himself, but the face that confronted him appeared to be that of a man rapidly changing under the pressures of great events, tense with the burden of them.

"Mr. President," he said, "I must first express my regrets for the ill health of former President Serapin, and the disruption this must have caused within your government."

"There was no disruption," Mikhail Yarkov said shortly. "I was here."

"Yes," the President said thoughtfully. "And now President Serapin no longer is." There was no response. "Well. In any event: thank you for deciding to talk to me. It seems to me very advisable to converse, now that things have reached the point they have."

"What point is that, Mr. President?" General Yarkov inquired with an apparent curiosity that conceded nothing.

"The point at which your city of Baku and its oilfields lie utterly destroyed," Ham Delbacher said. "The point at which, if you and I and China do not stop the unraveling of the world, it may finally explode altogether. *That* point, Mr. President."

"Baku and the oilfields lie in ruins, Mr. President," Yarkov said sharply, "because you conspired with the madman who runs Iran and with the devils of Pakistan to engage in the ultimate act of war against the Soviet Union. That is why Baku and its oilfields lie in ruins."

"I think not," the President said. "I think you oversimplify, Mr. President. I most certainly have done and am doing everything I can to promote the Moslem rebellion and the rebellions in Eastern Europe. And," he added, his voice as cold and deliberate as Yarkov's own, "I shall continue to do so. But I did not encourage nor have I in any way assisted in the use of the bomb on Baku. I was as shocked and appalled as you."

"I do not believe you," Yarkov said.

"I do not care whether you believe me or not," Ham Delbacher retorted, "it is the truth. Nor do I have the slightest idea whether the Young Fanatic, as we call him here, has another bomb or bombs, or whether he will use them on other targets in the Soviet Union to further his Pan-Islamic dream. I do know that you would be a fool not to accept my offer."

"Offer of what?" Yarkov shot out, and for a second the tension on his face flared into his eyes and the President could see that he was dealing with a very harried man; but not one, he could also see, who was anywhere near breaking under it.

"An offer to cooperate with you in trying to work out a peaceable solution of the problems on your borders and within your country before it is too late.''

"Too late for what?'' Yarkov demanded in the same contemptuous tone. "We have our own atomic bombs, you know; we have nuclear weapons directed at the United States, we have them trained on Teheran and Islamabad, and we have them trained on Warsaw, on Berlin, on Budapest and Belgrade—''

"And what good will it do you to destroy those cities or destroy us?'' the President asked. "We will simply destroy you in return. Even assuming you might survive, you personally or your government, you would preside over a graveyard. And what would be the point of that? It would be insanity . . . No, Mr. President, I am offering you a helping hand before it is too late. You had best think very carefully before you say no.''

"What can you do?'' Mikhail Yarkov inquired. "What control do you have over the antidemocratic forces in Eastern Europe? What can you do to stop the Fanatic? You are as helpless as I am, Mr. President. Furthermore, I do not trust you to help the Soviet Union. Your country has always wished to destroy the Soviet Union. Why are we to think you have changed now?''

"We have never wished to destroy the Soviet Union,'' the President said quietly, because there was no point in venting frustration in shouting. "We have only wanted the Soviet Union to leave us in peace and leave the rest of the world in peace. We have only wanted to live and let live.''

"Therefore you would not help to restore the Soviet Union,'' Mikhail Yarkov began—realized the admission of incipient defeat in what he had said—quickly amended, "you would not help the Soviet Union to repel her enemies, because you think the Soviet Union wants to destroy you. *You* are the fool, Mr. President. You would not help us at all, even if you could!''

Ham Delbacher studied his gray, unyielding face for several moments before he responded.

"Let me make clear, Mr. President,'' he said. "I do not propose that we help you to reestablish your dictatorship over Eastern Europe—no. I do not propose that we help you to suppress the legitimate desires of your own Moslem people for self-determination and self-expression—no. Those are tides of history that have now been set in motion and they are tides that neither you nor I can stop unless we utterly destroy the world. I do not want to do that. I assume you and your colleagues have at least an ounce of sense between you and do not want to do it either.

"But what I *do* propose and what I *can* do is offer my good offices, plus a very substantial amount of aid and assistance of all kinds, in helping to work out some arrangement between the Soviet Union and its former satellites—its *former* satellites," he repeated firmly as anger rose in Mikhail Yarkov's eyes, "and its *former* subject Moslem peoples that will preserve the security of the Soviet Union from outside attack and at the same time permit the former satellites and the former subject peoples to live in harmony together."

"Do you realize," General Yarkov said in a voice that trembled a little with the intensity of his emotion, "that we have more than fifty diverse races and nations within the Soviet Union? Do you realize that we, the Communist Party of the U.S.S.R., are the *only* thing that holds them all together? Do you realize that if we permit these rebellions to succeed they will turn on us and destroy us everywhere in Russia? Do you realize—"

"I realize that a handful of ruthless people would lose their special privileges, yes," Ham Delbacher said sharply. "But I do not see that this would be such a bad thing for the rest of their countrymen or the world, Mr. President. I am offering you what may be your last chance to work out some cooperative arrangement with Eastern Europe and with your own subject peoples, particularly the Moslems, so that they will *not* destroy you or your Party. But this means, of course," he added with a quietness that in no way decreased his firmness, "that it will be a very different Party . . . and it will treat the world, and its own peoples and its own allies, in a very different way than it has done since 1917."

For a long moment General Yarkov looked at him unblinking and apparently unmoved. Then he reached out a hand to turn off his machine and break the connection, speaking also with a quiet and adamant firmness as he did so.

"*You* are the one who is insane, Mr. President. We have nothing to discuss."

And he faded from the screen, eyes still unwavering and expression still adamant, until he was utterly gone.

Very well, my friend, Ham Delbacher thought. You do it your way and see where it gets you, now that all these forces greater than a million bombs have been released in the world at last . . .

Three calls were waiting when he turned back to his desk.

Chauncey Baron called to report that the Pope had appeared in Czechoslovakia, where he had been received by screaming millions whom he had hastily blessed and encouraged before vanishing again, reportedly to go on to Hungary and from there to Yugoslavia. Word of his coming had apparently been spread by the underground. The Soviets were taken by surprise, and though there had been a halfhearted attempt to herd back some of the crowds, the soldiers had not quite dared to shoot or bomb him, so enormous was his welcome and so overwhelming was the determination of the people. He had made little attempt to shelter himself and had stood in a warm fall rain for ten minutes in full view of the occupiers before being whisked away by friendly welcomers into the surrounding forests.

Linda called, tearful and ecstatically happy, to report that Mark had said a sleepy, "Hi," and taken her hand. The doctors were now convinced that in a relatively short time all would be well. The President called Elinor in the family quarters to tell her the good news. She was as relieved and happy as he.

From Peking came the call he had been expecting at any moment as the news from Moscow and the battlefields appeared to be turning ever more rapidly in his favor.

Again he suggested the Picturephone; quickly Ju obliged. He materialized, smiled briefly and began to speak in a gentle voice as though he did not have a care in the world. But his words were far from innocuous.

"Mr. President!" he said. "Congratulations! The flower of peace begins to bloom amid the smoke of war."

"Thank you, Vice-Premier," he said with a smile. "I'm glad you think so."

"Indubitably," Ju said. "Now we must begin to think what we will do with Russia."

" *'Do with Russia?'* " he echoed. "You take my breath away,

Vice-Premier. Russia is hardly in a state yet to 'do' anything with, is she?"

"She will be," Ju Xing-dao said with a dismissive little wave of his tiny hand. "She is dying—*they* are dying. It is only a matter of time now, and very little of that. *We* think she should be partitioned. Do you not agree?"

"I'll admit something like that has crossed my mind from time to time," Ham Delbacher said. "But I think it's a little early—"

"The curse of the West!" Ju interrupted with sudden severity, relieved by a sudden smile. "You never think ahead. You never plan. In the midst of peace you should plan war. In the midst of war you should plan peace. You have lost the fruits of two world wars because you refused to plan until the guns fell silent. Then old hatreds, old fears and old ambitions leaped back, and it was too late. Now, Mr. President, *now!* Now is the time to plan."

"What kind of partition do you have in mind?" he asked cautiously. "East-West like Germany, or—"

"Much too simple," Ju said sternly. "Much too good for them. Also, much too conducive to eventual reuniting, just as is happening in Germany today. Do you have a map beside you, Mr. President?"

"I have a globe."

"Good. So have I. Now," Ju said, raising his right index finger like the schoolteacher he once had been, far back down the years before the Long March and all the great days, "let us observe this Russia and see logically what becomes of her . . .

"First of all," he said emphatically, "she must be reduced to Russia proper—to Old Muscovy, if you will, and outlying areas."

"How outlying?" the President asked.

"About ten miles," Ju said promptly. Then he chuckled. "You look very alarmed, Mr. President, and yet why not? Have they deserved more?"

"Perhaps not," the President said. "But still—"

"Oh, I jest," Ju said. "You are familiar with me; I always jest." He became serious. "Not ten miles, nor a hundred. But certainly no more—*no more* than a thousand. Let them keep the heart of Russia, if they wish. But," he added, "completely disarmed and under occupation, of course."

The President whistled.

"You don't want much, Vice-Premier. A modest plan, if I ever heard one."

"Very practical," Ju said. "Obviously they must be disarmed so they won't attempt anything again. Obviously Moscow must be occupied to guarantee this. And obviously from that it follows that the present government must be abolished, the Communist Party must be dismantled and some new form of state must be set up—possibly on the basis of your favorite panacea in the West—'free elections.' "

"Go on," the President suggested. "It's fascinating. And very easy to do, too, with a couple of globes and a good imagination."

"We will have more than that to assist us," Ju predicted, "when our friends in Moscow collapse. So, then," he added like a child contemplating a new toy, "what next?"

"What next, indeed," Ham Delbacher said. "You're conducting this exercise, not I."

"Oh, but you will," Ju said comfortably. "It cannot be done without you. You will."

"Vice-Premier," he said, "there are so many things involved and such a long, hard road ahead, that I wouldn't venture at this point to predict what—"

"Then I am glad I am braver than you," Ju interrupted, but again with his twinkling little smile. "I am not afraid to sail these uncharted but necessary seas . . . So, then; now we have Russia confined. What do we do with the rest of her?"

"Exactly."

"Trust the globe and follow the map, Mr. President. It all becomes clear. Kazakhstan is in revolt right now. Aided by the other Moslem portions of the Soviet Union and the Islamic pressures from outside, Kazakhstan is going to succeed. He who is not called Foreign Minister is very shortly going to be called Prime Minister or President of a new Islamic state. This we should all recognize at once."

"That I am prepared to do," the President said, "the moment there are signs of victory there."

"Good," Ju said. "That is one partition—Islamasthan, or whatever they wish to call it—comprising Kazakhstan, Uzbekistan,

Kirghizia, Tadzhikistan, Turkemistan. Under our general protection and supervision—"

"Oh?"

"As the remaining superpower nearest the scene," Ju said smoothly.

"I see," the President said. "You *are* planning ahead."

"Certainly," Ju said.

"And Mongolia?"

"Returned to China, of course," Ju said firmly, "where it historically belongs and has always belonged before it was stolen from us by the robbers in Moscow. Joined with Inner Mongolia to form the Chinese Mongolian Autonomous Republic. We also intend to take the Sakhalin Peninsula."

"And with it all the missile sites and installations—and the missiles, no doubt," the President said.

"We believe we deserve them," Ju said blandly.

"*I* believe all the sites must be destroyed and all the missiles likewise," the President said. "That is *my* belief."

"Do not worry, Mr. President," Ju said airily. "They will be in good hands."

"Fortunately this is all on a couple of globes and a lot of imagination, Vice-Premier," the President said, "or you would have very grave problems with the United States."

"You are so far away," Ju said dreamily. "It would not be easy to impose your will—"

"There are means," Ham Delbacher said, sounding as absolutely firm as he knew he must. "So I warn you not to try to move too hastily, Vice-Premier. Many, many long consultations lie ahead, and much, much compromise. China cannot do this single-handedly. China *must not* try to do it single-handedly."

Ju stared at him like some brightly cheerful little bird, very old but still chirpy. Then he smiled and shrugged.

"Simply in the interests of planning Mr. President," he said in the same dreamy way. "Simply in the interests of planning . . ."

"Is there anything else, while we're remaking the globe?" the President inquired dryly.

Ju smiled comfortably.

"Only the Siberian Autonomous Republic—"

"Of China?"

"Again," Ju said with a vague smile, "propinquity . . ."

"You're contemplating enough land there to accommodate a dozen medium-sized nations," Ham said. "You think that it should run from east to west as far as a thousand miles out from Moscow? That's more than half the present Soviet Union."

"Well, perhaps fifteen hundred, let us say—from a point roughly straight north from the present western boundary of Mongolia. That we think would make a nice counterbalance to any resurgence out of Moscow. After all the Soviet officials have been removed, of course, and the whole area has been purged of potentially divisive elements."

" 'Purged?' "

"Oh, yes," Ju said. "*We* don't want to have to support three million Soviet communists in jail for the rest of their lives. Do you, Mr. President? Would your people stand for it?"

"We would try to treat everyone in a humanitarian way—"

"You would try," Ju said calmly, "but you would not succeed. Then would come tasks which, if you are too delicate to perform, we are not. Perhaps it would be best if you did not worry about them but simply left them to us."

"Well, Vice-Premier," Ham Delbacher said, "I'll admit you open up an astounding prospect. And a most interesting one. But I think it would be much better if you kept it to yourself for the time being, don't you? Any mention of it now would only strengthen Russian resistance."

"Perhaps," Ju said. "Perhaps not. The rulers of Moscow are hated, you know, by all these peoples and regions. The Soviet empire as such has no sentimental resonance for them. Russia as we know it hangs together by the merest thread. That is one reason they have always been so fiercely defensive, in Moscow. They know what will happen the minute their control starts to slip. And it *is* slipping. It is on its way off history's stage. Right now."

"You may be right," the President said. "God knows I hope you're right. A world without the Soviets, without that constant push out from the center, that constant meddling with the whole wide world, always inflaming everything, always making everything worse, deliberately creating trouble all the time so they can take advantage of it—I cannot imagine such a world, the other has been with us so long. But, Vice-Premier, that does not mean that you would not be playing into their hands by announcing this plan of yours too early. I know I can only give advice as a friend of China—''

"For the moment," Ju said with an amiable smile.

"You said that, I didn't. As a friend of China, I most strongly urge you to keep these ideas to yourself for the time being. After the Soviet collapse, then we can begin to talk about what comes next. But I do most strongly urge—''

"We shall see," Ju Xing-dao said cheerfully. "When the time is ripe, Mr. President. When it is ripe. I am sorry you will not join us, when it is."

"I didn't say that, either," Ham Delbacher said.

"But you are *not* joining."

"Not at the moment," he said firmly, "no. And if you do announce any such scheme to the world, I should probably be forced to denounce it."

"Aha," Ju said with his gentle, wry little smile. " 'Probably!' ''

"Yes," the President said. " *'Probably!'* ''

"It would be so much more effective if you *could* join us," the Vice-Premier said wistfully. "So much more . . .''

"Not now," the President said, not yielding. "And perhaps not for a long time to come."

"There is no 'long time' left," the Vice-Premier said as he prepared to take his leave with another little wave and smile. "Everything is moving so fast, now."

And so it was, the President thought with a strange mixture of hope and foreboding as he prepared to address the brave Russian people, as the preliminary announcement had put it with calculated and deliberate flattery, at noon the next day.

On the battlefields there continued to be heavy fighting in Eastern Europe, where the biggest Soviet forces had been concentrated; more scattered but also more successful risings all over Kazakhstan and the other Soviet Moslem "republics" enumerated by Ju Xing-dao; and in the Far East, uneasy silence along the four-thousand-mile Soviet-Chinese border.

In the areas where the late (as Ham Delbacher was almost certain, now, he was) Yuri Serapin had started conflicts, and in Cuba, all was relatively quiet: mopping-up operations were underway. Yuri's legacies, the major battles and the major shifts in world power, were occurring where Soviet leaders had always thought they could be avoided, on their own borders.

But still their atomic bombs had not fallen, their poison gas and bacteriological weapons had not appeared. Still they did not quite dare, in spite of Baku and being as hard-pressed as they were.

Still some lingering responsibility to humankind remained; but for how long, the fearfully watching world could not know.

Having failed with Mikhail Yarkov, whose fate no longer concerned him except that he wished him and his whole murderous crew out of there as fast as possible, the President was now prepared to go over his head directly to the Russian people. It was to them exclusively that he spoke at noon.

"My friends in Russia," he said gravely, his words carried to Russia in translation by the Voice of America and Radio Free Europe, and throughout the world in English by every other means of television and radio transmission available, "my friends the great Russian people:

"Evil men who control your government have now placed the Motherland in the greatest jeopardy she has known since World War II.

"It is you, the brave Russian people, among the bravest in all history, who must save her now.

"Three days ago a man named Yuri Serapin led the little group of murdering criminals and thieves who claim to represent you, the great Russian people. Today it is a man named Mikhail Yarkov. Tomorrow it may be someone else. But whoever it is, the government he heads means only three things: death for many fine young men and many civilians—destruction for the Russian state—disaster for the Motherland as long as this murderous gang is in control.

"It is time for you to rise against them, brave Russian people! It is time for you to throw off their control which means only evil for the Motherland!

"Revolt and rebellion now rage all along the western borders. Eastern Europe is aflame. Poland, East Germany, Czechoslovakia, Hungary, Yugoslavia, Latvia and Lithuania have risen for their freedom—that same freedom for which you, brave Russian people, made so many sacrifices in the Great Patriotic War—that freedom which you can understand, because it means so much to *you*. And because you too know what it is to have your freedom destroyed by the evil gang of men who sit in Moscow.

"In the same spirit of freedom, Moslem peoples in Kazakhstan and the other Moslem areas of the U.S.S.R. have risen against the gang in Moscow. Their quarrel is not with you, brave Russian people: it is with those evil men who have suppressed and enslaved all of you for so many long, weary years.

"The sooner you join the freedom fighters in throwing out the gang in Moscow, the sooner there will again be peace and security for the Motherland. The longer war continues, the greater danger there is that Mother Russia will suffer long-lasting damage. The quicker war ends, the more quickly will Mother Russia and all of you return to peace and freedom.

"Join the freedom fighters, my gallant Russian friends! We in the West stand ready to help you overturn the gang in Moscow. We stand ready to help heal the Motherland's wounds and restore her to her just place as a peace-loving member of the family of nations.

"We in the West, and especially we in the United States, have only the greatest admiration, sympathy and friendship for you, the great, brave Russian people. As President of the United States, I have ordered all possible aid to be rushed to the brave freedom fighters in Eastern Europe and the brave freedom fighters in Kazakhstan and the Moslem areas of Russia. I stand ready to order all possible aid to all of you, freedom fighters within Russia, the moment you rise against your evil masters who have kept you as slaves for so long.

"When you have overthrown them and established a free government that represents *you*, the heroic Russian people, and not a gang of murderous corrupt men whose only interest is in plundering the Motherland for their own power and profit, we stand ready to give all possible aid to strengthen and confirm that government. We will help *you,* the brave Russian people.

"Join the freedom fighters, my friends of Russia! Take your freedom, seize your freedom, *now!* Get rid of the gang that has ruined the Motherland! Get rid of the corrupt murderers who have kept you in slavery! Be free, brave fighters of Russia! The whole world prays for your success!"

Which he thought should be fairly effective, bearing in mind the very limited level of sophistication and world understanding he was addressing. A few last gasps of horror were expressed in the American media at the renewal of his "crude appeal for the overthrow of the legitimate Soviet government," but they were dying out. Life was real now, life was earnest; the most vocal magpies of opposition were cackling less loudly now. Events were sobering them up. That fabric, too, was fraying. At last. And, he thought, about time.

The thing he was not prepared for, however, and the thing that made him and his advisers cringe, came in the headlines next morning:

CHINA RUSHES MILLION MEN TO SOVIET BORDER AS MOSCOW BRINGS TROOPS HOME AGAINST OWN PEOPLE! PEKING CALLS FOR PARTITION OF RUSSIA: WOULD SPLIT SOVIET GIANT INTO FOUR PARTS! WASHINGTON FEARS THREAT MAY REUNITE NATION!

"We suggest," Mikhail Yarkov shouted at the bland little face that stared back at him from the Picturephone, "that you remove your troops from the border, or the heaviest possible nuclear destruction will fall upon you! We will kill five hundred million Chinese!"

Xing-dao shrugged.

"Proceed. We have five hundred million more."

Contrary to the President's fears, the Soviet state continued to unravel. Either the Russian people did not hear the Chinese message—or their leaders had jammed it for fear they might react in unpredictable ways if they did hear it—or the prospect of their own freedom was too compelling. He hoped and prayed it was this. Whatever the reason, the Motherland was apparently not going to be put back together again as the Soviets had known it.

> ### RUSSIAN REVOLT SPREADS NORTH!
> ### FIGHTING BREAKS OUT NEAR MOSCOW AND GORKI!
> ### U.S. RUSHES AID TO NEW "PEOPLE'S FREE-DOM MOVEMENT" IN LENINGRAD!
> ### SOME TOP MINISTERS REPORTED FLEEING TO WEST AS YARKOV HOLD THREATENED!

Two days later, very late at night, he received the call he had been expecting from Moscow. Before he took it he got up from his desk, walked to the window and stood for several minutes staring out at the Rose Garden. It was a sharp fall night, turning rapidly toward winter. Soon snow would fly and blanket the District of Columbia. It might also blanket the world.

Foolishly, he had thought that with the Soviet collapse, of which he knew this call would be the final acknowledgment, peace would come. Yet he knew now there would be no peace. There would never be "peace" as the idealists dreamed it. There would only be a continuation of conflict under different names.

War is a continuation of diplomacy by other means, von Clausewitz had said. In this sad, sick century, peace was a continuation of war by other means. The Soviet communists, more than any other single force in history, had turned "peace" upside down, perverting the language of man and man's intentions until finally the world had arrived at the last conundrum: War is peace—peace is war. And of the fatal marriage of the two there now shall be no divorcing to the furthest reaches of time.

Foolishly for a little while he had thought that China would be a partner in peace, but he knew now that this potentially was as fatal an error as the assumption in 1945 that the Soviet Union would be a partner in peace. Peace did not exist in either lexicon, though it now existed—too late—in the lexicon of the more stable and sophisticated nations of the West. No one there wanted war, or the perversion of peace into war. But there were others who still did, and they were strong and getting stronger, and when one of them fell, there were others to take its place. The desire for conquest and the desire for revenge no longer ever slept, no matter how fine the words to dress them up. The cold reality lay beneath, not as it always had—because there had been some times in history when humankind had made a real attempt—but now as it always would—because the desire for "permanent," peace, along with the capacity to achieve it, no longer existed in the world . . . if it ever really had.

Somewhere along the way in the years since 1945, the will and the ability had died in the human mind. The cliché was still mouthed, the words were still pretty; but the condition did not, could not, anymore, exist. It had become impossible.

This time, nuclear destruction had been narrowly avoided—he suspected that, even now, Mikhail Yarkov did not intend to blow up the world. That ultimate insanity humankind, with a great deal of luck and the blessings that attend the progress of fools, might be spared. But the constant existing on the brink, the constant living with the imminence of death, the constant underlying awareness that there never could be the "genuine and lasting peace" of the bravely spouting orators and the naively hoping souls—these would be with mankind now, he suspected, as long as mankind existed.

He sighed, an odd sound composed equally of irony, frustration, impatience and despair.

It never ended—it never would—the jockeying for position—the struggle for power—the striving for peace, the almost-happened and the might-have-been.

"Permanent peace" and a stability that humankind could depend upon without anxiety were an impossible dream. The wistful wishing and the ever-elusive hope were all the good Lord was going to allow His children from now on.

The *certainty* of peace would never come. The reality of endless conflict was now settled permanently upon the roads of earth.

The wishing, the hoping, the golden, ever-elusive dream—

never to be answered, never to be satisfied—that, he thought, is all there is.

There isn't any more.

The task of statesmanship now is the task of survival. Beneath that umbrella people may still be able to lead good lives. But in its ultimate essence, the purpose of existence has now become—to exist.

He turned back to his desk.

As he did so his eye caught momentarily the flag behind it.

He thanked God again, as he had so many times before, that his had been the good fortune to have been born into a country which, for all its faults and present perils—and both at times seemed overwhelming—was still a free country and was still what its sixteenth President had called it: the last, best hope of earth. There was some solace, if limited, in that.

He straightened his shoulders and lifted the phone: a big man for a big time, but not a miracle worker.

There were no miracles, and no miracle workers, left.

"Comrade President," he said, "you and I have nothing further to say to one another."

And listened without comment to Yarkov's furious cries of protest, exhortation, threat and fear; and, very soon, put down the receiver and cut off his harshly babbling voice.

January 1983–January 1984

SHOCKING TRUE CRIME STORIES

THE BEAUTY QUEEN KILLER
by Bruce Gibney
The true account of a twisted mind and the killing spree that
horrified a nation!
☐ 42380-2/$2.95

**DISAPPEARANCES: TRUE ACCOUNTS OF CANADIANS WHO HAVE
VANISHED**
by Derrick Murdoch
The chilling reconstruction of fourteen missing Canadians who
have vanished over the last thirty years.
☐ 43198-8/$3.75

EDWARD GEIN: AMERICA'S MOST BIZARRE MURDERER
by Judge Robert H. Gollmar
The terrifying true story of the Wisconsin mass murderer—told
by the judge who convicted him!
☐ 42210-5/$3.50

KILLER CLOWN
by Terry Sullivan with Peter T. Maiken
The horrifying true story of a man convicted of more murders
than any other person in U.S. history!
☐ 42274-1/$3.95

LADIES WHO KILL
by Tom Kuncl and Paul Einstein
The true-crime story of the deadly women awaiting execution on
death row.
☐ 42494-9/$2.95

THE PROSTITUTE MURDERS
by Rod Leith
The true-crime shocker of Richard Cottingham, who killed and
tortured Manhattan prostitutes.
☐ 42281-4/$2.50

FOUR FROM
GERALD PETIEVICH

"Gerald Petievich is...
a fine writer...his dialogue
is pure entertainment."
—Elmore Leonard,
Author of *Stick*

LEWIS PERDUE

THE TESLA BEQUEST
A secret society of powerful men have stolen the late Nikola Tesla's plans for a doomsday weapon; they are just one step away from ruling the world.
☐ 42027-7 THE TESLA BEQUEST $3.5☐

THE DELPHI BETRAYAL
From the depths of a small, windowless room in the bowels of the White House, an awesome conspiracy to create economic chaos and bring the entire world to its knees is unleashed.
☐ 41728-4 THE DELPHI BETRAYAL $2.9☐

QUEENS GATE RECKONING
A wounded CIA operative and a defecting Soviet ballerina hurtle toward the hour of reckoning as they race the clock to circumvent twin assassinations that will explode the balance of power.
☐ 41436-6 QUEENS GATE RECKONING $3.5☐

THE DA VINCI LEGACY
A famous Da Vinci whiz, Curtis Davis, tries to uncover the truth behind the missing pages of an ancient manuscript which could tip the balance of world power toward whoever possesses it.
☐ 41762-4 THE DA VINCI LEGACY $3.5☐

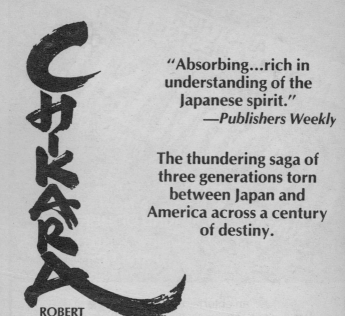